'Are you saying that I wouldn't be a good father?'

Her head snapped back at his growl. Crossing one long leg over the other, she held her hands in a tight bunch on her lap. 'Oh, come on—you're constantly travelling, your social life keeps at least three celebrity magazines in business. Are you seriously telling me that you have time to fit being a father into that schedule? That you even *want* to be a father?'

Irritation tightened his chest. She might be right in everything she said, but a sense of being cheated out of something he hadn't even begun to understand had him asking quietly, 'And you think you have the right to make that decision for me?'

She grabbed her black leather handbag off the floor of the car and sat it on her lap. She lobbed her notebook into it and hugged the hard lines of the small rectangular bag to her stomach. 'When it comes to protecting my baby—yes.'

THEIR BABY SURPRISE

BY
KATRINA CUDMORE

MILLS
BOON

First Published in Great Britain 2017
By Mills & Boon, an imprint of HarperCollins*Publishers*
1 London Bridge Street, London, SE1 9GF

© 2017 Katrina Cudmore

ISBN: 978-0-263-92313-1

23-0717

A city-loving book addict, peony obsessive **Katrina Cudmore** lives in Cork, Ireland, with her husband, four active children and a very daft dog. A psychology graduate, with a MSc in Human Resources, Katrina spent many years working in multinational companies and can't believe she is lucky enough now to have a job that involves daydreaming about love and handsome men! You can visit Katrina at www.katrinacudmore.com.

To Mum and Dad and the love you shared.

CHAPTER ONE

YOU CAN'T OUTRUN your past.

And right now Lucien Duval's past was staring at him from the radio studio's anteroom with as much warmth as a canister of liquid nitrogen.

That past being Charlotte Aldridge, the *verbal assassin* of Huet Construction's legal department.

Ten minutes ago, like an avenging angel to his guilty conscience, she had stalked into the anteroom, presumably sent to monitor every word he uttered in his early morning radio interview.

Ash-blonde hair coiled into a tight bun. Dark suit with buttoned-up blouse. Professional. Serious. A walking, talking, breathing human *Hands Off!* sign.

The type of woman he typically gave a wide berth to.

But those sea-green eyes of hers, which always observed him as though he was a disappointment, somehow also managed to burn something hot and liquid through his veins. Every. Single. Time.

And two months ago, he had learned that that tense mouth of hers was capable of softening and sending his pulse into another year.

And that those sea-green eyes, so cool and detached normally, could melt into a gaze of vulnerability and caution that had tripped over his heart. Two months on and he was still trying to shake off whatever hold she had on him.

The old scar just above his right ear began to tighten and itch.

He already had his board of directors haranguing him for his outspoken criticism of how the UK housing and infrastructure crisis was being managed—he didn't need the added disapproval of an employee he had recklessly slept with.

Charlotte had been an error in judgement, a slip in his usual strict self-control.

His honeymoon period as the new CEO and majority shareholder of Huet Construction was rapidly coming to an end. If he didn't start producing the results the City expected, the share price and investor confidence of one of the world's largest construction companies would soon be heading south.

And all of those who were sceptical of his buy-out of Huet, who said he was an opportunist, a maverick, would be proved right.

Never.

He shifted in his seat; he needed to get out of this radio studio.

Now.

He didn't have time to be listening to yet more empty promises from a politician.

He had a gigabyte worth of emails waiting for him... and points to prove.

He leaned forward across the studio table and growled, 'Enough.'

Mid-sentence, the Housing Minister, his fellow interviewee on the UK's largest breakfast radio show, leapt in his seat, his studio headphones twisting around, momentarily leaving him unable to speak as he tugged them back into place.

A quick look towards Charlotte's glacial gaze intensified his need to agitate, revolt, defy.

He switched his attention back across the table. 'Minister, I think you have bored the listeners enough, don't you? Let's allow them to enjoy their breakfasts in peace. It's the least you can do considering that the majority of them are actually having to live on a daily basis with the circumstances of this housing crisis: spiralling rents, the inability to provide a home for their families, couples unable to start families. And yet again, you're waffling and making excuses while not taking a single worthwhile action. When are you going to actually tackle the issues around land banking, compulsory purchase orders and the transparent disposal of public sector land? Look at innovative ideas like pre-fab housing? I say never because you have neither the courage nor the ability to do so. I'd have more faith in a bunch of toddlers with a box of play building bricks to sort out this crisis.'

With the minister grappling for words, an amused-looking radio presenter took the opportunity to wrap up the interview.

Lucien stood and approached the minister, who reluctantly accepted his handshake. Lucien gave him a brief nod and turned away. His plane was waiting for him at London City Airport.

Lucien swept through the anteroom and out into the corridor without as much as a glance in her direction.

Charlotte tried not to wince.

They had not spoken since their night together. It had been excruciating enough the few times they had passed one another in the corridors of Huet headquarters to nod in his direction, knowing what it was like to feel the weight of his powerful, hard body on hers, knowing the havoc his hands could cause.

But now, knowing that this would be the only time she got him alone, she chased after him as he strode towards the elevators. Instead of waiting for an elevator, he headed through the double doors to the stairwell so she followed him. Out in the empty concrete space she called to him on the landing below. 'Can I speak with you for a moment?'

He reached for the staircase handrail, looked at her impatiently and shook his head. 'I have a flight to catch.'

She dragged down the humiliation that he wouldn't even afford her a minute of his time deep into her stomach and followed him with resolve hardening her spine.

Struggling to keep up with him thanks to the narrowness of her knee-length pencil skirt, she called down to him, 'It won't take long.'

Now a full flight of stairs below her, he called back in a bored tone, 'Speak to my PA.'

Cursing under her breath, while a new wave of nausea folded her stomach into a cube of horribleness, Charlotte yanked off her shoes and hoisted her skirt. They had to talk. Now. 'I did yesterday evening—she told me that you will be away on business for the next fortnight.'

As he descended the last flight of stairs, she finally caught him up, with only the open iron bannister separating them. He slowed and his eyes ran the length of her bare legs. A surge of heat burnt in his eyes. She dropped her skirt. She moved down a step so that she was at eye level with him. Six inches or so taller than her, he usually towered over her.

The last time they had been like this, at eye level, was when they had been in his bed. When their senseless rushed, frenzied, unexpected, kissing and touching and exploring in his garden had been followed by him making the slowest, most incredible love to her in his bedroom.

Had it all been a dream?

She searched his eyes now for some remembrance, a hint that it too had been different for him...that she hadn't been just another conquest of this renowned serial dater.

He blinked hard. Long dark eyelashes sweeping over narrowed, alert, brilliant green eyes.

A deep frown cut down through the centre of his tanned forehead, reaching the top of his perfectly straight nose. A nose at odds with the rugged handsomeness of his face, the thin line of his mouth, the boxer-like quality of the deep cleft in his chin.

Lucien carried himself with the street-savvy smarts of a man who had worked his way from nothing to being the CEO of a billion-dollar company. To not have acquired a broken nose or two on his journey from construction labourer to the majority owner of Huet Construction by the age of thirty-six proved his intelligence and shrewdness... and made the prospect of getting him to agree to her plans for the future even more daunting. He wasn't the type to roll over easily, but hopefully in this instance he'd be more than willing to see her head off into the sunset.

He came a little closer, his hand almost touching hers on the handrail.

Her heart kicked against her ribs.

His green liquid eyes blazed into hers, sending burning heat into her cheeks.

His gaze dropped to her mouth. Her lips, useless traitors that they were, parted.

A door banged higher up on the stairwell.

She jumped and he jerked away before making his way down the remaining stairs. 'Send me an email.'

She followed him out of the stairwell in her bare feet and ran after him as he swept out of the building, the receptionists and a group of visitors signing in, turning to stare at her.

Outside, seeing her opportunity to talk to him slip away, she reached for his arm and pulled hard.

He came to an immediate stop.

Eyes glinting darkly, he stepped towards her, lowered his head and murmured in that lightly French-accented voice that always managed to hold a sexy threat, 'I'm not interested in having a lecture on libel laws right now.'

His nearness, his voice, his warm breath tangling on her hair played dangerous games with her long-held resolve never to let a man get to her again.

She stepped back and prayed her cheeks didn't look as hot as they felt. She affected a laid-back air, in defiance of her galloping heart, refusing to bend to the blistering male chemistry swirling towards her. 'Well, that's lucky because I'm a construction lawyer, not a defamation one. I'll travel with you as far as the airport.'

'Didn't Simon send you?'

Simon was her boss. 'No. He did mention last week that he had threatened to send someone to monitor your interviews. So when my radio alarm woke me this morning to the news that you were to be interviewed alongside the minister, I decided it would be a good opportunity to get you on your own.'

A stalker alert flickered in his eyes. He stepped away. 'I have calls to make.'

A fresh wave of nausea hit her.

Maybe she should just leave it for now.

Get her head straight first.

But she needed him to know.

The only way she was going to get through this sudden turn in her life was by having a clear plan for the future. She needed certainty in her life.

If they had to do this on the footpath, so be it. But he couldn't leave without her personally telling him. She needed to keep him onside. 'I wanted you to be the first to know that I'm resigning from Huet.'

He gave an impatient sigh, called to his driver, who was waiting by the open rear door of a black saloon, to start the engine, and then shifted his attention back to her, '*Tu plaisantes?* You're kidding? Isn't that an overreaction to my interview? I wouldn't have been so easy on the minister if I hadn't been in such a rush for my flight. I know you legal heads are born pedantic worriers but you really need to relax a little.'

'This has nothing to do with the interview.'

Realisation dimmed his brilliant eyes to suspicious wariness. He walked to the car door and held it open, silently but grudgingly gesturing for her to get in.

His driver pulled out onto Regent Street and headed south to Oxford Circus. The stores on the iconic shopping street were still closed but the pavements were bustling with early morning commuters, coffees in hand, earphone leads dangling, heading to work. There was a buzz in the air; only now in late April were they having the first true warm days of spring.

He twisted to face her, drumming his phone on his knee like an insect at night tap-tap-tapping against a window pane desperate to reach the light inside. 'I take it that you're resigning because of our night together.'

She tried to stay impassive. She had been through worse. And survived. But having to share the most wonderful but scary news of her life with a man she barely knew had her rehearsed words stick in her throat and she only managed to eke out a pathetic, 'Yes.'

'I thought we had both agreed to put it behind us.'

Oh, God. There was no easy way to say this.

Get it over and done with. Then you can move on with your life.

A fresh bout of nausea joined her pounding heart.

The car was suddenly way too hot.

The panicked, terrified void that had almost consumed her in her doctor's consulting room reared up again. How would she cope? She couldn't possibly raise a child on her own. She knew nothing about child-rearing, being a parent.

And what if her depression returned? What would she do then? But it wouldn't. She was strong now.

And then there were all those selfish thoughts that had eaten her up with guilt: what of her aspirations to become head of Legal, to move into a larger apartment in London, to travel?

She gulped in some air and forced herself to look into those green heartbreaker eyes. 'I'm pregnant.'

He jerked away.

Behind him, they swept past Trafalgar Square.

Brow furrowed, he stared at her. 'Because of that night?'

'Yes! Of course it was that night. I wouldn't be here telling you if I had any doubt about that. I'm eight weeks pregnant—it has to be you.'

Lucien was once again tapping his phone against his knee, the silver case banging against the charcoal wool of his trousers. She had wrapped her legs around his that night, felt the hard muscle of his thighs. A night of insanity that had knocked her life completely off course.

Lucien shook his head. 'We used protection.'

She fiddled with the window switch on the door and lowered her window, needing relief from the heat rising in her. Not able to meet his eye, she muttered, 'Not in the garden…' She trailed off and looked at him, praying he didn't need further explanation.

He winced and looked away.

Lucien had held a reception in his Mayfair home for all of his HQ senior management on the night of his first AGM. Lucien's takeover of Huet had heralded a bonanza for the hairdressers and fashion stores in the vicinity of Huet HQ as the entire female workforce fell for his rugged looks and alpha charisma. But Charlotte knew a player when she saw one. And she refused to join his fan club. Having her heart broken once in a lifetime was once too often for her liking. No man would ever get the opportunity to do so again. In fact she went out of her way to ignore him whenever she saw him at work.

But a week before the party she had to meet with him to discuss issues on a bid contract. And, despite herself, his astute charm and lightning intelligence had threatened to melt her cynicism. At the end of the meeting, dizzy from the effect of being so close to him, she had almost tripped over a low coffee table as she had struggled to leave his office. While he had worn an amused lethal grin.

Brief glances were all they had shared the night of the reception. He had shown no interest in talking to her, and as the party had broken up she had gone out into the garden to find her phone that she'd left there, relieved to get away from her pretence that she was oblivious to him, but also a little miffed that he had spoken to practically everyone else except her. About to go back inside, she had felt her heart somersault when he had walked down the cobbled garden path towards her, his large frame even bigger as his shadow had moved towards her and engulfed her. She had offered a polite thanks and said she should leave with everyone else. But he'd told her that they were alone. Everyone else had already left.

He had smiled down at her. A kind, easy smile. A *Well, what will we do now?* type of smile. And she had foolishly stepped towards him, all thought and caution abandoned to that wonderful, what seemed sincere, glistening green gaze.

She had reached out her hand towards his open suit jacket with an unbearable urge to touch the dark grey material, to make contact with him.

And he had stepped towards her. Run his fingertips along her cheek.

And the next thing she'd known, his mouth had been on hers, hot, seeking, exploring.

In an instant her body had been aflame. His fingertips, his mouth, his scent, his hard, hard, hard body making her lose every inhibition, every memory, every protective layer she had grown over her heart and soul in the past six years.

Frenzied, they had unbuttoned and unzipped without thought, driven by a desperate hunger for one another. But when he had claimed her against that cold garden wall, she had stilled and her heart had gone into free fall. All of those memories of her ex's betrayal, of how lonely and ugly and beaten she had felt during her depression, had gushed back and threatened to drown her. Lucien had gently drawn away and watched her with a soul-destroying questioning, as though wanting to understand. Only after did it dawn on her that this was a key skill of any Lothario. The pretence to care.

But that night he had brought her to his bedroom and, her body weak with longing though her heart had been afraid, she had willingly gone. And he had made love to her, slowly and tenderly. And after she had cried in his bathroom when she'd realised how empty her life was... and how stupid, stupid, stupid she was to have slept with her womanising boss.

Now, as he faced the consequences of that night, he ran a hand across the deep frown lines of his forehead and muttered, *'Zut!'*

Unexpected sadness pulled hard in her chest. A baby should bring joy, not this shock. What was he even thinking?

Did he hate her for this?

Bitterly regret the fire that had raged between them in the garden and the seconds when they had become one and senselessly forgot all thoughts as to the need to use protection?

Regret the baby growing inside her?

A fierce protectiveness surged through her.

Dismayed at how her hands were trembling, she pulled her notebook from her handbag and opened it to the pages where she had bullet-pointed her action plan. Needing the comfort of seeing in black and white her strategy for coping with this shocking but incredible turn in her life. 'My doctor confirmed two days ago that I'm almost eight weeks pregnant. My apartment here in London is too small to raise a baby so I've decided I'll move to the countryside, close to where my parents live. I will get work locally.'

He waved off her words with an impatient flick of his hand.

For five, ten, twenty seconds he stared at her intently, his gaze burning a hole in her heart.

He leaned a little closer, his shoulders tense, his eyes scanning her features like an interrogator searching for tell-tale body-language slips in a crime suspect. 'Are you certain that I'm the father?'

The lawyer in her knew that it was a reasonable question. But the woman in her, the mother-to-be, the idealist who believed in truth, fairness and honour, felt his question like a slap. She felt her throat constrict, a heaviness invade her sinuses, a burning sensation in her eyes. She was *not* going to cry. She was strong. A fighter. She sucked in some air. He was the serial dater, not her.

'I haven't slept with another man in a very long time. What happened between us was not typical for me,' she said fiercely.

She paused and cringed at having given him too much information and wondered why she felt she had to justify herself to him. Annoyed that she was doing so, she pulled in a steadying breath. 'I want nothing from you. I don't need financial support and I know a baby will not fit into your lifestyle. I want to give my child security and stability, a happy childhood. I've told you that you will be a father because you have the right to know but I don't *want* or *need* you in our lives.'

CHAPTER TWO

'I DON'T *WANT* or *need* you in our lives.'

Charlotte's words smashed into him.

His car, now opposite the entrance to the darkly historic Tower of London, was snarled up in a herd of London double-decker red buses and he had to rein in the desire to leap from the car and run. To run off the adrenaline twitching in his muscles, drying out his mouth, spinning his heart in crazy arcs.

He was going to be a father.

Something he'd never wanted to be.

Never wanting the responsibility, the fear of failing his child, never wanting to mess up, never wanting to have to face the fact that he was no better than his own father.

And he had always believed that a child deserved to be brought up in a loving environment with committed, responsible parents. Everything he didn't have.

But a failed, tempestuous, torturous marriage when he was in his late teens had proved to him that he was totally incapable of any such commitment.

And now, before he could even start to process it all, to make sense of this turn in his life, Charlotte was trying to snatch it away.

Those sea-green eyes steadily held his stare when he looked back at her, the only hint of her nervousness in how she fingered the cream lined pages of her notebook.

He leaned a little closer to her. She backed away, her hand rising to touch against the edge of her delicate jawline.

Pain radiated in his own jawline, moving up through his clamped teeth and into his cheekbones. The scar above his ear throbbing, throbbing, throbbing. 'As you're pregnant, I'm going to ask you nicely to explain exactly what you mean when you say you don't *want* me in your lives.'

She recoiled a little at first but then sat more upright in her seat, both hands running over the material of her black skirt. She settled challenging eyes on him. 'You don't want to be a father, not with your lifestyle and commitments... Let's not get into an argument about this.'

'Are you saying that I wouldn't be a good father?'

Her head snapped back at his growl. Crossing one long leg over the other, she held her hands in a tight bunch on her lap. 'Oh, come on, you're constantly travelling, your social life keeps at least three celebrity magazines in business. Are you seriously telling me that you have time to fit being a father into that schedule? That you even *want* to be a father?'

Irritation tightened his chest. She might be right in everything she said, but a sense of being cheated out of something he hadn't even begun to understand had him ask quietly, 'And you think you have the right to make that decision for me?'

She grabbed her black leather handbag off the floor of the car and sat it on her lap. She lobbed her notebook into it and hugged the hard lines of the small rectangular bag to her stomach. 'When it comes to protecting my baby, yes.'

He inhaled a deep breath. 'Are you seriously saying that you have to protect this child from *me*?'

'Well, you're hardly "father of the year" material, are you? I don't believe for one minute that you really want the responsibility of a child.'

She had to be kidding.

'I'm a CEO of a company with a thirty-billion turn-over, for crying out loud. Responsible should be my mid-dle name.'

She gave him a satisfied look, the look of a prosecu-tor knowing they had caught the defendant out. 'Tell me, just how many companies have you acquired in the past ten years?'

He folded his arms. 'Sixteen.'

'And how many countries have you lived in?'

'What are you getting at, Charlotte?'

'The way you constantly move around the globe is hardly the sign of a man able to give stability and com-mitment to a child, is it?'

This conversation had gone too far. He leaned closer to her and growled, 'Let me get this straight. You want me out of your lives but yet are expecting me to blindly trust you in raising *my* baby?'

The words *my baby* leapt from his mouth unconsciously.

Charlotte looked at him aghast. 'I'll give *my* baby secu-rity, routine. I'll be the best mother that I can be.'

Beneath her defiant tone, there was a nervousness she didn't quite manage to disguise. Was she as confident about being a parent as she was trying to portray? 'Did you want this—to be pregnant? To be a mother?'

She lifted one of the gold chain handles of her bag, the only hint of flamboyance in her entire wardrobe, and twisted it around her index finger, the metal tightening as she twisted once, twice, three times. 'Not until now.'

'Why?'

She gave a shrug. 'I was focused on my career.'

Dieu! This was such a mess. A thought tugged in his heart and leaked out into his chest: this baby deserved bet-ter than this. He needed to start focusing on the practicali-ties, understanding just where they stood. 'Are you seeing anyone else?'

She eyed him warily. 'Why are you asking?'

He fisted his hands, a stab of jealousy sideswiping him at the possibility that she was dating someone. 'I want to understand who will support you.'

She unravelled the chain from her finger, in one fast, furious movement. 'You're the father. There's no one else in my life.' She paused and vigorously rubbed the red welts the chain had left. 'I know you might find all of that hard to believe given your social life, but it's the truth.'

He itched with the desire to reach for her finger and soothe her skin himself. That night she had touched him lightly, tenderly, almost reverentially with those delicate hands. That feather-light touch just one of the many inexcusable reasons why he had broken his own ethical code that he never dated employees, never mind slept with them. Exasperated at his own weakness and lack of honour that night, he said sharply, 'Don't believe everything you read in the media.'

She rose a disbelieving eyebrow. 'I saw a picture of you with Annabelle Foster online over the weekend.'

Yes, Annabelle Foster, a TV news reporter, had accompanied him to a Homelessness charity ball, but they had left early, his driver dropping Annabelle directly home. Alone.

Since his night with Charlotte he had dated a few women, but he had ended each date early, a restlessness making his bones itch as he had tried but failed to focus on his date across the restaurant table from him, images of Charlotte's vulnerable, tender, passionate gaze when they had made love in his bed leaving him with no appetite. For anything.

'It's tiresome to attend functions on my own. I enjoy having company, but that doesn't mean it's anything more serious than a night out.'

She considered his answer with a suspicious frown but then, with an *it doesn't matter anyway* shrug, swung her bag back to the floor. She gave him the faintest whisper of an understanding sigh. 'I know this must have come as a shock to you. It did to me. But I want this baby… I want to give him or her the same happy childhood I had, with lots of love, laughter, happiness, certainty.'

All of the things he hadn't had as a child. Instead he'd had arguments and accusations and animosity.

The worst being the night he'd woken to hear his mother sob downstairs that she hated her life, hated being married to his father, hated being tied down with a child with no way out.

His father had lashed back demanding to know if she seriously thought he wanted any of this, a nightmare marriage, his dreams of university, of a better life, long abandoned as he was now straddled with a wife and child to support.

It was another four years before they divorced, five years until his mother eventually threw Lucien out for punching her new boyfriend. Her boyfriend had caught Lucien stealing his beer and had flung a beer can at him. Lucien, sick of the controlling bully who spent his days belittling his mother, had launched himself at him, long past caring about the consequences of anything he did in life. He had ended up with a permanent scar over his ear and living in a fleapit in Bordeaux at the age of seventeen. But at least there, there wasn't the constant silent, frightening tension of waiting for another bitter argument to start.

History could not repeat itself. This baby was never to feel unwanted.

That thought hit him hard in his gut, in his heart.

'So who will support you in raising the baby?'

Her arms folded tightly on her waist. 'My parents will be nearby. I know they will adore being grandparents.'

Which was something…but a feeling of loss, of not being in control of how his life was changing, of needing to make sure he got this right had him warn, 'Being a single parent won't be easy.'

She closed the window beside her and gave a shrug. 'I'll manage.'

But would she? He didn't know her, not really. For a few crazy hours he had experienced a connection with her that had flummoxed him, but with hindsight he had recognised that it had been nothing more than a mutual powerful attraction.

And now she was expecting him to be happy with entrusting her with raising his child. What was the best thing to do? For the baby? Neither he nor Charlotte mattered in all of this. 'Don't you think a child has the right to know its father, to benefit from that support?'

White teeth bit down on the soft, tender plumpness of her lips. He cursed silently at the drag of attraction that barrelled through him.

She pulled on the collar of her plain lilac blouse and eyed him impassively before she answered, 'Perhaps, but only if the father wants and is capable of doing so.'

Fresh irritation swept through him. He set furious eyes on her. 'You're making a lot of dangerous assumptions.'

She held his gaze, her mouth now a thin line of scepticism. 'Am I?'

'Let me be clear. I'll make the decision as to my role in this baby's life. Starting with understanding just how you propose to raise it. Are you going to work full-time? Who will take care of it when you do? Have you thought through the financial implications? Who else in your life will support you? What happens if something happens to you, you get sick or are in an accident—who will care for the baby then?'

'Nothing's going to happen to me.'

She spoke with a tremor in her voice. For a moment he paused, taken aback by the fear in her eyes…the same fear and vulnerability he had seen the night they'd spent together. Inexplicably he was hit with the urge to reach out for her again, to pull her soft body against him, to whisper that everything would be okay. Just as he had done that night.

Canary Wharf Tower, a touchstone for the command of commerce and finance in London, was now visible in the distance. Until thirty minutes ago he had thought of nothing but business and stamping his mark as the most successful owner in the global construction sector. He had worked for almost twenty years to achieve that position, moving from labourer to site management and then into operations. Moving companies, moving countries, working, working, working. Acquiring small companies in the early days and rapidly and aggressively expanding those by taking risks, all the time defying economic predictions. Needing to prove he was strong, that he wasn't a failure, wasn't a coward.

The feeling that he was at a critical crossroads in his life moved through him, dancing from his whirling brain down to the confusion plugging his chest. 'How can you be sure nothing will happen? None of us know what the future holds—you need support in raising a baby.'

She reached down for her handbag again and, placing it on her lap, searched through it, not looking towards him when she answered, 'I'm sure friends will help me.'

'And your parents?'

Her fingers clasped the sharp, firm ridges of her handbag bottom. She eyed him warily before mumbling, 'They'll be supportive but they're elderly.'

'Have you siblings?'

'No and I don't see what the issue is here. Lots of people are happily brought up in single-parent homes.'

'The *problem* is that I don't like being given ultimatums. I will decide what involvement I want, when I'm ready to do so.'

She turned to stare out of her window.

When they passed a signpost for the Docklands Light Railway, Blackwall Station, he knew they were close to the airport.

Her gaze fixed on the outside world, she said in a low voice, 'Even though I don't *want* you in our lives.'

He closed his eyes for a moment, her words stinging hard.

He was another mistake in a woman's life.

Too angry to speak, he willed away the remaining ten minutes of his journey.

He needed space and time to think.

He needed to get away from the woman next to him. The soon-to-be mother of his child. He see-sawed from an infuriation at her coldness, her icy assertion that she didn't want him in her life, to a deep desire to tug her to him and kiss away that frozen exterior to the warm, passionate woman he had spent the night with.

When his driver pulled up at the departure terminal at City Airport, he turned to her. His words were lost for a moment when he once again was pulled under by her fragile beauty: the pale skin over high cheekbones, the plumpness of her lips, the high arched eyebrows over sea-green eyes that mostly belonged to the Arctic Circle but occasionally reminded him of the sun-kissed warmth of the turquoise sea by his villa in Sardinia. 'What *you* want isn't important. I'll do what's best for *our* baby. We'll speak again when I return from my business trips.'

He jumped out of the car and stalked away but pulled up when he heard her call his name.

She stood behind the door he had exited, her hands clutching the frame. 'I'll still be handing in my resignation letter later today.'

He walked back to her and stared down into those defiant eyes. She pulled the car door even closer against her body.

He leant down close to her ear and whispered words that came from the very centre of his being. 'Trust me, I'm not going to let you go that easily.'

Later that evening, Charlotte left the open expanse of the Thames river walkway in Bankside to scoot down Clink Street. The dark narrow cobbled street once again sent an involuntary shiver through her. Now a fashionable part of London, this historic area, famous for Clink prison, still held a hint of menace. And she loved it.

She loved all of London. It was why she walked to and from her work in St James's to her home in Borough every day. Her journey took her past Big Ben and the Houses of Parliament. Then the London Eye, the giant wheel always making her smile when she remembered her mum's terror when they had ridden it for her fourteenth birthday. And towards the end of her walk came her favourite, Shakespeare's Globe Theatre. The timber construction embodying the history that this city was steeped in and the determination of its people to continue its rich and vibrant culture.

And now she was going to have to leave all of this. Leave her apartment, leave her challenging but exhilarating work, leave this buzzing city. She was leaving for all of the right reasons, but she would miss this life she had worked so hard to achieve.

Lucien's question earlier that day as to who would care for her baby should something happen to her came back to plague her again. She yanked the strap of her rucksack tighter on her shoulder, her sports-trainer footsteps falling silently on the cobbled street. What if her depression did return? Not that he knew anything about her past illness.

A tight, tight, tight cord lashed itself around her throat.

How would she care for her baby if it did come back?
That's not going to happen. I'm strong now.

She passed a noisy popular fusion restaurant and looked away from the smiling and animated couples and large groups of friends dining there. They all seemed so carefree.

In her final year at university she had been sucked deeper and deeper into depression. Not that she had understood any of that at the time.

At first it had just been a feeling of being overwhelmed by her workload, her looming exams and the self-imposed pressure of achieving a first-class degree. Unable to concentrate, constantly tired, her mind swamped by a sense of hopelessness. She'd kept it hidden for months. Not wanting to be thought of as weak. Feeling a complete failure. Not wanting to be a burden to anyone. Eventually she had told her boyfriend Dan and best friend Angie. And had somehow managed to drag herself through her final exams.

On the night of her final exam she had told Dan once again that she was too tired to go out. To her relief, for once he hadn't become quietly irritated with her. But later she had changed her mind. Hoping that now that the exams were over just maybe she would be herself again.

With that glimmer of hope sustaining her, she had made her way to the riverside pub. And had found Dan and Angie in the beer garden. Kissing. Intimately. Lovers intimately.

Dan had been the first to see her. He had broken away and approached her with a guilty but almost relieved look on his face. Within minutes she had learned that they had been dating for weeks. And it was over between herself and Dan.

She had gone home to her parents that night. Broken. And had spent the following year slowly dragging herself out of the swamp of depression.

In the years since, she had wrapped up all the memories of that year into a tiny capsule that sat deep within her.

Knowing that she needed to mind herself, protect herself against the depression returning. And she did that by telling herself that she *was* strong, protecting herself in relationships, and guarding herself against men who might hurt her again.

She passed an upmarket burger restaurant and walked on by. But a few steps on she came to a stop and turned around.

She needed a milkshake.

Twenty minutes later, she turned right onto Kipling Street, sucking hard on the thick sweet vanilla mixture, fears at bay for now, just glad to see her apartment block further down the street and the prospect of watching escapism TV for an hour.

The drink straw dropped from her mouth.

And her shock was much too quickly superseded by the hot heat of embarrassment and soul-destroying attraction.

Leaning against the door of this dark saloon, Lucien was talking on his phone. Earthy, menacing, sexy.

He hadn't seen her yet.

She pushed away the impulse to run away and instead put the milkshake carton in a nearby bin, tidied the strands of hair that had escaped her ponytail, grimaced down at her purple and blue leggings and dark navy sweatshirt, and tightened her grip on her rucksack handle.

He became aware of her when she was twenty paces away. He continued to talk on the phone but he watched her intently. Every. Single. Step. Of. The. Way. Green eyes narrowed, lazily travelling down her body and back up again.

He was tieless, top button undone, his shirt sleeves rolled up. His dark brown hair was cut tightly into his scalp at the side, the top a little longer and curling slightly, adding to his air of menace. The powerful strength of his fighter body was clear in his muscular forearms, the broad width of his shoulders, the long length of his legs, planted wide apart.

Lucien didn't look like the other suave CEOs that

swarmed London. Instead he looked like a dock worker from Marseille who modelled and took part in mixed martial arts in his spare time.

She hated how attracted she was to him.

She hated how her body melted just seeing him, the tight longing that pulled hard within her.

She hated the physical hunger that froze her brain and all logic.

Destructive, crushing chemistry.

She came to a stop a few steps away from him and he finished his call.

They stared at each other and she raised an eyebrow. Determined not to be the first to talk. To ask him why he was here. To say that she thought he was away on business for the next fortnight.

His gaze dropped down along her body again. And stopped on her stomach. Heat blasted through her at the intimacy, protectiveness, ownership of his look.

Her heart thudded in her chest.

He was the father of her child.

They would be bound for ever.

A thought that was mystifying, incredible, terrifying.

She cleared her throat loudly and dropped her rucksack down in front of her, to swing against her legs. Her arms now shielded her belly.

'We need to talk,' he said.

She wanted to say no. This morning had been way more difficult than she had ever anticipated. In perhaps complete naivety she had thought Lucien would be shocked but accepting of her plans for the future. He wasn't father material, after all. She had sat at her desk all day thinking about what he had said. And come to the realisation that she needed to reassure him of her ability to care for their baby.

He gestured down the street. 'We can talk in a café on the High Street.'

'The smell of coffee makes me nauseous.' She hesitated for a moment as the lines around his eyes tightened. In concern or dislike at another reminder of her pregnancy? With a sense of inevitability and a need to get this over and done with, she added, 'We can talk in my apartment.'

Lucien said something quickly to his driver and then she led the way into the 1960s redbrick block.

Inside the foyer, he reached for her rucksack. 'I'll carry your bag.' For a brief moment their fingers met. Their gazes clashed and all of the intimacy, the intensity, the closeness of their night together rushed back.

She yanked her hand away and, not welcoming the prospect of being stuck in the tight confines of the lift with him, led him to the stairwell instead.

Walking alongside him up the stairs, she asked, 'What explanation did you give Human Resources for wanting my address?'

He looked at her with a hint of bemusement. 'The HR director has enough sense not to ask.' Then his features fixed back into their usual hard shrewdness. 'I also spoke to Simon. He made no mention of your resignation.'

They had reached the third floor and she paused on the stairwell and answered, not quite able to meet his eye. 'I didn't resign… I'll do so tomorrow.'

'Why?'

His now dispassionate tone, so in contrast to the heat of his gaze in the foyer, his lack of understanding of how her life was being turned upside down and his insistence on questioning everything she needed to do had her answer crossly. 'Simon was busy, and frankly I couldn't face it… not after this morning. I couldn't take another difficult conversation today.' She paused, and as the true realisation of what she was giving up hit home she grabbed her rucksack off him. 'I love my job. I've worked so hard over the years to get to this position.' A lump suddenly formed in her throat.

She knew of her reputation as a tough negotiator within the wider organisation, but within her department, where she was one of the most senior staff members and often mentored the younger staff, she was more relaxed, more herself. 'It's going to be hard to say goodbye to everyone.'

She twisted around and stormed through the door into the corridor that led to her apartment. As she searched her rucksack for her keys he joined her at her front door and said, 'You don't have to resign.'

'Yeah, that would work out just fine—me pregnant with the CEO's baby and we can't even bring ourselves to say hello in the corridors.'

'That's why I came back from Paris. We need to sort this out now.'

With tense fingers she opened the front door of her apartment, a heavy knot of anxious speculation landing in her stomach at his words, while simultaneously managing to worry about the trivial: what would he make of her minuscule apartment, especially in comparison to his vast five-storey Mayfair town house? But her love for her apartment's bright open interior and pride that she had finally managed to get a foothold on the crazy London property market had her march in ahead of him.

In the open-plan lounge and kitchen she gestured to her grey velvet couch, silently inviting him to sit, and asked, 'Can I get you something to drink?'

He didn't sit but instead paced around the room. The room shrank around his restlessness, the power and strength of his body. Needing some oxygen against the tension in the room, she moved to the lounge window and opened it to the still-warm April air.

When she turned back to face him, he hit her with a non-compromising stare. 'I want to be a part of this baby's life on a daily basis.'

The knot of anxiety inside her twisted. 'That's not possible, you know that. I'm moving away from London.'

'Don't move away.'

She gestured around her apartment. 'I need more space. I need to be near my parents. To have family close by.'

'I agree, that's why I believe you should move in with me…and, for that matter, why we should marry.'

She sank down onto the window seat below the open window. 'Marry!'

'Yes.'

A known serial dater was proposing marriage. This was crazy. He had the reputation for being impulsive and a maverick within the industry, but his decisions were always backed up with sound logic. And that quick-fire decision-making, some would even say recklessness, often gave him the edge over his more ponderous rivals. But he had called this one all wrong. She gave an incredulous laugh. 'I bet you don't even believe in marriage?'

He rolled his shoulders and rubbed the back of his neck hard, his expression growing darker before he answered, 'It's the responsible thing to do when a child becomes part of the equation.'

This was crazy. She lifted her hands to her face in shock and exasperation, her hot cheeks burning against the skin of her palms. 'Have you really thought about what it takes to be a father? A child needs consistency, routine, to know that they are the centre of the parent's life. Have you considered the sacrifices needed? Your work life, the constant travel, all of the partying—everything about the way you live now will be affected. Are you prepared to give up all of that?'

Standing in the centre of the room, he folded his arms on his wide imposing chest, his eyes firing with impatient resolve. 'I don't have a choice. This child is my responsibility and duty. I will do whatever it takes to ensure that it has a safe and happy childhood.'

'I can give my baby all of that.'

'You admitted this morning that you have limited support.'

'I have my friends.'

'Are they going to be there in the middle of the night when the baby is crying? Are they going to be there when you're exhausted, when you're sick, when you have work demands, when you need to be with your elderly parents?'

She flinched and lowered her head. Needing time to think.

Bitterly she accepted that he was right… She loved her two best friends, Tameka and Jill, both ex-colleagues from a previous employer, but she knew only too well the fragility of friendship.

When she'd had depression she had lost friends. Not wanting to be seen as being weak she had isolated herself, especially after Dan and Angie's betrayal, but also their reaction when she had told them about feeling down and unable to cope. At first they had been understanding and supportive but as the weeks had passed she'd felt their impatience, their nervousness. Their eyes had said, *Can't you pull yourself together?*

She stared down at the floorboards she had lovingly painted a pale pink last year, emotions sweeping through her.

Anger at those memories, anger at him for hitting so many raw nerves.

Frustration and guilt at being so daunted at the prospect of being the sole carer for a newborn, at the years that stretched out before her, knowing she was the only person protecting this precious life.

Fear about what would happen if her depression returned.

Anxiety about her parents' slowly declining health.

Perplexity at how stupidly attracted she was to this heartbreaker.

Overloaded with all of those emotions, she rounded on him. 'And are you going to be there in the middle of the night, when I'm exhausted, or are you going to be away travelling or out on a date?'

His expression tightened and he tilted his head back defiantly. 'I *will* take my marriage vows seriously, including to be always faithful.'

The absolute resolution in his voice, the deceitful, guilt-inducing thrill in her heart at his words, blew her usual coolness even further out of the water. 'Oh, please! You? Celibate? Are you kidding me?'

Heat entered his eyes, pinning her to the seat. 'Who said anything about being celibate?'

She leapt up. 'No way are we sleeping together again.'

He walked across the room and right up to her, inches separating them. He stared down at her, his eyes dangerously challenging her, daring her to lie about the attraction whistling through the air in the room. 'Why?'

He spoke in a low whisper.

She swallowed hard, a shiver running through her. 'Because you're not my type.'

'Which is?'

'A serial dater who probably gets a kick out of breaking women's hearts.'

A dangerous spark lit up in the corner of his eye. He moved even closer. She willed herself not to lean towards his heat, his gorgeous faint-inducing scent of leather and soap, his invisible pull that yanked on every cell in her body.

'Afraid I might do the same to you?'

She stepped back. Away from his power. 'No! Let me set you straight...my career and now my baby are all that matters to me. I don't have time or interest in relationships.'

'Good, so a working marriage will suit you perfectly.'

'A working marriage?'

'Think of it as a business relationship. We'll both be clear that the only reason we're married is for the welfare of *our* baby. Our mission will be to nurture and protect our child by working closely together and supporting each other in parenting him or her. It will be a team effort.'

He made it all sound so simple and logical. She shook her head and walked away, towards the kitchen counter, muttering, 'I think I'm in a nightmare.'

'This is the best solution. Our baby will have both parents in its life, you get to stay in London, stay working in the job you obviously love.'

Why was he doing this? There had to be more reasons than just because he felt responsible. Why would a player, a man known to live for his work, be willing to change his life so much when he didn't have to? A horrible thought took hold. Was this proposal nothing more than appeasing his board and protecting his reputation? It wouldn't look too good for a CEO to have got an employee pregnant. Even if he was the majority shareholder in the company. With a bitter taste in her mouth, she asked, 'Do you want to marry so as not to damage your reputation?'

He considered her with amusement, a faint smile on his lips. 'My reputation! *Je m'en fiche complètement!* I couldn't care less. I'll happily tell people that it was an accidental pregnancy and we decided to marry in order to raise our baby together. There is no shame in either. We're simply being responsible and mature parents.'

Her mouth dropped open. 'You'll do no such thing.'

'Why?'

'My parents are elderly and conservative…they believe in the sanctity of marriage. They would be deeply upset if they knew I didn't marry for love.'

Lucien threw his eyes upwards.

She eyed him angrily. 'My parents have the most wonderful, loving marriage imaginable. Just because you're totally lacking in any romance doesn't mean that it doesn't exist for other people.'

'Don't tell me that *you* were waiting to be swept off your feet.'

She fixed him with her iciest stare. 'Hardly.'

He looked at her warily. 'Do you want romance, love… all of that fairy-tale stuff?'

She folded her arms and threw him an unimpressed look. 'And here I was thinking all Frenchmen were romantics.'

'A lot of us are grounded in reality.'

'You're so grounded I can practically see roots emerging from your shoes. To answer your question, no, I don't want romance. Thanks to a few too many run-ins with men like you, I've been cured of all such desires… What my parents have is unique, but certainly not for me.'

'Good, so there's no reason why we shouldn't marry. My PA has set up a meeting for us at the marriage registrar's office tomorrow morning to give notice. You will need to bring your passport and proof of address. She also provisionally booked a slot for us to marry there in a month's time.'

She swallowed the yelp of disbelief that barrelled up inside her. And fixed him with a deadly stare. 'Wasn't that a tad presumptuous on your part?'

'Simply forward planning in the knowledge that your logical legal brain would see the sense of this plan. We have only seven months to get to know one another, to establish an effective working marriage. I want any potential issues resolved before the baby arrives.'

His words should have brought comfort; what he was proposing could, just maybe, work…on paper. Her baby would benefit from having another person in his or her life.

But what if Lucien proved to be unreliable?

And what of her attraction to him, how vulnerable she already felt around him? How she was always waylaid by her attraction to him, abandoning logic and self-preservation to the sound of his voice, the sight of his rugged face, powerful body, the pull of his clean, masculine scent.

She paced the room.

Dizzy, overwhelmed, giddy.

She had to think of her baby. And one thought kept snaking around her brain, around her heart. What if her depression returned? Who would take care of her child then?

She went to the kitchen counter and poured a glass of water.

The cold liquid calmed the nausea swishing around in her belly. 'Do you mean it when you say that it will be a business relationship and nothing more?'

'Let's call it a team effort—we will raise our baby together and support one another at home and in our careers.'

His voice was calm, conciliatory, at peace with the decisions he had taken. A red rag to all of the fears coursing through her. 'But will we be a team…or are you expecting me to make all of the changes? It's me who has to leave my home, my independence. The plans I had already made for our future, the baby and me. Will you accept my desire to have a career of my own? Will you accommodate my friends, my parents, my interests? Or will I have to flex to your way of life? Will you change the way you work, your socialising? Will you welcome me and the baby into your life or will you always begrudge us?'

She had spoken angrily, her fear sitting at the base of her throat. She expected him to respond just as angrily but instead he walked towards her. He held her gaze while gently fixing a loose strand of hair behind her ear. 'I will never make our child feel unwanted.'

His expression grew even gentler; concerned eyes swallowed her up. Just as they had the night they made love. 'Don't be so afraid.'

'I'm not afraid.'

His smile told her she wasn't kidding anyone. So she added, 'It's just that this is the craziest idea ever. We don't know each other.'

'We'll get to know one another. You don't have to do everything in life by the book.' He lowered his head closer to her and whispered, 'We can make this work, trust me.'

Her heart dipped and then soared in her chest.

He spoke with such strength, determination, even kindness, she forgot every reason why this could never work and said with a gulp, 'Can we?'

His hand reached out and for a moment rested just above her hip. She stopped breathing. She fought the urge to move in closer. Longing to feel his arms wrapped around her, his body pushed against hers.

His gaze moved to her tummy and then back up to hers. He lowered his head, his lips not far away from hers.

She fell into the green burning depths of his eyes.

His breath whispered across her lips.

She swayed closer.

His eyes burnt even brighter. And then his lips brushed against her cheek until he reached her ear. In a low voice he whispered, 'We'll make this work.' His hand cupped her hip even more. 'I'll make sure it does.'

And then he was moving to the door. 'Our appointment is at nine-thirty tomorrow. I will collect you at nine-fifteen.'

Dazed, she stared after him.

A gut-wrenching thought hit her.

Had she just witnessed a master manipulator at work?

She followed him to the front door, resolute that she was going to say no to everything he was proposing. There was no way she was agreeing to marrying this expert schemer… player…heartbreaker.

But before she could speak he turned and, with a quiet, intent dignity, he said, 'I will be the best father and husband that I can. I'll change my way of working, my socialising. I will be faithful to *all* of my marriage vows.' He paused and his hand moved close to where her belly lay beneath her sweater top, his fingers tipping against the navy cotton. 'Why wouldn't I, when I have something so special waiting for me at home?'

CHAPTER THREE

Wednesday 20th April, 10:45 p.m.

This is my private number. Contact me any time you need me.

LATER THAT EVENING Lucien pressed 'send' on his text and went back to the never-ending stream of emails awaiting his attention. His stomach growled. He needed food. He had missed the gala dinner he had been scheduled to attend tonight in Palais Brongniart in favour of returning to London.

Knowing that decisive action was needed.

Knowing that he had to cut off any ideas Charlotte had of excluding him from their lives before that idea became entrenched.

And if that took marrying her, so be it.

He was doing the right thing.

He had a duty to his unborn child.

Unlike his own parents, he *would* be a responsible parent.

But that did not stop the whispers of doubts that were creeping into his bloodstream. Could he make this work? Would he mess up as a father, as a husband? He had failed as a husband once before. Would he do so again?

His phone pinged and the screen glowed in the low light

of his home office. He grabbed it impatiently, annoyed to admit to himself that he had been waiting for her response.

I understand why you want to be part of my child's life. But why do you want us to marry? C

After his first marriage had failed he had sworn never to marry again. Hurt and angry at the endless arguments, sick in his heart at his own weaknesses that led to the marriage imploding. Sick at the knowledge that he was no better than his own spineless father. He had been repulsed the day he had found his father in the act of betraying his mother with another woman.

But not repulsed enough to fight the weak nature he had obviously inherited from him. For Lucien had gone on to betray his first wife, Gabrielle. A betrayal driven by anger and jealousy and hurt and pain. He had found Gabrielle semi-naked in the arms of another man and in pathetic revenge had gone out and slept with another woman. Frantic to ease the panic and loneliness that had threatened to crush him, knowing that there was no one in this world he could trust.

But now an unexpected need to protect his own was hammering through him and it pushed even his fears of marriage, of how it would expose the coward at the heart of him, to the side. He stabbed out his response.

I don't want our child to have any doubt about how much he's wanted, or about our commitment to raising him together. This is a public commitment to our baby.

After ten minutes of waiting for a response, he gave in to his hunger and was cooking fresh spinach and ricotta ravioli he had found in his fridge when her response finally came.

It might be a girl. C

Puzzled, he checked back on his previous text and saw he had unwittingly referred to the baby as a boy.

He popped a white grape from a bunch he had also taken from the fridge into his mouth. And then crunched down on another. And another. The sweet but sharp juice easing the dryness in his throat. His heart did a funny little shiver. He was going to be the father of a boy. How he knew he had no idea. But he knew. The knot of tension eating into his neck all day tightened even more.

He texted back.

It's a boy.

He was plating his pasta when his phone lit up again.

Do you really want to do this? I know you are impulsive in work, in the decisions you take, but this is about a baby, not a business deal you can walk away from if it doesn't work out. C.

He dropped the bottle of olive oil he was holding onto the smooth concrete of the kitchen counter. He could still back out of this. See the baby at weekends. And at other agreed times.

He wouldn't have the same opportunity to mess up his son's life when he wasn't a constant presence in his life.

He wouldn't have the constant fear of his marriage descending into a toxic mess.

He wouldn't have to deal with the fire that burned between him and Charlotte whenever they were in the same room. A fire that could easily derail their plans to raise their child together if expectations and emotions became confused.

But he owed it to his son to make him feel the most wanted child in this world. And he would do anything to ensure that his son *never* doubted his father's love.

He punched in his response.

I will never walk away from my son.

He ate his pasta in silence. What was Charlotte thinking? Was she getting cold feet? He typed in another text.

Will collect you at nine-fifteen tomorrow. I'm travelling to Rome after the register office and then on to Asia and the US but I'll keep in contact.

Again silence. He tossed his now empty plate into the dishwasher and grabbed his phone.

I will curtail my travel when the baby is born.

Sitting on her sofa in her pyjamas, Charlotte laid her hand on her stomach. Was it slightly more rounded than usual?

Was there really a life growing inside there?

She sighed in confusion at the conflicting thoughts looping through her brain: why would she want to lose her independence?

But then why would she choose to face being a parent on her own?

Why would she choose to marry a maverick heart-breaker?

But then why would she deny her child the right to have her father in her life on a daily basis?

And what of her career? She would struggle to get a job as challenging and rewarding and with so much potential for progression outside London.

But would Lucien be a feckless father?

Or could he love his child as much as her own father loved her?

A large lump swelled in her throat. She adored her father, his old-fashioned gentlemanly ways, his sense of fairness, his love for her mum, his dry sense of humour. The way his eyes lit up whenever he saw her.

But against all of this constant jabber and these conflicting thoughts, one solid feeling pumped in her heart.

She had to do everything to protect her child's future.

Which had to include taking steps now to protect her baby should anything ever happen to her. She inhaled a deep breath and with trembling fingers managed to type.

The only reason I'm agreeing to this marriage is so that my baby has a hands-on, loving and attentive father in her life. If you aren't those things, if work and your social life interferes, we are walking away. C

After pressing 'send' she switched off the phone and threw it into the far corner of the couch. Instead of resigning tomorrow she would be registering to marry her CEO. She stood and walked towards her bedroom. Praying she knew what she was doing.

Thursday 21st April, 11:10 p.m.

Why aren't you answering my calls?

Sorry. Was busy. Had to work late to catch up after our appointment at the registrar's office this morning. What do you want? C

To check how you are.

I'm fine. Thanks. Night. C

Friday 22nd April, 4:54 p.m.

Still busy, I take it? Or is it just my calls you aren't taking?

I'm at work. Personal calls aren't allowed. C

Funny. Ring me. I want to speak to you about the Poole project. It's almost midnight here in Singapore so call within the next half-hour.

Sorry can't. In a meeting. C

How are you?

Great. Got to go. C

Saturday 23rd April, 12:30 p.m.

Just arrived into Tokyo. What are your plans for the weekend?

Going to visit my parents. Will tell them about baby and our wedding. C

How will they react?

I don't know. C

Wait for me to return to London. I'll be back on 30th.

Why? C

I want to support you. And I'm guessing they'll want to meet me.

I need to do this by myself. C

Why?

It's easier to pretend to be in love with you when you're not standing in the same room. C

Tuesday 26th April, 10:30 p.m.

How's Tokyo? C

In Las Vegas now.

Mixing with lots of pretty showgirls? C

I'm on a construction site.

I told my mum and dad. They're thrilled about the baby. Shocked but happy about the wedding. C

Good.

Wednesday 27th April, 9:14 p.m.

Won your fortune in Las Vegas yet? C

Moved on to New York last night.

Lucky you. Love New York. C

How are you?

I'm okay. Morning sickness still here. C

'You didn't tell me.

It's not important—most women suffer when pregnant. C

Take time off work. You should have told me.

You didn't tell me that you had been married before. C

You're annoyed?

I'd have preferred not to have found out when we were in the register office. C

It was a long time ago. Have you seen a doctor about your sickness?

Yes. She assured me it's completely normal. C

You have to take care of yourself and the baby.

We haven't spoken about telling people at work yet. C

I have a plan that I'll discuss with you when I'm back in London on Saturday. Come to my house for dinner.

There's a new restaurant in Soho I've been wanting to try. Let's meet there. I'll book and send you the details. We also need to talk about a pre-nuptial agreement. I don't want anything from you. C

We'll have more privacy to talk in my house.

Somebody at the door. Have to go. C

* * *

Charlotte grimaced at the gingernut biscuit crumbs that had landed on her desk. *And in her keyboard!* Just—*yuck*.

Now she remembered why she had quickly given up eating at her desk as a young intern.

She twisted the keyboard upside down and shook vigorously. A woman in an online pregnancy forum swore that ginger biscuits kept her nausea at bay.

Charlotte wasn't convinced but at least the biscuits might give her a temporary sugar high to beat the tiredness that sat heavy in her bones.

She wasn't sleeping well.

In a matter of days she had gone from avoiding calls and texts from Lucien to being addicted to checking her phone to see if he had left a message.

In the first few days when he had gone, she had been unable to handle talking to him. Too overwhelmed with how her life had changed. And shocked to know that he had been married before. It shouldn't have been a surprise, but it left her feeling more vulnerable. It brought home how little she knew him.

She had needed space and time away from him. Away from how she seemed to lose her ability to think logically when in his presence, even if that was an electronic one. So she hadn't answered his calls and kept her texts brief, immersing herself instead in finalising the new mentoring programme she was introducing into the department for their new interns.

But when he had stopped texting over the weekend, she realised how much she missed hearing from him, missed knowing that he was thinking about her, even if it was only because she was carrying his child.

But last night when he had suggested that they meet at his house on Saturday to talk it had hit home just how difficult it would be to live under the same roof as him, especially in a house full of memories and reminders of their night together.

Was she doing the right thing?

A large crumb stubbornly refused to budge from under the space bar. She shook the keyboard hard and it dropped down to her desk.

Only when she had settled the keyboard back onto the desk did she realise that the entire office was staring at her. Even Simon, in the midst of a phone call, was staring out at her from his office window with his mouth open.

And then she realised that all of the eyes were trailing from her to a point behind her shoulder.

She turned slowly in her swivel chair.

Standing there, green eyes fixed on her, almost devouring her, wearing a smile that pinged her heart right out of her chest, a huge hand-tied bunch of tulips in his arms and, most worrying of all, a robin-egg-blue jewellery box in his hand, was Lucien.

Her throat sealed over. But aware of all of her colleagues staring at her, she managed to garble out, 'You're back early.' Two days early to be precise.

That incredible smile broadened. Who was this imposter? Lucien Duval scowled. He didn't smile.

He handed her the white and pink tipped tulips.

She accepted them, gave her flabbergasted colleagues who worked behind her a faint smile and said in a rush, 'Maybe we should go and talk somewhere more private.'

But instead, he dropped down to one knee and said, 'I know we're only dating a short while but you have become the centre of my world, especially now that you're to be the mother of my child.'

There was a collective gasp from the audience surrounding them, which did absolutely nothing to knock Lucien off course.

Opening the blue box, he lifted a much too beautiful

and elegant three-diamond and platinum ring towards her. 'Charlotte, *veux-tu m'épouser*? Will you marry me?'

She wanted to scream *no*. She wanted to shout at him for doing this. For asking her in such a low, sensual, sexy voice that she couldn't stop her legs from jingling against the central frame of her chair. For mortifying her like this. For piercing her heart with those intense green eyes.

But she had no option but to nod her acceptance, hoping that her colleagues thought that her hand was clasped to her mouth in shocked happiness rather than horror.

Wolf whistles, applause and cheers sounded in the room.

Lucien stood and, taking the ring from the box, placed it on her finger.

She tried to yank her hand away but he only tightened his grip more firmly and pulled her up to stand before him.

'Kiss, kiss, kiss.'

Charlotte looked beseechingly towards the intern corner, willing them to stop their chant. But her appeal only egged on the duo of mischievous male interns who shouted even louder for them to kiss, their female counterparts openly ogling Lucien close to swooning at any moment.

With a quick tug he pulled her towards him, an amused glint in those sinful green eyes the last thing she saw before his lips landed on hers.

It was a soft kiss.

Teasing, torturous, tantalising.

She stumbled closer into him, her hand reaching out to balance herself.

The hard thump of his heart beat against her palm beneath his lightweight grey suit jacket.

For a moment she became lost to the weight of his hand on her waist, the hardness of his chest, the scent of a freshly showered man.

When he pulled away, her already burning cheeks fired

even hotter with the crazy compulsion to have their kiss continue.

She stumbled back from him.

Tried to smile as her colleagues clapped once again.

She plastered a rictus smile on lips that felt stupidly swollen for what was a relatively chaste kiss. On tippy toes she reached up to his ear, her colleagues probably thinking she was whispering a sweet nothing to him when in fact she snarled, 'We need to talk. *Now.*'

On the top floor, inside his office, Charlotte shut the door and leaned against it with an infuriated sigh. 'Do you care to explain what on earth the past ten minutes has been about?'

'Assertive public relations.'

'Meaning?'

'The key to any public relations is to get in there first with how you want to present a story. My proposing to you publicly has taken away the power of any speculation as to why we're marrying. Now that it's out in the open it will only be office gossip for ten minutes max rather than weeks of water-cooler gossip.'

'I didn't think you cared.'

'I want my staff focused on work not their CEO's relationship with another employee. Also, you now have a ring and a story to tell your parents, if you're still determined to pretend to them that we're in love.'

Charlotte gritted her teeth. She was so annoyed on so many different levels she didn't know where to start. Lucien Duval needed to be taken down a peg or two. And he had to learn that this was a relationship of equals, which included not always being the one with the upper hand. A hard lesson to learn for a CEO who liked to always have things his way.

She smiled at him sweetly.

He looked at her suspiciously.

She dropped her head to the side and shrugged innocently. 'That's okay. I already told my parents that I took you to Paris and proposed to you there.'

His familiar scowl reappeared with a vengeance. 'Well, you can *un*-tell them.'

'Nope. Can't do. My mum, though shocked at first, was actually chuffed that I took matters into my own hands. I told my parents that on balance I thought you'd make an ideal father, I'm guessing you're good at sport so you'll be handy on sports day, you speak native French so the baby will be bilingual and I'm hoping you'll be handy around the house.' She gave him an unapologetic smile. 'Anyway I'm sticking by my story…especially after the stunt you just pulled.'

He considered her for a moment, dark brows pinched, shrugged off his jacket and placed it on his desk and advanced towards her, a wicked gleam now shining brightly in his eyes. 'You didn't object to our kiss.'

He was doing it again.

Invading her personal space, his big body making her feel tiny, making her body swim with want.

She stared at the crisp brightness of his white shirt and tried to ignore the pull of his clean soapy scent. The image of him in his shower…

She had to remember that he was a player. That she couldn't trust him. If her *'regular guy'* ex could break her heart, imagine what devastation an astute alpha charmer could inflict.

Memories of her shattered heart, the hollowing-out loneliness of being heartbroken coupled with her depression, shot steel back into her spine. She placed her hand on the door handle and said icily, 'I'm good at faking my responses.'

His eyes duelled with hers. She tried not to blink. Not

to look away. The gleam in his eye shifted from wicked to evil. 'You enjoyed it and you know it.'

She pressed the door handle down. 'Not enough for it to happen again.'

'That sounds like a challenge.'

What was she doing? Antagonising, provoking, challenging a man who thrived on confronting obstacles. It was like poking a sleeping grizzly bear with a stick. She pushed down on the door handle even more, ready to make a quick exit once she had said her piece. 'Well, it's just as well then that we both know that our marriage is nothing more than a front for raising our child. I'm sure I can rely on you not to jeopardise our child's happiness by confusing the reasons why we're together.'

His brows slammed together.

And then as though he couldn't help himself, that risk-taking maverick at the heart of him shining through, he placed his foot against the base of the door, preventing her exit, and said with a glint in his eye, 'Deny away, Charlotte. There's nothing I like more in life than to prove others wrong.'

CHAPTER FOUR

SHE HAD TO be kidding.

The following month, Lucien watched Charlotte emerge from a classic silver Bentley, festooned with white ribbon, to the applause of the 'small' wedding party.

Dressed in a knee-length, full-skirted white bridal dress, Charlotte accepted her father's outstretched hand—well, he was guessing it was her father—and cuddled into his side, a wide smile on her mouth. Her father, tall and upright, handsome with slicked-back steel-grey hair, slowly leaned down and kissed her forehead.

Dieu! The Verbal Assassin had turned into a blushing bride.

The wedding party began to make their way up the tree-lined cobbled forecourt. Charlotte said something to her father and broke away, approaching him on her own, her father stopping to chat to a woman wearing a flying-saucer-sized hat.

He smiled at her, the ever dutiful groom, temporarily forgetting all of his grievances as he was sucked into this pantomime, for a moment almost believing that the gorgeous woman smiling and blushing shyly at him was his willing and loving bride.

He pulled himself together, his frustration spiking dangerously, and when she was close enough he growled, 'The registrar is running late. We have to wait outside here until they are ready.'

Just then a photographer arrived and in a stage whisper said, 'Don't mind me, I'll just snap away. Try to be as natural as you can be.'

Lucien reined in the urge to grab his camera and toss it in the nearest bush and instead pointed the photographer in the direction of his friend Rakesh. 'Take some photos of him and the other witness.' He paused and waited while Charlotte directed him towards her friend Tameka.

When the photographer had scuttled away he said, 'I thought this was going to be a simple ceremony. It makes a royal wedding look tame.'

She glanced at the pedestals of pink, lilac and white flowers lining the pathway, the pink and silver balloons tied to the trunks of the trees flapping in the warm May air and gave a guilty smile. 'My mum got a little carried away.'

'You don't say. I was half expecting you to arrive in a horse and carriage. Why didn't you warn me?'

She smiled at him sweetly but her eyes damned him. 'If I'd seen you during the past two weeks maybe I would have.'

A thread of guilt poked his gut and, not wanting to think about it, he answered with a shrug, 'I had to be in Asia for negotiations.'

'So you said.'

Her hair was coiled into a low bun to the side of her head, a large white silk flower threaded just above her right ear. The picture-perfect bride. A wave of frustration and panic swirled in his chest. This was supposed to be a quick, no-nonsense ceremony. A business deal. Had Charlotte already confused the nature of their agreement? 'Why didn't you stop your mother? Surely you don't want all of this fuss too?'

She adjusted the satin bodice of her dress. 'Obviously

not, but as my mum had hoped I'd get married in my village church with the entire village in attendance, I wasn't going to deny her a few flowers and balloons, was I?'

He tried not to stare at her, to fully acknowledge to himself just how stunningly pretty she looked.

He flexed his jaw and nodded towards the noisy, laughing crowd behind them, mostly made up of men who looked like retired army officers and their stalwarts-of-the-community wives. Good people who would be horrified at the truth of their marriage. 'Flowers and balloons I could handle, but did they have to invite such a large crowd?'

She nodded and scowled towards where Rakesh was blatantly chatting up Tameka, the photographer snapping Rakesh's rakish smile and Tameka's blush. 'Twenty-four people is hardly a crowd. There's over two hundred people in the village. So count yourself lucky. Just because you decided to only invite a fellow playboy to the wedding didn't mean that I was going to restrict the number of guests my parents wanted to invite. It's a moment of celebration for them, even if it's closer to being a funeral for you.' She regarded him with an evil smile playing on her lips. 'I'm guessing it would have been too humiliating to have more than one witness to the death of your womanising days.'

Dieu, she had a special gift for needling him.

He had only invited one guest because this was no more than an agreement to raise their child together. The last thing he had wanted was a circus around what should be a simple ceremony.

He ignored the voice that came from deep within him, pointing out that in truth he had no one else close enough to him to invite.

With irritation gnawing his insides, he leaned down towards her.

For a moment he became disorientated. She smelt different. Gone was the smell of starched cotton and paperwork. Now she smelt of light and sunshine.

Who was he marrying?

The ice-cool lawyer of work or the vulnerable, gentle woman he had made love to in his bed?

He drew back.

Familiar unimpressed sea-green eyes held his gaze.

This woman, the tough, cynical lawyer, he could handle.

Reassured, he gave her a slow smile and a husky whisper. 'Trust me, I'm looking forward to being a one-woman man.'

She dropped her head to the side. 'Best of luck in finding her. Anyway, I guess I should introduce you to my parents. Or do you have a sudden need to get away again? Any crisis in the New York office that only Super Lucien can sort out?'

He cupped her cheek and stroked her skin with his thumb. Lifted her chin, forcing her to meet his gaze. 'I've already told you, you're the only woman in my life from now on. Get used to that fact.'

Something shifted in her expression. She bit her lip and said softly,, 'You can still call this off. It's not too late.'

Her gaze was nervous, almost pleading. Doubt swirled in his chest. Should he call it off? Could he be a good husband to this woman? But then his eyes drifted down to the waistband of her dress, her gently rounded belly catching slightly on the material.

A reminder of why they had to go through with this.

He caught her by the elbow and twisted her around slowly towards the wedding guests, shards of sunshine breaking through the leafy trees overhead, dancing on the cobbled path. 'And cause a scandal in the village? I don't think so.'

As they approached the guests Charlotte's father and a

flustered-looking woman in her mid-seventies broke away from the other guests to meet them.

'Mum, Dad, this is Lucien.'

From her dad he received a firm handshake and an un-flinching military stare. Her mum rushed forward and yanked him down into a mama-bear-type hug. For a moment he thought he had whiplash.

Disconcerted, he cleared his throat and moved back two steps. 'Monsieur and Madame Aldridge, my apologies for cancelling our lunch last Sunday.'

A bundle of feathers and what looked like painted pink straw in Charlotte's mum's short grey hair quivered when she answered. 'Oh, call us by our first names, Robert and Carol, and don't worry about last weekend. Lottie explained how you decided to go on a weekend course called How to be a Good Husband—what will they think of next? But such a good idea. I must say between your weekend course and accepting Lottie's proposal, you really are one of these *New Men* I read about in the newspapers.'

Charlotte patted him on the arm. 'Oh, Lucien really is a *New Man*, ready to embrace his softer side. I already see a change in how he's communicating with me. And he's so in tune with my needs. Aren't you, darling?'

He gritted his teeth and addressed her mother, 'Lottie?'

Taken aback, her mum gestured towards Charlotte. 'Lottie, of course, it's our pet name for Charlotte—didn't she ever tell you that?'

Her father and mother moved closer to one another and stared at him dubiously. He placed an arm around Charlotte's shoulders and tucked her against his chest. '*Dieu!* You have to forgive me... I'm a little jet-lagged right now. I've got into the habit of calling Charlotte *ma minette*: my pussycat.'

Charlotte swung her hand up to rest beneath his jacket and gave a loud chuckle. Her fingertips dug into his side.

'I've told you, darling, just call me Charlotte. Lottie and *ma minette* don't suit me.'

He forced himself to smile down at her, his skin stinging.

Her father cleared his throat and said sombrely, 'Lottie said that your parents are unable to make the wedding. It's a shame they couldn't be here.'

Fed up of all the lies and how Charlotte kept playing games with him, he gave an extravagant shrug. 'Not really. We haven't spoken in almost twenty years. We don't get on.'

For a moment alarm bells flashed in both of her parents' eyes. And rather satisfyingly, Charlotte looked up at him as if she was ready to take him apart.

Her mum was the first to break the tense silence. With a loud sigh she said, 'Oh, well…never mind. You'll be part of our family now.'

Charlotte's body stiffened beneath his hold. 'Mum, please.'

He dropped his arm and stepped away.

Her mother continued, looking at him with earnest ecstasy, 'We can't tell you, Lucien, how thrilled we are about the baby.'

Charlotte's frown dropped and she looked at her mum with a wistful indulgent smile.

Her father interjected by stepping forward. 'We hope that you're both very happy together. Lottie means the world to us, when—'

Charlotte interrupted her father in a low pleading voice, 'Dad, please.'

For a moment all three shared looks that spoke of family bonds, of family secrets. Bonds and secrets that excluded him. A wave of loneliness caught him unawares. Had he ever been as close to anyone in his life where a single look could communicate so much?

His voice unsteady, Charlotte's father continued, 'We

hope more than anything that you have a long and happy life together. Be kind and patient with one another.'

Charlotte hugged her dad and then her mum, who was busy wiping away tears.

Lucien fisted his hands against the guilt and inadequacy that exploded inside him. He already had a failed marriage, parents who were the antithesis of role models when it came to parenting. He should end this charade. Her parents should know the truth: that he couldn't give their daughter all of the things they wanted for her—he was not capable of being the husband they expected. He wasn't even certain he was capable of being the father their grandson deserved.

Was Charlotte right? Should they call this off?

He muttered something in agreement and was relieved when Charlotte suggested that she introduce him to her friends.

When they were out of earshot he said furiously, 'We need to tell them the truth.'

Charlotte came to a stop and, with a pained smile on her lips, muttered through clenched teeth, 'If you hurt my parents I will never forgive you.'

With that she walked away.

His soon-to-be infuriating wife.

Could he, should he go through with this? His life was going to be turned upside down. A new baby, a wife, in-laws. How on earth was he going to focus on work and the daily crises needing his attention? How on earth was he going to handle the suffocating bonds of family, the fear of messing up his marriage, the fear of failing his son?

If Charlotte had ever allowed herself to stop and think about what her perfect wedding ceremony would look like, this would probably be it. A small intimate venue in a historic house, her parents present, spring sunshine flooding into the room from a large bow window, a garden outside filled with vibrant-coloured gladioli swaying in the light breeze and the promise of another long energetic and exciting summer in London. A violin soloist playing. And at her side a man who made her heart leap every time she saw him. A man who took her normal physical reserve and tore it into strips just by being him, all six-foot-two, muscular, hard, sneering him. A tough-skinned business maverick who got what he wanted in life through brutal persuasion and a dangerous intelligence. A player. A heartbreaker.

The registrar invited them to stand to say their vows.

She stood and clasped her trembling hands.

And looked into the clear green eyes of the man she was about to marry.

They had emailed each other back and forth various versions of their vows for the past week, until they had found a version they were both comfortable with.

His attention focused solely on her, Lucien repeated after the registrar, 'I, Lucien Duval, take you, Charlotte Aldridge, as my wife. I promise to create and protect a family and home that's full of love, understanding, respect and honour.'

Lucien paused and swallowed hard.

The lines around his eyes tightened.

Her stomach somersaulted, sadness, tenderness dragged in her chest.

Lucien Duval, street-savvy maverick CEO, looked lost.

Without thinking she reached out to him.

He took her hand in his. For the longest moment he held her gaze, doubt in his eyes.

Was he about to back out?

She closed her eyes.

Her heart sank down into her chest.

Heavy with...what? Was it disappointment that was weighing it down so fiercely?

His fingers gripped hers and pulled her ever so slightly closer to him.

She opened her eyes to his intense stare.

And for that moment they were the only people in the room.

It would be so easy to fall in love with him.

Her heart went into overdrive. She mustn't. But it would be so easy.

In a low sombre voice, his eyes not wavering from hers, Lucien continued with his vows. 'I promise to be always open and honest. And, whatever may come, promise to provide you with comfort and support through life's joy and sorrow.'

It was her turn.

But her mouth wouldn't co-operate.

I'm about to marry this man who takes my breath away. This totally unsuitable man. I've lost my mind.

She smiled guiltily to the registrar, who had whispered her name a number of times. Nodded to say that she was okay.

Looked back at Lucien.

Her pulse pounded even harder.

Could she go through with this?

Lucien stepped in towards her. And held her hand with both of his. As though offering her his strength. He regarded her with a dignity that tightened her chest.

She took a deep breath and repeated her vows. 'I, Charlotte Aldridge, take you, Lucien Duval, as my husband. I promise to create and protect a family and home that's full of love, understanding, respect and honour.'

She paused and fought the tears that sprang up in her eyes, saying the words aloud, in front of friends and family, reminding her of why they were marrying. To create a family. This was all about their baby.

Handing Lucien their marriage certificate, the registrar invited them to stand. With a smile she introduced them to their guests as man and wife. And after the applause died down, she invited them to kiss.

Her stomach headed south.

Lucien gave her that *Well, what are we going to do now?* smile, which had proved her undoing that night they'd slept together. Beguiling, playful, safe, inviting.

His hand reached up and his thumb slowly ran along her jawline.

As though treasuring what was before him.

His green eyes didn't hold their usual shrewdness. Instead he considered her almost tenderly…sweetly.

His fingers ran down the side of her neck.

Her back arched.

The room was in silence. Without looking she knew their guests were staring at them, breaths held, waiting for their kiss.

He angled his head. His eyes darkened. The flattering, intoxicating, hard-to-resist gaze of a man who was looking at something he wanted. A lot.

She moved a little closer. Moved up onto her tippy toes.

He gave a small smile, pulled her towards him and kissed her gently. His lips teasing hers.

In an instant she was melting against him, drugged by the taste of his mouth, his clean leathery scent, the pull of his big body.

She felt his hand rest on her tummy. Lightly, protectively, possessively.

A silent reminder of why they were standing here as husband and wife, kissing.

The pretence of a relationship for the sake of their child.

Half an hour later, the Bentley slowly passed the Elephant and Castle, the early Friday rush hour slowing their journey northwards to their reception venue.

Beside her, Lucien was still pulling grains of rice from his hair and suit pocket.

Every now and then their driver would gaze at them in his rear-view mirror, obviously puzzled at the tense silence between the newlyweds.

She ran her hands down over the satin of her dress. Despite everything this dress represented—a sham marriage, the loss of her independence, having to pretend she wasn't magnetised to her groom—she loved its simple elegance. Though it had got a little too tight in the past week—the changes in her body were becoming more pronounced with each passing day—she had actually been pleased when she had looked at her reflection in the mirror in her bedroom earlier. But now she just felt deflated.

The need to end the awful and telling silence between them had her say, 'Well, I guess we must hold the record for the shortest ever wedding photoshoot.'

'The photographer had ten minutes—how long more did he need?'

'The poor man looked crushed when you refused to stand in for more photos. And there I was hoping for a few shots of us paddling in the fountain in the park next door—I thought it would look cute on—' she paused and forced herself to say '—our mantelpiece.' Was she really going to live with Lucien Duval? Her CEO. The playboy serial dater. Live with him…as his wife. Would this ever feel normal and not half fantasy, half nightmare?

Lucien's only response was a disbelieving exhalation before he began to flick through his phone.

Irritated, she said, 'We don't have to go to the reception if you don't want to.'

He threw her a quick glance, but there was a hint of amusement lurking there. 'And miss whatever wonderful surprises your mother has organised? I don't think so.'

Stupidly buoyed up by this change in his humour, she

said with a wry teasing smile, 'It's nothing really special—just a champagne reception, a five-course meal with an accompanying jazz band in Claridge's.'

He threw his eyes to heaven and dropped his phone down onto the seat between them. He turned and stared at her for a moment, the humour in his eyes slowly fading. 'Why is this wedding so important to your parents?'

After Dan's and Angie's betrayal, she had boxed away any thoughts and dreams she had of boyfriends, a fiancé, a husband. Too hurt and scared to even contemplate those things any more.

But despite her terrible relationship history, propelled by a low-lying loneliness, over the past few years she had occasionally scurried out of her comfortable world of work and gym classes to date. And after a few skirmishes she would quickly retreat, hating the games involved, the second guessing, the vulnerability of putting yourself and your heart on the line. The need to mind and protect herself easily defeating the need for intimacy and closeness.

Now, to answer his question she gestured to her dress with a wry grimace. 'I've always said I wanted to focus on my career and that relationships weren't important to me, so they never expected to see me dressed in a meringue. They weren't the only ones.' Her mocking tone died in her mouth and she cleared her throat, her heart pounding, not sure why she felt so compelled to share with him what was scaring her so much. 'My dad isn't well—he has heart problems.'

He considered her for much too long, those green eyes eating her up, the usual hardness in his expression softening. 'I'm sorry to hear that.'

Her heart dropped into her stomach and bounced back at double its normal speed. He had spoken in a low, kind voice. The voice he had whispered to her with, that night they had spent together. She bit the inside of her lip, trying to stop the thickness in her throat from building any more.

He twisted further in his seat, laid a hand on the seat between them, his fingertips almost touching the satin of her skirt. 'You worry about them?'

Without thinking she answered, 'Almost as much as they worry about me.'

She had argued with her mum and dad the weekend she had told them about the baby and her engagement, over whether she should tell Lucien about her depression. They insisted that she should. But she had refused to even discuss the issue with them.

Talking about her depression still felt as if she had to rip her soul out and expose it for the whole world to see.

What good could come from burdening Lucien with her past health history anyway?

It *was* in the past.

Aware that Lucien was waiting for her to explain what she meant about her parents worrying about her, she opted to focus the conversation on him instead. 'Why don't you talk to your parents?'

The mellow, empathic Lucien disappeared in a long slow blink of his dark eyelashes to be replaced by the familiar street-fighter blank stare. 'I hit my dad when I found him in bed with another woman. Two years later I hit my mum's new boyfriend even harder.'

She gasped at the bluntness of his answer. The lack of emotion in his voice. She muttered, 'Why?' while wincing inside at the brief disappointment that flickered on his features at her shocked response.

In a bored tone he said, 'I don't think this is a subject matter for a wedding day, even a convenience one like ours.'

They were now driving through Green Park via Constitution Hill, past tourists heading to and from Buckingham Palace, past commuters rushing home for the weekend. Hearing the bitterness in his voice, his dismissal of their wedding day, had her turn to him and ask a question that she knew was going to lead to a whole series of questions she had to ask, questions that were starting to drive her insane.

She tried to keep her voice neutral, the voice of a colleague passing time on a shared journey. 'How old were you when you married the first time round?'

He considered her for a moment, a chess master sizing up his opposition. 'Eighteen.'

'And your wife?'

He now seemed intrigued as to where she was going with this. 'Eighteen too.' He rose an eyebrow as though to say, *Well, what's coming next?*

Inside logic was screaming at her not to ask. But she couldn't stop herself. How could she compete with an eighteen-year-old? No wonder he hadn't said one thing about how she looked today. Couldn't he at least have said she looked *nice*? That innocuous word that covered general okayishness and all sorts of wardrobe malfunctions?

'Was she beautiful?'

He looked at her in exasperation. But then turned and stared out at the hotels on Park Lane. 'I don't remember.'

She gave a tight laugh full of mocking derision. Derision for her own vain stupidity and her own lack of self-esteem, driven by the prowling image of herself, thin and grey and exhausted, facing a too-loved-up-to-hide-the-evidence Dan and Angie that had her wanting, needing Lucien to find her attractive on their wedding day, even if it was all a charade. 'And you said you don't like to lie.'

He twisted back to her. Frustration burned in his eyes. 'Yes, she was pretty…but not as beautiful as you look today.' He inhaled, ran a hand down over his face. He settled now softer, sad even, eyes on her and in a quiet voice he added, 'Please…don't make this any harder than it has to be. There's too much at stake.'

Something cracked inside her heart. She had to work

against the tightness in her throat before she managed to say, 'You're right. Sorry.'

His hand gently landed on hers, his fingers splayed across hers. Followed by a look full of resigned regret but also a hint of warmth and understanding.

His fingers curled around her hand and he looked back out into the streets of London.

He held her hand all the way to Claridge's.

And for the first time she fully realised that for better or worse they were now a couple, a team, a husband and wife. Not in the conventional sense, of course, they hadn't got traditional romantic love, but they did have something just as important bonding them together for ever: a love for their child.

CHAPTER FIVE

FOUR HOURS LATER, Lucien led Charlotte into the kitchen of his Mayfair home.

Now her home too, of course.

His wife.

The mother-to-be of his child.

Dieu! Would he ever get used to all of this?

He swung open the folding doors that ran the length of the back kitchen wall, a brilliant sunset just about to drop below the coach house to the rear of the garden.

It was still warm enough to sit outside so he gestured to the garden furniture out on the terrace. 'You must be tired. Take a seat and I'll get you a drink.'

Her gaze trailed out into the garden and paused for the briefest moment on the garden wall in the near right corner. To the spot where their child had been conceived in a moment of intoxicating, passionate madness.

She gave him a tight smile. 'Tea would be nice. Do you have any decaf?'

He nodded and twisted away. Hoping that with time both of their memories would fade of that night. Because right now, those memories were torturing him with unleashed desire.

He jerked on the water tap, filled the kettle and placed it on the hob. And then snapped open his coffee machine. Until he remembered.

He switched it off. And yanked open his fridge and took out a bottle of sparkling water.

Charlotte considered the bottle and then him. 'You can have a coffee if you want. I'm able to tolerate the smell now.'

'It's fine.'

She shrugged, and sat down on a stool at the far side of the breakfast counter, a hand running along the poured concrete countertop surface. 'Or have something stronger if you'd like. You haven't drunk all day. Just because I can't drink alcohol, doesn't mean you aren't able to.'

In her white princess dress, her hair coiled to the side of her head, she looked like the ballerina figure that used to twirl around and around when he opened his mother's jewellery box.

Would he ever manage to look at her without it doing something peculiar to his heart, without being possessed with a burning need to reach out and touch her?

Dieu!

He was worn out from spending the day trying not to notice her.

Their first dance on the small dance floor in the private dining room where their reception had been held had been an uncomfortable blend of awkwardness and a strange intimacy, the vivid memories of their night together alive and intense as he held her slight frame in his arms, and the bond of creating a child tying them together more powerfully than if they had known each other for years.

'I don't drink alcohol.'

'Really?'

He rested against the kitchen countertop opposite her and folded his arms. 'Not what you expected from a serial dater who enjoys breaking women's hearts?'

She shrugged with a hint of guilty admission at his reminder of her previous accusation and said, 'I have to admit that I had assumed drinking went along with your lifestyle.'

Once upon a time it had. In his late teens he had used alcohol to numb the gnawing emptiness inside him, but it had only made the emptiness more overwhelming and had fuelled a self-destructive anger that had led him to ending his marriage through the weakest, most cowardly, most pathetic act possible.

'We have a lot to find out about each other,' he said, turning away to make her tea, adding with his back to her, 'I hate not being in control.'

'Should I be worried—you're not a control freak, are you?'

Her voice was teasing.

He turned and raised an eyebrow. 'Hardly. I put up with the extravaganza that was our supposedly simple wedding ceremony today, didn't I?'

She grimaced and asked, 'Was today really that horrible for you?'

Despite himself he admitted the truth. 'All things considered, it was a nice day. Your mum did a good job.'

She smiled and lifted the cup he had placed before her. 'Thanks for playing along today, for keeping up the story...' she cleared her throat, and stared down at her cup '...that we're in love... It means a lot to me. I would hate to upset my parents. As you probably could tell, they're very protective of me.'

They looked at each other in silence for a few seconds too long, awkwardness, tension, the enormity of what they were doing hanging between them once again.

He forced himself to speak. 'Why so?'

Her eyes shifted away from him, she shrugged, moved in her seat, adjusting her gown beneath her. 'My parents were relatively old when I arrived. They had been told they couldn't have children so I was a surprise...a much-wanted surprise. They were pretty strict and old-fashioned in their ways. I wasn't spoiled but I always knew that I was adored.'

How different their childhoods had been. 'You were lucky.'

'Why?'

'Not every child is wanted so much.'

She jerked back in her stool, her eyes wide in alarm. 'You mean our child?'

Was she serious? He dropped his water bottle down on the concrete counter with a thud. 'No. Of course not. I want this child—didn't today prove that to you? Why else would I have gone through with it?'

For the longest while she stared at him and then quietly answered, 'I appreciate the sacrifice you've made.'

He gritted his teeth, hating the hurt in her voice, and tried to steer their conversation back on track. They had to learn to work together, not constantly be tense and wary of one another. 'What excuse did you give to your parents for us not going on a honeymoon?'

'I said that we planned on going away later in the pregnancy, when I was feeling less poorly.'

He placed both hands on the breakfast counter and scanned her face for any signs of illness. 'Are you unwell? I thought your nausea had gone.'

'It comes and goes but it's nothing serious. I had to find an excuse for us not having a honeymoon.'

'You must tell me if you're feeling ill.'

Her expression tightened. 'Out of concern for the baby?'

He reined in his disquiet at the angry hurt in her voice that he was guilty of causing by recklessly sleeping with her and said, 'For you too.' He moved towards her. 'You're my wife, Charlotte.' It was his first time saying that. My wife.

A blush formed on her cheeks and a knot formed in his heart.

She smiled nervously. 'I have something I want to give

to you.' She paused and worried her lip. 'It's a wedding present of sorts.'

She got up and walked back out into the hallway where her suitcase lay. His driver had collected it from her apartment earlier that morning prior to the wedding ceremony. All of her other items were to be delivered by a removal company tomorrow.

When she came back she stood by the breakfast bar and stared down at the small piece of paper in her hands.

Slowly, almost reluctantly, she passed it to him along the surface of the counter separating them.

The photograph-sized light piece of paper held a black and white image. He stared at it not understanding.

His heart began to thud.

He picked it up and swallowed hard.

He could just make out the image of a head, a long body, curled up legs.

In the distance, he heard Charlotte say, 'It's a sonogram of our baby.'

Confused, he looked up sharply, 'When did you get this?'

She gave him a pensive smile. 'Wednesday, when I went for my twelve-week scan and obstetrician appointment at the Claremont.'

He stared at her in disbelief. They had had a heated discussion a few weeks back as to where her maternity care should take place. Charlotte had intended attending a hospital close to her old apartment but he wanted her care to be closer by. The Claremont, located only a five-minute drive away from here, was world-renowned for its consultant-led maternity care. Charlotte had eventually given into his arguments why she should attend the Claremont, but was this exclusion of him her way of getting him back for his insistence that he have an equal say in her maternity care? 'Why didn't you tell me? Shouldn't the father go too?'

'You weren't around.'

Angry that she had excluded him, angry at no longer feeling in control of his life, he waved the piece of paper at her. 'You should have told me. I should have been there with you.'

She reached up and pulled the white silk flower from her hair. 'You spend most of your time trying to avoid me.'

'What do you mean? I called you every day while I was away.'

Patting her hair, she gave a resigned shrug. 'Since our engagement you've been away constantly. If you're as absent as this when the baby is born our marriage won't survive.'

Thrown, he fought back. 'I've given you my word that I won't be absent. I *will* be there for my child.'

'We'll see.'

Her unconvinced, resigned tone dissolved his righteous anger.

Which was replaced with a heavy dose of guilt.

She was right.

He had been avoiding her.

Unconsciously needing time away, the distraction of work to bury the dread of messing up with his child... with his wife.

Not trusting himself around her.

Not trusting himself not to kiss her and a whole lot more.

He had to change. She and the baby deserved better.

He went and fetched his phone from the kitchen table where he had dropped it earlier. 'When's your next appointment?'

'I have my twenty-week scan on July fourteenth.'

He angled away from her and inhaled deeply. Old memories of his parent's broken promises to celebrate the French National holiday of Independence together as a family tugged hard in his chest. Instead he would join his best friend Yann's family to celebrate, their warm welcome only emphasising the coldness of his own home. Without turning he mindlessly scrolled through his phone calendar and said, 'Bastille Day.'

'Do you go back to France to celebrate it?' Without waiting for his answer, she said in a rush, 'I can go to the scan by myself. It won't be a problem.'

She didn't want him at the scan.

When was she going to understand that he wanted to be a full participant in this pregnancy? He *was* the father. With rights and responsibilities.

He turned back to her and through gritted teeth asked her for the time of the scan appointment and entered it into his phone.

He had fifty-seven unread emails. He should look at them. He normally would still be working at this time on a Friday night.

His new wife looked at him, perplexed.

Freezing her out, going to his home office to work, would clearly be counterproductive. They needed to work on their relationship—his last marriage failed because they never spoke properly, never were clear in what they could give to the other person, or what they expected of one another.

He was not making that mistake with this marriage.

Reluctantly he dropped his phone back onto the counter. 'I left France when I was twenty. I was offered an apprenticeship with a German construction company. I've only returned to France since for business reasons.'

'Do you miss it?'

'I guess.'

'Do you ever think of returning, living there?'

'I haven't thought about it. I grew up in the Charente region amongst the vineyards. I guess I miss the open spaces there, the slower pace of life. When I was growing up I used to dream of owning my own vineyard.'

Yann's family had owned a vineyard; their fifteenth-century chateau set in the centre of the property had been filled with endless love, laughter and acceptance.

Back then, he had thought that one day he too might be able to create his own world of family and love and belonging when he was older.

But the bitterness of his first marriage had shown him just how ridiculous those dreams had been.

He was just as incapable as his parents of selflessly loving a partner, of not sabotaging it all.

Charlotte gave a light laugh. 'I used to dream of being a tortoise. I thought it would be so cool to be able to carry my house around on my back!' Shaking her head in playful mockery of her childhood dream, she added, 'At least your dream is still feasible.'

No, it wasn't feasible.

He wasn't capable of the selfless love that a marriage demanded.

And now he was married to a woman who didn't trust him, who didn't want to marry him in the first place.

And she was right not to trust him.

Look at how he destroyed his first marriage.

Shame pulled like a tight fist in his chest; he took a slug of his water, the bubbles popping harshly at the back of his throat.

'Maybe one day you'll take our baby to France. Show her where you grew up.'

Taken aback by her suggestion, he stared at her.

And despite the painful memories of his childhood with his parents, there was so much he loved and still missed about his childhood home place, the endless fields of vineyards and sunflowers, swimming in the meadow-lined Charente River with his school friends, the trips to La Rochelle, climbing Dune du Pilat in Arcachon.

But would going back just be a painful reminder of all the hurt and the constant, twisting, painful knowledge that he wasn't wanted? That he wasn't loved.

He shook off those thoughts and narrowed his eyes, challenging her insistence that the baby was a girl. 'I'm sure *he'd* love it.' His throat tightened and he asked, 'Did you find out the sex of the baby at the scan?'

She lifted a hand to rest on her stomach. 'No. I want to keep it a surprise until the birth.' She gave him a cautious look. 'Is that okay with you?'

He nodded in agreement, his heart hammering at how tantalising his new bride looked in her white gown, perched on the breakfast stool, her hand cradling his unborn son.

He had been avoiding her.

The least he could do was apologise. 'My first marriage ended over fifteen years ago. I haven't been in a serious relationship since. Our relationship…our marriage, it's all so new. Give me some time to get things right.'

Charlotte nodded but she was clearly still unconvinced. And looked rather sad at that fact.

He shifted on his feet. 'I want this to work out.'

Her sombre eyes held his. 'I guess you need to prove it now.'

Hating her wariness, her doubt, even if they were justified, he lifted up the sonogram picture and studied it deliberately. 'It takes two to make a marriage work. We clearly need to establish how we communicate. How we work together. But most important of all is that we start as we mean to go along, in every aspect of our relationship.'

'Meaning?'

'Meaning no more surprises like today. We take decisions together as a couple, and that includes the pregnancy.

I want to be present at all appointments. Plus we need to meet at least once a day to talk.'

'That won't be a problem for me.' Her tight tone implied that it would prove to be a problem for him.

They regarded each other cagily.

The distance between them once again thrown into sharp relief.

He planted his hands on his hips. 'Nor me.'

Her head dropped to the side, a sceptical eyebrow raised. 'Fine, let's have breakfast every morning.'

He dropped his hands from his hips. 'I go to the gym at six.'

'At seven so.'

He met with his PA every morning at seven. His day would be a nightmare if he started any later. 'I go straight to work.'

She let out a disbelieving breath.

Raising his hands in surrender, he said, 'Okay, we'll have breakfast at seven.'

She gave a satisfied nod. 'When the baby is born I expect you to be home by seven at the latest. For now I'll accept you being home by eight.'

He loosened his tie and opened his top shirt button. How was he going to manage the demands of work with this new domestic regime? For now he countered her proposition with a more feasible figure. 'Nine.'

She pursed her lips, a combative spirit emboldening the brightness in her eyes. 'I thought we were going to set a routine.'

'Eight-thirty.'

She shook her head and sighed dramatically as though terribly disappointed.

Dieu! She was enjoying this.

She gave him a tight smile. 'Until September, after that we'll pull it back each week by half an hour until it's seven.

And with regards to travel, you'll have to cut that back too. The baby will need her father here. I'm happy to accept you travelling for two weeks a month until September and after that a week per month.'

She was testing his resolve to put the baby first.

Well, two could play at that game. 'Fine. If we're going to be so prescriptive in setting our daily routine then we should do the same with our sleeping arrangements. We'll sleep in the same bedroom.'

He moved away, ignoring her aghast expression, and added, 'Starting tonight. You look tired. I'll take your suitcase up to our bedroom.'

Charlotte chased after Lucien up the three flights of stairs that led to his top-floor bedroom suite, abandoning her shoes on the first floor.

Averting her eyes from his super-king-size bed, she followed him into his adjoining dressing room and watched him deposit her luggage onto a suitcase rack. She gave a disbelieving laugh. 'You're actually serious, aren't you?'

'*Absolument*. Absolutely. Our baby will not grow up in a house with parents who sleep in separate bedrooms.'

'Why not?'

'What type of message would it give if we sleep in separate rooms? I'm assuming you want our child to believe we're in love too?'

He had a point. But still, this was crazy. They couldn't sleep in the same bed. 'Yes, but—'

'And what about my housekeeper—what is she to think? And your parents when they visit and see that we're sleeping apart?'

'I'll say that I'm not sleeping well at the moment, which is the truth.'

'*Pour l'amour du ciel!* For heaven's sake, Charlotte, as

if they are going to believe that a young and healthy couple who are supposedly in love would want to sleep apart.'

She stared at him aghast and then blankly down at her suitcase.

He was right…to a point.

But she also knew he was testing her.

Testing her continual assertions that she was committed to raising their baby in a happy, loving environment, while at the same time being sceptical of his pledges to do likewise.

It would be excruciating to have to share his bed.

To have to lie there and try not to remember their night together and how she had responded to him. How she had cried out in pleasure. Time and time again.

But there was no way she was going to admit any of that to him and she certainly wasn't going to give him the satisfaction of calling her bluff.

She bent down and twisted the suitcase to face her and opened it, the lid flying backwards. 'You want us to sleep in the same bed. Fine. Just stay to your side of the bed.'

He stepped towards her and she forced herself not to move.

He brought with him his scent, the pull of his large body, the memories of her nipping at the tender skin at the base of his throat the last time she had been in this bedroom suite.

His head dropped until only inches separated them. 'I promise to be a gentleman at all times.'

A deep shiver ran through her at his softly spoken words.

She fisted her hands and dared to look up and into his eyes. Eyes that held a hint of mischief but also shared intimate memories.

Her heart came to a standstill.

Crushed by how much she still wanted him, crushed by knowing it could never happen again, crushed by her deep craving to have him stare with the same want and tenderness as he had that cold March night, she lashed out, 'I'm already paying the consequences of our poor judgement. I don't think it's something we should repeat.'

He jerked back.

His mouth hardened.

Intense impersonal icy green eyes held hers. 'You're right. It was ill-judged. And I'm sorry that you're having to pay the cost of my lack of judgement.' He moved beyond her and added, 'I'm going for a shower. I'll leave you to unpack.'

Once inside the bathroom he shut the door with a heavy thud.

Charlotte dropped her head and ran her hands tiredly over her face, drawing in a deep breath.

Sleeping in the same bed was his idea—surely he didn't expect her to embrace it without argument?

She hesitated for a moment at the suitcase but then began to unpack, her thoughts alternating from agreeing with his reasoning to wondering if she was losing her mind. A constant thought worming its way through her mind—was getting her to sleep in his bed some scheme to manipulate her?

Had he another agenda other than keeping up the pretence of their marriage.

Was she being manoeuvred and controlled by a master tactician…for purposes that she couldn't even start to understand?

Was she way out of her depth without realising it?

It was another ten minutes before he emerged from the bathroom.

She jumped up guiltily from where she had been waiting on the side of the bed.

One glance in his direction and her throat went drier than the ginger biscuits she was still having to eat to keep her now early morning nausea at bay.

She clutched her bundle of nightclothes and toiletries

closer to her. 'I'll…ahem… I'll…' Heat bunched in her cheeks.

He did not say a word but walked towards the dressing room, wearing nothing but a white towel slung low on his hips.

She swallowed at the sight of a large drop of water that was slowly travelling down the length of his tanned muscular back, the outline of his bottom beneath the towel, the shape of his calves.

His wet hair was slicked back, the colour now a much darker shade, just like his mood.

She placed her bundle onto a bathroom stool and reluctantly went back outside and stood close to the dressing-room door. 'I need help with my dress.'

His large frame, now dressed in only wine-coloured cotton pyjama bottoms, soon filled the doorway.

She twisted away from the menace in his expression. Her back to him, she explained, 'I can't undo the buttons.'

She waited for him to respond. The silent chasm between them laying bare the reality of their marriage on what *should be* a unique, intimate and special night between a husband and wife.

A groom should happily undress his bride.

She shivered when he walked behind her, his height and size dwarfing hers.

She crossed her arms and closed her eyes.

One by one his fingers released the buttons.

She squeezed her eyes more firmly shut. Pushing away the desire to turn to him. Pushing down on the giddy butterflies in her tummy thanks to the skim of his slightly calloused fingers on her skin. Pushing away the memories of that night they were together and how he had fervently undressed her, and how cruelly it compared to his detached, controlled unbuttoning now.

Would she ever get used to not being truly wanted, to not being desired?

To being in a marriage that only existed because they had conceived a child together.

When he had reached as far as her waist, she stepped away and muttered with her back still to him, 'I can manage the rest,' and scuttled into the bathroom.

Inside she locked the door and undressed, her whole body trembling.

After a quick shower, she brushed her teeth, rehearsing in her mind the plan for when she got into bed with him. She would be polite. Say goodnight. Turn on her side. And fall asleep.

It didn't need to be anything more complicated or dramatic than that. They were both grown adults with a child to raise.

But having finished brushing her teeth, she stupidly became undone again.

Where should her toothbrush live?

In the holder next to Lucien's?

It seemed too intimate. Too permanent.

Tears blinded her for a moment.

And just how lonely she was going to be in this marriage hit her hard.

She was about to make a life with a man who only married her because she was carrying his baby.

She would never have the bond, intimacy, attachment or trust her parents shared.

But your baby will have a father. Isn't that enough for you?

She plonked her toothbrush into the holder and twisted away.

And twisted back, shoving it as far away from Lucien's as possible.

Outside in the bedroom he was sitting up in bed, reading a book, unfairly displaying his naked and formidable tanned chest, taut with powerfully defined pecs and a mind-blowing six-pack. She had kissed each of those muscles on that night, her lips slowly moving over the beautifully juxtaposed smooth skin and hard muscle beneath.

She skirted to the other side of the bed.

He lowered the hardback tome he was reading, his gaze wandering over her dark leggings and baggy yoga sweater. 'Going to the gym?'

'I get cold during the night.' She lay down in the bed, switched off her light and, clinging to the edge of her side of the bed, said, 'Goodnight.'

Long slow minutes ticked by.

Behind her she heard no movement.

'I meant it earlier when I said I won't touch you.'

Her heart was pumping faster than it ever did in her weekly spinning classes. Her throat was stupidly dry once again. She eventually managed to say, 'I know.'

Lucien plunged the room into darkness by switching off his bedside lamp. 'Goodnight, Charlotte.'

She bit her lip.

It would be okay.

She would fall asleep soon.

And she had Lucien here to protect her.

Or was he scarier than the dark?

'Lucien?'

'Yes?'

'Would you mind if I put on the bathroom light? I don't like sleeping in the dark.'

He didn't say anything for a few minutes. He was probably too busy asking himself why he had ever thought that marriage was a good idea.

On a loud exhale he got out of the bed.

She twisted onto her back.

His footsteps were barely audible on the carpeted floor.

Instead of the main light he switched on the shaving light over the sink mirror.

When he rejoined her in the bed she whispered, 'Thank you.'

He didn't say anything in response.

She cringed, certain now that he was majorly hacked off.

She thought he had fallen asleep when he suddenly said, 'How come the dark wasn't an issue the last time you slept here?'

Without thinking she admitted, 'I was too exhausted to notice.'

There was a moment of silence and she died inside.

But then he chuckled.

And she giggled in relief and mortification.

But their light laughter quickly died.

To be replaced by tight tension that filled the room.

Was he remembering their endless lovemaking as she was?

Even now, leaving her pregnancy aside, which she would never ever regret, she would never be sorry that she had slept with Lucien. It had been too special. It had held an almost dreamlike quality. It was as if they had been two different people, happy to find each other for a few incredible hours where only they existed. It had been intense, beautiful, extraordinary.

He deserved to know the truth of how she felt about that night. What she had said earlier had sounded all wrong. 'You said earlier that you were sorry about our night together... I wanted that night to happen as much as you did. I knew what I was doing.'

The mattress sagged a little as he moved. She twisted her head to see him gazing in her direction.

'I'm your CEO. I should have known better.'

'But it just happened...it's just one of those things. Nobody's to blame.' That night, they hadn't had a hope of stopping such intense, insane chemistry and attraction.

'There was a point in the garden when you looked unsure. We should have stopped then.'

'I didn't want to.' She paused and knew he deserved a better explanation. 'I was hurt in the past, that's why I was unsure. It had nothing to do with you.'

'Who hurt you?'

She scrunched her eyes shut. This was something she didn't want to speak about.

Could their wedding night be more different from the norm? A gap you could drive a double-decker bus through between them in their bed. No shared history or reference points. She didn't even know what his favourite food was, the type of movies he liked to watch.

'When I was twenty-two my then boyfriend cheated on me with my best friend.'

'Ouch.'

'Exactly.'

Silence fell on the room again.

She twisted her head. Across the expanse of the bed, Lucien was watching her with a frown.

Her heart ricocheted around her chest.

It felt so right yet so wrong to be lying here with him.

'You loved him?'

She blinked hard at his question, the gentleness of his tone puncturing through all the defences she had spun around herself these past six years. For the first time she admitted to herself just what she had lost back then.

Through a knotted throat she confessed, 'With all of my heart.'

Lucien looked away, his focus now on the ceiling above him. 'Did you try getting back together?'

'There was no point. Even I could tell how deeply in

love they were. They're now happily married with three children by all accounts.'

In the resumed silence of the room, she stared at the silhouette of the modern gold and crystal chandelier that hung at the centre of the ceiling, feeling totally exposed, wondering why she had told him all of this.

Did he pity her?

Did he understand what it was like to have a broken heart?

Would he think her weak?

Be more wary of her?

After all, he only knew her as a coolly detached, logical professional. He was probably recoiling at this much too personal and emotional conversation.

She should say something to end the silence, reassure him that she wasn't a complete emotional wreck. Erect the barriers around herself once again.

But before she could do so, he spoke. 'It still hurts?'

His question was asked without judgement. Was there a hint of understanding? In a quiet voice she said, 'Yes.'

Oh, why was she talking to him like this?

She never spoke to anyone about what had happened between her and Dan. Preferring to consign it to a bitter lesson learned in life, not to be revisited.

'I'm sorry you had to go through that...what your ex did was unforgivable.' Why did he sound so angry, so vehement?

'I guess.'

'You sound like you forgive him.'

Did she? 'No... I don't know.'

He waited for her to speak but she didn't know what to say. How would she explain to her new husband that Dan, that entire year of being ill, had shaken her to the core? Had ripped away the happy person she once had been. And left her floundering as to who she could trust and annoyed at her own naivety in believing that love could conquer all. Annoyed for thinking you could rely on others for support and care when ultimately there was only one person you could count on: yourself.

A truth she had to remember in this marriage.

Lucien was her husband but in name only. All she could hope for was that he would be a good father to her child. 'I just wished I had known at the time that nothing stays the same in life... I thought I'd be in pain for ever.'

'How are you doing now?'

His quietly spoken question sounded so genuine, so caring that for a moment she actually wanted to cry. But she pushed aside the heavy weight of emotion jamming her throat to answer. 'I'm okay. How about you? Are you getting used to the idea of being a father?'

A husband?

He shrugged one of those impossibly wide shoulders. 'A little. How about you being a mum?'

'I'm daunted, to be honest. I'm trying not to think about giving birth. And I'm even more worried about taking care of something so tiny after. I've barely ever held a baby. I've never fed one, or changed a nappy.'

'I'm the same. Maybe we should both do a parenting course. My trainer on the How to be a Good Husband course highly recommended a holistic retreat that encourages a birthing-in-the-woods-while-chanting approach. We could give that a go.'

Despite herself, she giggled and the sudden bubble of happiness that floated in her chest grew bigger when she saw the teasing mischief glinting in his eyes. If only their relationship could always be as relaxed as this. 'You know, hanging out with you mightn't be so bad after all.'

The room grew still.

His gaze worked from her eyes down to her mouth.

She couldn't read his blank expression.

A reckless urge to move towards him, to place her hand on his exposed chest, to feel his taut, warm skin, the tightness of the muscle beneath, to inhale him, to connect with him in the most potent and powerful way a man and woman could do so swept through her.

A dangerous charge whipped around the room.

It would be so easy to reach out. To touch her fingers to his arm. To invite him to move towards her.

Desire and need coiled tight inside her but she forced herself to say, 'I think we should go to sleep.'

His answer was a quick nod and he turned away from her.

And the loneliness of her new marriage hit her again. An empty, hollow sensation pumping through her heart.

Dieu! He was such a hypocrite.

Lucien stared at his bedside clock and gritted his teeth.

Two hours after they had said goodnight to one another and sleep still eluded him thanks to the desire, anger, irritation swirling inside him.

He wanted to track down Charlotte's ex and make him pay for causing her such obvious pain.

But at the same time he wanted to move across the bed and make love to her, to drive away all those memories of her ex. To recreate the passion of their one night together. To hear her hold her breath time and time again and the explosion of sound as she responded to him.

What a hypocrite.

He wanted to punish her ex while at the same time thinking and wanting to act in a way that would cause her even greater hurt in the long-term by complicating the delicate truce they had set in place to raise their child together.

A bigger hypocrite because he had behaved much more

despicably than her ex in the past. In an act that had confirmed that he was as weak willed and lacking in honour as his father.

He needed to be careful. Already he was feeling a closeness to Charlotte. Her stubborn, sharp-witted, vibrant personality beneath that detached image was getting to him. Weakening his resolve that he would keep his distance from her. And now that he knew of her past, he had an even greater urge to protect her from any other hurt. The irony being, of course, that he would have to protect her from himself.

His first marriage had quickly descended into endless rows and frustration as they had realised that passion and a shared love for partying could not sustain their relationship and the responsibilities they had needed to face in life. But they had been so entwined emotionally, so believing that the other person would save them from a life of loneliness, so invested in each other, that their break-up had been both brutal and cruel as they had tried to extract themselves from their passionate and all-consuming marriage.

This marriage could not be like that. He had to keep his distance from Charlotte. For her sake. For the baby's sake. For his own sake.

He turned in the bed.

His heart karate-chopped against his chest.

Charlotte was awake and staring in his direction.

He wanted to move towards her. To touch the long length of her hair that looked like silver threads in the dark shadows of the room. To kiss that soft, beautiful mouth. To make her his.

Wasn't that what was supposed to happen on your wedding night? Long glorious hours of lovemaking.

Instead he forced himself to ask, like any dutiful father-to-be, 'Is everything okay? Can I get you something? A glass of water?'

She shook her head and turned away.
He flipped onto his back.
Feeling more alone than ever.

CHAPTER SIX

TWO WEEKS LATER Charlotte roamed a Mayfair art gallery on Cork Street, trying to avoid actually looking at the exhibition of modernist paintings that were threatening to turn her hovering headache into a full-blown migraine.

At the rear of the room, standing next to a particularly lurid painting full of lime green and yellow splatters and daubs, Lucien was deep in conversation with Selina Hutton, the only current female chairperson of a UK investment bank.

Earlier when Charlotte had spoken to Selina as they had both puzzled over the meaning of a twisted steel sculpture, Selina had been charming and funny. And at forty, she was not only strikingly good-looking but carried the easy confidence of a woman perfectly content in her own skin. Her fitted ankle-length teal trousers and loose cream silk blouse hung perfectly on her trim body, her mane of chestnut hair holding just the right amount of bounce and glossiness.

Charlotte turned away from them. And pulled on her black shift dress. Suddenly feeling invisible.

She fanned herself with the exhibition price list. And sneaked a look back towards Lucien.

His slim-fitting white shirt over wheat-coloured chinos unwittingly revealed her Achilles' heel: his sharp broad shoulders and ridiculously defined torso that were reducing her to feverish insomnia every night.

And she was completely hacked off about it.

Couldn't he at least once in a while go to bed before her? Spare her the sight of him emerging from the bathroom night after night, freshly showered and pyjama bottoms slung low on his hips.

While she pretended to be asleep.

Which was a joke. Because she lay awake each night reliving their night together.

The way her heart had spun in wonder.

Memories of how he had looked at her with such passionate amazement.

As though he would never tire of her.

As though it had all been special.

How foolish she had been.

For two weeks now they had been sleeping together. And keeping to his word, he had proved to be the perfect gentleman.

He had tired of her after one single night.

Okay, so maybe that was a little unfair.

If they hadn't been CEO and employee in the first instance, if she hadn't ended up pregnant, maybe the fire between them would have been able to burn a little longer. But it would have burned out eventually.

Lucien would have wanted to move on.

And so would she.

Wouldn't she?

Lucien turned in her direction. His gaze moved down over her.

The fire of want and embarrassment pulled hard inside her.

She ducked behind a pillar.

What did he think when he looked at her? Did he find her ever-growing belly, how her entire body seemed to be softening into lush curves, unattractive? Did he wonder what on earth he had done in marrying her?

She tried to ignore a tearing sensation in her heart.

Why did she even care?

Her headache was worsening.

She needed air.

She needed to get away from the sight of Lucien and Selina flirting together.

An hour later, Charlotte meandered her way around the Mayfair square that led to her new home, still struggling to fathom how her life had changed direction so dramatically since she had rung in the New Year with her parents less than six months ago.

Back then, as they had watched the village fireworks together, her biggest worry had been how she was going to secure her next promotion.

Now she had childbirth, being a mother, and being a wife to the sexiest man she had ever met but who was blind to her to worry about.

The worst part was that instead of being attracted to Lucien she should be furious with him.

He wasn't meeting half of the promises he had agreed to.

Placing her key in the lock of the front door, she cursed the fact that she was allowing her attraction to him to get in the way of all her usual good sense and logic.

Lucien was a heartbreaker, a go-getter who liked novelty, who could make you feel as if you were the most special, most cherished woman in the world until the next woman came along.

She had known so many like him in university, dating them in her first few years there. She had allowed herself to be charmed by them, forgiven them when she should have booted them out of her life, and invariably ended up hurt and humiliated when they had dumped her for someone else.

That was why she'd fallen for Dan. He had seemed so different. So genuine.

And he had been kind and generous, until she had become ill.

And now she was foolishly falling for Lucien's charm and allowing herself to be blind to the fact that he was full of empty promises.

'Where were you?' Lucien stalked down that hallway towards her.

She gripped her milkshake carton tighter. 'I went for a walk.'

He gave her an infuriated stare. 'Why didn't you tell me that you were leaving the gallery?'

'You were busy chatting to Selina Hutton.'

'So? You could have interrupted us.' He lifted both hands in exasperation. 'You're my partner, my wife, you don't just walk out without telling me. I felt ridiculous having to ask others if they had seen you. And you didn't answer your phone when I called you.'

She opened her clutch bag and lifted her phone to see seven missed calls from him. 'My phone was on silent. There's some problems with the Estonia project I'm working on that I wanted to think through by going for a walk.'

He didn't respond but looked at her with a disbelieving frown. In the excruciating silence that followed, her skin heated uncomfortably as those green eyes studied her unflinchingly. Eventually, unable to handle his stare any longer, she mumbled, 'I was feeling ill. I needed some air.'

He shook his head and turned around while muttering, 'And a milkshake apparently.'

She followed him into the lounge that had a double-height bay window overlooking the residents-only park set at the centre of the square.

Lucien stood in front of the large marble fireplace, his stiff and menacing reflection showing in the gilt mirror hanging above it. 'Why didn't you tell me that you were feeling ill?'

'It didn't look as though you'd appreciate being disturbed in your conversation with Selina.'

His eyes narrowed and he drew his shoulders back. 'You don't trust me, do you?'

She swallowed hard.

This was the first time she'd ever seen him this angry, this cold and formidable.

Deep down she knew she should be reasonable, make allowances for the demands and pressure of his position at work, but the foolish pain within her that he didn't find her attractive, the loneliness of her marriage, her ongoing fears for what type of father and son-in-law he would be, the loss of her own independence had her say bitterly, 'Let's see. You agreed that we'd meet for breakfast every day. This week you made it twice. You were home when it was past ten o'clock, three nights. I barely see you. Everything seemed to be working so well our first week together but in the past week it's all falling apart. I'm honestly questioning your commitment to this marriage, to our baby.'

Lucien tried to breathe deeply into his lungs, fighting to steady his heart, to shake off the adrenaline still coursing through his veins.

He had been angry and humiliated when he'd realised she had left the gallery.

And guilty, because he had been avoiding her all evening, trying to keep a firm hold on how much he wanted to place his hand on her growing stomach, how sexy she looked this evening with her hair hanging loose, a bold *come and get me* slash of red lipstick on her mouth. How much he wanted to run his hands over her curves, the warmth of her naked beauty again.

With each passing day he was growing more and more

attracted to her. In their first week together, when he'd got home from work in the evenings he had often found her on the living-room floor practising yoga or on the sofa, curled up reading a book. She shouldn't have looked sexy dressed in her yoga wear, her hair tied back into a messy ponytail. But she had. And when she'd smiled in his direction and asked if he wanted something to drink, to eat, in that first week he had said yes, please. Which had been a big mistake. Because in those few short days his attraction, need for her, had gone shooting off the Richter scale as they'd chatted over food, as they'd washed up over supper.

And then he would have to feign nonchalance when they went upstairs, pretend that he didn't see the shape and swell of her body beneath her light cotton pyjamas. Maybe it would have been better if she had stuck to wearing her gym clothes in bed.

And the following morning as she had yawned over breakfast, her make-up-free skin pink from sleep, he would have to leave for work tense with the desire to kiss her. And twice they had attended work meetings together and his concentration had been shot to pieces. In one meeting with his board, Charlotte had made a presentation on the funding due diligence for a port construction project in Estonia. He had watched his astute wife handle the assertive questioning of the board with pride, and with vastly inappropriate thoughts of how he would like to get her alone in the boardroom and strip her bare before making love to her.

Last week, knowing he had to create distance between them before he did something he'd regret, he had started coming home later, the ever looming demands of work giving him a legitimate justification.

The same justification he had used tonight when he had spoken to Selina Hutton about his plans for Huet when in truth all he had wanted to do was take Charlotte by the hand and walk through the summer streets of London with her.

Perhaps walk to St James's Park, hire a deckchair, eat ice cream. Chat and argue with her. Laugh with her. Kiss her.

His anger that Charlotte had walked out on him had flicked to panic when he had arrived home to find the house empty.

With each unanswered phone call that panic had intensified. Images of her falling in those sexy high-heeled red sandals she had insisted on wearing tonight persecuting him as he had waited and waited and waited for her to return.

He had feared for the baby. For her.

He knew he should walk away, get his emotions under control. But the rage, the panic still in him had him growl out, 'This is exactly why I never wanted to marry again. Stupidly arguing and pulling each other apart. Never being able to satisfy the other person.'

With her long blonde wavy hair hanging loose about her face she looked incredibly young and sweet…the exception being the sharp fury firing from her sea-green eyes. She folded her arms, her mouth twisting. 'I wouldn't be bringing any of this up if I thought you were even trying—for crying out loud, last weekend when my parents visited you were completely withdrawn and it was obvious that you resented them being here in your house. I spent the whole afternoon trying to pretend all was happiness and light between us. I was actually glad when you said that you had to go into the office.'

'It's your house too. And, no, I didn't resent them being here. That's just a ludicrous idea.' He paused and thought back to their visit, the laughter between them, the baskets of food her mum had arrived with, their fussing over Charlotte, their pride in her.

And he had felt like a fraud.

They thought he was in love with her.

They thought he would do everything in his power to protect her.

When in truth he wanted to wreck her heart, their baby's future, by sleeping with her again, by growing closer to her, getting to know her, which would confuse the basis of their relationship, cause misunderstandings, create emotional bonds he would eventually tear apart.

And if he managed to keep his distance emotionally and physically, if he protected her heart by keeping himself distant, there was still no guarantee that he would be a good father to their child.

Was Charlotte's lack of trust in him, the fact that she was constantly judging him, justified? Was he proving to be as irresponsible and self-serving as his parents?

Because surely he should be man enough to be able to push his attraction to her aside, to fulfil his side of the bargain to be a responsible husband and father.

Now, the anger in her eyes was burning less brightly, and a hurt expression was rising up instead.

He hated to see her upset, a raw pain he didn't understand pierced his chest, and words exploded out of him. 'I don't know how to act when you're with your parents. I'm overwhelmed by the love between you.'

He backed away. Stunned at his own words.

Charlotte came towards him. 'I don't understand.'

He looked away. Fighting the temptation to walk out of the room.

The only other person he had ever described his past to was his first wife. And she had used it like a weapon when their marriage had ended, accusing him of being as weak willed as his own father, shouting that he was no different and would always be greedy and self-centred in any relationships.

Did he want to give Charlotte that power?

But maybe if she understood his past she'd know to stay away from him.

He went and stood at the bay window and stared out at the street and park beyond.

When he turned back, Charlotte was still in the same spot, waiting for him to speak.

'My upbringing was the polar opposite of yours. You said yours was full of happiness and love—well, I spent my childhood trying to appease my parents, constantly trying to stop their arguments.'

Trying to make them love me.

His stomach rolled in distaste at what he was about to say but the earlier surge of adrenaline because of his panic over her disappearance from the gallery drove him on recklessly. 'When I was fifteen I arrived home early one day and found my father in bed with a work colleague. My father refused to admit it to my mum so I had to tell her. She didn't believe me, said that I was lying. Until she saw them together herself one day at a café. She threw him out and he moved to Spain with the other woman.'

He paused as Charlotte walked towards him.

He glanced out into the park beyond the iron railings on the opposite side of the road, to the ancient plane trees weighed down in their dark green summer foliage.

He had come so far from his childhood, but not in what was important.

His new wife should fully understand what type of person he was.

Then perhaps she would know not to have too many expectations of him, too many hopes. 'My mother couldn't cope with living on her own. I didn't help. I was angry all of the time and getting into trouble at school. She moved a boyfriend in with us. He threw a beer can at me one day for stealing his beer. It smashed into my head. We ended up fighting on the floor. Blood pumping from my head. My mother screamed at me for ruining her new shoes and threw me out. Probably deservedly so.'

When Charlotte didn't respond he looked towards her furiously.

But the angry words that were about to demand if she was disgusted to be married to a man with such an awful family history, when hers was so damn normal and lovely, died when he saw the sadness in her eyes.

A sadness that was matched by the gentle tone of her voice when she spoke. 'How old were you?'

'Seventeen.'

'You were still a child.'

He shook his head. He fully accepted his role in his estrangement from his mother. 'I was out of control.'

'Where did you go?'

'I moved to Bordeaux and quickly fell in with other troubled teenagers. We all lived in a derelict house. It's where I met my first wife, Gabrielle.'

Should he tell Charlotte about his ex...the relationship they'd had?

The need to share his past with her was burning inside him.

For the first time ever he wanted to speak out loud about that time, to try to make sense of his teenage past and how much he'd messed up.

'Gabrielle moved into the apartment a few months after I did. Her mum had just died, she never knew her dad. She had no one else to turn to. We thought we could fix each other's loneliness. But our initial love and hope turned to hurt when we realised we couldn't make life better for one another. We couldn't fix one another, repair the damage within us. We were both selfish, wrapped up in our own wants and needs, and blamed each other for our marriage crumbling. It lasted less than a year.'

There was more he should tell her—that last night when he had delivered the final fatal blow to their marriage.

But he couldn't bring himself to.

The shame and guilt of his actions were too overwhelming.

The shock, the agony, the torture, the anger of Gabrielle's betrayal with one of the other men who lived in the apartment. He had found them kissing, Gabrielle dressed in only her underwear, her dress strewn on the kitchen floor.

After he had confronted them and realised their affair had been going on for months he had gone out.

And got drunk.

And slept with Gabrielle's friend.

A pathetic, weak, contemptible act that showed he was as weak as his own father.

He had spent more than fifteen years trying to distance himself from that selfish, egotistical person.

But he was still the same person at heart despite all of his achievements. 'I'm a selfish person, Charlotte. From a messed-up family.'

He fisted his hands in hopeful intention. 'But I will do my best to be a good father.'

His stomach churning, he added bitterly, 'I overheard my parents arguing one night and it was clear that they considered me a mistake. My mother was only twenty when she became pregnant with me. My parents resented me for tying them down, for burdening them.'

He drew in a breath, thrown by just how passionate he felt about what he was going to say, 'So help me God, my child will never feel like he's a mistake or a burden. I will try to be a good husband to you, but I will probably never be the husband you need.'

Outside the evening was disappearing into night, sucking all of the light out of the lounge. Before her, Lucien stood with a dark dignity.

How little she knew her husband.

She needed some time and space to think about what he'd said.

But most of all she wanted to comfort him, give him the care and respect that had been missing from his childhood. 'Would you like a cup of tea?'

He gave her a quizzical look and shrugged.

She led the way into the kitchen and made their tea in silence. She placed their cups and the teapot on the old oak farm kitchen table. Lucien's interior designer had chosen well in selecting the table; it lent a much-needed homely feel to the hard lines of the concrete and minimalist white kitchen.

Lucien sat at the head of the table, facing out into the garden, she to his side. The same places they sat at, each time they shared a meal. An arrangement that had happened naturally, evolved without discussion, just one of many small, outwardly couple-like behaviours so at odds with the frustrations and distance of their relationship.

She poured their tea and sipped hers before she spoke. 'I don't think you're selfish. You married me for your child. To give her security. A family. That's the most selfless, loving act possible.'

He shook his head, not buying her words. 'Is it, though? Or is this all about my ego? Is it a crazy macho need to protect my own that belongs to caveman times rather than the modern day? You're perfectly capable of raising a child. Maybe I should have left you to it.'

'I want my child to have her father in her life. Hearing you describe your past, I now understand just how difficult it must have been for you to marry me.' She paused, struggling to talk against the rock of emotion wedged in her throat. 'I'm really moved that you would do that for our child. You'll be a great dad.'

He sat back in his chair and inhaled deeply.

Rubbed his hand along the back of his neck. Looking as though he was trying to fight her words. Find a reason not to believe her. Eventually he said with a bitter twist to his voice, 'I'm making for a lousy husband, though.'

She shrugged. 'I'm not exactly making for a great wife either. Let's face it, you'd have been better off married to someone like Selina Hutton.'

'Why on earth would you say that?'

Wasn't that obvious to him? Selina Hutton, sensible and pragmatic, would be able to keep her emotions at bay for the greater good of the family unit. 'You'd have been the ultimate power couple.'

He drew back in his chair. 'Selina and I were talking business, that's all.' He arched his neck, loosening out some kink. 'I don't want to hurt you, Charlotte. I like you…but my past history shows that I mess up relationships. This is one relationship I can't afford to wreck.'

Charlotte nodded as he held her gaze.

It *was* pointless falling for this man.

She would only end up hurt and destroying any hope of them raising their child together in harmony.

Yet a burning need rebelled inside her; she wanted to throw caution to the wind and to lean across the table and touch her fingers to the strong column of his neck, run her hand along the hard lines of his collarbone, touch her lips to the evening shadow on his jawline, inhale his brain-stupefying scent.

With a sage wisdom that was totally at odds with her attraction to him, her need for him, she said, 'Maybe we should try harder at being friends, be more supportive of one another.'

He gazed at her for long scorching seconds.

Oh, to be held in his arms again if only for a few minutes.

To feel his mouth on hers.

To lose herself to him. To his warmth and strength. To

have his eyes hold her heart in the suspended time of care and comfort and promise.

Lucien cleared his throat. 'We can try.'

She pulled her mouth into the semblance of a smile. 'They say the best relationships are those founded on friendship.'

They smiled at each other.

Pained smiles that didn't reach their eyes.

Both knowing that there was so much more that they wanted from each other.

CHAPTER SEVEN

CHARLOTTE TRIED TO open her eyes but the pain was too intense. It felt as if someone had poured acid onto her brain. The epicentre just beneath her right temple.

Lying on one of the living-room sofas, she wanted to cry.

But it would hurt too much.

She couldn't move.

She heard the front door open.

It was Lucien's housekeeper's day off. She knew she should be worried but in truth she didn't care if they were about to be burgled. As long as the burglars got her a cold press while rifling through the kitchen cupboards they were welcome to whatever they wanted.

Familiar-sounding footsteps bounded up the stairs.

She tried to call out but when she lifted her head the acid burrowed even deeper into her brain.

She pushed the heel of her hand against her right eye, trying to ease the pressure there.

Within minutes he was rushing back down the stairs, calling her name.

In a croaky voice, pain slaying every facial muscle, she called, 'I'm in here.'

His footsteps tapped, tapped, tapped furiously on the wooden floor. 'Simon told me that you had gone home ill. Why didn't you tell me?'

This time she whispered, hoping not to stir the beast of

pain currently living in her brain. 'You were busy...you had your meeting with the government guys from Denmark.'

'Why are you lying here? Why not upstairs in bed?' His voice was now anxious, the anger gone.

'I couldn't make it...pain too bad.'

She heard him come closer, his hand rested on her arm. Soothing. 'Another migraine?'

'The worst yet.'

'I'll call my doctor.'

'No point, I can't take anything. I just need to sleep for a while. Later I need to go back into the office to work on a sub-contractor adjudication.'

'You're not going anywhere but your bed today. I'll carry you upstairs—you'll sleep better there.'

She should object. She knew she should. But the pain outweighed the guilt of being out of work sick and the thought of the warmth and comfort of her bed was too great to resist. And even more, she wanted to be held by him if only for a few minutes. 'Please...and sorry, I can't open my eyes. It hurts too much.'

With surprising ease he gently lifted her up.

Just minutes ago she had felt alone and vulnerable.

Now she wanted to weep in relief to have him here, to be minded, to be cared for.

Upstairs, he lowered her onto the cool cotton of their bed quilt and, before she had the chance to do so, pulled off her high-heeled work shoes.

Still unable to open her eyes, she waited for him to speak.

He cleared his throat. 'Do you want me to undress you?'

So many women would give their eye teeth to hear Lucien Duval ask that question of them. And here she was preferring if he would just lie down beside her and hold her. 'No, it's fine. I'd like a blanket, though.'

After he had placed a blanket over her, his hands tucking the sides against her body, she heard him close the shutters and the swoosh when he drew the heavy silk curtains together on all three Georgian sash windows.

She curled up onto her side, wincing as the acid tunnelled into her brain once again.

'I've dampened a face cloth. Would you like to use it?'

She made the tiniest movement with her head to indicate yes and croaked out, 'Lay it on my temple.'

He laid the cool cloth down against her skin and she gave an involuntary groan. 'That's so nice, thank you.'

'*Dieu!* I feel so responsible. It's awful to see you in such pain.'

His voice, which came from very close by, as though he was crouched down before her, sounded tortured. She wished she could open her eyes to see him, to reassure him. 'It's okay…it's nice to have you here.'

He repositioned the cloth on her temple and when he'd finished his hand slowly moved down, gently, soothingly, over her hair. 'I'm glad I'm here. What can I do?'

Lie down beside me, hold me. Tell me that all this will go away.

'I just need to sleep. I'll be fine. You go back to work.'

He didn't say anything for the longest while but eventually, repositioning the cloth against her skin, whispered, 'I'll be downstairs, but I'll check on you throughout the afternoon.'

'Go back to work. I know how important your meeting is.'

He lifted up the blanket to cover her shoulders. 'It's more important that I stay with you. Try to sleep. I'll be here if you need me.'

At the backs of her eyes she felt tears form. She nodded and hoped he would leave before they fell onto her cheeks. Lucien had said the words she had willed Dan to say all those years ago but never did.

'I'll be here if you need me.'

She curled up on her side even more, hugging her knees into her chest, allowing his low whisper, the comfort, the reassurance, the care it brought to lull her to sleep.

Later that evening, Charlotte sat on the side of their bed and blinked hard, trying to focus on the time showing on Lucien's bedside clock. She had been asleep for more than three hours.

Though groggy and light-headed, she made her way into the bathroom, sending up silent thanks that sleep had washed away the burning acid from her brain.

For a moment she considered locking the bathroom door, but to do so now seemed petty.

When she had moved in with Lucien she had locked the bathroom door behind her as an act of defiance. An act to exclude him, push him away from her.

A silent way of communicating that she didn't trust him.

But they had to trust one another. It was the only way this marriage was going to survive.

She couldn't spend the next couple of decades locking the bathroom door on him. No married couple did that, did they?

Her parents certainly didn't.

Was she being foolhardy though?

Was she lowering her defences around him too much?

Was she confusing his care and kindness and attention towards her as being about her, when in truth it was all about protecting his child?

She turned on the shower, undressed and stepped under the warmth of the water. She turned the temperature up high, needing to feel the heat on her tense shoulders.

Since the night in the gallery when she had left early, they had been working on 'being friends'. But the downside of opening up to one another and spending time together was that she was growing even more attracted to him.

Last night she had persuaded him to go to the cinema at the British Film Institute on Southbank to watch a Norwegian crime thriller. He had been reluctant at first, pointing out that they had a home cinema in the basement. But though his basement cinema was more luxurious than any commercial cinema, the idea of watching a film in the darkness all alone with him had been too much for her. And anyway, she liked being out with him, walking the life-affirming streets of London together. Window-shopping along Piccadilly. The vibrancy and chaos of Piccadilly Circus. It was easier to talk to him when they were walking side by side rather than facing each other. It was less personal, less distracting when his piercing gaze wasn't focused on her.

They had arrived early to the cinema.

As had a couple who had sat in front of them.

Of similar age to them, the couple had flirted and teased, completely at ease with one other. They had continually touched one another affectionately, whispered to one another, shared brief kisses.

Their intimacy had laughed at the awkwardness that still existed between her and Lucien. An awkwardness, a lack of connection that would be the hallmark of their marriage for ever.

And to see up close just how it really should be between a couple had left a hollowness deep inside her for the rest of the evening.

When she was with Lucien she always got a temporary high from laughing, arguing, getting to know him. But then, as she had last night, she would be pulled up with a reminder that their relationship was only one of co-parenting their child.

The same reminder that mocked her every night when

they lay in bed together and her body hummed with the need for him to roll over and touch her. The need to move across the wide expanse of their bed. Touch her mouth to his. Feel his hands on her body. As her stomach grew larger, her breasts more tender, an acute need to be intimate with the father of her baby was destroying her. But she forced herself to hold back. To stay away from him. For their baby's sake. And because she knew the pain of a broken heart and dreams.

Knew just how much you could damage a relationship when you grew too close.

When you depended on the other person for strength.

She switched off the shower and quickly dried. In their dressing room, she pulled on a short-sleeved navy jersey dress. It clung a little too tightly, but this evening she needed comfort above all. She would need to go maternity-clothes shopping soon as her jeans and work clothes no longer fitted. She loved how her body was changing as her pregnancy progressed. She felt more sensual, more womanly…and occasionally she caught Lucien staring at her stomach, at her heavier breasts, with intimate heat in his eyes. But then he would look away and her heart would slam to a stop, bereft at his silence.

Back out in the bedroom she opened the curtains and shutters, and lifted up the bottom of one of the sash windows. Birdsong and the distant, constant hum of traffic greeted her. For a moment she paused and looked out at the church spires in the distance, the tall building cranes that brought constant renewal to this ever-changing city.

Sitting at her new dressing table, she began to dry her hair. Lucien had surprised her with the dressing table earlier in the week. The Art Deco table had a delicate round mirror and a bronze-plated drawer at the front where she stored her lipsticks and eyeshadows. Two further drawers sat at either side of the table, before tapering down to colt-like legs tipped with silvered bronze on the feet.

A matching stool with similarly tapered legs and up-holstered in a heavy cream wool fabric had arrived with the table when it was delivered by one of London's leading auction houses.

Even with her limited knowledge of the antique market she had realised that the table must have cost a great deal. Lucien had refused to allow her to return it, saying that she deserved to sit at something so pretty every day.

His words and indulgent smile had stupidly thrilled her and she had stopped arguing and accepted the gift with the grace it deserved.

She was slowly learning to pick her battles with her new husband.

Halfway through drying her hair, she switched off the drier with a smile when Lucien entered the room. He dropped a number of bright yellow department-store bags onto the bed.

She gave him a teasing smile. 'Been out shopping?'

He threw her a *What do you think*? look and said, 'Who-ever invented online shopping was a genius.'

He came closer and his eyes slowly trailed over her face, and for a brief second his hand touched against her shoulder. 'How are you feeling?'

She swallowed and tried to ignore how her heart was melting. 'Much better than your poor back, I bet.'

He gave her an indignant frown. 'I squat press the equivalent of two of you every morning.' His expression sobering, he considered her for a while, as though wanting to make certain she was better. 'I ordered in dinner—are you up to eating?'

'I'd kill for a milkshake right now.'

'*Dieu!* How can you say that to me…a Frenchman who

loves good food? I've ordered in light food from Gallery—
a beef consommé and steamed hake to follow.'

Gallery, one of London's top restaurants, was located
only a five-minute walk away from Lucien's house. From
what she could gather, until she had moved in and started
cooking meals, he had ordered from them most nights when
he was alone in London and not out entertaining.

She turned in her chair and folded her arms. 'Are you
trying to avoid my cooking?'

'Now what gave you that idea? Those chickpea burgers
last night were…interesting.'

Okay, so they had been on the dry side, but they were
healthy…apparently.

'I'll leave you to finish.' He paused and gestured to the
parcels. 'They are for you.'

Intrigued, she got up and opened the first bag.

Inside she found a cashmere-blend pale blue throw. She
unfurled it on the bed, running her hands over the soft
material. In the second bag she found a similar-coloured
lounge top and bottoms. She shook her head, laughing. 'I
keep telling you, it's a girl, not a boy.'

'If it's a girl I'll do every night feed for the first month.'

Her husband the risk-taker. 'Now that's fighting talk.'
She folded up the blanket and opened the smaller third bag.
Inside she found a month's supply of her favourite brand of
vanilla caramel fudge. She lifted it up accusingly. 'I've noticed that my fudge has been disappearing from the pantry
cupboard. Hands off these ones. They're all mine.'

Standing at the bedroom door, he propped his hand on
the doorframe. 'I thought marriage is all about sharing.' A
cheeky smile broke on his mouth.

And her legs almost gave way.

She playfully conceded, 'I'll allow you to have the occasional one.'

They stood there smiling for much too long.

Until it began to get awkward.

Until it felt as if this was how married couples should be together.

She gestured back to his gifts, needing to break the tension. 'The presents are great, thank you, but there really was no need.'

Lucien approached the bed again and lifted up the throw. He shuffled it from hand to hand.

His eyes met hers.

'I hate to see you in pain.'

When he was like this it was impossible to resist him. It would be so easy to forget why they could never be a true couple.

She forced herself to look away and said with a laugh, 'You'd better not come to the birth so.'

A hint of something, worry or perhaps guilt, flickered in his eyes. 'I wouldn't miss it for the world. I've cleared my diary for that week.'

'I could go early or late.'

He shrugged and walked back towards the door. 'I'll have my plane on standby at all times. Come downstairs when you are ready. Dinner will be delivered in twenty minutes.'

Switching the hairdryer back on, she gazed at his gifts lying on the bed and then stared at her reflection.

Seeing for herself the heat of pleasure in her cheeks at his thoughtfulness.

He was a master at worming his way into her heart.

And at times, like now, she just wanted to give into it all, to allow herself to fall for him totally, to enjoy his company without constantly second-guessing him, second-guessing her own ability to cope with another love affair gone bad.

Later that night, Lucien rolled up the set of architectural drawings he'd had his chief architect work on for the past week. Each day the two men had met to revise the plans until Lucien was satisfied that they were perfect.

He had intended giving them to Charlotte last night but had pulled back after their trip to the cinema. Seeing the ease and intimacy of the couple in front of them, and Charlotte's quietness beside him as she had watched them, had brought home what he was denying her by their marriage.

She had claimed that she had never wanted to marry, wanting to focus on her career instead. But it was obvious that her break-up with her ex was the true reason why she shied away from relationships.

With time she would probably have met a man capable of breaking down her defences and teaching her how to love again. But he had denied her that opportunity by marrying her.

Now she would never have the intimacy, the true closeness of a love marriage.

Guilt at that realisation and at how his attraction to her was getting in the way of them being friends only, partners in raising their child, was tearing him apart.

Since the night of the art exhibition, when he had told her about his parents and his first marriage, she was more open to him and in small subtle ways she was sucking him right into her world.

A world that he wanted to resist but was failing to.

When he had flown in from Madrid last Saturday he had joined her and her group of friends in a King's Road restaurant towards the end of their meal. She had excitedly shuffled along the booth to make space for him, including him in every conversation and insisting that he share her chocolate roulade.

Her friends, cautious at first, had accepted him enough to tease him about Charlotte's description of his impatience when it came to driving in London traffic.

She was texting him throughout the day, chatting freely

in the evenings about how her day had gone. Asking him in turn about his day.

And when he needed to work late into the evening, she would bring him cups of coffee, playfully pinching her nose so as not to smell it.

But their attraction to one another, the chemistry between them, was acting like a barrier; it kept them wary of one another. A barrier that was needed. Because if they were intimate again, then their relationship would move to a level of complexity that neither might be able to control.

Seeing her so ill today, though, had shown him that he needed to balance this wariness and need to keep a distance between them with the support and care she obviously needed. Charlotte deserved to have a marriage, a relationship that was considerate and reassuring.

Downstairs, he found her out on the terrace, reading a pregnancy magazine, tucked beneath her new blanket.

Sitting beside her, he unrolled the plans, and pointed to the coach house to the rear of the garden. 'I've had plans drawn up for renovating the coach house into a two-bedroom mews.'

She stared at the plans and then at him. 'You want me to move into the coach house?'

What? Where had she got that idea?

'No. I—'

Jumping to her feet, she interrupted him. 'I'm taking the baby with me.'

She stepped back from him, clasped her forehead with her hand, heat exploding in her cheeks. 'It's a good idea. We should have thought about it before now.'

He stood. 'You're not moving out—don't be crazy. This is for your parents. I'm sure they'll want to spend a lot of time with you and the baby. I thought they'd like their own space when they do.'

'For my parents?'

'I know how much you worry about them.' He pointed towards the plans. 'I have specified that there is a lift to take account of their mobility in the future. Long-term they could move in permanently if it suited everyone.'

Charlotte stared at the plans again and then at him, agog. Tears shone in her eyes.

His heart did a little kick-start.

She shook her head, still looking bewildered. 'Are you serious? Really?'

When he nodded yes she gave him a shaky smile. Her fingers slowly and tentatively touched against his arm. 'That's the nicest thing anyone has ever done for me.'

She came closer and he moved towards her without thought, helplessly lost to her smile, the cautious happiness shining in her eyes, and wrapped his arms around her waist, pulling her in close.

He inhaled the scent of her freshly washed hair, sweet and clean.

Into the material of his shirt, she whispered, 'Thank you.'

Her waist was tiny beneath his grasp.

He edged his hand down, his thumb stroking just above the swell of her hips. Hips that had danced beneath him the night they had made love.

They both pulled back, only an inch or two separating their heads, their noses angled, their mouths aligned.

Her breath settled on his skin.

He wanted to taste those lips, to feel the warmth and softness of her mouth. He wanted to kiss her neck, run his fingers along her spine, undress her.

He wanted her. He wanted to make love to his wife. To the woman carrying his child.

Her body pressed in against his.

Desire sliced through him.

This was madness.

He pulled back. Before this went too far. 'I need to do some work.'

Charlotte, dazed, her lips parted, nodded frantically. 'Of course. Thank you again. My mum and dad will be thrilled.' She considered him for a moment with hungry eyes. Attraction and desire swarmed between them.

She backed away towards the terrace sofa. And distractedly said, 'They…my parents…they really like you.'

His heart turned over.

He hadn't realised until now that he wanted them to like him, approve of him. 'Good.'

Charlotte gave him a dazed but happy smile.

And his heart sank.

What would her parents think of him if they knew the truth of their marriage, the truth of his past? Guilt clogged his throat.

'They'd like to get to know you even better. Will you come with me tomorrow to see them? We can tell them about the coach house together.'

It was the last thing he wanted to do. 'Wouldn't you prefer to go on your own?'

'I'd like you to be there.'

He stretched his shoulders against the tension in them and reached down to roll up the plans. He handed them to her. 'I'm working tomorrow.'

She folded her arms, refusing to take the plans from him. 'It's a Saturday.'

A silent standoff ensued, he holding out the plans to her, she defiantly ignoring them. With a sigh he said, 'Okay, I'll come.'

She took the plans from him. 'I'm glad.'

Cautiously she moved towards him.

Standing on her tippy toes, she gave him a tight hug.

And against his hair she whispered again, 'Thank you.'

It was not a hug driven by physical attraction but a tender, appreciative hug from a wife to a husband.

The type of hug he had been missing all of his life.

nothing.

Charlotte

CHAPTER EIGHT

SOON AFTER MIDDAY on the following day, Charlotte heard
the front door open and then close downstairs.

Lucien was back from the office.

She stepped into her fuchsia-pink kitten heels and looked
in the mirror dubiously.

This morning, in a moment of madness on Regent's
Street, she had bought a new dress and heels that were
nothing like the functional, conventional clothes she normally wore.

Given the soft, pretty design of the dress, she could only
conclude that her pregnancy hormones were definitely creating a nesting instinct in her.

Downstairs she found him in the kitchen, standing at the
kitchen island studying the coach house renovation plans
with a cup of coffee in his hand, her bag of vanilla fudge
to the side.

He didn't look as if he would be ready to leave the house
in less than five minutes' time. She had told him this morning that they would need to leave by twelve-fifteen at the
latest to make sure that they reached her parents' house in
time for lunch.

Had he changed his mind?

Disappointed, she plucked her handbag off the dark navy
kitchen sofa and asked, 'Having second thoughts?'

He twisted around to her. And did a double take. 'Your hair—it's different.'

'I was at the hairdresser's this morning. She cut a few inches off.'

His gaze travelled down over her. 'And your dress—that's new too?'

Unable to handle how self-conscious she felt, she fingered her 1940s-style crepe dress with its box-pleat skirt. The dress had an off-white background with the tiniest prints of iconic lipsticks and perfume bottles produced during the 1940s.

Her kitten heels matched perfectly one of the lipstick colours.

Lucien placed his coffee cup down and propped himself against the edge of the island with a lazy sexiness. He was wearing navy chinos and a brilliant white polo shirt. Everything about him glowed. His white shirt, the glint in his eye, the bright, healthy caramel tone of his skin, his raw, street-fighter athleticism.

She clenched her hands together. Fighting the lick of desire whipping through her. The empty ache inside her.

'You look beautiful today.'

She gave a weak smile and said, 'Thank you.'

He smiled. And didn't say anything.

From outside she heard a lawnmower.

In the kitchen there was only a thick silence full of temptation.

Her gaze fell for a moment on the garden wall. Where she had lost her mind to him. Her heart pounding, needing to kill the torturous silence, she began to babble. 'I fell in love with the dress the moment I saw it. It's not my usual style but it's such a beautiful day, and my clothes aren't fitting me any more. I hope it's not too mumsy.'

She ran out of breath.

'Your dress is lovely, but I was talking about *you*, Charlotte. *You* are beautiful.'

His eyes bored into hers. Weak-kneed, she smiled. She needed to get out of here before she did something stupid. Like walk into his arms, kiss that gloriously smiling but yet menacing mouth, run her hands under his polo shirt to the warmth and strength of his chest beneath.

Shuffling her heavy handbag to her other hand, she brought them back to how their conversation had started. 'So, have you changed your mind?'

He gave her an amused smile and began to roll up the plans. 'About the coach house? No. I just wanted to double-check the lighting plan.'

'I meant about visiting my parents.'

He laid the plans down on the counter. 'You want me there, so I'll come.'

'But you're not happy about it.'

His mouth tightened. 'I don't like lying to them.'

She nodded and looked out to the garden. Pleached lime trees ran the length of the boundary walls of the garden, low lines of box hedging edging the paths, both giving the garden a formal, elegant structure, which was softened by glorious planting of large clusters of lupins and hollyhocks. In a few years' time their baby would be toddling through that beautiful garden, sometimes to continue on to the coach house to visit her grandparents.

I will not hurt my parents. Why should they carry the burden of my mistakes?

She turned back to him. 'I see it as protecting them. What good would it serve to tell them the truth? Now can we go? We're going to be late.'

He didn't move when she took a few steps towards the hall.

But then his expression softened and his gaze wandered over her again, lingering for the longest while on her stomach.

A wicked glint grew in his eyes. 'We're going to have a very handsome son, you know.'

Relieved that his good humour had returned, she began to walk towards the hallway again. 'A very pretty daughter, you mean.'

Lucien followed her into the marble-floored hallway and said, 'A daughter hopefully as pretty as you.'

He moved in front of her and held open the front door. His silver Aston Martin was parked on the kerb outside.

Thrown by his words, annoyed by how stupidly pleased they made her, how much she wanted to believe them, she paused on the top step and turned back to him. 'You don't need to use your chat-up lines with me. I'm your wife, remember?'

His jaw tensed ever so slightly. He checked his watch.

For a split second he hesitated.

And then in one swift move he pulled her back into the house and shut the door.

He backed her against the hallway wall.

'What are you doing? We're going to be late. My dad is a real stickler for time.'

One hand landed on the wall above her, trapping her.

He was standing way too close to her. Towering over her.

Shrewd green eyes challenged her.

He lowered his head and asked, 'Do you think that I've forgotten that you're my wife?'

She swallowed against the sexy drawl of his voice, against the chemistry thumping between them. 'No.'

He cocked his head and raised an eyebrow.

Desire tugged hard inside her.

'Do you think that I lie when I say you're beautiful?'

If she moved forward a few inches and rose up onto her tippy toes she would be able to lay her lips on that sharp, arrogant mouth and stop him asking all of these awkward questions. 'Maybe.'

He drew back a little. The heat was still beating between them but his mouth was an even harder, more alarming line of displeasure. 'Why do you doubt yourself?'

She gulped against the wild thumping of her heart, but managed to give him a haughty glare. 'I don't.'

He dropped his hand from the wall.

And touched his fingers along the inside of her arm. At first he skimmed beneath the cuff of her short sleeve before moving down the skin of her inner arm, torturous inch by torturous inch, toying with her. Light-headed, she fought against how badly her eyes wanted to close, trying not to let the groan of delicious desire in her throat escape. His fingers lingered at her wrist, drawing lazy circles over her artery. Could he feel her pulse throbbing there?

She should move away. But his dangerous eyes and even more dangerous body held her captive.

His eyes darkened.

Her heart dipped as he stared at her as though he was trying to look into her soul. 'At work you like to portray yourself as cool and logical, an ice queen. It's who I thought you were at first, but the reality is that you're *une tigresse*. A tigress who protects her family, who protects her heart.'

And I need to protect it from you.

She pressed hard against the wall behind her. Trying to ground herself. Lost in a world where nothing mattered more than to feel the weight of her husband on her again. 'Perhaps.'

His fingers threaded down to hers. 'Your ex was a fool to have lost you.'

But you would have been happy to let me go too.

Sobering, remembering the truth of their relationship, she fell away from him on weak legs, desperately trying to pull herself together. 'Can we go now? My dad likes to have his lunch at precisely one-thirty every day.'

He studied her for a moment before opening the front door.

Outside, he opened the passenger door of the car for her, and when she passed him to sit in the car, he held her arm and said quietly, 'Some day you're going to let me in and allow me to see what's really going on in that brain, in that heart of yours. Some day you're going to actually trust me.'

Unable to meet his eye, she looked out blankly as he drove much too quickly through Mayfair following the sat-nav instructions to head south-east towards her home village close to Maidstone in Kent.

Knowing that she could never tell him why she doubted herself so much. How diminished, dismissed, worthless she had felt when the man she had loved had looked at her with such confusion and impatience when she had been depressed. She couldn't tell him because she didn't want to remember that time. She didn't want him to think her weak. Anyway, why burden him with all of that? What purpose could it serve?

Charlotte's parents lived in a house that would have been old even when Shakespeare was a boy. Set down a narrow lane off the main street of the village, it had a cottage garden to the front and a long lawn to the rear with fruit trees at the rear boundary wall.

Inside the rooms were timber-beamed with several open fireplaces, and low doorways Lucien had to duck through while trying not to tread on their tiny 'Yorkie-poo', Billy.

Billy was now repeatedly ramming a soft toy into his ankle, waiting for him to play yet another game of tug-of-war, as he sat out on the terrace with Charlotte at the garden dining table, her dad in the process of pouring them both home-made lemonade.

Charlotte's mother Carol paused from carrying out platters of food to the table from the kitchen, having refused to allow either of them to help, and eyed Charlotte with obvious pleasure. 'It's so lovely to see you wearing such a pretty dress.'

Charlotte touched the dress and shrugged. Again uncomfortable and disbelieving of any compliments.

Her mother's gaze narrowed. 'You look tired, though. Are you sleeping well at night, darling?'

Charlotte glanced at him and then away. 'Mum! Honestly.'

For a few seconds Carol looked at her, perplexed, before flapping her hands, an embarrassed expression on her face. 'Oh…no, that's not… I meant are you not sleeping well because of the pregnancy.'

Charlotte gave her an incredulous look.

Carol backed away, clearly anxious to make a quick exit. 'I'll get the salads.'

Her father walked away too, muttering something about checking on the barbecue.

Charlotte gave Lucien a cheeky smile, amusement glittering in her eyes, and he laughed. She leaned into him, her arm touching his, her head dropping against his shoulder for a moment before she pulled away.

Something strong and beautiful pinged between them. A connection.

Was this what it meant to be a married couple?

The intimacy you shared from spending hours together, the easy ability to read one another with a single look, to tease each other without uttering a word?

Her mum and dad soon reappeared and they settled down to a lunch of barbecued salmon and salads.

Halfway through the lunch, after much talk and gossip on village happenings, the intricacies of which made office politics sound like a walk in the park, Charlotte lowered her cutlery and said to her parents, 'When you visited you would have seen a coach house at the bottom of Lucien's garden.'

He grimaced a little that she still referred to *their* house as *his* but, oblivious to this, Charlotte continued on, 'Lucien has had a terrific idea. He's drawn up plans to renovate the coach house so that when you visit you'll be able to stay there.'

Carol clapped her hands excitedly. 'Oh, that's a wonderful idea. But are you sure? We wouldn't want to be getting in your way. You're a newly married couple, after all.'

Beside him Charlotte groaned.

Amusement and guilt stirred simultaneously inside him. He pushed both down and addressed Carol with sincerity. 'Charlotte and I will welcome your support and company. I'm sure your grandson will also love to have his grandparents so close by.'

His child would only have one set of grandparents in his life and he would do everything to make sure this warm and loving couple were an integral part of his life. Even if at times their love and happiness for one another, for Charlotte, painfully reminded him of just how lacking his own parents were.

Would he ever be able to match the Aldridges' easy love and openness?

With tears in her eyes, Carol exclaimed, 'It's a boy!'

Charlotte darted him a dirty look. 'We don't know yet, Mum. We've decided not to find out until the birth but Lucien keeps insisting it's a boy. But I know it's a girl.'

Robert, who had remained silent up to this point, stood up and raised his wine glass. 'I think it's time for a toast. Carol and I are delighted to welcome you into the family, Lucien. I have to admit that at the start we were concerned that you were marrying too quickly…' he stopped and gave a little cough, reddening a little as he glanced towards Charlotte's stomach '…even given your circumstances, but we can see now that Charlotte was a lucky woman when she met you. You're an honourable and considerate man.' Robert's chin wobbled. 'What more could parents wish for their daughter?'

Lucien drew back in his chair, about to drown in his own guilt. 'I'm not sure—'

The rest of his sentence was lost as Charlotte interrupted, 'You're right, Dad. Lucien is incredibly considerate. Every year he donates millions personally to charities that provide much-needed housing to vulnerable and homeless young adults.' She stopped and inhaled a deep breath. Her mum and dad looked at her, a little confused, clearly not following why she was telling them this right now.

But he wasn't fooled for a second.

She interrupted because she had been afraid that he was going to say something that would give away the true nature of their marriage. Her words were hollow.

But then she turned to him, her cheeks growing hot, an intensity and admiration in her eyes. 'And just this week he announced at work a new apprenticeship scheme that will be rolled out in Huet this year, which will provide a training scheme for hundreds of vulnerable teenagers.' She smiled at him. 'I'm so proud to be the wife of a man who has worked so hard to achieve what he has, often with little support and in difficult circumstances, and the fact that he's so determined to help others now.'

His heart turned over.

He stared at Charlotte.

He stared at his wife.

He had been alone for ever.

With no one believing in him.

And now he had her.

He took a gulp of his lemonade.

His heart in free fall.

Her cheeks flushed, Charlotte turned to him and smiled at him shyly.

He wanted to kiss her. Right then and there.

He wanted to push her away. Terrified about what she was doing to him.

He wanted to be her husband, in every sense. To have her heart and soul. To connect with her emotionally and physically. Sleep with her. Make love to her time and time again.

But those weren't thoughts he should be having with her parents staring at him. Sitting in their garden on a blue-skied summer's day, when life suddenly felt as if it was full of possibilities.

He shook his head, pretending to be amused, modest, laid-back about all she said. When in truth they were the most meaningful words anyone had ever said to him. Words that were terrifying and wonderful at the same time. 'Thank you for the compliments but I'm far from perfect.'

A sparkle lit up in Charlotte's eyes. With an exaggerated sigh she said to her parents, 'He's right, he does have his faults.'

In unison Carol and Robert said, 'Really?'

'He drives too quickly.'

Carol looked appalled. 'Oh, Lucien, you mustn't—especially with Lottie being pregnant. With her past problems we—'

Before Carol could finish her sentence, Charlotte interrupted, 'And he steals my fudge.'

Robert shook his head. 'That's not a good idea.'

Charlotte shot him a narrowed gaze. 'And he works way too hard.'

'Well, that's to be expected,' her dad conceded.

Confused, Lucien turned to Carol. 'What problems?'

A tense silence fell on the table. Carol, clearly flustered, glanced at Charlotte, reddened a little but then acted as though she didn't hear him. 'When are you going to go on your honeymoon?'

There was something they weren't telling him. He fixed his gaze on Charlotte but she suddenly had the need to grind a ridiculous amount of pepper onto her salmon. Carol and Robert managed to avoid his gaze too as they busied themselves with their meal. He bit down on the frustration that uncurled in him at being excluded and said in retaliation, 'We're going next Thursday to my villa in Sardinia, for a long weekend.'

Charlotte turned to him with her prosecutor stare. 'Darling, you didn't tell me.'

He gave his best smile to her parents. 'It was to be a surprise but I'm sure you don't mind me sharing it with your parents.'

She lifted her glass and muttered, 'I can't wait.'

He met her eye and spoke the truth. 'Me neither.'

CHAPTER NINE

EVEN WHEN ASLEEP Lucien held the alertness and rawness of a street-fighter ready for action.

Propped up on an elbow, Charlotte watched her sleeping husband.

This, the first morning of their so-called *honeymoon*, was the only time since they had married that she had woken to find him still asleep beside her.

Was there a significance to that?

All week she had given Lucien a hard time for announcing the break to Sardinia in front of her parents but he had retaliated by teasingly asking her why she was so reluctant to go away with him.

As if he was oblivious to the tension that was mounting between them all week at the idea of being alone together for four days in the sun, on their *honeymoon*, and all the connotations that that brought.

She had grumbled on Monday evening about her old swimwear not fitting any longer. His answer to that, his eyes blazing, a sexy grin on his mouth, had been that they could always go skinny-dipping.

Completely flustered at that suggestion, she had made an excuse to leave the house and ten minutes later had been ordering a milkshake in a diner in Soho.

She edged a little closer to him in the bed. Bristle lined his jawline and down the thick column of his neck. His mouth was a sharp horizontal line, as dangerous as any blade. The faint hint of a lone acne scar close to his left ear made her think of him as a teenager, fighting to make his way, to escape his past. What strength and resilience he must have had. Could she wish for a better man to be the father of her baby?

She should get up and explore. And stop ogling her husband. They had arrived late last night but even in the darkness she had been blown away by the sprawling six-bedroom single-storey property with its extensive grounds located close to the exclusive resort of Porto Cervo on Sardinia's north-eastern Emerald Coast: Costa Smeralda.

She should get up and go for a walk on the golden sands of his private beach or perhaps go for a swim in the shimmering blue Mediterranean Sea, both visible through the open French doors from where she lay in the bed.

She should get up and keep her distance.

But instead she stared at him. Her husband. As usual sprawled over his half of the bed, limbs thrown in every direction. The sheet twisted around his body revealing the power and hard beauty of his golden chest. His nearest arm tossed behind his head, the muscles of his biceps taut and bulging.

'The light is killing me.' His voice groggy, he scrunched his eyelids even more firmly shut.

She threw herself down onto her pillow, hoping he hadn't realised she had been staring at him for the past ten minutes. Trying to sound as though she had just woken too, she said in a low voice, 'I can't imagine a nicer way to wake up—to this view and the sound of the sea.'

'We're shutting the blinds and doors tonight.'

'Oh, don't be such a spoilsport.'

He twisted his head to her and opened up an eye. 'Spoilsport?'

She tried not to smile, not to react to how he was now watching her with sexy mischievousness. 'You heard me.'

'You're the one who refused to go swimming last night.' His sleepy voice was sexy, adorable, toe-curlingly tempting.

'You woke me in the middle of the night!' The desire to move to him, to lay her head on his chest, feel his arms around her, be wrapped up in his warmth, was crushing.

A slow grin formed on that lethal mouth. 'Where's your sense of adventure?'

'I'm adventurous!'

'Really? How about you prove that?'

In one quick movement he was out of the bed and staring down at her. 'First to the pool gets to decide if we swim... with or without clothes.'

He was joking. Wasn't he?

'No way!'

He smirked at her protest and sauntered to his dressing room.

She was adventurous.

She didn't need to prove it to him.

Who was she kidding? She lived life by the book. Maybe it was time to throw caution to the wind. And regain the light-hearted girl she once was.

She rushed into her dressing room; the bedroom suite had 'his and hers' dressing rooms with doors that led to a shared palatial bathroom.

She searched her suitcase for a bikini and shouted out to him, 'This isn't fair. I have two pieces to change into.'

He answered back in a drawl, 'I'll help you if you want.'

Time to get him back. 'That would be great. I'll need to tie up my hair—my elastic bands are in my wash bag in the bathroom. Would you mind getting me one?'

The crash of something falling came from the bathroom, followed by a low curse.

With fumbling fingers she tied her bikini top while making for the open terrace door.

Outside she rushed down the pale yellow stone path that led to the infinity pool, her feet brushing against the coarse ticklish grass of the manicured lawns bordering the path.

She glanced behind her.

Lucien, in short-legged navy swim trunks, watched her from the terrace. A menacing smile on his face. Like any predator, happy to toy with his prey before he went in for the kill.

She gave an involuntary but heartfelt yelp and walked more quickly.

Genuinely scared. Thrillingly so.

She held a hand to her bikini bottoms, her forearm resting on her swollen belly, the other hand resting on her top. Praying that her newly purchased bikini continued to preserve her modesty.

Goosebumps serrated her skin.

She prayed that she wasn't waddling but it was difficult to pull off a graceful walk when eighteen weeks pregnant.

Light, assured footsteps sounded behind her.

She gave another yelp and tried to lengthen her stride.

In a few steps she would be at the wide terrace surrounding the pool.

Another few steps after that and she would have the safety of the water. She was about to win.

But suddenly a muscular arm was about her waist, lifting her up, carrying her forward along the terrace and away from the direction of the pool.

They passed a row of sun loungers and then she saw where he was taking her: a four-poster canopied double sunbed.

He gently placed her down onto the mattress so that they lay on their sides.

At first she giggled, but then she pushed him hard on the chest. 'I win.'

'Nope, I don't think so.'

'You manhandled me!' She eyed him evilly and tried to get up but his arm once again circled her waist.

'I think on this occasion that I win.'

His tone was sexy, dark, full of suggestion. She went to respond but the heat of his voice, the heat in his eyes, the heat of his hand on her back, stole all of her words away.

Their thighs were touching.

Only a few inches separated their chests.

A hunger for him stormed through her. So fierce, so intense, so pointless, she couldn't breathe.

His thighs moved forward. Pressing more firmly against hers.

Desire moved through her body like a cascade of falling dominos.

He angled his head closer to hers.

Beyond caring any more about hiding her attraction to him, she whispered, 'Can we get up? Because I can't handle this for much longer.'

He didn't answer but continued to hold her gaze.

His bright green gaze so devastating her heart looped and looped and looped in her chest.

His mouth hovered over hers.

Their breaths mingled.

And with deliberate, heartbreaking slowness his lips moved onto hers.

Soft, enquiring, tentative.

But when she gave a give-away moan, his kiss turned hot and seeking. Urgent. Turbulent.

Six weeks of denial of the chemistry between them exploding into an endless kiss of release, hunger, desperation.

His mouth was hard. Demanding. Taking.

She groaned against his mouth when his leg wrapped

around hers, his torso cradling into her side. His hand moved over her ribs and skimmed her breasts.

And still his mouth was on hers.

She wrapped her arms around his neck.

Needing more.

Glorying in the feel of his hard, powerful, domineering body entwined with hers.

His hand moved down, over her hip bone.

Deep desire ached inside her.

She wanted him.

She had wanted him from the first moment she had ever seen him, walking towards her on the executive floor at work. His long stride, dangerous air, streetwise gaze, fascinating and intimidating.

An innate potent attraction she had never experienced before that had her trying to convince herself that she had imagined it.

Now his hand moved up and over her swollen belly.

The kiss lightened.

His hand no longer frantic but a light caress.

His mouth still on hers, he whispered, 'The baby.'

Her heart turned over.

This was the father of her child. She was carrying his baby inside her.

Her heart felt as if it were about to burst with the bond, the closeness she felt for him.

She wrapped her hands more firmly on his neck, tried to pull him back to her. Needing his mouth, needing his body, needing him.

But he jerked away.

Punch drunk, she stared at him, lost in a jumbled world of connection and desire.

He inhaled deeply and untangled his body from hers. 'We can't…you'll only end up hating me. There's too much at stake.'

She edged away from him. Sat on the corner of the sun-bed. Light-headed with desire and disappointment. 'What do you mean I'll hate you?'

He stared at the pale yellow stone beneath his feet, his jaw tense. 'I'll never be the husband you need or deserve.'

Humiliation, frustration and fear combined into fury. 'Isn't that up to me to decide?'

He didn't answer but instead stood up and walked to the side of the pool.

She waited for him to dive in, but he turned away and walked back up the path to their bedroom. Not once look-ing back towards her.

She collapsed back onto the sunbed, tears of frustration and loneliness burning the backs of her eyes. She dragged the light blanket that sat at the bottom of the bed around herself. Feeling cold and silly lying there in her bikini.

He'd done the right thing.

But right now she hated him for it.

Hated him for persuading her into this lonely marriage.

Later that evening, Lucien inhaled a lungful of dread when he turned to see Charlotte make her way down the path from their bedroom, to the pool terrace where he was wait-ing for her.

She was wearing what must be more of her recent pur-chases: a short gold miniskirt, a loose spaghetti-strap cream silk top and gold sandals; her hair hung in loose waves down her back.

A troubled goddess.

Her gaze met his only fleetingly.

He couldn't bear this any longer.

How was he supposed to take her to dinner and pretend that this morning didn't happen?

How was he supposed to not give into the temptation of touching his lips to her already sun-kissed skin?

And later on, to lie in the same bed as her but not be able to draw her into him, to taste her, to make love to her?

All day they had avoided making eye contact. As they had shared lunch, spent the afternoon on his yacht moored out of Porto Cervo, tension had bounced between them.

He had wanted nothing in life as desperately as he had wanted to untie Charlotte's mouth-watering apple-green bikini this morning. To love her body again.

To lose himself in her warmth.

To have the soft swell of her body beneath his.

To hear her cries of contentment.

But how could they do any of this when they had a child to raise together?

They had at least twenty years ahead of them where they needed to be able to support each other and work together. Mixing the emotions and expectations of being lovers into that would jeopardise their ability to get along.

And anyway, if Charlotte knew the full truth of his past, she would realise that she couldn't trust him.

She needed to know that truth.

Damning shame twisted in his chest and he reluctantly gestured to the beach. 'Let's go for a walk before we leave for dinner. There's still enough light.'

Her mouth tightened and she pointed a foot towards him, her raspberry-painted toenails, her long toned legs almost undoing his resolve to go through with this conversation. 'These sandals weren't made for the beach. We can talk at the restaurant.'

'We need to talk in private.'

She studied him unhappily for a few seconds before sitting down on a lounger and whipping off her sandals.

He removed his own moccasins.

Down on the beach, they sank into the fine sand, the light lap of the sea the only sound.

He steeled himself, suddenly overheating despite the

fading sun to the west. 'I haven't told you everything you should know about my first marriage.'

She slowed her pace, caution replacing her annoyance.

He tried to speak but the words tangled and stuck in his throat.

She was the first person he would tell this sorry, pathetic tale to.

She stopped and turned to face him, her hand shielding her stomach. 'Our marriage isn't conventional. I don't expect you to tell me everything. Our past can be our own business.'

'After this morning, you need to know. You *need* to know why we can't sleep together. I hate lies. Ever since I found my father in the act of betraying my mother I've abhorred dishonesty. And to my shame I've been dishonest with you.'

A light breeze caught her hair and it swirled around her. She gathered it together and twisted it into a rope. 'What do you mean?'

He needed to walk. He couldn't face her when telling her this. He turned away and she joined him to walk along the crescent-shaped beach.

'Towards the end of my first marriage, Gabrielle and I were constantly arguing. We both hated where we lived, sharing with so many others, the noise, the rodents, how run-down and unsafe the property was. I wanted to move to Paris for better opportunities. Gabrielle refused to. We were growing apart but neither of us wanted to face that fact. Until I arrived home one night and found her semi-naked in the kitchen with another man who shared the apartment. She eventually admitted that it hadn't been the first time they were together.'

She pulled him to a stop, her hand resting on his arm. 'That's horrific.'

He moved away. Not able to bear her touch. Knowing

how much she would hate him when he told her every-thing. 'It tore me apart. Despite our problems, I thought she was the one person I could rely on. Trust. I wanted to hurt her, as much as she had hurt me. I went out and got drunk.' He looked into Charlotte's troubled and horrified eyes and admitted his darkest secret, saying the words, fighting the crunching tightness in his chest. 'And then I slept with her friend.'

Charlotte gasped. Backed away, stumbling in the sand. 'You betrayed her, with her friend.'

He looked away from her crestfallen expression, the hurt in her eyes.

'Oh, Lucien, how could you?'

He winced at the pain in her voice but forced himself to look back and face her disappointment in him. 'I'm not going to try to defend myself.'

Her expression hardened. 'I should hope not. Did you tell your ex what had happened?'

'The next day.'

She planted both hands on her hips and lifted her chin. Fury pouring from her every pore. 'What you did was self-ish, stupid and immature. How could you? I know Gabrielle betrayed you first. But what you did was no better.'

At that she walked away from him, furiously striding down the beach, her body rigid with anger.

He stayed put. Knowing there was no point in following her. Knowing there was nothing else to be said. She now knew what type of person he really was. A man who be-trayed his wife. A man a thousand times more contempt-ible than her ex who had broken her heart.

For well over ten minutes she stared out at the sea at the far end of the beach.

And as the minutes ticked by his self-disgust turned to dread.

What if she wanted nothing to do with him after this?

Had he just compromised his child's future because of his past, because he couldn't handle his feelings for Charlotte?

What had he done?

Her eyes closed, Charlotte lifted her chin, desperate to ease the tight tension in her neck, the onshore breeze lifting her hair away from her shoulders.

He had betrayed his wife.

And she had no idea how to respond.

She flung her eyes open.

He still stood where she had left him, further up the beach.

Over black trousers he was wearing a light soft-knit black sweater. His dark clothing adding to his intensity, dignity, pride even when admitting something so terrible.

She had always said he was a heartbreaker. A manipulating charmer. Unreliable and selfish. And if he had told her this before they had married, before she had got to know him, she would have walked away.

She stalked back towards him, needing to lash out.

Still not quite sure what she was going to say.

She had to think of the baby.

But she also had to think of herself. Of her heart.

She came to a halt before him and the words tumbled out furiously. 'I hate what you did. You're a better man than that. Why did you do something so horrible, so stupid?'

He winced but held her gaze.

The self-recrimination in his eyes blunted her anger.

She inhaled a shaky breath, her heart dipping to see the tight lines of distress at the corners of his eyes. She bit her lip against the uncertainty, the broken dreams twisting inside her, but mostly in compassion for Lucien's pain. 'But I know what it's like to hurt, to be afraid. We don't always act well when we're scared.' She had isolated herself from others when depressed, pushing them away. How many people had she inadvertently hurt? 'You were young. Young and stupid. What you did was wrong, really wrong, but we've all done things we regret.'

He shook his head and said bitterly, 'I'm sure you never did anything quite as stupid as I did.' He stopped and his expression tightened further. 'I'm particularly sorry that it only acts as a reminder of how Dan betrayed you.'

She closed her eyes at the memory of how Dan and Angie had stared at one another in the pub garden after they had broken away from their kiss. Their love for one another puncturing endless holes in her already depression-ravaged heart. Now she looked at Lucien and said, 'Knowing what you did does hurt. But I have done things I too regret. I regret how I was with Dan towards the end of our relationship…things were tense and sad between us.'

She paused and drew in a breath into her unbearably tight chest. She had pushed Dan away, not wanting to contaminate him with her unhappiness. While at the same time unfairly willing him not to allow her to push him away, wanting him to believe in her, fight for her. 'It doesn't excuse what Dan and Angie did, but I do know that things are never black and white in life, and that relationships are complex and messy.'

Lucien reached forward and repositioned the thin strap of her top that had fallen down her shoulder. His touch as gentle, as intimate as his voice when he asked, 'What went wrong between you?'

Her heart pinched. A shiver darted up her spine. She should tell him about the depression.

But she couldn't.

She gestured back up the beach. 'I'm getting cold. I need to go to the villa for my wrap.'

They walked back up the beach, a wide gap separating them. She needed to give him an explanation as to why she pushed Dan away. To explain at least part of her regrets. 'Back then, Dan and I were growing apart. We just weren't able to talk like we used to, university was coming to an end, we had careers to think about, I wanted to move to London, Dan wanted to move to Manchester for work.'

'Were you still in love with him?'

Emotion the size of a bowling ball landed on her chest. 'Yes.'

At the bottom of the steps leading back up to the terrace he stopped and looked at her soberly, his jaw working. 'Are you still in love with him?'

She looked her husband in the eye and answered, 'No.'
But I am with you. Stupidly.

She shrugged and continued, 'We all make mistakes. It's only human. It's not making them again…that's the important part.'

At the top of the steps Lucien stamped his bare feet on the flagstones to remove the sand clinging to his soles. 'But do we ever change? What if those mistakes happen because they are an integral part of you? What if it's genetic? And you do it again.'

'What are you saying?'

'I grew up with selfish parents who were irresponsible, who sabotaged every relationship they ever had. What if I'm the same?'

'Are you saying that you might sabotage our relationship?'

His eyes held hers with a steady strength full of pride but a keen awareness of his past and the hurt he had caused. 'I'll do everything in my power not to. But with my background how can I swear to you that I won't hurt you at some point in the future? And the worst part is I know you'll never rightly trust me after hearing this.'

'Maybe I will.'

He shook his head. 'No, you won't.'

She picked up her sandals and stabbed them towards him, angry to hear the stubborn defiance in his voice. ' I won't pretend that I'm not really disappointed that you betrayed Gabrielle, but I will trust you and do you know why? Because I now understand that, with your background, it would have been so much easier for you not to marry me. But you still went ahead for the sake of our baby. You turned your life around when you were so young, when everything was going against you, and that takes immense strength and courage. You did all of that alone, without support. It's about time you had support, someone who believes in you.'

She swallowed hard and stepped towards him. She touched the soft wool of his sweater, her heart thundering. 'I'd like to be that person. If you'll let me.'

His hand moved down and covered hers. He pulled her into him, his arms wrapping around her waist. 'Why?'

She spoke her words into the warmth of his throat. 'Because you're the father of my child. My husband.'

Because I'm in love with you.

His hands tightened around her waist. His lips brushed against her ear. In a voice full of dark emotion he breathed out, 'I want to be your husband in the fullest meaning of that word. I want to make love to you.'

'You do?'

He answered with a soft groan. But then he held her gaze with serious burning green eyes. 'I'll never want to hurt you.'

He meant it, for now. But she knew better than anyone that life could change you, change how you thought you would act and behave.

She smiled at him shyly, her heart thumping with need to connect with her husband. Whatever the future might bring for them.

On the nearest sun lounger, he wiped her feet clean of sand. His movements gentle and tender.

A precursor to the night ahead.

CHAPTER TEN

THE FOLLOWING MORNING a warm body cradled Charlotte and a rainfall of soft kisses dropped down along the side of her neck and over her bare shoulders.

Her eyes closed. She wanted to stay in this dreamlike state for ever, and she murmured little moans of appreciation when his hand moved down over her hips, along the length of her thigh and back up to caress her bottom.

His mouth nibbled on her ear.

She giggled and tried to move away, but he pulled her in closer, wrapping her in the cocoon of his heat and tight, taut body.

She had almost fallen back to sleep when he whispered against her cheek, 'Come and watch the sunrise with me.'

Drowsily she twisted around to him.

The corners of his mouth were crinkled; happiness, mischievousness, lingering want shone brightly in his eyes.

A long luxurious feeling moved through her: the feeling of being sated, contented, worn out.

She stretched lazily. 'I'm too tired.'

Playfully he ran kisses over her cheeks and down her throat. She giggled and tried to push him away. Which only encouraged him to run his kisses further down until his mouth was playing havoc once again with her breasts.

She moaned and her body lifted, desperate to press against him.

He lifted his head, triumphant, and asked, 'Still too tired?' He didn't wait for her answer but instead climbed out of the bed.

He disappeared into his dressing room but soon re-emerged dressed in jeans and a tee shirt. His feet bare.

He plucked his sweater from the evening before off the floor and brought it to her. 'Wear this.'

Sitting up, she reluctantly pulled on the gorgeously soft sweater, her sleepy haze intensifying as she inhaled his lingering scent on the wool fibres, all while trying to protest that it was too early, too dark outside. She wanted him back in bed with her. Holding her. Distracting her from her thoughts. Thoughts that had her panicking about just how deeply she was in love with him.

Last night he had made love to her so slowly, so tenderly, so intimately that she had completely lost her heart to him.

Now he listened to her protests with amusement, clearly not prepared to give in to her.

She shuffled back in the bed, pulling his sweater down to cover the tops of her thighs, her back against the headboard. And pulled an ace from her sleeve. 'I'm pregnant… cut me some slack here. I've barely slept all night.'

He wasn't falling for it. He flashed her an evil grin and swooped her into his arms.

He carried her through the open terrace door and followed the lit path down to the pool terrace.

She tried to pull her sweater down over her bottom where it had ridden up but his fingers, clasping her at the top of her thigh, flicked her hand away.

She groaned as those fingers then teasingly caressed the sensitive skin at the top of her thighs. She wriggled but he only tightened his grip. And in retaliation she nibbled the skin just below his hammering heart.

He cursed lowly.

And when he dropped her onto the double sunbed, he

loomed over her and said, 'I think we have unfinished business here, don't you?'

Later, wrapped in each other's arms, they watched the sun, cautiously at first, but then in a fiery bold blaze, rise up in the east. And she pushed away all of the fears for the future that ebbed and flowed in her brain like the sea below them, knowing the only way she would cope was by not overthinking this situation. Yes, he was with her only because she was pregnant with his child. But maybe that was enough. Maybe his affection and friendship would suffice instead of love.

A week later, Charlotte locked the coach-house door that led out into the main garden and paused to dust herself down.

The builders had begun work on Monday and, five days in, they had demolished all of the internal structure that needed removing, insulated the inside and had begun to build new partition walls.

Lucien had left for meetings in Brussels Wednesday morning.

Two nights without him and she felt completely lost.

As much as she hated to admit it, she was in deep. Deeper than she wanted to be. But she was so consumed by him, so hungry to be in his presence, so distracted by him that she couldn't think rationally.

The pink and white tea roses and peonies now blooming in the garden glistened under the evening sun. It had rained earlier. London was being hit by short and fierce thunderstorms, and the air was filled with a mixture of rose blossom and damp earth.

A movement on the terrace had her start.

And then she smiled.

He was home early.

He wasn't due home until tomorrow afternoon in time for a charity ball they were attending in Somerset House.

She stood still.

And drank him in. Her heart flapping. Her entire body trembling.

Her husband. Dressed in a dark navy suit, his purple and silver tie loosened, the top button undone.

With his hard body, solid neck, sharp jawline and cleft chin, he was still a street-fighter. But one with honour and integrity.

He cocked his head to the side.

Waiting for her to go to him.

About to go, she wavered. Needing to stay in control.

He pulled off his tie.

Threw his jacket onto a nearby chair.

And sauntered towards her.

Night after night for the past week, they had made love time and time again, waking each other during the night with a never-ending hunger to connect again. And during the day they sneaked out of work at lunchtime and spent the hour in bed, Lucien poker faced when they returned to HQ, Charlotte blushing at the speculative glances of the receptionists.

He came closer.

Dark, dangerous, all-consuming, his expression one of absolute desire.

He towered over her. She was unable to breathe against the fire in his eyes.

A single finger touched against her stomach.

She shivered. Closed her eyes with a sigh.

Both hands clasped her face, his long fingers threading through her hair.

She opened her eyes and mouth at the same time.

And she moaned hard and long when his mouth claimed hers.

He unbuttoned her dress in the garden.

Removed it in the kitchen.

Made love to her on the thick, inviting wool of the living-room rug.

Not a single word passed between them.

The following evening, butterflies dancing in her belly, Charlotte ran out into the hallway from the kitchen when she heard Lucien rush down the stairs.

'We're going to be so late. Did you have to go into work on a Saturday? You…' The rest of her admonishment for him being so late home faded as she drank him in.

Standing a few steps up on the stairs, he was unbearably handsome in his bespoke tuxedo.

Her cruel, sexy assassin…with a heart full of honour and kindness.

Her king amongst men.

But he wasn't quite perfect.

She dashed up the stairs towards him. 'You can't go to the ball with wet hair.'

'It'll dry on the way there.'

'It's not even a ten-minute journey away. Come on, I'll dry it for you.'

In their bedroom she pulled out her dressing table stool and gestured for him to sit.

He did so reluctantly.

The moment she touched his hair, she knew that it was a bad idea.

Now they were definitely going to be late.

Her fingers ran through his hair, the tips skimming the hard contours of his scalp. The ever restless ache inside her for him igniting.

And he stared at her in the reflection of the mirror. Stared hard. Stared with the look of a man who liked what he saw.

Hungry. Compelling. Formidable.

Overwhelmed, she twisted to the side, so that the reflection would only show her back. And she bowed her head so that he wouldn't be able to catch her eye. Embarrassed by how much she wanted him, at how weak, how defenceless and vulnerable she was around him.

Male power oozed from him.

Her fingers danced through his dark brown hair. Above his right ear, her fingers touched against his scar. She had felt it on the first night they had been together but hadn't learnt how he had acquired it until he had told her of his childhood. It represented so much about this strong man who had defied what life had thrown at him.

He turned his head a tad towards her. His gaze shifting up, devouring her.

She glanced away, heat and an intense intimacy for her husband firing through her.

She longed to move her hand down further, to feel the strength of his neck, touch her lips to his skin, and inhale his earthy, leathery scent.

But they were already late.

She switched off the hairdryer.

Needing to break the tension, she joked, 'I don't suppose a milkshake will be on the menu tonight? My cravings for one are off the scale at the moment. It must be the humidity.'

Instead of answering, he reached forward and placed one hand on her waist, anchoring her to the spot while the other gently landed on her ever increasingly rounded stomach.

Her legs wobbled beneath her.

He pulled her towards him and down onto his lap.

At the same eye level now, his green gaze engulfed her. 'You're truly beautiful tonight.'

She swallowed and smiled. Incapable of speaking.

The yearning ache inside her for him widening.

His hand moved up over the loose jersey folds of her full-length gown, caressing her legs beneath.

She shivered.

And he groaned before his mouth lightly touched against hers.

She twisted in his lap. Aching for him to touch all of her.

He deepened his kiss and she moaned when his hand moved up over the satin sash at her waist to the floral lace of the gown top, his fingers lightly teasing her heavy breasts, before they moved to the deep V at the back of the dress.

She squirmed into his lap and deepened their kiss when his fingers ran along her exposed spine.

They were *definitely* going to be late.

His hand moved down to her stomach. Their kiss lightened. Became tender. A soul-destroying connection to this man, her husband, the father of her child slammed into her.

They pulled away from one another.

And she could see in his eyes that he felt it too.

She loved him.

It was reckless and stupid.

But she loved him.

She was looking heartbreak in the eye and couldn't do anything about it.

She wanted to cuddle into him. Have him hold her for ever. She wanted him to make crazy, passionate love to her. She wanted to get up and never turn back, walk away now while she could.

And then she gasped and looked down in astonishment to where Lucien's hand lay on her belly.

A second ripple travelled through her stomach.

'Was that the baby?' he asked softly.

Her hand flew to her mouth. Tears popped up in her eyes. 'Yes…yes…oh, Lucien, our baby moved.'

He let out a shaky breath. Gave her the most incredible smile. And pulled her into his lap even more tightly. Tucked her head against his collarbone. One hand tightly holding her to him, the other hand resting on her stomach, protecting their child.

Charlotte pulled back her tears. Knowing she needed to be strong for this baby. She needed to remain logical and realistic in what she could expect from him. He would be a good, perhaps even brilliant father. But as his wife she could never expect or demand his unconditional love.

But now, for five minutes even, she wanted to be held in the safety of his arms and forget reality.

Four hours later Lucien walked down the steps from the cloakroom to the courtyard of Somerset House, his heart tightening once again when he spotted Charlotte standing watching the iconic fountain show that had water jets hidden in the cobblestones, shooting synchronised powerful spurts of water upwards.

He juggled from one hand to the other her heavily beaded red silk wrap he had gone inside to retrieve.

His attraction, his affection…his love for her was spiralling out of control.

He was besotted by her.

And it made him feel ridiculous. All night, instead of being focused and concentrating on his conversations with some of the City's big hitters, first out on the river terrace overlooking the Thames where the drinks reception had been held and later during dinner in Somerset House's vast neoclassical courtyard, he had been distracted by the sight of Charlotte in her full-length red gown. Hating to see her chatting with her male legal acquaintances, the way she flicked back her loose hair, smiled at them openly, a crazy urge to snarl and claim her as his wiping away all reason.

He loved her.

But he wasn't sure if he would ever be able to tell her. In telling her, he could destroy what they had. He could frighten her away. He could open emotional floodgates neither of them could contain.

He couldn't lose her.

He couldn't lose this baby.

He couldn't risk telling her he loved her because he couldn't bear the thought of her not loving him back. He couldn't bear the thought of failing her in the future. He couldn't bear the thought of ever losing her. Of being rejected. Again.

Now, despite the noise of the swing band playing on the stage and the chatter of the other guests, she turned to him as he approached, as though she sensed his presence without looking. Across the crowd for a brief second he caught her worried expression. But then she smiled at him shyly.

They were leaving the ball early. Dancing together on the crowded dance floor, beneath the night sky of the courtyard, the historic buildings surrounding them bathed in a pale blue light, he had whispered into her ear that he wanted to take her home and make love to her. She had looked at him, her eyes heavy with desire, her cheeks flushed, lips slightly parted, and nodded.

And a sudden need to be truly intimate with his wife had rocked him.

An intimacy that was more than just about making love.

He wanted to be closer to her emotionally. To really understand her.

But he didn't know how to get fully inside her head.

Was that even possible?

Was he being unrealistic? Surely the physical attraction and burgeoning friendship between them should be enough. But yet…but yet a kernel of dissatisfaction, of something not being quite right, gnawed away inside him.

He placed her wrap around her shoulders and planted a light kiss on her forehead.

Took her hand in his.

And together they walked towards the archway that led out onto the Strand, where his driver was waiting for them.

He pushed away all doubts and focused on the here and now by asking, 'Any more movement?'

She shook her head with a wry smile, her hand clasping his more tightly. 'Not since you last asked me ten minutes ago.'

He gave her a guilty smile.

Laughing, she added, 'I promise to tell you when she does kick again.'

He should work tomorrow. He had to fly to South Africa on Monday. The quarterly results for Huet were positive but the next quarter's projections were worrying him. South America's growth was falling way behind target. Despite all of that he heard himself say, 'Let's go shopping for the nursery tomorrow. We can have brunch in my club and then look at the specialist nursery furniture stores we saw on King's Road the night we had dinner with your friends.'

Last week they had agreed to convert the bedroom across the corridor from theirs into a nursery. With windows overlooking the rear garden, the room would be perfect.

Despite the warmth of the night, he felt her shiver. She pulled her hand free of his and drew her wrap in closer around her shoulders. 'I'd prefer to wait until nearer my due date.'

Her voice echoed sharply against the neoclassical columns and stonework of the archway. He drew her to a stop with a sense of foreboding. 'Are you worried?'

'No, but I suppose I'm just being cautious… I don't want to tempt fate.'

He wasn't following. Charlotte liked order and logic. He didn't have her down as someone who was superstitious. 'Tempt fate?'

'What if we buy things and something goes wrong.'

The worry in her eyes had him step towards her. 'Nothing will go wrong.'

She backed away and glanced out towards his waiting car. 'Let's wait at least until after the scan next week.'

He followed her, and pulled her to a stop. 'Why do you think something might go wrong? Is there something you're not telling me?'

'No.' She worried her lip and said in a rush, 'It's just that you never know, do you?' Her wildly blinking eyes clung to his, before she looked down to the ground. 'If you can't make the scan on Thursday, it's okay.'

Where did that come from? She knew he was determined to go to the scan. 'Don't you want me there?'

Charlotte looked away from the sharp intelligence in Lucien's eyes. 'No…no, of course I want you there. I just know how busy you are.'

Guilt rushed through her. Twisting her stomach into a tight knot. The truth was that she didn't want him there.

At her twelve-week appointment she had discussed at length her past history of depression with her obstetrician consultant.

But what if the consultant, whom she was also scheduled to meet, said something at the appointment?

Logic kept telling her that it wouldn't happen.

She could always ring and ask for it not to be mentioned in front of her husband…but even the thought of that made her cringe with guilt and embarrassment.

She needed to stop panicking.

She attempted a bright smile and said, 'You're cutting your trip short to come back for the appointment. It just seems excessive. I can bring my mum if you would prefer for someone else to be there.'

He eyed her dubiously. 'I'll be there. I told you that I

would.' His hand moved under her elbow and he led her towards his car.

It was close to midnight and the streets and pavements of Trafalgar Square and Piccadilly were alive with Saturday-night revellers. They spent the journey home in silence. Lucien's steadfast gaze out towards the passing streets. She had insulted him by suggesting he might not want to go to the scan.

Once home and in the kitchen, he was as attentive as ever, asking if she wanted something to drink, but there was a distance between them. A distance she had created.

A jolt of realisation slammed into her. She shuddered and for a moment grew light-headed.

How would I cope if he ever shut me out of his life? Just with this silence I feel like I'm being scissored in two.

Unable to bear the tension between them, she said, 'I'm sorry.'

Those streetwise, uncompromising eyes held hers. 'I will be at the scan on Thursday. I *want* to be there. You don't have to test me on it, by giving me a way out.'

Was that what he thought?

'I wasn't...' She stopped at his questioning frown, having no alternative explanation to give to him. 'I'm sorry.' She gave him a small smile. 'I hate it when you're annoyed.'

The faintest hint of a sparkle of amusement grew in his eyes. It freed something in her and she added, 'You're pretty scary when you're annoyed, you know.'

For the longest while he stared at her. And then he walked to stand before her on the far side of the kitchen island. His hand cradled her cheek and then ran down the length of her hair, skimming the side of her breast. 'Scary good or scary bad?'

With a gulp she admitted, 'Don't-dare-mess-with-this-sexy-tough-guy scary.'

At that he delivered her a sinfully dazzling smile. 'I'll take sexy scary.'

And she smiled at him goofily.

His eyebrow lifted and he stepped closer. 'Take your dress off.'

Her pulse went into overdrive at his growl. Heating up by at least twenty degrees, she jumped away.

There was an evil glint in his eye.

'Seriously?'

His expression darkened. 'I think you should prove just how sorry you really are.'

He was calling her bluff again. A deep vulnerability stirred in her, all of her old insecurities threatening. But the fire blazing in his eyes torched all those vulnerabilities. She wanted to undress for her husband.

She reached around and pulled down her zip. Dropped one lace shoulder and then the other.

Lowered the dress to her waist.

He groaned when his eyes lighted on her red lace bra.

She eased the dress over her bump and the material dropped to the floor.

He ran a hand along his stubbled jawline, muttering, 'I guess you are sorry.'

His eyes skimmed over her. Over her breasts, her stomach, her matching red panties. Down to her red stiletto heels and back up again. His gaze burning into her.

Please let him come to me. Wrap me in his arms. Wrap me in his warmth. Wrap me in his softly murmured words when he makes love to me.

He moved in front of her. Cupped a cheek into the warmth of his hand. And smiled with a sexy badness before he turned away and walked out into the hallway and up the stairs.

Bewildered, she stood there unable to move for what felt like a lifetime.

But then she reached down and yanked up her dress.

But before she made it out of the kitchen, to head up-stairs to tell him precisely what she thought of his mean little trick, he was back. With a pair of her maternity jeans, a cosy sweater and trainers.

He handed them to her. 'I know a great diner in Camden that does the best milkshakes ever.'

She'd prefer him…but a milkshake sounded pretty good too. Especially with him at her side. She pulled on her jeans and then her sweater, happiness bubbling through her. 'You're a genius, Lucien Duval, and I think I'm fall-ing in love with you!'

Lucien's smile faded.

Panicked by what she'd said, panicked by his surprised gaze, panicked by the intensity of her feelings for this man who was her husband of convenience, she added, 'I'm warn-ing you, though, the diner better not be closed when we get there. Or you'll be way down on my list of favourite people.'

She rushed to the door, cringing. And was relieved when he opened the door and gave her a laid-back smile. 'I called ahead earlier…they are staying open especially for you.'

She breathed in a sigh of relief that he hadn't taken her words seriously.

And then breathed out a sigh of regret that he hadn't done so. But why would he think she might love him when the only reason they were together was for their baby's sake?

Tuesday 12th July, 8:32 p.m.

Missing me?

Sorry, who's this? C

Funny. I miss you.

Bet you're out in a club with clients right now. C

A Cape Town restaurant, in fact.

Pretty girls there? C

I haven't noticed. Send me a photo of yourself.

I'm not that sort of girl! C

I meant fully dressed...unless you'd prefer otherwise.

Wow, Charlotte. Crossed eyes suit you.

Bet you're regretting marrying me now. C

Meeting you was the best thing that ever happened to me.

Wednesday 13th July, 6:43 p.m.

Meeting delayed here. Won't get back tonight. But will be back in time to collect you for the scan appointment at twelve tomorrow.

I'll have the sonograms to show you if you don't. C

I'll be there. I'll call you later. I'm about to make a presentation to the clients.

I'm meeting Tameka and Jill later. I'll speak to you tomorrow. C

I miss you.

You too. C

Only now do I realise what was missing from my life.

A cross-eyed pedantic legal head? C

Family and belonging.

I'm glad. C

CHAPTER ELEVEN

ON THURSDAY MORNING, Charlotte sat alone in the Ultrasound waiting room at Claremont Hospital waiting to be called for her scan. Thanks to a French air traffic controllers' strike Lucien's plane had landed into City Airport late and he was likely to miss the appointment.

He had sounded exasperated when he had rung her earlier at work to tell her that he had organised for a company car to take her to the appointment. And she, like a traitor, had breathed out a sigh of relief that there would be no danger of her history with depression being revealed to him.

What kind of wife am I to be glad that my husband won't be able to attend our baby's scan? Am I that selfish that I'll put my panic, my fears above his happiness?

Needing a distraction from her guilt and the nervous energy bubbling in her stomach at the prospect of the scan and the ever-present worry that a problem with the baby might be detected, she went and rifled through a pile of magazines left on a console table in the corner of the room next to the water fountain.

She searched through the tall column of magazines not taking them in, too overwhelmed by the guilty ache twisting and twisting and twisting inside her.

Towards the end of the tower of magazines, she came to a stop. And let out a disbelieving sigh as she yanked out a glossy magazine.

Below the magazine's main front cover of the royal family attending church in Sandringham on Christmas Day last year, there was a photo of Lucien attending a West End premiere. His date that night had been one of the UK's top female track athletes, who was leaning into him, a wide ecstatic smile on her face.

Despite Lucien's moody scowl at the camera, the body language between them was so relaxed, so intimate, it was obvious they were close…lovers close.

She tossed the magazine away. And shut her eyes. Jealousy heating her stomach. With a groan she sank her head into her hands.

She was in love with Lucien and it terrified her. She didn't know where she stood with him. How he really felt towards her. *Family and belonging.* That was what his text last night had said had been missing from his life. But what did he mean by that? Was he only growing close to her because of their child? Was this still only a *business marriage*…that had veered into the confusing depths of lovemaking?

He had opened up to her about his past. That spoke volumes, didn't it? But maybe he saw her as a partner, a friend, someone he was fond of rather than in love with.

'Is everything okay?'

She yelped at the sound of his voice.

Standing at the waiting-room door, suit jacket in his hand, and despite needing to shave and his shirt being a little wrinkled, Lucien was as big and formidable and sexy as ever.

Adrenaline zipped through her.

She went to speak. But her mouth refused to co-operate. Pleasure, relief at seeing him, the dizzying realisation that in fact she did want him here, all competing with a rush of fear that he might now find out about her depression from someone other than her.

How would he react? Would he slowly but inevitably distance himself as Dan had? Would he think of her as weak? Would he be wary of her because her depression might one day return? Would he find her less attractive? Could he even use the knowledge of her depression against her somehow?

He walked to her and his hands came to a rest on her shoulders, concern and anxiety shining in his eyes. '*Qu'est-ce que tu as?* What's the matter? Is there something wrong with the baby?'

She shook her head.

He bent down to look her in the eye. He gave her a small concerned smile. Willing her to speak.

She swallowed against how much she wanted him to hold her, against how her heart was banging wildly against her chest in pleasure to see him.

She dragged in a deep breath, a sense of unreality washing over her. Was she really going to tell him? She hadn't spoken about her depression with anyone other than her medical team in such a long time. Her stomach lurched violently and suddenly she was shivering. She had to force the words out. 'I have something I need to tell you.'

Lucien paled.

Horrified, she said in a rush, 'It's nothing to do with the baby. I haven't been seen yet. The couple before me only went in five minutes ago.'

He led her to the wooden chairs set into the semi-circle of a large bow window and sat beside her, his body tense, his expression a mixture of concern and confusion.

She gripped her hands against the churning in her stomach.

'There's something you should know about my past medical history.' She paused and inhaled a shaky breath, cringing at how hot her cheeks felt.

His expression grew grave. Oh, God, was she doing the right thing in telling him? He had married her because she was going to be the mother of his child. He hadn't signed up to be burdened with this.

Her knees were jiggling like crazy but she couldn't control them.

Just say the words. Why are you making such a big deal over this?

'In my final year of university I had depression.'

He looked at her blankly. And then his eyes grew wide. He drew back in the chair. 'Depression?'

Hating to see his shock, she nodded and stood, backing away from him until her back was pressed against the wall on the opposite side of the room.

For the longest while he just stared at her. As though he wasn't able to process her words.

After an excruciating few minutes he stood and took a step towards her. A sadness flooded his eyes. He shook his head as though perplexed. 'Why didn't you tell me about this before?' The sadness in his eyes was nothing in comparison to the hurt in his voice.

Guilt squeezed her heart painfully. But the panic rolling through her was even more intense. She didn't want to talk about this any more. 'It was ages ago and I've been well for such a long time. I'm not on medication now. It's not a big deal.'

He looked at her as though mystified. And then he twisted away and walked to the other end of the room. And back towards her. And away again. This time he didn't turn back but stood staring at a noticeboard filled with leaflets on antenatal care at the opposite end of the room.

She wanted everything to go back to how it had been. 'It's great that you got here in time.'

He didn't respond. Didn't turn around.

She moved closer, clutched her hands together and said, 'I missed you.'

Now he did turn. But it was as if he didn't hear her. His expression dark, shrewd, wary. 'Why are you telling me about this now?'

Her mind went blank. Fresh panic unfurled within her. There was a weariness, a distance to him that was frightening her.

'Why, Charlotte?'

She moved back from him. The urge to run away overwhelming. 'I wanted you to hear about it from me rather than someone at the hospital.'

His jaw tightened. 'If I hadn't insisted on coming to the appointments would you have told me?'

She felt all hot and clammy. Her heart was beating way too fast. She closed her eyes, her stomach churning, and said, 'I'm not sure.'

When she opened her eyes again, he was staring at her with disbelief.

She began to babble. 'I'm better now... I was on medication for a few years, but I no longer am. I practise yoga and mindfulness every day—I take care of myself.'

A horrible silence settled on the room.

She wanted to get away from him.

She wanted him to offer her comfort. She wanted him to see the terror inside her at the prospect of having to tell him about her depression. How she couldn't bear to have to relive all of that hurt and pain and fear again. She wanted him to recognise how vulnerable, how fragile, how weak she felt right now.

But instead he looked at her as though he didn't know her any more.

It was to this hideous silence that the sonographer swung open the door, cheerfully calling out Charlotte's name with a warm smile of welcome.

* * *

In the darkened room, Lucien stared at the images of his baby on the screen, a thick wad of emotion stuck in his chest, making it difficult to breathe.

He could make out his nose, his hand, his foot.

He should feel joy.

But instead he felt numb.

For a few crazy weeks he had thought he had found a family. A woman he trusted and loved. But she hadn't trusted him.

Had she always intended to keep her depression from him? Or was it when he had told her about sleeping with Gabrielle's friend that she had decided not to?

From the corner of his eye he saw her look towards him.

The wad of emotion in his chest hardened.

He was never going to get away from his past. She was never going to trust him.

He should have kept their marriage strictly business. Not revealed so much about himself.

He stared at his baby on the monitor screen.

For the first time in his life he had thought he had found a connection, a closeness, a safe harbour with Charlotte but it had all been wishful thinking on his part.

For years he had numbed himself to the need for closeness, for care. Needing to erect a barrier against the pain of parents who resented him and then a failed marriage.

The bitter taste of sadness and shame grabbed his throat. Charlotte did not accept him. Value him enough to share something so significant.

He stared at the monitor, the numbness spreading through his body like a virus.

An hour later, back home, Charlotte stood on the terrace and listened to the thud of music coming from an open window of the coach house. The builders' radio. The music was drowned every now and again by the sound of heavy banging.

The music and building noise were oddly reassuring after the tight silence of her trip home with Lucien after the hospital appointments. Both the sonographer and her consultant, whom they'd met after the scan, were pleased with the baby's development.

And she had forced herself to ask her consultant to explain to Lucien the consequences of her past mental-health history. Lucien had listened intently and asked his questions in a matter-of-fact manner.

Lucien was now upstairs changing. They were both going to head back into work once he was showered and changed. When they had got home he had made her tea and asked if she was okay, in a formal, stiff, distant manner.

They were like strangers once again.

A light movement fluttered in her stomach. She placed her hand there and stared down, trying not to let the tears at the backs of her eyes escape.

How was it possible to love someone you hadn't yet met so much?

To feel such love even when your heart was beginning to crumble?

Saturday afternoon Charlotte went to the front door and for a moment placed her hand on the wood panel. Steadying herself against the nervous energy that was coursing through her body.

The doorbell rang again.

She forced herself to smile and opened the door to her parents.

Her mum swept towards her and dragged her into a quick hug before bustling past her, heading in the direction of the kitchen. Her dad stepped into the hallway and lowered the umbrella they had been sheltering under.

His kind blue eyes ran over her. 'How are you, Lottie?'

A lump lodged in her throat.

Please let nothing happen to him. Please let him know his grandchild for years and years.

'It's great to see you, Dad.'

His slow hug almost undid her. The heavy weight of his arms on her back, the reassuring familiar scent of his damp tweed jacket. The comfort it brought bringing home just how alone she felt in this house, in her marriage.

She glanced up the stairs as they went to the kitchen. Lucien knew her parents were visiting this afternoon. Her stomach knotted. Would he be as remote with them as he was with her?

Since Thursday, he was at home more than he had ever been before. They were talking but it was perfunctory. Stilted conversations on how their day had been. How she was feeling. It felt as if he thought he had to be at home rather than wanting to be there.

In bed at night she craved his touch. Wished with all of her heart that he would pull her into his arms and hold her. Tell her that he was there for her. More than anything she wanted his comfort, to feel safe with him again.

They were living in the same house, but it was as if he were absent. He was there, but out of her reach.

And with each passing day the fear inside her that he had never really been there for her grew. The heart-shattering confirmation that this marriage was never anything more for him than a means for raising their child together. And growing close to her had been nothing more than a sensible approach to making their marriage tolerable.

Another summer storm had hit London, bringing brief relief from the heatwave that had sat over the city for weeks now. Rain lashed against the kitchen windows.

Her mum stood at the kitchen island unpacking a heavy carrier bag filled with dented old tin Christmas biscuit boxes that brought back memories of school bake sales. With a smile of satisfaction her mum opened each tin. 'Fruit scones, apple squares and, especially for Lucien, the coffee and walnut cake he likes so much.'

Charlotte opened a kitchen cupboard to get some plates, the sense of being a visitor in this house overtaking her again. The sense of being an imposter in her own life. It felt wrong to be entertaining her parents in his house. It felt wrong to be pretending to her parents that her marriage was a happy one.

'Is Lucien home?' her dad asked, taking a seat at the kitchen table she had earlier set for their afternoon tea.

'He's working at the moment but he hopes to be able to get down to see you at some point, in between his conference calls.'

They poured tea and ate the scones while her mum recounted in detail what had happened at the village fete that had taken place the previous weekend. Charlotte sipped her tea but struggled to eat.

As usual her mum noticed. 'Are you okay, Lottie? You're…' she paused and her eyes flickered anxiously over her face, taking in the dark circles under her eyes that Charlotte hadn't been able to erase even with the aid of concealer '…you're looking tired.'

Before she could answer, her parents' attention was diverted by the sound of Lucien's footsteps out in the hallway. For a split second when he came in the door she saw displeasure in his eyes when his gaze moved over their little tea party. Did he resent them all being in his house?

Her heart stumbled.

Please don't drag my parents into this.

But then he smiled affably towards her parents and allowed her mum to hug him and he shook her dad's hand.

He didn't move to sit with them so, attempting a relaxed voice, she asked, 'Will you join us?'

His gaze moved over her and then settled on the rain-soaked windows. 'I need to get back to work,' he said, looking back to her mum and dad, 'but I thought you might like a tour of the coach house—if you don't mind going back out into the rain.'

Charlotte felt relief and disappointment at the same time. Relief that he was welcoming to her parents, relief that he still envisaged them visiting and staying here in the future. But disappointment that not once since he had come downstairs had he looked her in the eye.

Her mum answered first. 'That would be lovely…and a little rain never hurt anyone. But first you must show us the scan pictures from Thursday.'

Charlotte got up and retrieved them from her bag on the kitchen sofa. The set of pictures from her twelve-week scan sat proudly next to Lucien's computer upstairs. But neither of them had thought of these scan pictures since Thursday. Their poor baby had been forgotten in the stand-off between them.

She brought the pictures back to the table and gave one to each of her parents. She glanced quickly at Lucien. In a quiet voice she said, 'You must take one for your office.'

For a moment something softened in his expression. But then he looked away.

Her mum oohed and aahed and asked, 'Did you find out whether it's a girl or boy?'

'No, as I've said before we want to wait until the birth to find out,' Charlotte answered, pushing away the small voice in her head asking if there would be a *we* by then.

Then her father, who had been carefully studying the sonogram, said, 'The details are incredible. I can see a foot and hand. After everything you went through that time you were unwell I never…' Her dad came to a stop and glanced at Lucien in alarm.

His expression unreadable, Lucien said quietly, 'Charlotte told me about her depression during the week.'

Both her mum and dad visibly winced at the word depression. They still preferred to call it *the time she was unwell*.

'That's a relief. Lottie should have told you from the start. But she's always been closed about the whole thing,' her mum said.

Charlotte shot her mum a warning glance. 'Mum.'

'But you have, Lottie. You would never talk to your dad and me about it. And it's not something that you should keep from your husband.'

At this point her dad cleared his throat loudly. 'I think we should take that visit of the coach house now, don't you, Lucien?' He stood without waiting for Lucien to respond.

Lucien stood but tension whipped off him. His jaw tightened before he glanced down at her. 'Do you want to come with us?'

She shook her head, her throat tightening to see a brief flicker of disappointment in his eyes before they once again became guarded. 'I'll stay and tidy up.'

When they had gone, she stood at the kitchen island, midway in clearing up, holding a tin box in her hands, watching Lucien guide her parents down through the garden, slowing his pace for them, holding an umbrella in both hands to protect them both from the rain. And the ache of loneliness in her deepened…she wanted so badly to be able to turn to him for comfort and care, to know that he was there for her.

How long more could she keep up this exhausting pretence of a happy marriage?

When they eventually returned from the coach house, her parents speaking enthusiastically about the space, her dad especially animated over the plumbing and bathroom fixtures, Lucien held back and watched her silently.

Seeing afresh his distance, the constantly closed way he observed her now, when her dad, who was always nervous of driving in London, said that they should be leaving soon, she blurted out without thinking, 'I've been thinking that I will take annual leave next week.'

All three stared at her.

'You're right, Mum, I am feeling tired at the moment. The heat here in London is stifling.' She glanced briefly towards Lucien but it hurt too much so she turned to her parents. 'Lucien is leaving early tomorrow morning for Toronto and will be away all week so would it be okay if I come home with you now?'

CHAPTER TWELVE

SATURDAY EVENING LUCIEN stared at his semi-packed suitcase and realised he hated it. Hated everything it symbol-
ised. Before he had married he had loved to travel. Loved
the anticipation of the new and exciting. But the sad fact of
it all was that travel was only another way of him trying to
escape the loneliness of his life.

Living with Charlotte, coming home to her each night,
chatting over dinner, making love to her, talking after-
wards in the dark, he had felt truly connected to another
person for the first time. And it had given him a sense of
acceptance and security that had quietened the agitation,
the unhappiness that had rattled inside him all of his life.

Until the scan appointment on Thursday.

*'It's not something that you should keep from your hus-
band.'*

For crying out loud, even her mother understood that.

He slammed the suitcase lid shut and stormed downstairs.

Restless, hating the silence in the house, he went into
the lounge on the first floor and switched on the television.
He flicked it off after five minutes, unable to concentrate.

On the library shelves surrounding the television, next
to his collection of biographies, were the books Charlotte
had brought with her when she moved in. He ran a finger

along the spines of the mostly pregnancy books and romance novels.

For someone who professed she didn't believe in love she certainly read enough about it.

I think I'm falling in love with you.

Had she meant it when she had said that the night of the Somerset ball? Or had she been joking? He had seen her shock at having said those words and, not knowing how to react himself, had chosen not to ask her to elaborate on what she meant. He hadn't wanted to ruin what they had, their delicate burgeoning relationship, by pushing her. But now, all he could think about was how could she possibly say those words with any sincerity but yet keep something so personal and intimate from him?

From outside came the loud squeal of a child's laughter.

He went to the window and saw a family playing out in the park at the centre of the square. The mum and little girl giggling as the father tried to retrieve an errant Frisbee from dense and thorny rose bushes.

He turned away and went down to the kitchen.

There he opened the fridge door, knowing he should eat something.

His eyes were drawn to a bottle of Sauvignon Blanc on the wine rack at the bottom of the fridge.

It was years since he had last had a drink.

Would there be any harm in starting again? Just one glass?

His stomach churned.

And he slammed the fridge door shut.

She had gone home.

But this was supposed to be her home.

He grabbed his keys and wallet from the console table in the hallway. He had to get out of this house now. The silence was unbearable.

* * *

On the way to the River Bourne, Charlotte passed through the kissing gate to cross Carpenters Lane and heard the whack of a cricket bat from the village cricket green. As a child, she had spent her summers at the river, swimming and hanging out with her friends. Those friends, just like her, had all left the village for careers and marriages. Would she be the first to return?

It was four days since she had last seen Lucien. He texted and called every day but their conversations were stilted and remote.

What was she going to do?

She missed him. She loved him. But could she stay in a marriage that left her feeling so insecure and vulnerable?

Could she stay married to a man who didn't love her enough?

She skirted along the side of Stewarts Field, the late afternoon sun warming her, bees and butterflies fluttering and dipping around the vibrant yellow rapeseed crop.

She passed through another kissing gate and followed the bare earth path that wound its way down to the river, tall hedges thick with blackberry bushes on either side. She used to come here every September to pick plump blackberries with her friends after school.

Would she be bringing her little girl here too?

She drew in a ragged breath. Would she be a single mum then? Would it be only the two of them, with Lucien visiting at weekends? Hot pain grabbed her heart. How would she cope with having him in her life but yet having him so distant, so disconnected from her? To not feel his arms around her again, his breath on her skin, his whispers of affection.

At the river she walked alongside the riverbank until she came to the point where it had collapsed down into a gentle slope of soft earth that allowed access to a deep pool of water. She dropped her rucksack onto the grass and placed her picnic blanket beneath the dappled shade of an ash tree.

She lay down and closed her eyes. Tired to the marrow of her bones.

She had hoped that in staying with her parents she would finally manage to get some sleep in her childhood bed, away from the torture of having to lie in Lucien's bed and all of the memories that existed there. But she lay awake most nights, twisting and turning, thinking about him. Wondering where he was, what he was doing at that precise time. At times angry that he had shut down on her. And at other times resigned to it with a sadness that chewed ferociously at her heart. He had married her because of their child; he had never said that he would love her.

A thought flickered through her mind. She tried to catch it but it flickered away. He hadn't said he'd love her…but…

Charlotte shot up to a sitting position on the blanket.

Their wedding vows.

Her heart thumping in her chest, she remembered the words.

I promise to be always open and honest. And, whatever may come, promise to provide you with comfort and support through life's joy and sorrow.

She sank her head into her hands.

How had they come to fail one another so badly?

Early Friday morning Lucien wearily opened the front door.

He had packed five days' worth of meetings into four, needing to get home. Knowing he had to go to Charlotte at her parents' house and talk with her.

He had destroyed one marriage.

He couldn't do the same with this one. Not when there was a child involved.

But first he needed to shower and change.

And drink a litre of espresso to fight his jet lag.

He left his suitcase in the hallway but brought his carry-on bag upstairs and into the spare bedroom across from theirs. From his carry-on he pulled out a cross-eyed tortoise he had found in the window of a toy store on Queen Street yesterday when travelling to a construction site meeting.

His first present for his son. He placed it on the double bed of the room, fixing the little blue bow tie the tortoise was wearing.

They had planned for this room to be the nursery. But that was no longer a certainty. Just like their marriage.

He flinched as a hollowing-out pain twisted his heart.

Their marriage couldn't continue like this. How could they raise a child in the tense, awkward atmosphere that was between them now? An atmosphere that possibly would only disintegrate further and further into blame and bitterness.

There was no way his child was going to be brought up in a household like that. History was *not* going to be repeated.

He turned to leave but then spotted a small snow-white Babygro on the room's chest of drawers.

When had that appeared?

It hadn't been there on Saturday night when he had sat in here after he had come home from his club at two in the morning, having taken part in a late-night poker game with other members in preference over the silence awaiting him at home.

He picked up the tiny piece of soft fabric.

And swallowed against the tightness at the back of his eyes.

He shook himself.

He placed the Babygro back where he had found it and inhaled a deep breath.

Please let me be right on this...please let this mean that she has come home.

He opened the door to their bedroom. His heart tripped over. Charlotte was asleep...lying on his side of the bed.

He came closer and stood watching her chest rise and fall beneath the soft pink lace of her nightdress. Only a sheet covered her, the beautiful swell of her bump clearly visible beneath the light cotton. How he missed placing his hand there, the surge of emotion, the intimacy, the connection that knocked him for six every time he touched her and their baby beneath her taut, warm skin.

He wanted to climb in beside her. Hold her.

Would she turn to him? Or curl herself into the tight ball of limbs and silence she had recently adopted. Shutting him out, silently saying, *I don't trust you. I don't need you.*

He didn't want to wake her but they needed to talk. Before his jet lag worsened and he was incapable of any coherent thought. Reluctantly he crouched down before her and called her name.

Her drowsy eyes opened. Groggily she smiled at him. Her lips a gentle curve of contentment.

For a few glorious seconds hope surged through him.

But then the drowsiness cleared and she shot up in the bed and retreated away from him, pulling the sheet up around her. 'I thought you were in Toronto until Saturday.'

He tried to ignore the pain of her withdrawal, the wary caution in her eyes. 'I need a quick shower but I'll make us breakfast after. We need to talk.'

She nodded with a sad acceptance and shuffled further against the pillows at her back, readjusting the sheet.

He went into the bathroom and switched on the shower. His whole body and soul aching for her. Needing to be close to her again. But panic was churning in his stomach. Would she ever fully let him know her? Or was his past always going to haunt him?

* * *

He found her in the garden after he had showered and dressed.

Wearing a grey jersey tank dress, she was sitting on the terrace drinking her usual first-thing mug of decaf tea.

He settled for tea too and sat at the garden table alongside her.

The tips of her shoulders were red. He bit back the urge to tell her off for not wearing sunscreen and asked instead, 'I thought you were staying with your parents for the week.'

She dropped her mug to the table. Touched her hand to her forehead. For a few seconds blocking him out. Then she looked at him with sad, sad, sad eyes. And gave an even sadder smile filled with sorrow. 'I was out walking yesterday and I thought about our vows. Do you remember what we said?'

Confused, he shrugged while trying to recall the exact words.

'I promise to create and protect a family and home that's full of love, understanding, respect and honour.' Charlotte paused and her gaze met his before she continued, 'I promise to be always open and honest.' She went to speak again, but couldn't get past, 'And whatever may come…'

He clenched his hands around the wooden slats of his seat, guilt and regret clogging his throat. And finished off the words he had said on their wedding day. 'I promise to provide you with comfort and support through life's joy and sorrow.'

Charlotte forced herself to remain looking at Lucien. Even though it tore her apart to hear him say those words again. Tore her apart to have such tension, so many unsaid words between them.

Despite his shower and fresh clothes he still looked exhausted. The hard lines on his face deeper, the shadows beneath his eyes adding to the bewildered pain in his eyes.

'Why didn't you tell me about your depression?' he asked quietly.

I promise to be always open and honest.

She had broken those vows. Despite the dread and fear crawling along her skin, the embarrassed heat on her cheeks, she met his gaze and answered, 'We barely knew each other. I...' She closed her eyes, unable to continue.

'But we did get to know one another.' With an expression of sad bewilderedness, he added, 'At least I thought we did.'

She clenched her hands. 'I didn't want to burden you... I was worried about how you would react.'

Lucien recoiled in his chair and then came forward again. 'What do you mean, how I would react?' The softness of his tone was gone and was now replaced by angry disbelief. 'I'm your husband, for crying out loud. I thought you trusted me... I told you everything about my past. Everything. Every single pathetic thing. I opened up to you. And you kept your depression from me. How can we function as a couple if you don't trust me enough to really let me into your thoughts, into your past?'

She knew he was right, but the pain and loneliness in her, the fear that she wanted so much more from this marriage than he did, weren't about to be silenced so she cried out, 'The only reason you married me was for the baby. You weren't signing up to be burdened with my mental-health history. You heard my consultant—the risk of me developing postnatal depression is higher because of it, I didn't want to burden you with that possibility.'

He closed his eyes for a moment, his jaw tightening. Her heart dropped down to her feet. Was he about to say out loud what she already knew: that he couldn't handle, support, be there for her should her depression ever return?

Please. Please. Don't.

She jumped up and fled while muttering, 'I'll go and make us breakfast.'

In the kitchen she yanked open the fridge and pulled out random items with trembling hands.

She yelped when she turned around to find him standing only feet away from her. His expression sombre. 'If your depression did recur we would deal with it, as a couple, as a family.'

She swallowed hard. So desperately wanting to believe him. But knowing that in reality he was only saying it because he wanted them to stay together for the sake of their child. 'I don't expect you to. I'd understand it if you wanted to walk away.'

'Of course I would be there for you. You're my wife. I told you when I asked you to marry me that I would take my vows seriously. I won't walk away from you. You mean too much to me.' His jaw tightened and a raw vulnerability entered his eyes before he continued, 'Is it because of my past…my parents' marriage, how I destroyed my first marriage, that you don't trust me?'

'No! Of course not. Not telling you…it had nothing to do with your past.'

His cynical stare told her he didn't believe her.

She had to be honest with him. Her legs weak, an emptiness opening up inside her, she propped herself against the fridge door and admitted her deepest fears. 'When I told Dan about my depression, he wasn't there for me, not really, at first he tried to be, but the reality of having a girlfriend with depression soon took its toll on him and he resented it. I was terrified that you would be the same. That you'd see me as a burden. Think less of me.'

He stepped back from her. 'I thought you knew me… How could you think that I would see you, my wife, as a burden?'

His voice, his expression, were filled with pain.

Matching her own heart churning confusion and fear. 'But since I've told you about the depression you've been so watchful, so detached. It has felt as though you're worried about me...but only because I'm carrying your baby.' Unable to stop, the hurt and vulnerability of the past week bubbling in her chest, she added, 'I've been so lonely without you.'

Lucien sank his head into his hands, tiredly rubbing his face. When he looked back, his tortured eyes held hers. 'I'm sorry.' He twisted away and walked to the kitchen island where he placed his hands on the counter, and stretched his back. When he eventually turned back to her, he said, 'I couldn't understand why you hadn't told me. It ripped me apart. I wanted you to trust me enough to tell me. I felt like a failure, knowing you couldn't trust me. A failure because my wife couldn't rely on me, didn't need me the way I needed her. But how could you trust or rely on me? Knowing the destructive environment I grew up in. Knowing how it has messed with my head as my first marriage demonstrated.'

He was so wrong.

A surge of protectiveness for him steamed through her. 'No. I'm not having that. You're a strong and honourable man. Why on earth do you think I fell in love with you?'

'You're in love with me?'

Her heart somersaulted and fell over at the disbelief in his voice. 'Of course I am.'

'You said you loved me on the night of the Somerset House ball but I didn't know if you were serious.' He stopped and looked at her, bewildered. 'But how can you love a person you don't trust?'

She stepped back, punched by his sadness, by his words. 'I do trust you. I love you.'

He gave her a resigned look full of regret. 'But if you don't let me know you fully how can we survive as a couple?'

Tears of hope and confusion and terror stung at the backs of her eyes. She bit her lip, squeezed her hands, her nails digging into her palms, and asked the hardest question of her entire life. 'But do you want us to survive?'

Lucien's heart crumbled at her softly spoken question. She loved him. But he needed more. He needed to fully know his wife. 'Yes, I want us to survive, but you have to let me know you.'

'For the sake of our baby?'

Was that what she thought?

He wanted to move to her, take her into his arms and comfort her as he should have done days ago.

I promise to provide you with comfort and support through life's joy and sorrow.

He had said those words. And had meant them.

But at the first hurdle in their marriage he had not honoured them.

Shame washed over him. But he pushed it away. Now had to be about Charlotte, not his guilt. 'I want our marriage to survive because I want *you* in my life. *Je veux être avec toi pour toujours.* I want to be with you for ever. But to do so, I need to know you.' He stopped and tried to fight the inadequacy swelling up inside at voicing his fears, for showing weakness. But he needed her to know *him* too. 'I need to feel safe with you and while you continue to guard yourself from me I will never feel that you trust me.' A plug of shame clogged his throat but he forced himself to continue. 'I grew up knowing I wasn't wanted by my parents. I can't handle a marriage where I'm not truly wanted, accepted, needed. Where I feel insecure.'

She came towards him, the anguish in her eyes matched by that in her voice. 'I do want you. I do love you.'

A thousand emotions choked him, leaving him struggling for air. Did she love him enough to let him in, to share her most intimate thoughts?

'Tell me about the depression.'

Charlotte looked at him with terrified eyes before grabbing a box of eggs and studying it uncertainly. Eventually she said, 'I was twenty-two. Apart from the usual dramas of falling for the wrong guys and exam worries, I was sailing through life.' She stopped and shrugged, her expression haunted. 'But in my final year, with exams looming and the pressure to get a first-class honours degree, I started to feel overwhelmed, unable to cope. I kept telling myself that I needed to be stronger, but I got more and more exhausted. I couldn't concentrate. Everything started to feel grey. I was constantly anxious. I had panic attacks. Life…life felt so hard. I had no interest in anything. Especially the future.'

Without warning she turned away and pulled open the pan drawer beneath the hob. 'You must be hungry. Would you like an omelette?'

When he didn't answer she turned to him, a frying pan in her hand.

He went to her and took the pan from her. 'Speak to me, Charlotte. Tell me about that year.'

She backed away until she was pressed against the hob. Disquiet in her eyes. For a moment she hesitated but then said impatiently, 'I didn't tell anyone for ages, especially my parents. I hated failing them. I hated being so weak.'

She grabbed the frying pan out of his hands and said, 'I'll make you a mushroom and ham omelette.'

He wanted to take the pan back off her. But could see that she needed to be busy. She cracked three eggs into a jug and whisked them furiously before peeling and chopping mushrooms like a woman possessed.

Eventually she said, her voice angry and sad all at once, 'My parents were so upset when my GP eventually diagnosed depression that I knew I couldn't really talk to them about it. I felt so guilty. I didn't want to be a burden to them. So I pretended that I was okay.'

'But you weren't?'

'No. I was so, so sad.' Her face crumpled into a mask of distress but after a few seconds she inhaled a shaky breath and continued, 'I did tell Dan and Angie. At first they were supportive and understanding, but after a few weeks I could tell that they were getting impatient with me. They would change the subject if I spoke about how I felt. Or tell me that I needed to try to see the positives in my life. Which used to drive me crazy.' She threw her hands up irritably. 'If only I could have. If only it was that simple. And as the weeks and months passed Dan and I grew further and further apart. We met less and less often, and when we did it was awkward and we struggled to even talk.'

She turned back to the counter and clicked the gas ring of the hob on. And switched it off again. Her back to him, she said, 'All I wanted was for Dan to hold me and tell me everything would be okay. But he didn't. I hated him seeing me so ill. I hated how awful I looked. And then I found out about him and Angie.' She turned to him with tears in her eyes. For a brief second she held his gaze before she bowed her head and said in a quiet voice choked with hurt, 'When I found out about their affair I felt so useless, so hopeless, so worthless. I had lost too much weight and looked ten years older. I felt so ill and tired.'

Sharp thorns stabbed his heart to see her pain. No longer able to stay away from her, he went and placed a hand on her arm. The other reaching up to cup her face. Slowly and reluctantly she lifted her head. 'No wonder you doubt just how beautiful you are.'

A single tear dropped down along her cheek. She scrunched her eyes shut. 'The loneliness was the worst. I had no one to turn to. No one to offer me comfort. I was all alone…and I was scared of reaching out.'

No wonder she had kept it from him. 'And you still are.'

She opened her eyes and her fingers touched his hand that was cupping her cheek. He held his breath at the relief in her eyes. The connection, the intimacy that had been missing between them for much too long surged back. 'I decided the only way for me to cope was to be tough and not get hurt in a relationship again, to only focus on what I could control: my career, minding myself by being insular. I wanted to forget the past and focus on the future.'

He stepped even closer to her and said, 'Your future is with me now.'

'Is it?' Her question was asked with such trepidation and wonder and disbelief he found it difficult to breathe.

He ran his hand down over her hair. Time and time again. Wanting to touch her, soothe her, care for her. 'Of course it is.'

Her eyes wide, her cheeks flushed, she whispered, 'Why?'

'Because I love you. I want you in my life. I want to care and comfort you.'

'Even knowing about my depression?'

'There's no shame or weakness to having had depression. I don't think any less of you for it. I love you regardless. You said before that you wanted to support me. Well, I want to support you too.'

He smiled at the hope that was beginning to shine in her eyes. 'Your depression is only a small part of who you are. I love so much about you. I love you in the morning when you're sleepy and cling to me.'

He swung her around so that he was now leaning against the kitchen counter. He pulled her in against him, her baby bump nestling against his hip. 'I love you during the day when you're smart and bright and feisty at work. I love you in the evenings when I come home to you, come home to your happiness and teasing and gorgeous smile. I love you when you make me dinner with such enthusiasm, each meal making me feel more loved than any words could do.' She smiled at that. His heart tripped over.

He pulled her into him so that her cheek was resting on his chest. Into her hair he whispered, 'I love you in the nights when I can make love to you, when I can kiss your soft skin, when I can lose myself in you, when I feel complete for the first time in my life.'

Slowly and reluctantly Charlotte pulled herself out of the embrace she would happily stay in for the rest of her life and backed away. 'Can I have five minutes to get my head together?'

A flicker of apprehension crossed his expression.

Quickly she explained, 'I vowed to you that I would be open and honest with you. And I'm trying to be…but there's more I want to say. Words to explain how I feel for you. I want to get those words right.'

A smile lifted his lips gloriously upwards. 'But you're the *Verbal Assassin.*'

Happiness rolled through her. 'Yes and look what you've reduced me to—a jabbering wreck!'

Out in the garden she paced the decking.

He loved her. He loved her. He loved her!

He accepted her depression. She had seen it in the kind, understanding sincerity of his gaze.

He wanted her. Not just because she was carrying his baby. He wanted *her.*

Her husband loved *her.*

And I love him with every fibre of my being. I love him with all my soul.

Back inside the kitchen, Lucien was waiting for her, propped against the kitchen island. Looking nervous. She loved him even more seeing how edgy he was…how he waited for her to speak as though it was the most important thing in the world to him.

It was time she opened her heart to him. Completely. 'You say you really want to know me?'

At his encouraging nod she took a deep breath. 'Well, here goes—I fancied you the first time I saw you but thought you were a player. So I used to tell my colleagues who thought you were *"hot"* that they needed to have their heads examined. And then one cold March night you simply smiled at me and I lost my heart to you. That night we slept together was so special, so tender, I wanted more but knew I couldn't. And when I found out about my pregnancy I didn't want to marry you because I was terrified I'd fall in love with you while you'd have no feelings for me other than I being the mother of your child. But over the past few months you have showed yourself to be fair, full of integrity, a man who wants family and love. I have so much respect for everything you have achieved, for how generous and supportive you are to others... I just refused to believe that you would be the same with me. But now I can see how wrong I was.'

Lucien came towards her, his large body looming above her, sexily, protectively. Green brilliant eyes, assured and confident, held hers and he said, 'I saw you on my second day at Huet, at ten in the morning to be precise. I was heading to the boardroom and you passed along the corridor.' His voice dipped even further into a low sexy whisper. 'You were wearing a navy pencil skirt, a white blouse with gold buttons and navy heels.'

She shivered when his fingertips ran down the length of her arm. 'I think I fell in love with you right then and there. Even though you almost froze me to the spot with the icy stare you threw in my direction. I tried to convince myself I was crazy. I have never dated employees.'

His hip edged towards hers. She inhaled him, and grew

even dizzier. He continued, 'But the night we made love, I couldn't stay away from you. And after we made love, deep down inside me I knew I was never going to let you go. But I didn't know how to get beyond my past and fear of messing up a relationship again.'

His hand reached down to her stomach and with a smile he said, 'But Robbie decided to make an appearance before I had worked out how to get you into my life permanently.'

She laid her hand on his. Her heart soaring. 'Robbie?'

'After your dad.'

She blinked away the tears. It proved a little more difficult to dislodge the lump blocking her throat. 'Will I make you that omelette?'

His eyes twinkled. 'Nope.'

She blushed at the suggestive smile on his lips and muttered, 'You're looking a little tired. Maybe you should lie down.'

His mouth dipped to her ear. 'I was going to suggest the same to you… I did wake you early on your day off, after all.'

A tremor ran through her body at his low whisper, and how he was now nibbling the lobe of her ear, a hand moving up to skim at the sensitive side of her breasts. 'I had hoped to spend the day in bed,' he whispered before drawing back, those brilliant green eyes, full of love, consuming her. 'In fact, we're spending the entire weekend there. We've a lot of catching up to do.'

And then he kissed her.

A kiss full of intimacy and closeness and connection.

A dizzying kiss so full of love and tenderness that she wobbled against him, light-headed and weak-kneed.

With an affectionate laugh he lifted her into his arms.

And for three days they closed off the rest of the world.

Loving and cherishing each other for every precious second.

EPILOGUE

EARLY CHRISTMAS MORNING Charlotte paused at the downstairs lounge door, her heart skipping a beat.

Inside, the only light came from the golden tree lights, shimmering like a thousand wishes on the Christmas tree. And in a chair next to the tree, Lucien stared down at their sleeping baby daughter cradled in his arms.

Lucy was already three weeks old.

It had been the hardest and most wonderful three weeks of her life.

She was sleep deprived. Her breasts were aching. Sometimes she cried over nothing. But she was doing okay. It was still early days but Lucien's constant love and attention were helping her stay strong. She was minding herself too. Not stressing over the moments she felt down, accepting that all new mums did. Sleeping, eating healthily and exercising as much as she could. And most of all talking to Lucien. Reaching out to him and letting him into her thoughts and fears.

Her husband. Her daughter.

She felt complete.

She felt loved.

She felt safe and secure.

She knew just how lucky she was. To have met a man who loved her so much. A man who, though apprehensive, had taken to fatherhood with enthusiasm and pride and love. A man who held her and whispered his love for her at every opportunity.

A man who had insisted that her parents move into the coach house for the entirety of Christmas. A man who had insisted on finding their Christmas tree himself and that they decorate it together while Lucy had slept in her downstairs cot. Christmas carols had played as he had cursed the lights that had become horribly tangled as they'd wrestled them onto the enormous tree that had had to be specially delivered by a delivery truck.

She stepped into the room.

His soft smile for Lucy grew even wider when he spotted her.

He beckoned her over with his eyes.

And when she was close enough he held out his hand to her and pulled her gently down onto his lap.

They smiled at each other.

And finally he whispered, '*Joyeux Noël*, Lottie.'

She rested her head against his chest. His lips touched reverently against her bed-head hair, as though he worshipped everything about her. And then he whispered, playfully, wickedly, 'Next time I know it will definitely be a boy.'

* * * * *

If you loved this story, check out
HER FIRST-DATE HONEYMOON *by Katrina Cudmore,*
part of the ROMANTIC GETAWAYS *quartet.*
Available now!

If you're looking forward to another emotional
feel-good romance then you'll love
CAPTIVATED BY THE ENIGMATIC TYCOON
by Bella Bucannon.

This isn't real.

It wasn't real, but it felt real. It even looked real.

Diana was dressed in a strapless chiffon gown, midnight blue, with a dangerously low, plunging neckline. A glittering stone rested between her breasts. A sapphire. The sapphire necklace from the photo shoot.

"Please stop staring." She turned and met his gaze. At last.

Franco's body hardened the instant his eyes fixed with hers. As exquisite as the sapphire around her neck was, it didn't hold a candle to the violet depths of those luminescent eyes. "You're lovely."

She stared at him coldly. "Save it for the cameras, would you? There's no one here. You can drop the act."

"It's not an act. You look beautiful." He swallowed. Hard. "That's quite a dress."

"Just stop it, would you? I know we're supposed to be madly in love with each other in public. But in private, can we keep things professional? Please?"

Something about the way she said *please* grabbed Franco by the throat and refused to let go.

Had he really been so awful to her all those years ago?

Yes. He had.

* * *

Drake Diamonds:
Looking for love that shines as bright
as the gems in their window!

IT STARTED WITH
A DIAMOND

BY
TERI WILSON

First Published in Great Britain 2017
By Mills & Boon, an imprint of HarperCollins*Publishers*
1 London Bridge Street, London, SE1 9GF

© 2017 Teri Wilson

ISBN: 978-0-263-92313-1

23-0717

Our policy is to use papers that are natural, renewable and recyclable products and made from wood grown in sustainable forests. The logging and manufacturing processes conform to the legal environmental regulations of the country of origin.

Printed and bound in Spain
by CPI, Barcelona

Teri Wilson is a novelist for Mills & Boon. She is the author of *Unleashing Mr. Darcy*, now a Hallmark Channel Original Movie. Teri is also a contributing writer at HelloGiggles.com, a lifestyle and entertainment website founded by Zooey Deschanel that is now part of the *People* magazine, *TIME* magazine and *Entertainment Weekly* family. Teri loves books, travel, animals and dancing every day. Visit Teri at www.teriwilson.net or on Twitter, @teriwilsonauthr.

For Brant Schafer, because naming a polo pony
after me will guarantee you a book dedication.

And for Roe Valentine, my dear writing friend
and other half of the Sisterhood of the
Traveling Veuve Clicquot.

Chapter One

"It's hard to be a diamond in a rhinestone world."
—Dolly Parton

Diana Drake wasn't sure about much in her life at the moment, but one thing was crystal clear—she wanted to strangle her brother.

Not her older brother, Dalton. She couldn't really muster up any indignation as far as her elder sibling went, despite the fact that she was convinced he was at least partially responsible for her current predicament.

But Dalton got a free pass. For now.

She owed him.

For one thing, she'd been living rent free in his swanky Lenox Hill apartment for the past several months. For another, he was a prince now. A literal Prince Charming. As such, he wasn't even in New York anymore. He was somewhere on the French Riviera polishing his crown or sitting on a throne or doing whatever it was princes did all day long.

Dalton's absence meant that Diana's younger brother, Artem, was the only Drake around to take the full brunt of her frustration. Which was a tad problematic since he was her boss now.

Technically.

Sort of.

But Diana would just have to overlook that minor point. She'd held her tongue for as long as humanly possible.

"I can't do it anymore," she blurted as she marched into his massive office on the tenth floor of Drake Diamonds, the legendary jewelry store situated on the corner of 5th Avenue and 57th Street, right in the glittering center of Manhattan. The family business.

Diana might not have spent every waking hour of her life surrounded by diamonds and fancy blue boxes tied with white satin bows, as Dalton had. And she might not be the chief executive officer, like Artem. But the last time she checked, she was still a member of the family. She was a Drake, just like the rest of them.

So was it really necessary to suffer the humiliation of working as a salesperson in the most dreaded section of the store?

"Engagements? *Really?*" She crossed her arms and glared at Artem. It was still weird seeing him sitting behind what used to be their father's desk. Gaston Drake had been dead for a nearly a year, yet his presence loomed large.

Too large. It was almost suffocating.

"Good morning to you, too, Diana." Artem smoothed down his tie, which was the exact same hue as the store's trademark blue boxes. *Drake* blue.

Could he have the decency to look at least a little bit bothered by her outburst?

Apparently not.

She sighed. "I can't do it, Artem. I'll work anywhere in this building, except *there*." She waved a hand in the direction of the Engagements showroom down the hall.

He stared blithely at her, then made a big show of looking at his watch. "I see your point. It's been all of three hours. However have you lasted this long?"

"Three *torturous* hours." She let out another massive sigh. "Have you ever set foot in that place?"

"I'm the CEO, so, yes, I venture over there from time to time."

Right. Of course he had.

Still, she doubted he'd actually helped any engaged couples choose their wedding rings. At least, she hoped he hadn't, mainly because she wouldn't have wished such a fate on her worst enemy.

This morning she'd actually witnessed a grown man and woman speaking baby talk to each other. Her stomach churned just thinking about it now. Adults had no business speaking baby talk, not even to actual babies.

Her gaze shifted briefly to the bassinet in the corner of her brother's office. She still couldn't quite believe Artem was a dad now. A husband. It was kind of mind-boggling when she thought about it, especially considering what an abysmally poor role model their father had been in the family department.

Keep it professional.

She wouldn't get anywhere approaching Artem as a sibling. This conversation was about business, plain and simple. Removing herself from Engagements was the best thing Diana could do, not just for herself, but also for Drake Diamonds.

Only half an hour ago, she'd had to bite her tongue when a man asked for advice about choosing an engagement ring and she'd very nearly told him to spend his money on something more sensible than a huge diamond when the chances that he and his girlfriend would live happily ever after were slim to none. *If* she accepted his proposal, they only had about an eighty percent chance of making it down the aisle. Beyond that, their odds of staying married were about fifty-fifty. Even if they remained husband and wife until death did them part, could they reasonably expect to be happy? Was *anyone* happily married?

Diana's own mother had stuck faithfully by her husband's side after she found out he'd fathered a child with their housekeeper, even when she ended up raising the boy herself. Surely that didn't count as a happy marriage.

That boy was now a man and currently seated across the desk from Diana. She'd grown up alongside Artem and couldn't possibly love him more. He was her brother. Case closed.

Diana's problem wasn't with Artem. It was with her father and the concept of marriage as a whole. She didn't like what relationships did to people…

Especially what one had done to her mother.

Even if she'd grown up in a picture-perfect model family, Diana doubted she'd ever see spending three months' salary on an engagement ring as anything but utter foolishness.

It was a matter of logic, pure and simple. Of statistics. And statistics said that plunking down $40,000 for a two-carat Drake Diamonds solitaire was like throwing a giant wad of cash right into the Hudson River.

But she had no business saying such things out loud since she worked in Engagements, now, did she? She had no business saying such things, period. Drake Diamonds had supported her for her entire life.

So she'd bitten her tongue. Hard.

"I'm simply saying that my talents would be best put to use someplace else." *Anyplace* else.

"Would they now?" Artem narrowed his gaze at her. A hint of a smile tugged at the corner of his mouth, and she knew what was coming. "And what talents would those be, exactly?"

And there it was.

"Don't start." She had no desire to talk about her accident again. Or ever, for that matter. She'd moved on.

Artem held up his hands in a gesture of faux surrender. "I didn't say a word about your training. I'm simply pointing out that you have no work experience. Or college education, for that matter. I hate to say it, sis, but your options are limited."

She'd considered enrolling in classes at NYU, but didn't bother mentioning it. Her degree wasn't going to materialize overnight. *Unfortunately.* College had always been on her radar, but between training and competing, she hadn't found the time. Now she was a twenty-six-year-old without a single day of higher education under her belt.

If only she'd spent a little less time on the back of a horse for the past ten years and a few more hours in the classroom…

She cleared her throat. "Do I need to remind you that I own a third of this business? You and Dalton aren't the only Drakes around here, you know."

"No, but we're the only ones who've actually worked here before today." He glanced at his watch again, stood and buttoned his suit jacket. "Look, just stick it out for a while. Once you've learned the ropes, we'll try and find another role for you. Okay?"

Awhile.

Just how long was that, she wondered. A week? A month? A year? She desperately wanted to ask, but she didn't dare. She hated sounding whiny, and she *really* hated relying on the dreadful Drake name. But it just so happened that name was the only thing she had going for her at the moment.

Oh, how the mighty had fallen. Literally.

"Come on." Artem brushed past her. "We've got a photo shoot scheduled this afternoon in Engagements. I think you might find it rather interesting."

She was glad to be walking behind him so he couldn't see her massive eyeroll. "Please tell me it doesn't involve a wedding dress."

"Relax, sister dear. We're shooting cuff links. The photographer only wanted to use the Engagements showroom because it has the best view of Manhattan in the building."

It did have a lovely view, especially now that spring had arrived in New York in all its fragrant splendor. The air was filled with cherry blossoms, swirling like pink snow flurries. Diana had lost herself a time or two staring out at the verdant landscape of Central Park.

But those few blissful moments had come to a crashing end the moment she'd turned away from the showroom's floor-to-ceiling windows and remembered she was surrounded by diamonds. Wedding diamonds.

And here I am again.

She blinked against the dazzling assault of countless engagement rings sparkling beneath the sales floor lights and followed Artem to the corner of the room where the photographer was busy setting up a pair of tall light stands. A row of camera lenses in different sizes sat on top of one of glass jewelry cases.

Diana slid a velvet jeweler's pad beneath the lenses to protect the glass and busied herself rearranging things. Maybe if she somehow inserted herself into this whole photo-shoot process, she could avoid being a part of any-one's betrothal for an hour or two.

A girl can dream.

"Is our model here?" the photographer asked. "Be-cause I'm ready, and we've only got about an hour left until sundown. I'd like to capture some of this nice view before it's too late."

Diana glanced out the window. The sky was already tinged pale violet, and the evening wind had picked up, scattering pink petals up and down 5th Avenue. The sun was just beginning to dip below the skyscrapers. It would be a gorgeous backdrop…

…if the model showed up.

Artem checked his watch again and frowned in the di-rection of the door. Diana took her time polishing the half-dozen pairs of Drake cuff links he'd pulled for the shoot. Anything to stretch out the minutes.

Just as she reached for the last pair, Artem let out a sigh of relief. "Ah, he's here."

Diana glanced up, took one look at the man stalking toward them and froze. Was she hallucinating? Had the blow to the head she'd taken months ago done more dam-age than the doctors had thought?

Nothing is wrong with you. You're fine. Everything *is fine.*

Everything didn't feel fine, though. Diana's whole world had come apart, and months later she still hadn't managed to put it back together. She was beginning to think she never would.

Because, deep down, she knew she wouldn't. She couldn't pick up the pieces, even if she tried. No one could.

Which was precisely why she was cutting her losses and starting over again. She'd simply build a new life for herself. A normal life. Quiet. Safe. It would take some getting used to, but she could do it.

People started over all the time, didn't they?

At least she had a job. An apartment. A family. There were worse things in the world than being a Drake.

She was making a fresh start. She was a jeweler now. Her past was ancient history.

Except for the nagging fact that a certain man from her past was walking toward her. Here, now, in the very real present.

Franco Andrade.

Not him. Just...no.

She needed to leave. Maybe she could just slink over to one of the sales counters and get back to her champagne-sipping brides and grooms to be. Selling engagement rings had never seemed as appealing as it did right this second.

She laid her polishing cloth on the counter, but before she could place the cuff links back inside their neat blue box, one of them slipped right through her fingers. She watched in horror as it bounced off the tip of Artem's shoe and rolled across the plush Drake-blue carpet, straight toward Franco's approaching form.

Diana sighed. This is what she got for complaining to Artem. Just because she was an heiress didn't mean she had to act like one. Being entitled wasn't an admirable quality. Besides, karma was a raging bitch. One who didn't waste any time, apparently.

Diana dropped to her knees and scrambled after the

runaway cuff link, wishing the floor would somehow open up and swallow her whole. Evidently, there were indeed fates worse than helping men choose engagement rings.

"Mr. Andrade, we meet at last." Artem deftly side-stepped her and extended a hand toward Franco.

Mr. Andrade.

So it *was* him. She'd still been holding out the tiniest bit of hope for a hallucination. Or possibly a doppelganger. But that was an absurd notion. Men as handsome as Franco Andrade didn't roam the Earth in pairs. His kind of chiseled bone structure was a rarity, something that only came around once in a blue moon. Like a unicorn. Or a fiery asteroid hurtling toward Earth, promising mass destruction on impact.

One of those two things. The second, if the rumors of his conquests were to be believed.

Who was she kidding? She didn't need to rely on rumors. She knew firsthand what kind of man Franco Andrade was. It was etched in her memory with excruciating clarity. What she didn't know was what he was doing here.

Was he the model for the new campaign? Impossible.

It had to be some kind of joke. Or possibly Artem's wholly inappropriate attempt to manipulate her back into her old life.

Either way, for the second time in a matter of hours, she wanted to strangle her brother. He was the one who'd invited Franco here, after all. Perhaps joining the family business hadn't been her most stellar idea.

As if she had any other options.

She pushed Artem's reminders of her inadequate education and employment record out of her head and concentrated on the mortifying matter at hand. Where was that darn cuff link, anyway?

"Gotcha," she whispered under her breath as she caught sight of a silver flash out of the corner of her eye.

But just as she reached for it, Franco Andrade's ridiculously masculine form crouched into view. "Allow me."

His words sent a tingle skittering through her. Had his voice always been so deliciously low? The man could recite the alphabet and bring women to their knees. Which would have made the fact that she was already in just such a position convenient, had it not been so utterly humiliating.

"Here." He held out his hand. The cuff link sat nestled in the center of his palm. He had large hands, rough with calluses, a stark contrast to the finely tailored fit of his custom tuxedo.

Of course that tuxedo happened to be missing a tie, and his shirt cuffs weren't even fastened. He looked as if he'd just rolled out of someone's bed and tossed on his discarded Armani from the night before.

Then again, he most likely had.

"Thank you," she mumbled, steadfastly refusing to meet his gaze.

"Wait." He balled his fist around the cuff link and stooped lower to peer at her. "Do we know each other?"

"Nope." She shook her head so hard she could practically hear her brain rattle. "No, I'm afraid we don't."

"I think we might," he countered, stubbornly refusing to hand over the cuff link.

Fine. Let him keep it. She had better things to do, like help lovebirds snap selfies while trying on rings. Anything to extricate herself from the current situation.

She flew to her feet. "Everything seems in order here. I'll just be going…"

"Diana, wait." Artem was using his CEO voice. Marvelous.

She obediently stayed put, lest he rethink his promise and banish her to an eternity of working in Engagements.

Franco took his time unfolding himself to a standing position, as if everyone was happy to wait for him, the Manhattan sunset included.

"Mr. Andrade, I'm Artem Drake, CEO of Drake Diamonds." Artem gestured toward Diana. "And this is my sister, Diana Drake."

"It's a pleasure to meet you," she said tightly and crossed her arms.

Artem shot her a reproachful glare. With no small amount of reluctance, she pasted on a smile and offered her hand for a shake.

Franco's gaze dropped to her outstretched fingertips. He waited a beat until her cheeks flared with heat, then dropped the cuff link into her palm without touching her.

"El gusto es mio," he said with just a hint of an Argentine accent.

The pleasure is mine.

A rebellious shiver ran down Diana's spine.

That shiver didn't mean anything. Of course it didn't. He was a beautiful man, that was all. It was only natural for her body to respond to that kind of physical perfection, even though her head knew better than to pay any attention to his broad shoulders and dark, glittering eyes.

She swallowed. Overwhelming character flaws aside, Franco Andrade had always been devastatingly handsome... emphasis on *devastating*.

It was hardly fair. But life wasn't always fair, was it? No, it most definitely wasn't. Lately, it had been downright cruel.

Diana's throat grew thick. She had difficulty swallowing all of a sudden. Then, somewhere amid the sudden fog in her head, she became aware of Artem clearing his throat.

"Shall we get started? I believe we're chasing the light." He introduced Franco to the photographer, who practically swooned on the spot when he turned his gaze on her.

Diana suppressed a gag and did her best to blend into the Drake-blue walls.

Apparently, any and all attempts at disappearing proved futile. As she tried to make an escape, Artem motioned her back. "Diana, join us please."

She forced her lips into something resembling a smile and strode toward the window where the photographer was getting Franco into position with a wholly unnecessary amount of hands-on attention. The woman with the camera had clearly forgiven him for his tardiness. It figured.

Diana turned her back on the nauseating scene and raised an eyebrow at Artem, who was tapping away on his iPhone. "You needed me?"

He looked up from his cell. "Yes. Can you get Mr. Andrade fitted with some cuff links?"

She stared blankly at him. "Um, me?"

"Yes, you." He shrugged. "What's with the attitude? I thought you'd be pleased. I'm talking to the same person who just stormed into my office demanding a different job than working in Engagements, right?"

She swallowed. "Yes. Yes, of course."

She longed to return to her dreadful post, but if she did, Artem would never take her seriously. Not after everything she'd said earlier.

"Cuff links." She nodded. "I'm on it."

She could do this. She absolutely could. She was Diana

Drake, for crying out loud. She had a reputation all over the world for being fearless.

At least, that's what people used to say about her. Not so much anymore.

Just do it and get it over with. You'll never see him again after today. Those days are over.

She squared her shoulders, grabbed a pair of cuff links and marched toward the corner of the room that had been roped off for the photo shoot, all the while fantasizing about the day when she'd be the one in charge of this place. Or at least not at the very bottom of the food chain.

Franco leaned languidly against the window while the photographer tousled his dark hair, ostensibly for styling purposes.

"Excuse me." Diana held up the cuff links—18-carat white-gold knots covered in black pavé diamonds worth more than half the engagement rings in the room. "I've got the jewels."

"Excellent," the photographer chirped. "I'll grab the camera and we'll be good to go."

She ran her hand through Franco's hair one final time before sauntering away.

If Franco noticed the sudden, exaggerated swing in her hips, he didn't let it show. He fixed his gaze pointedly at Diana. "You've come to dress me?"

"No." Her face went instantly hot. Again. "I mean, yes. Sort of."

The corner of his mouth tugged into a provocative grin and he offered her his wrists.

She reached for one of his shirt cuffs, and her mortification reached new heights when she realized her hands were shaking.

Will this day ever end?

"Be still, *mi cielo*," he whispered, barely loud enough for her to hear.

Mi cielo.

She knew the meaning of those words because he'd whispered them to her before. Back then, she'd clung to them as if they'd meant something.

Mi cielo. My heaven.

They hadn't, though. They'd meant nothing to him.

Neither had she.

"I'm not yours, Mr. Andrade. Never have been, never will be." She glared at him, jammed the second cuff link into his shirt with a little too much force and dropped his wrist. "We're finished here."

Why did she have the sinking feeling that she might be lying?

Chapter Two

Diana Drake didn't remember him. Or possibly she did, and she despised him. Franco wasn't altogether sure which prospect was more tolerable.

The idea of being so easily forgotten didn't sit well. Then again, being memorable hadn't exactly done him any favors lately, had it?

No, he thought wryly. *Not so much.* But it had been a hell of a lot of fun. At least, while it had lasted.

Fun wasn't part of his vocabulary anymore. Those days had ended. He was starting over with a clean slate, a new chapter and whatever other metaphors applied.

Not that he'd had much of a choice in the matter.

He'd been fired. Let go. Dumped from the Kingsmen Polo Team. Jack Ellis, the owner of the Kingsmen, had finally made good on all the ultimatums he'd issued over the years. It probably shouldn't have come as a surprise.

Franco knew he'd pushed the limits of Ellis's tolerance. More than once. More than a few times, to be honest.

But he'd never let his extracurricular activities affect his performance on the field. Franco had been the Kingsmen's record holder for most goals scored for four years running. His season total was always double the number of the next closest player on the list.

Which made his dismissal all the more frustrating, particularly considering he hadn't actually broken any rules. This time, Franco had been innocent. For probably the first time in his adult life, he'd done nothing untoward.

The situation dripped with so much irony that Franco was practically swimming in it. He would have found the entire turn of events amusing if it hadn't been so utterly frustrating.

"Mr. Andrade, could you lift your right forearm a few inches?" the photographer asked. "Like this."

She demonstrated for him, and Franco dragged his gaze away from Diana Drake with more reluctance than he cared to consider. He hadn't been watching her intentionally. His attention just kept straying in her direction. Again and again, for some strange reason.

She wasn't the most beautiful woman he'd ever seen. Then again, beautiful women were a dime a dozen in his world. There was something far more intriguing about Diana Drake than her appearance.

Although it didn't hurt to look at her. On the contrary, Franco rather enjoyed the experience.

She stood at one of the jewelry counters arranging and rearranging her tiny row of cuff links. He wondered if she realized her posture gave him a rather spectacular view of her backside. Judging by the way she seemed intent on ignoring him, he doubted it. She wasn't posing for his benefit, like, say, the photographer seemed to be doing. Franco could tell when a woman was trying to get his attention, and this one wasn't.

He couldn't quite put his finger on what it was about her that captivated him until she stole a glance at him from across the room.

The memory hit him like a blow to the chest.

Those eyes…

Until he'd met Diana, Franco had never seen eyes that color before—deep violet. They glittered like amethysts. Framed by thick ebony lashes, they were in such startling contrast with her alabaster complexion that he couldn't quite bring himself to look away. Even now.

And that was a problem. A big one.

"Mr. Andrade," the photographer repeated. "Your wrist."

He adjusted his posture and shot her an apologetic wink. The photographer's cheeks went pink, and he knew he'd been forgiven. Franco glanced at Diana again, just in time to see her violet eyes rolling in disgust.

A problem. Most definitely.

He had no business noticing *any* woman right now, particularly one who bore the last name Drake. He was on the path to redemption, and the Drakes were instrumental figures on that path. As such, Diana Drake was strictly off-limits.

So it was a good thing she clearly didn't want to give him the time of day. What a relief.

Right.

Franco averted his gaze from Diana Drake's glittering violet eyes and stared into the camera.

"Perfect," the photographer cooed. "Just perfect."

Beside her, Artem Drake nodded. "Yes, this is excellent. But maybe we should mix it up a little before we lose the light."

The photographer lowered her camera and glanced around the showroom, filled with engagement rings. You couldn't swing a polo mallet in the place without hitting a dozen diamond solitaires. "What were you thinking? Something romantic, maybe?"

"We've done romantic." Artem shrugged. "Lots of times. I was hoping for something a little more eye-catching."

The photographer frowned. "Let me think for a minute."

A generous amount of furtive murmuring followed, and Franco sighed. He'd known modeling wouldn't be as exciting as playing polo. He wasn't an idiot. But he'd been on the job for less than an hour and he was already bored out of his mind.

He sighed. Again.

His eyes drifted shut, and he imagined he was someplace else. Someplace that smelled of hay and horses and churned-up earth. Someplace where the ground shook with the thunder of hooves. Someplace where he never felt restless or boxed in.

The pounding that had begun in his temples subsided ever so slightly. When he opened his eyes, Diana Drake was standing mere inches away.

Franco smiled. "We meet again."

Diana's only response was a visible tensing of her shoulders as the photographer gave her a push and shoved her even closer toward him.

"Okay, now turn around. Quickly before the sun sets," the photographer barked. She turned her attention toward Franco. "Now put your arms around her. Pull her close, right up against your body. Yes, like that. Perfect!"

Diana obediently situated herself flush against him, with her lush bottom fully pressed against his groin. At last things were getting interesting.

Maybe he didn't hate modeling so much, after all.

Franco cleared his throat. "Well, this is awkward," he whispered, sending a ripple through Diana's thick dark hair.

He tried his best not to think about how soft that hair felt against his cheek or how much her heady floral scent reminded him of buttery-yellow orchids growing wild on the vine in Argentina.

"Awkward?" Diana shot him a glare over her shoulder. "From what I hear, you're used to this kind of thing."

He tightened his grip on her tiny waist. "And here I thought you didn't remember me."

"You're impossible," Diana said under her breath, wiggling uncomfortably in his arms.

"That's not what you said the last time we were in this position."

"Oh, my God, you did *not* just say that." This was the Diana Drake he remembered. Fiery. Bold.

"Nice." Artem strode toward them, nodding. "I like it. Against the sunset, you two look gorgeous. Edgy. Intimate."

Diana shook her head. "Artem, you're not serious."

"Actually, I am. Here." He lifted his hand. A sparkling diamond and sapphire necklace dangled from it with a center stone nearly as large as a polo ball. "Put this around your neck, Diana."

Diana crossed her arms. "Really, I'm not sure I should be part of this."

"It's just one picture out of hundreds. We probably won't even use it. The campaign is for cuff links, remember? Humor me, sis. Put it on." He arched a brow. "Besides, I thought you were interested in exploring other career opportunities around here."

She snatched the jewels out of his hands. "Fine."

Career opportunities?

"You're not working here, are you?" Franco murmured, barely loud enough for her to hear.

Granted, her last name was Drake. But why on earth would she give up a grand prix riding career to peddle diamonds?

"As a matter of fact, I am," she said primly.

"Why? If memory serves, you belong on a medal stand. Not here."

"Why do you care?" she asked through clenched teeth as the photographer snapped away.

Good question. "I don't."

"Fine."

But it wasn't fine. He *did* care, damn it. He shouldn't, but he did.

He would have given his left arm to be on horseback right now, and Diana Drake was working as a salesgirl when she could have been riding her way to the Olympics. What was she thinking? "It just seems like a phenomenal waste of talent. Be honest. You miss it, don't you?"

Her fingertips trembled and she nearly dropped the necklace down her blouse.

Franco covered her hands with his. "Here, let me help."

"I can do it," she snapped.

Franco sighed. "Look, the faster we get this picture taken, the faster all this will be over."

He bowed his head to get a closer look at the catch on the necklace, and his lips brushed perilously close to the elegant curve of her neck. She glanced at him over her shoulder, and for a sliver of a moment, her gaze dropped to his mouth. She let out a tremulous breath, and Franco could have sworn he heard a kittenish noise escape her lips.

Her reaction aroused him more than it should have, which he blamed on his newfound celibacy.

This lifestyle was going to prove more challenging than he'd anticipated.

But that was okay. Franco had never been the kind of man who backed down from a challenge. On the contrary, he relished it. He'd always played his best polo when facing his toughest opponents. Adversity brought out the best in Franco. He'd learned that lesson the hard way.

A long time ago.

Another time, another place.

"You two are breathtaking," the photographer said. "Diana, open the collar of your blouse just a bit so we can get a better view of the sapphire."

She obeyed, and Franco found himself momentarily spellbound by the graceful contours of her collarbones. Her skin was lovely. Luminous and pale beside the brilliant blue of the sapphire around her neck.

"Okay, I think we've got it." The photographer lowered her camera.

"We're finished?" Diana asked.

"Yes, all done."

"Excellent." She started walking away without so much as a backward glance.

"Aren't you forgetting something, *mi cielo*?" he said.

She spun back around, face flushed. He'd seen her wear that same heated expression during competition. "What?"

He held up his wrists. "Your cuff links."

"Oh. Um. Yes, thank you." She unfastened them and

gathered them in her closed fist. "Goodbye, Mr. Andrade."

She squared her shoulders and slipped past him. All business.

But Franco wasn't fooled. He'd seen the tremble in her fingertips as she'd loosened the cuffs of his shirt. She'd been shaking like a leaf, which struck him as profoundly odd.

Diana may have pretended to forget him, but he remembered her all too well. There wasn't a timid bone in her body, which had made her beyond memorable. She was confidence personified. It was one of the qualities that made her such an excellent rider.

If Diana Drake was anything, it was fearless. In the best possible way. She possessed the kind of tenacity that couldn't be taught. It was natural. Inborn. Like a person's height. Or the tone of her voice.

Or eyes the color of violets.

But people changed, didn't they? It happened all the time.

It had to. Franco was counting on it.

Chapter Three

Diana was running late for work.

Since the day of the mortifying photo shoot, she'd begun to dread the tenth-floor showroom with more fervor than ever before. Every time she looked up from one of the jewelry cases, she half expected to see Franco Andrade strolling toward her with a knowing look in his eyes and a smug grin on his handsome face. It was a ridiculous thing to worry about, of course. He had no reason to return to the store. The photo shoot was over. Finished.

Thank goodness.

Besides, if history had proven anything, it was that Franco wasn't fond of follow-through.

Still, she couldn't quite seem to shake the memory of how it had felt when he fastened that sapphire pendant around her neck…the graze of his fingertips on her collarbone, the tantalizing warmth of his breath on her skin.

It had been a long time since Diana had been touched in such an intimate way. A very long time. She knew getting her photo taken with Franco hadn't been real. They'd been posing, that's all. Pretending. She wasn't delusional, for heaven's sake.

But her body clearly hadn't been on the same page as her head. Physically, she'd been ready to believe the beautiful lie. She'd bought it, hook, line and sinker.

Just as she'd done the night she'd slept with him.

It was humiliating to think about the way she'd reacted to seeing him again after so long. She'd practically melted into a puddle at the man's feet. And not just any man. Franco Andrade was the king of the one night stand.

Even worse, she was fairly sure he'd known. He'd noticed the hitch in her breath, the flutter of her heart, the way she'd burned. He'd noticed, and he'd enjoyed it. Every mortifying second.

Don't think about it. It's over and done. Besides, it wasn't even a thing. It was nothing.

Except the fact that she kept thinking about it made it feel like something. A very big, very annoying something.

Enough. She had more important things to worry about than embarrassing herself in front of that polo-playing lothario. It hadn't been the first time, after all. She'd made an idiot out of herself in his presence before and lived to tell about it. At least this time she'd managed to keep her clothes on.

She tightened her grip on the silver overhead bar as the subway car came to a halt. The morning train was as crowded as ever, and when the doors slid open she wiggled her way toward the exit through a crush of commuters.

She didn't realize she'd gotten off at the wrong stop until it was too late.

Perfect. Just perfect. She was already running late, and now she'd been so preoccupied by Franco Andrade that she'd somehow gotten off the subway at the most crowded spot in New York. Times Square.

She slipped her messenger bag over her shoulder and climbed the stairs to street level. The trains had been running slow all morning, and she'd never be on time now. She might as well walk the rest of the way. A walk would do her good. Maybe the spring air would help clear her head and banish all thoughts of Franco once and for all.

It was worth a shot, anyway.

Diana took a deep inhale and allowed herself to remember how much she'd always loved to ride during this time of year. No more biting wind in her face. No more frost on the ground. In springtime, the sun glistened off her horse's ebony coat until it sparkled like black diamonds.

Diana's chest grew tight. She swallowed around the lump in her throat and fought the memories, pushed them back to the farthest corner of her mind where they belonged. *Don't cry. Don't do it.* If she did, she might not be able to stop.

After everything that had happened, she didn't want to be the pitiful-looking woman weeping openly on the sidewalk.

She focused, instead, on the people around her. Whenever the memory of the accident became too much, she tried her best to focus outward rather than on what was going on inside. Once, at Drake Diamonds, she'd stared at a vintage-inspired engagement ring for ten full minutes until the panic had subsided. She'd counted every tiny diamond in its art deco pavé setting, traced each slender line of platinum surrounding the central stone.

When she'd been in the hospital, her doctor had told her she might not remember everything that had led up to her fall. Most of the time, people with head injuries suffered memory loss around the time of impact. They didn't remember what had happened right before they'd been hurt.

They were the lucky ones.

Diana remembered everything. She would have given anything to forget.

Breathe in, breathe out. Look around you.

The streets were crowded with pedestrians, and as Diana wove her way through the crush of people, she thought she caught a few of them looking at her. They nodded and smiled in apparent recognition.

What was going on?

She was accustomed to being recognized at horse shows. On the riding circuit she'd been a force to be reckoned with. But this wasn't the Hamptons or Connecticut. This was Manhattan. She should blend in here. That was one of the things she liked best about the city—a person could just disappear right in the middle of a crowd. She didn't have to perform here. She could be anyone.

At least that's how she'd felt until Franco Andrade had walked into Drake Diamonds. The moment she'd set eyes on him, the dividing line between her old life and her new one had begun to blur.

She didn't like it. Not one bit. Before he'd shown up, she'd been doing a pretty good job of keeping things compartmentalized. She'd started a new job. She'd spent her evening hours in Dalton's apartment watching television until she fell asleep. She'd managed to live every day without giving much thought to what she was missing.

But the moment Franco had touched her she'd known the truth. She wasn't okay. The accident had affected her more than she could admit, even to herself.

There'd been an awareness in the graze of his fingertips, a strange intimacy in the way he'd looked at her. As if she were keeping a secret that only he was privy to. She'd felt exposed. Vulnerable. Seen.

She'd always felt that way around Franco, which is why she'd been stupid enough to end up in his bed. The way she felt when he looked at her had been intoxicating back then. Impossible to ignore.

But she didn't want to be seen now. Not anymore. She just wanted to be invisible for a while.

Maybe she wouldn't have been so rattled if it had been someone else. But it had been *him*. And she was most definitely still shaken up.

She needed to get a grip. So she'd posed for a few pictures with a handsome man she used to know. That's all. Case closed. End of story. No big deal.

She squared her shoulders and marched down the street with renewed purpose. This was getting ridiculous. She would *not* let a few minutes with Franco ruin her new beginning. He meant nothing to her. She was only imagining things, anyway. He probably looked at every woman he met with that same knowing gleam in his eye. That's why they were always falling at his feet everywhere he went.

It was nauseating.

She wouldn't waste another second thinking about the man. She sighed and realized she was standing right in front of the Times Square Starbucks. Perfect. Coffee was just what she needed.

As soon as she took her place in line, a man across the room did a double take in her direction. His face broke into a wide smile. Diana glanced over her shoulder, convinced he was looking at someone behind her. His wife, maybe. Or a friend.

No one was there.

She turned back around. The man winked and raised his cardboard cup as if he were toasting her. Then he turned and walked out the door.

Diana frowned. People were weird. It was probably just some strange coincidence. Or the man was confused, that was all.

Except he didn't look confused. He looked perfectly friendly and sane.

"Can I help you?" The barista, a young man with wire-rimmed glasses and a close-cropped beard, jabbed at the cash register.

"Yes, please," Diana said. "I'd like a…"

The barista looked up, grinned and cut her off before she could place her order. "Oh, hey, you're that girl."

That girl?

Diana's gaze narrowed. She shook her head. "Um, I don't think I am."

What was she even arguing about? She didn't actually know. But she knew for certain that this barista shouldn't have any idea who she was.

Unless her accident had somehow ended up on You-Tube or something.

Not that. Please not that.

Anything but that.

"Yeah, you are." The barista turned to the person in line behind her. "You know who she is too, right?"

Diana ventured a sideways glance at the woman, who didn't look the least bit familiar. Diana was sure she'd never seen her before.

"Of course." The woman looked Diana up and down. "You're her. Most definitely."

For a split second, relief washed over her. She wasn't losing it, after all. People on the sidewalk really had been staring at her. The triumphant feeling was short-lived when she realized she still had no idea why.

"Will one of you please tell me what's going on? What girl?"

The woman and the barista exchanged a glance.

"The girl from the billboard," the woman said.

Diana blinked.

The girl from the billboard.

This couldn't be about the photos she'd taken with Franco. It just couldn't. Artem was her brother. He wouldn't slap a picture of her on a Drake Diamonds billboard without her permission. Of course he wouldn't.

Would he?

Diana looked back and forth between the woman and the barista. "What billboard?"

She hated how shaky and weak her voice sounded, so she repeated herself. This time she practically screamed. *"What billboard?"*

The woman flinched, and Diana immediately felt horrible. Her new life apparently included having her face on billboards and yelling at random strangers in coffee shops. It wasn't exactly the fresh start she'd imagined for herself.

"It's right outside. Take two steps out the front door and look up. You can't miss it." The barista lifted a brow. "Are you going to order something or what? You're holding up the line."

"No, thank you." She couldn't stomach a latte right now. Simply putting one foot in front of the other seemed like a monumental task.

She scooted out of line and made her way to the door. She paused for a moment before opening it, hoping for one final, naive second that this was all some big mistake. Maybe Artem hadn't used the photo of her and Franco for the new campaign. Maybe the billboard they'd seen wasn't even a Drake Diamonds advertisement. Maybe it was an ad for some other company with a model who just happened to look like Diana.

That was possible, wasn't it?

But deep down she knew it wasn't, and she had no one to blame but herself.

She'd stormed into Artem's office and demanded that he find a role for her in the company that didn't involve Engagements. She'd practically gotten down on her knees and begged. He'd given her exactly what she wanted. She just hadn't realized that being on a billboard alongside Franco Andrade in the middle of Times Square was part of the equation.

She took a deep breath.

It was just a photograph. She and Franco weren't a couple or anything. They were simply on a billboard together. A million people would probably walk right past it and never notice. By tomorrow it would be old news. She was getting all worked up over nothing.

How bad could it be?

She walked outside, looked up and got her answer.

It was bad. Really, really bad.

Emblazoned across the top of the Times Tower was a photo of herself being embraced from behind by Franco. The sapphire necklace dangled from his fingertips, but rather than looking like he was helping her put it on, the photo gave the distinct impression he was removing it.

Franco's missing tie and the unbuttoned collar of his

tuxedo shirt didn't help matters. Neither did her flushed cheeks and slightly parted lips.

This wasn't an advertisement for cuff links. It looked more like an ad for sex. If she hadn't known better, Diana would have thought the couple in the photograph was just a heartbeat away from falling into bed together.

And she and Franco Andrade were that couple.

What have I done?

Franco was trying his level best not pummel Artem Drake.

But it was hard. Really hard.

"I didn't sign up for this." He wadded the flimsy newsprint of *Page Six* in his hands and threw it at Artem, who was seated across from Franco in the confines of his Drake-blue office. "Selling cuff links, yes. Selling sex, no."

Artem had the decency to flinch at the mention of sex, but Franco was guessing that was mostly out of a brotherly sense of propriety. After all, his sister was the one who looked as though Franco was seducing her on the cover of every tabloid in the western hemisphere.

From what Franco had heard, there was even a billboard smack in the middle of Times Square. His phone had been blowing up with texts and calls all morning. Regrettably, not a single one of those texts or calls had included an offer to return to the Kingsmen.

"Mr. Andrade, please calm down." Artem waved a hand at the generous stack of newspapers fanned across the surface of his desk. "The new campaign was unveiled just hours ago, and it's already a huge success. I've made you famous. You're a household name. People who've never seen a polo match in their lives know who you are. This is what you wanted, is it not?"

Yes…

And no.

He'd wanted to get Jack Ellis's attention. To force his hand. Just not like this.

But he couldn't explain the details of his reinvention to Artem Drake. His new "employer" didn't even know he'd been cut from the team. To Franco's knowledge, no one did. And if he had anything to say about it, no one would. Because he'd be back in his jersey before the first game of the season in Bridgehampton.

That was the plan, anyway.

He stared at the pile of tabloids on Artem's desk. Weeks of clean living and celibacy had just been flushed straight down the drain. More importantly, so had his one shot at getting his life back.

He glared at Artem. "Surely you can't be happy about the fact that everyone in the city thinks I'm sleeping with your sister."

A subtle tension in the set of Artem's jaw was the only crack in his composure. "She's a grown woman, not a child."

"So I've noticed." It was impossible not to.

A lot could happen in three years. She'd been young when she'd shared Franco's bed. Naive. Blissfully so. If he'd realized how innocent she was, he never would have touched her.

But all that was water under the bridge.

Just like Franco's career.

"Besides, this—" Artem gestured toward the pile of newspapers "—isn't real. It's an illusion. One that's advantageous to both of us."

This guy was unbelievable. And he was clearly unaware that Franco and Diana shared a past. Which was probably for the best, given the circumstances.

Franco couldn't help but be intrigued by what he was saying, though. *Advantageous to both of us...*

"Do explain."

Artem shrugged. *Yep, clueless.* "I'm no stranger to the tabloids. Believe me, I understand where you're coming from. But there's a way to use this kind of exposure and make the most out of it. We've managed to get the attention of the world. Our next step is keeping it."

He already didn't like the sound of this. "What exactly are you proposing?"

"A press tour. Take the cuff links out for a spin. You make the rounds of the local philanthropy scene—black-tie parties, charity events, that sort of thing—and smile for the cameras." His gaze flitted to the photo of Franco and Diana. "Alongside my sister, of course."

"Let me get this straight. You want to pay me to publicly date Diana." No way in hell. He was an athlete, not a gigolo.

"Absolutely not. I want to pay you to make appearances while wearing Drake gemstones. If people happen to assume you and Diana are a couple, so be it."

Franco narrowed his gaze. "You know they will."

Artem shrugged. "Let them. Look, I didn't plan any of this. But we'd all be fools not to take advantage of the buzz. From what I hear, appearing to be in a monogamous relationship could only help your reputation."

Ah, so the cat was out of the bag, after all.

Franco cursed under his breath. "How long do you expect me to keep up this farce?"

He wasn't sure why he was asking. It was a completely ludicrous proposition.

Although he supposed there were worse fates than spending time with Diana Drake.

Don't go there. Not again.

"Twenty-one days," Artem said.

Franco knew the date by heart already. "The day before the American polo season starts in Bridgehampton. The Kingsmen go on tour right after the season starts."

"Precisely. And you'll be going with them. Assuming you're back on the team by then, obviously." Artem shrugged. "That's what you want, isn't it?"

Franco wondered how Artem had heard about his predicament. He hadn't thought the news of his termination had spread beyond the polo community. Somehow the fact that it had made it seem more real. Permanent.

And that was unacceptable.

"It's absolutely what I want," he said.

"Good. Let us help you fix your reputation." Artem shrugged as if doing so was just that simple.

Maybe it is. "I don't understand. What would you be getting out of this proposed arrangement? Are you really this desperate to move your cuff links?"

"Hardly. This is about more than cuff links." Artem rummaged around the stack of gossip rags on his desk until he found a neatly folded copy of the *New York Times*. "Much more."

He slid the paper across the smooth surface of the desk. It didn't take long for Franco to spot the headline of interest: Jewelry House to be Chosen for World's Largest Uncut Diamond.

Franco looked up and met Artem's gaze. "Let me guess. Drake Diamonds wants to cut this diamond."

"Of course we do. The stone is over one thousand carats. It's the size of a baseball. Every jewelry house in Manhattan wants to get its hands on it. Once it's been cut and placed in a setting, the diamond will be unveiled at a gala at the Metropolitan Museum of Art. Followed by a featured exhibition open to the public, naturally."

Franco's eyes narrowed. "Would the date for this gala possibly be twenty-one days from now?"

"Bingo." Artem leaned forward in his chair. "It's the perfect arrangement. You and Diana will keep Drake Diamonds on the front page of every newspaper in New York. The owners of the diamond will see the Drake name everywhere they turn, and they'll have no choice but to pick us as their partners."

"I see." It actually made sense. In a twisted sort of way.

Artem continued, "By the time you and Diana attend the Met's diamond gala together, you'll have been in a high-profile relationship for nearly a month. Monogamous. Respectable. You're certain to get back in the good graces of your team."

Maybe. Then again, maybe not.

"Plus you'll be great for the team's ticket sales. The more famous you are, the more people will line up to see you play. The Kingsmen will be bound to forgive and forget whatever transgression got you fired." Artem lifted a brow. "What exactly did you do, anyway? You're the best player on the circuit, so it couldn't have been related to your performance on the field."

Franco shrugged. "I didn't do anything, actually."

He'd been cut through no fault of his own. Even worse, he'd been unable to defend himself. Telling the lie had been his choice, though. His call. He'd done what he'd needed to do.

It had been a matter of honor. Even if he'd been able to go back in time and erase the past thirty days, he'd still do it all over again.

Make the same choice. Say the same things.

Artem regarded him through narrowed eyes. "Fine.

You don't need to tell me. From now on, you're a re-formed man, anyway. Nothing else matters."

"Got it." Franco nodded.

He wasn't seriously considering this arrangement. It was borderline demeaning, wasn't it? To both himself and Diana.

Diana Drake.

He could practically hear her breathy, judgmental voice in his ear. *From what I hear, you're used to this kind of thing.*

She'd never go along with this charade. She had too much pride. Then again, what did he know about Diana Drake these days?

He cleared his throat. "What happens afterward?"

"Afterward?"

Franco nodded. "Yes, after the gala."

Artem smiled. "I'm assuming you'll ride off into the sunset with your team and score a massive amount of goals. You'll continue to behave professionally and even-tually you and Diana will announce a discreet breakup."

They'd never get away with it. Diana hadn't even set eyes on Franco or deigned to speak a word to him in the past three years until just a few days ago. No one would seriously believe they were a couple.

He stared down at the heap of newspapers on Ar-tem's desk.

People already believed it.

"You'll be compensated for each appearance at the rate we agreed upon under the terms of your modeling contract. You can start tonight."

"Tonight?"

Artem gave a firm nod. "The Manhattan Pet Rescue animal shelter is holding its annual Fur Ball at the Wal-dorf Astoria. You and Diana can dress up and cuddle with a few adorable puppies and kittens. Every photographer in town will be there."

The Fur Ball. It certainly sounded wholesome. Nauseatingly, mind-numbingly adorable.

"I'm assuming we have a deal." Artem stood.

Franco rose from his seat, but ignored Artem's outstretched hand. They couldn't shake on things. Not yet. "You're forgetting something."

"What's that?"

Not what. Who. "Diana. She'll never agree to this."

Artem's gaze grew sharp. Narrow. "What makes you say so?"

Franco had a sudden memory of her exquisite violet eyes, shiny with unshed tears as she slapped him hard across the face. "Trust me. She won't."

"Just be ready for the driver to pick you up at eight. I'll handle Diana." Artem offered his hand again.

This time, Franco took it.

But even as they shook on the deal, he knew it would never happen. Diana wasn't the sort of person who could be handled. By anyone. Artem Drake had no idea what he was up against. Franco almost felt sorry for him. Almost, but not quite.

Some things could only be learned the hard way.

Like a slap in the face.

Chapter Four

Diana called Artem repeatedly on her walk to Drake Diamonds, but his secretary refused to put her through. She kept insisting that he was in an important business meeting and had left instructions not to be disturbed, which only made Diana angrier. If such a thing was even possible.

A billboard. In Times Square.

She wanted to die.

Calm down. Just breathe. People will forget all about it in a day or two. In the grand scheme of life, it's not that big a deal.

But there was no deluding herself. It was, quite literally, a big deal. A huge one. A whopping 25,000-square-foot Technicolor enormous deal.

Artem would have to take it down. That's all there was to it. She hadn't signed any kind of modeling release. Drake might be her last name, but that didn't mean the family business owned the rights to her likeness.

Or did it? She wasn't even sure. Drake Diamonds had been her sponsor on the equestrian circuit. Maybe the business did, in fact, own her.

God, why hadn't she gone to college? She was in no way prepared for this.

She pushed her way through the revolving door of Drake Diamonds with a tad too much force. Urgent meeting or not, Artem was going to talk to her. She'd break down the door of his Drake-blue office if that's what it took.

"Whoa, there." The door spun too quickly and hurled her toward some poor, unsuspecting shopper in the lobby who caught her by the shoulders before she crashed into him. "Slow down, Wildfire."

"Sorry. I just…" She straightened, blinked and found herself face-to-face with the poster boy himself. Franco. "Oh, it's you."

What was he doing here? *Again?* And why were his hands on her shoulders? And why was he calling her that ridiculous name?

Wildfire.

She'd loved that song when she was a little girl. So, so much.

Well, she didn't love it anymore. In fact, Franco had just turned her off it for life.

"Good morning to you too, Diana." He winked. He was probably the only man on planet Earth who could make such a cheesy gesture seem charming.

Ugh.

She wiggled out of his grasp. "Why are you here? Wait, don't tell me. You're snapping selfies for the Drake Diamonds Instagram."

He was wearing a suit. Not a tuxedo this time, but a finely tailored suit, nonetheless. It was weird seeing him dressed this way. Shouldn't he be wearing riding clothes? He adjusted his shirt cuffs. "It bothers you that I'm the new face of Drake Diamonds?"

"No, it doesn't actually. I couldn't care less what you do. It bothers me that *I'm* the new face of Drake Diamonds." A few shoppers with little blue bags dangling from their wrists turned and stared.

Franco angled his head closer to hers. "You might want to keep your voice down."

"I don't care who hears me." She was being ridiculous. But she couldn't quite help it, and she certainly wasn't going to let Franco tell her how to behave.

"Your brother will care," he said.

"What are you talking about?" Then she put two and two together. Finally. "Wait a minute...were you just upstairs with Artem?"

He nodded. Diana must have been imagining things, because he almost looked apologetic.

"So you're the reason his secretary wouldn't put my calls through?" Unbelievable.

"I suppose so, yes." Again, something about his expression was almost contrite.

She glared at him. He could be as nice as he wanted, but as far as Diana was concerned, it was too little, too late. "What was this urgent tête-à-tête about?"

Why was she asking him questions? She didn't care what he and Artem had to say to each other...

Except something about Franco's expression told her she should.

He leveled his gaze at her and arched a single seductive brow. Because, yes, even the man's eyebrows were sexy. "I think you should talk to Artem."

She swallowed. Something was going on here. Something big. And she had the distinct feeling she wasn't going to like it. "Fine. But just so we're clear, I'm talking to him because I want to. And because he's my brother and sort of my boss. Not because you're telling me I should."

"Duly noted." He seemed to be struggling not to smile.

She lifted her chin in defiance. "Goodbye, Franco."

But for some reason, her feet didn't move. She just kept standing there, gazing up at his despicably handsome face.

"See you tonight, Wildfire." He shot her a knowing half grin before turning for the door.

She stood frozen, gaping after him.

Tonight?

She definitely needed to talk to Artem. Immediately.

She skipped the elevator and took the stairs two at a time until she reached the tenth floor, where she found him sitting at his desk as if it was any ordinary day. A day when Franco Andrade wasn't wandering the streets of Manhattan wearing Tom Ford and planning on seeing her tonight.

"Hello, sis." Artem looked up and frowned as he took in her appearance. "Why do you look like you just ran a marathon?"

"Because I just walked a few miles, then sprinted up the stairs." She was breathless. Her legs burned, which was just wrong. She shouldn't be winded from a little exercise. She was an elite athlete.

Used to be an elite athlete.

He gestured toward the wingback chair opposite him. "Take a load off. I need to talk to you, anyway."

"So I've heard." She didn't want to sit down. She wanted to stand and scream at him, but that wasn't going to get her anywhere. Besides, she felt drained all of a sudden. Being around Franco, even for a few minutes, was exhausting. "Speaking of which, what was Franco Andrade doing here just now?"

"About that…" He calmly folded his hands in front of him, drawing Diana's attention first to the smooth surface of his desk and then to the oddly huge stack of newspapers on top of it.

She blinked and cut him off midsentence. "Is that my picture on the front page of the *New York Daily News*?"

She hadn't thought it possible for the day to get any worse, but it just had. So much worse.

And the hits kept on coming. As she sifted through the stack of tabloids—all of which claimed she was having a torrid affair with "the drop-dead gorgeous bad boy of polo"—Artem outlined his preposterous idea for a public relations campaign. Although it sounded more like an episode of *The Bachelor* than any kind of legitimate business plan.

"No, thank you." Diana flipped the copy of *Page Six* facedown so she wouldn't have to look at the photo of herself and Franco on the cover. If she never saw that picture again, it would be too soon.

Artem's brow furrowed. "No, thank you? What does that mean?"

"It means no. As in, I'll pass." What about her answer wasn't he understanding? She couldn't be more clear. "No. N.O."

"Perhaps you don't understand. We're talking about the largest uncut diamond in the world. Do you have any idea what this could mean for Drake Diamonds?" There was Artem's CEO voice again.

She wasn't about to let it intimidate her this time. "Yes. I realize it's very important, but we'll simply have to come up with another plan." *Preferably one that doesn't involve Franco Andrade in any way, shape or form.*

"Let's hear your suggestions, then." He leaned back in his chair and crossed his arms. "I'm all ears."

He wanted her to come up with a plan *now*?

Diana cleared her throat. "I'll have to give it some thought, obviously. But I'm sure I can come up with something."

"Go ahead. I'll wait."

"Artem, come on. We can take the owners of the diamond out to dinner or something. Wine and dine them."

"You realize every other jeweler in Manhattan is doing that exact same thing," he said.

Admittedly, that was probably true. "There's got to be a better way to catch their attention than letting everyone believe I'm having a scandalous affair with Franco."

Please let there be another way.

"Not scandalous. Just high profile. Romantic. Glamorous." Artem gave her a thoughtful look. "He told me you'd refuse, by the way. What, exactly, is the problem between you two?"

Diana swallowed. Maybe she should simply tell Artem what happened three years ago. Surely then he'd forget about parading her all over Park Avenue on Franco's arm just for the sake of a diamond. Even the biggest diamond in the known universe.

But she couldn't. She didn't even want to think about that humiliating episode, much less talk about it.

Especially to her brother, of all people.

"He's a complete and total man whore. You know that, right?" Wasn't that reason enough to turn down the opportunity to pretend date him for twenty-one days? "Aren't you at all concerned about my virtue?"

"The last time I checked, you were more than capable of taking care of yourself, Diana. In fact, you're one of the strongest women I know. I seriously doubt I need

to worry about your virtue." He shrugged. "But I could
have a word with Franco...do the whole brother thing
and threaten him with bodily harm if he lays a finger on
you. Would that make you feel better?"

"God, no." She honestly couldn't fathom anything
more mortifying.

"It's your call." Artem shrugged. "He's rehabilitating
his image, anyway. Franco Andrade's man-whore days
are behind him."

Diana laughed. Loud and hard. "He told you that? And
you believed him?"

"When did you become such a cynic, sis?"

*Three years ago. Right around the time I lost my vir-
ginity.* "It seems dubious. That's all I'm saying. Why
would he change after all this time, unless he's already
had his way with every woman on the eastern seaboard?"

It was a distinct possibility.

"People change, Diana." His expression softened and
he cast a meaningful glance at the bassinet in the corner
of his office. A pink mobile hung over the cradle, decorated with tiny teddy bears wearing ballet shoes. "I did."

Diana smiled at the thought of her adorable baby niece.

He had a point. Less than a year ago, Artem had been
the one on the cover of *Page Six*. He'd been photographed
with a different woman every night. Now he was a candidate for father of the year.

Moreover, Diana had never seen a couple more in love
than Artem and Ophelia. It was almost enough to restore
her faith in marriage.

But not quite.

It would take more than her two brothers finding marital bliss to erase the memory of their father's numerous
indiscretions.

It wasn't just the affairs. It was the way he'd made no

effort whatsoever to hide them from their mother. He'd expected her to accept it. To smile and look away. And she had.

Right up until the day she died.

She'd been just forty years old when Diana found her lifeless body on the living room floor. Still young, still beautiful. The doctors had been baffled. They'd been unable to find a reason for her sudden heart attack. But to Diana, the reason was obvious.

Her mother had died of a broken heart.

Was it any wonder she thought marriage was a joke? She was beyond screwed up when it came to relationships. How damaged must she have been to intentionally throw herself at a man who was famous for treating women as if they were disposable?

Diana squeezed her eyes shut.

Why did Franco have to come strutting back into her life *now*, while she was her most vulnerable? Before her accident, she could have handled him. She could have handled anything.

She opened her eyes. "Please, Artem. I just really, really don't want to do this."

He nodded. "I see. You'd rather spend all day, every day, slaving away in Engagements than attend a few parties with Franco. Understood. Sorry I brought it up."

He waved a hand toward the dreaded Engagements showroom down the hall. "Go ahead and get to work."

Diana didn't move a muscle. "Wait. Are you saying that if I play the part of Franco's fake girlfriend by night, I won't have to peddle engagement rings by day?"

She'd assumed her position in Engagements was still part of the plan. This changed things.

She swallowed. She still couldn't do it. She'd never

last a single evening in Franco's company, much less twenty-one of them.

Could she?

"Of course you wouldn't have to do both." Artem gestured toward the newspapers spread across his desk. "This would be a job, just like any other in the company."

She narrowed her gaze and steadfastly refused to look at the picture again. "What kind of job involves going to black-tie parties every night?"

"Vice president of public relations. I did it for years. The job is yours now, if you want it." He smiled. "You asked me to find something else for you to do, remember? Moving from the sales floor to a VP position is a meteoric rise."

When he put it that way, it didn't sound so bad. Vice president of public relations sounded pretty darn good, actually.

Finally. This was the kind of opportunity she'd been waiting for. She just never dreamed that Franco Andrade would be part of the package.

"I want a pay increase," she blurted.

What was she doing?

"Done." Artem's grin spread wide.

She wasn't seriously considering accepting the job though, was she? No. She couldn't. Wouldn't. No amount of money was worth her dignity.

But there was one thing that might make participating in the farce worthwhile...

"And if it works, I want to be promoted." She pasted on her sweetest smile. "Again."

Artem's brows rose. "You're going to have to be more specific. Besides, vice president is pretty high on the food chain around here."

"I'm aware. But this diamond gala is really important. You said so yourself."

Artem's smile faded. Just a bit. "That's right."

"If I do my part and Drake Diamonds is chosen as the jewelry house to cut the giant diamond and if everything goes off with a hitch at the Met's diamond gala, I think I deserve to take Dalton's place." She cleared her throat. "I want to be named co-CEO."

Artem didn't utter a word at first. He just sat and stared at her as if she'd sprouted another head.

Great. She'd pushed too far.

VP was a massive career leap. She should have jumped at the opportunity to put all the love-struck brides and grooms in the rearview mirror and left it at that.

"That's a bold request for someone with no business experience," he finally said.

"Correct me if I'm wrong, but wasn't vice president of public relations the only position you held at Drake Diamonds before our father died and appointed you his successor as CEO?" Did Artem really think she'd been so busy at horse shows that she had no clue what had gone on between these Drake-blue walls the past few years?

Still, what was she saying? He'd never buy into this.

He let out an appreciative laugh. "You're certainly shrewd enough for the job."

She grinned. "I'll take that as a compliment."

"As you should." He sighed, looked at her for a long, loaded moment and nodded. "Okay. It works for me."

She waited for some indication that he was joking, but it never came.

Her heart hammered hard in her chest. "Don't tease me, Artem. It's been kind of a rough day."

And it was about to get rougher.

If she and Artem had actually come to an agreement,

that meant she was going out with Franco Andrade tonight. By choice.

She needed to have her head examined.

"I'm not teasing. You made a valid point. I didn't know anything about being a CEO when I stepped into the position. I learned. You will, too." He held up a finger. A warning. "But only if you deliver. Drake Diamonds must be chosen to cut the stone and cosponsor the Met Diamond gala."

"No problem." She beamed at him.

For the first time since she'd fallen off her horse, she felt whole. Happy. She was building a new future for herself.

In less than a month, she'd be co-CEO. No more passing out petit fours. No more engagement rings. She'd never have to look at another copy of *Bride* magazine for as long as she lived!

Better yet, she wouldn't have to answer any more questions about when she was going to start riding again. Every time she turned around, it seemed someone was asking her about her riding career. Had she gotten a new horse? Was she ready to start showing again?

Diana wasn't anywhere close to being ready. She wasn't sure she'd *ever* be ready.

Co-CEO was a big job. A huge responsibility—huge enough that it just might make people forget she'd once dreamed of going to the Olympics. If she was running the company alongside Artem, no one would expect her to compete anymore. It was the perfect solution.

She just had to get through the next twenty-one days first.

"Go home." Artem nodded toward his office door. "Rest up and get ready for tonight."

Tonight. A fancy party. The Waldorf Astoria. Franco.

She swallowed. "Everything will be fine."

Artem lifted a brow.

Had she really said that out loud?

"I know it will, because it's your job to make sure everything is fine," Artem said. "And for the record, there's not a doubt in my mind that your virtue is safe. You can hold your own, Diana. You just talked your way into a co-CEO job. From where I'm standing, if there's anyone who has reason to be afraid, it's Mr. Andrade."

He was right. She'd done that, hadn't she?

She could handle a few hours in Franco's company.

"I think you're right."

God, she hoped so.

Chapter Five

Franco leaned inside the Drake limo and did a double take when he saw Diana staring at him impassively from its dark interior.

"Buenas noches."

He'd expected the car to pick him up first and then take him to Diana's apartment so he could collect her. Like a proper date. But technically this wasn't a date, even though it already felt like one.

He couldn't remember the last time he'd dressed in a tuxedo and escorted a woman to a party. Despite his numerous exploits, Franco didn't often date. He arrived at events solo, and when the night was over he left with a woman on his arm. Sometimes several. Hours later, he typically went home alone. He rarely shared a bed with the same woman more than once, and he never spent the night. Ever.

In fact, the last woman who'd woken up beside him had been Diana Drake.

"Good evening, yourself," she said, without bothering to give him more than a cursory glance.

That would have to change once they arrived at the gala. Lovers looked at each other. They touched each other. Hell, if Diana was his lover, Franco wouldn't be able to keep his hands off her.

This isn't real.

He slid onto the smooth leather seat beside her.

It wasn't real, but it felt real. It even looked real.

Diana was dressed in a strapless chiffon gown, midnight blue, with a dangerously low, plunging neckline. A glittering stone rested between her breasts. A sapphire. *The* sapphire necklace from the photo shoot.

"Please stop staring." She turned and met his gaze. At last.

Franco's body hardened the instant his eyes fixed on hers. As exquisite as the sapphire around her neck was, it didn't hold a candle to the luminescent violet depths of those eyes. "You're lovely."

She stared at him coldly. "Save it for the cameras, would you? There's no one here. You can drop the act."

"It's not an act. You look beautiful." He swallowed. Hard. "That's quite a dress."

He was used to seeing her in riding clothes, not like this. He couldn't seem to look away.

What are you, a teenager? Grow up, Andrade.

"Seriously, stop." The car sped through a tunnel, plunging them into darkness. But the shadows couldn't hide the slight tremor in her voice. "Just stop it, would you? I know we're supposed to be madly in love with each other in public. But in private, can we keep things professional? Please?"

Something about the way she said *please* grabbed Franco by the throat and refused to let go.

Had he really been so awful to her all those years ago?
Yes. He had.

Still, she'd been better off once he'd pushed her away,
whether she'd realized it or not. She was an heiress. The
real deal. And Franco wasn't the type of man she'd bring
home.

Never had been, never would be.

"Professional. Got it," he said to the back of her head.
It felt more like he was talking to himself than to Diana.

She'd turned away again, keeping her gaze fixed on
the scenery outside the car window. The lights of the city
rushed past, framing her silhouette in a dizzying halo of
varying hues of gold.

They sat in stony silence down the lavish length of
Park Avenue. The air in the limo felt so thick he was
practically choking on it. Franco refrained from pointing out that refusing to either look at him or speak to
him in something other than monosyllables was hardly
professional.

Why the hell had she agreed to this arrangement, anyway? Neither one of them should be sitting in the back
of a limo on the way to some boring gala. They both belonged on horseback. Franco knew why he wasn't training right now, but for the life of him, he couldn't figure
out what Diana was doing working for her family business.

He was almost grateful when his phone chimed with
an incoming text message, giving him something to focus
on. Not looking at Diana was becoming more impossible by the second. She was stunning, even in her fury.

He slid his cell out of the inside pocket of his tuxedo
jacket and looked at the screen.

A message from Luc. Again.

Ellis still isn't budging.

Franco's jaw clenched. That information wasn't exactly breaking news. If he'd held out any hope of the team owner changing his mind before the end of the day, he wouldn't be sitting beside the diamond ice princess right now.

Still, he didn't particularly enjoy dwelling on the dismal state of his career.

He moved to slip the phone back inside his pocket, but it chimed again.

This has gone on long enough.

And again.

I can't let you do this. I'm telling him the truth.

Damn it all to hell.
Franco tapped out a response...

Let it go. What's done is done. I have everything under control.

Beside him, Diana cleared her throat. "Lining up your date for the evening?"

Franco looked up and found her regarding him through narrowed eyes. She shot a meaningful glance at his phone.

So, she didn't like the thought of him texting other women? Interesting.

"You're my date for the evening, remember?" He wasn't texting another woman, obviously. But she didn't need to know that. He hardly owed her an explanation.

She rolled her eyes. "Don't even pretend you're going home alone after this."

He powered his phone down and glanced back up at Diana. "As a matter of fact, I am. Didn't Artem tell you? You and I are monogamous."

She arched a brow. "Did he explain what that meant, or did you have to look it up in the dictionary?"

"You're adorable when you're jealous. I like it." He was goading her, and he knew it. But at least they were speaking.

"If you think I'm jealous, you're even more full of yourself than I thought you were." In the darkened limousine, he could see two pink spots glowing on her cheeks. "Also, you're completely delusional."

He shrugged. "I disagree. Do you know why?"

"I can't begin to imagine what's going on inside your head. Nor would I want to." She exhaled a breath of resignation. "Why?"

"Because nothing about this conversation—which *you* initiated—is professional in nature." He deliberately let his gaze drop to the sapphire sparkling against her alabaster skin, then took a long, appreciative look at the swell of her breasts.

"You're insatiable," she said with a definite note of disgust.

He smiled. "Most women like that about me."

"I'm not most women."

"We'll see about that, won't we?"

The car slowed to a stop in front of the gilded entrance to the Waldorf Astoria. A red carpet covered the walkway from the curb to the gold-trimmed doors, flanked on either side by a mob of paparazzi too numerous to count.

"Miss Drake and Mr. Andrade, we've arrived," the driver said.

"Thank God. I need to get out of this car." Diana reached for the door handle, but her violet eyes grew wide. "Oh, wait. I almost forgot."

She opened her tiny, beaded clutch, removed a Drake-blue box and popped it open. The black diamond cuff links from the photo shoot glittered in the velvety darkness.

She handed them to Franco as the driver climbed out of the car. "Put these on. Quickly."

He slid one into place on his shirt cuff, but left the other in the palm of his hand.

"What are you doing? Hurry." Diana was borderline panicking. The back door clicked open, and the driver extended his hand toward her and waited.

"Go ahead, it's showtime." Franco loosened his tie and winked. "Trust me, Wildfire."

She stretched one foot out of the car, aimed a dazzling smile at the waiting photographers and muttered under her breath, "You realize that's asking the impossible."

Franco gathered the soft chiffon hem of her gown and helped her out of the limo. They stepped from the quiet confines of the car into a frenzy of clicking camera shutters and blinding light.

He dropped a kiss on Diana's bare shoulder and made a show of fastening the second cuff link in place. A collective gasp rose from the assembled crowd of spectators.

He lowered his lips to Diana's ear. "I have everything under control."

I have everything under control.

Maybe if he repeated it enough times, it would be true.

The man is an evil genius.

Diana hadn't been sure what Franco had up his sleeve until she felt his lips brush against her shoulder.

The kiss caught her distinctly off guard, and as her head whipped around to look at him, she saw him fastening his cuff link. He curved his arm around her waist, murmured in her ear and she finally understood. He'd purposely delayed sliding the diamonds into position on his shirt cuff so it looked as though he was only just getting dressed, no doubt because their arrival at the gala had caught them in flagrante delicto.

The press ate it up.

Evil genius. Most definitely.

"Diana, how long have you and Franco been dating?"

"Diana, who are you wearing?"

"Look over here, Diana! Smile for the camera."

Photographers shouted things from every direction.

She didn't know where to look, so she bowed her head as Franco steered her deftly through the frenzied crowd with his hand planted protectively on the small of her back.

"What's the diamond heiress like in bed, Franco?" a paparazzo yelled.

Diana's head snapped up.

"Don't let them get to you," Franco whispered.

"I'm fine," she lied. The whole scene was madness. "But if you answer that question, I will murder you."

"A gentleman doesn't kiss and tell."

Their eyes met briefly in the chaos, and if Diana hadn't known better, she would have believed he was being serious.

Suddenly, the thought of doing this for twenty-one straight days seemed absurd. Absurd and wholly impossible.

"Good evening, Miss Drake, Mr. Andrade." The doorman nodded and swept the door open for them. "Welcome to the Waldorf Astoria."

"Gracias," Franco said. *Thank you.* He gave her waist a gentle squeeze. "Shall we, love?"

His voice rumbled through her, deliciously deep.

She swallowed. *It's all pretend. Don't fall for it. Don't fall.*

She'd told herself the same thing three years ago. A fat lot of good that had done her.

Everything was moving too fast. Even after they finally made it inside the grand black-and-white marble lobby, Diana felt as if she'd been caught up in a whirlwind. A glittering blur where everything was too big and too bright, from the mosaic floor to the grand chandelier to the beautiful man standing beside her.

"Miss Drake and Mr. Andrade, I'm Beth Ross, director of Manhattan Pet Rescue. We're so pleased you could make it to our little gathering this evening."

"Ah, Beth, we wouldn't have missed it for the world," Franco said smoothly, following up his greeting with a kiss on the cheek.

Beth practically swooned.

He was so good at this it was almost frightening. If Artem had really known what he was doing, he would have made Franco the new vice president of public relations.

Say something. You're not the arm candy. He is.

"Thank you for having us. We're so pleased to be here." Diana smiled.

From the corner of her eye, she spotted someone holding up a cell phone and pointing toward her and Franco. He must have seen it too, because he deftly wrapped his arm around her waist and rested his palm languidly on her hip. Without even realizing it, she burrowed into him.

Beth sighed. "You two are every bit as beautiful

as your advertising campaign. It's all anyone can talk about."

"So we've heard." Diana forced a smile.

"Our party is located upstairs in the Starlight Ballroom. I've come to escort you up there, and if you don't mind, we'd love to snap a few pictures of you with some of the animals we have up for adoption later this evening."

Diana stiffened. "Um…"

Franco gave her hipbone a subtle squeeze. "We'd be happy to. We're big animal lovers, obviously."

We're big animal lovers.

We.

Diana blinked. Franco seemed to be staring at her, waiting for her to say something. "Oh, yes. Huge animal lovers."

They moved from the glitzy, gold lobby into a darkly intimate corridor walled in burgundy velvet. Beth pushed a button to summon an elevator.

"That doesn't surprise me a bit," she said. "I just knew you must be animal lovers. Drake Diamonds has always been one of our biggest supporters. And, of course, both of you are legendary in the horse world."

The elevator doors swished open, and the three of them stepped inside.

"Diana has a beautiful black Hanoverian. Tell Beth about Diamond, love." Franco looked at her expectantly.

Diana felt as though she'd been slapped.

She opened her mouth to say something, anything, but she couldn't seem capable of making a sound.

"Are you all right, dear? You've gone awfully pale." Beth eyed her with concern.

"I just… I…" It was no use. She couldn't talk about Diamond. Not now.

For six months, she'd managed to avoid discussing her beloved horse's death with anyone. Not even her brothers. She knew she probably should, but she couldn't. It just hurt too much. And after so much silence, the words wouldn't come.

"She's a bit claustrophobic," Franco said.

Another lie. Diana was beginning to lose track of them all.

"Oh, I'm so sorry." Beth's hand fluttered to her throat. "I didn't realize. We should have taken the stairs."

"It's fine." Franco's voice was like syrup. Soothing. "We're almost there, darling."

The elevator doors slid open.

Diana burrowed into Franco as he half carried her to the entrance to the ballroom. She couldn't remember leaning against him in the first place.

Breathe in, breathe out. You're fine.

She took a deep inhale and straightened her spine, smiled. "So sorry. I'm okay. Really."

Her heart pounded against her rib cage. She desperately wished she were back at Dalton's apartment, watching bad reality television and curled up under a blanket on the sofa.

Don't think about Diamond. Don't blow this. Say something.

She glanced up at the stained-glass ceiling strung with twinkling lights. "Look how beautiful everything is."

Beth nodded her agreement and launched into a description of all the work that had gone into putting together the gala, a large part of which had been funded by Drake Diamonds. Diana smiled and nodded, as did Franco, although at times she could see him watching her with what felt like too much interest.

She was dying to tell him he was laying it on a little

thick. They were supposed to be dating, not engaged, for crying out loud. Besides, she'd shaken off the worst of her panic.

She was fine. She just hadn't expected him to mention Diamond. That's all. She'd assumed that Franco had known about her accident. Apparently, he hadn't. Otherwise, he never would have brought up Diamond.

She'd been shocked, and probably a little upset. But it had passed.

He didn't need to be worried about her, and he definitely didn't need to be watching her like that. But an hour into the gala they were still shaking hands and chatting with the other animal shelter donors. She and Franco hadn't had a moment alone together.

Not that Diana was complaining.

The limousine ride had provided plenty of one-on-one time, thank you very much.

"If we could just ask you to do one last thing…" Beth guided them toward the far corner of the ballroom where guests had been taking turns posing for pictures. "Could we get those photos I mentioned before you leave?"

Diana nodded. "Absolutely."

Franco's hand made its way to the small of her back again. She was getting somewhat used to it and couldn't quite figure out if that was a bad thing or a good one.

It's nearly over. Just a few more minutes.

One night down, twenty to go. Almost.

She allowed herself a subtle, premature sigh of relief. Then she noticed a playpen filled with adorable, squirming puppies beside the photographer's tripod, and any sense of triumph she felt about her performance thus far disintegrated. She couldn't handle being around animals again. Not yet.

"Well, well. What do we have here?" Franco reached

into the playpen and gathered a tiny black puppy with a tightly curled tail into his arms.

The puppy craned its neck, stuck out its miniscule pink tongue and licked the side of Franco's face. He threw his head back and laughed, which only seemed to encourage the sweet little dog. It scrambled up Franco's chest and showered his ear with puppy kisses.

Beth motioned for the photographer to capture the adoration on film. "Doesn't she just love you, Mr. Andrade?"

The puppy was a girl. Because of course.

Franco's charm appealed to females of all species, apparently.

Why am I not surprised?

"Come here, love." Franco reached for Diana's hand and pulled her toward him. "You've got to meet this little girl. She's a sweetheart."

"No, it's okay. You keep her." She tried to wave him off, but it was impossible. Before she knew what was happening, she had a puppy in her arms and flashbulbs were going off again.

"That's Lulu. She's a little pug mix."

"Franco's right. She's definitely a sweetheart." Diana gazed down at the squirming dog.

Before her brother Dalton got married and moved to Delamotte, he'd tried talking her into getting a dog on multiple occasions. At first she'd thought he was joking. Dalton didn't even like dogs. Or so she'd thought. Apparently that had changed when he met the princess. Then he'd practically become some sort of animal matchmaker and kept encouraging Diana to adopt a pet.

What had gotten into her brothers? Both of them had turned into different people over the course of the past year. Sometimes it felt like the entire world was moving forward, full speed ahead, while Diana stood completely still.

Everything was changing. Everything and everyone.

It didn't use to be this way. From the first day she'd climbed onto the back of horse, Diana had been riding as fast as she could. She'd always thought if she rode hard enough, she'd escape the legacy Gaston Drake had built. Escape everything that it meant to be part of her family. The lies, the deceit. She'd thought she could outrun it.

Now she was back in the family fold, and she realized she hadn't outrun a thing.

She swallowed hard. How could she even consider saving a dog when she wasn't even convinced she could save herself?

"Here. You take her." She tried to hand the puppy back to Franco, but he wrapped his arms around her and kept posing for the camera.

"You three make a lovely family," Beth gushed.

That was Diana's breaking point.

The touching…the endearments…the puppy. Those things she could handle. Mostly. But the idea of being a family? She'd rather die.

"It's getting late. We should probably go."

But no one seemed to have a heard a word she said, because at the exact time that she tried to make her getaway, Franco made an announcement. "We'll take her."

Beth squealed. A few people applauded. Diana just stood there, trying to absorb what he'd said.

She searched his features, but he was still wearing that boyfriend-of-the-year expression that gave her butterflies, even though she knew without a doubt it wasn't real. "What are you talking about?"

"The puppy." He gave the tiny pup a rub behind her ears with the tip of his pointer finger.

"Franco, we can't adopt a dog together," she muttered through her smile, which was definitely beginning to fade.

"Of course we can, darling." His eyes narrowed the slightest bit.

No one else noticed because they were too busy fawning all over him.

"Franco, *sweetheart*." She shot daggers at him with her eyes.

This wasn't part of the deal. She'd agreed to pretend to date him, not coparent an animal.

Besides, she didn't want to adopt a dog. Correction: she *couldn't* adopt a dog.

A dog's lifespan was even shorter than a horse's. Much shorter. She wouldn't survive that kind of heartache. Not again. *Never* again.

Franco bowed his head to nuzzle the puppy and paused to whisper in her ear. "They're eating it up. What is your problem?"

It was the worst possible time for something to snap inside Diana, but something did. All the feelings she'd been working so hard to suppress for the past few months—the anger, the fear, the grief—came spilling out at once. She gazed up at Franco through a veil of tears as the whole world watched.

"Diamond is dead. That's my problem."

Chapter Six

A *Page Six* Exclusive Report

The rumors are true! Diamond heiress Diana Drake and polo's prince charming, Franco Andrade, are indeed a couple. Tongues have been wagging all over New York since their sultry billboard went up in Times Square. The heat between these two is too hot to be anything but genuine!

Drake and Andrade stepped out last night at Manhattan's Annual Fur Ball, where witnesses say they arrived on the heels of what was obviously a romantic tryst in the Drake Diamonds limousine. During the party, Andrade was heard calling Drake by the pet name Wildfire and couldn't keep his hands off the stunning equestrian beauty.

At the end of the evening, Drake was moved to tears when Andrade gifted her with a nine-week-old pug puppy.

Chapter Seven

Franco shifted his Jaguar into Park and swiveled his gaze to the passenger seat. "I don't suppose I can trust you to stay here and let me do the talking."

Lulu let out a piercing yip, then resumed chewing on the trim of the Jag's leather seats.

"Okay, then. Since you've made no attempt at all to hide your deviousness, you're coming with me." He scooped the tiny dog into the crook of his elbow and climbed out of the car.

"Try to refrain from gnawing on my suit if you can help it."

Lulu peered up at him with her shiny, oversize eyes as she clamped her little teeth around one of the buttons on his sleeve.

Marvelous.

Franco didn't bother reprimanding her. If the past week had taught him anything, it was that Lulu had a mind of her own. Not unlike the other headstrong female in his life…

Diana hadn't been kidding when she said she didn't want anything to do with the puppy. As far as pet parenting went, Franco was a single dad. Which would have been fine, had he not known how badly she needed the dog.

She was reeling from the loss of her horse. That much was obvious. If anyone could understand that kind of grief, Franco could.

He'd had no idea that Diamond had died. But now that he knew, things were beginning to make more sense. Diana hadn't given up riding because she had a burning desire to peddle diamonds. She was merely hiding out at the family store. She was heartbroken and afraid.

But she couldn't give up riding forever.

Could she?

"Franco." Ben Santos, the coach of the Kingsmen, strolled out of the barn and positioned himself between Franco and the practice field. "What are you doing here?"

Not exactly the greeting he was hoping for.

Franco squared his shoulders and kept on walking. Enough was enough. He needed to stop worrying so much about his fake girlfriend and focus on resurrecting his career.

"Nice to see you too, coach." He paused by the barn and waited for an invitation onto the field.

None was forthcoming.

Ben squinted into the sun and sighed. "You know you're not supposed to be here, son."

Franco's jaw clenched. He'd never liked Ben's habit of calling his players *son*. Probably because the last man who'd called Franco that had been a worthless son of a bitch.

But he'd put up with it from Ben out of respect. He wasn't in the mood to do so now, though.

Seven nights of wining and dining Diana Drake at every charity ball in Manhattan had gotten him absolutely nowhere. He had nothing to show for his efforts, other than a naughty puppy and a nagging sense that Diana was on the verge of coming apart at the seams.

Not your problem.

"I was hoping we could talk. Man to man," Franco said. Or more accurately, man to man holding tiny dog.

Lulu squirmed in his grasp, and the furrow between Ben's brows faded.

"Nice pup," he said. "This must be the one I've been reading about in all the papers."

Thus far, Lulu's puppyhood had been meticulously chronicled by every gossip rag and website Franco had ever heard of, along with a few he hadn't. Just this morning, Franco had been photographed poop-scooping outside his Tribeca apartment. He supposed he had that lovely image to look forward to in tomorrow's newspapers. Oh, joy.

He cleared his throat. "So you've been keeping up with me."

Excellent. Maybe the love charade was actually working.

"It's been kind of hard not to." Ben reached a hand toward Lulu, who promptly began nibbling on his fingers.

"The publicity should come in handy when the season starts, don't you think?" Franco's gaze drifted over the coach's shoulder to where he could see a groom going over one of the Kingsmen polo ponies with a curry comb. The horse's coat glistened like a shiny copper penny in the shadows of the barn.

Diamond is dead. That's my problem.

"Except you're not on the team, so, no." Ben shook his head.

"This has gone on long enough, don't you think? You need me. The team needs me. How long is Ellis planning on making me sweat this out?"

"You were fired. And I don't think Ellis is going to change his mind. He's furious. Frankly, I can't blame him." Ben removed his Kingsmen baseball cap and raked a hand through his hair. He sighed. "You went too far this time, son. You slept with the man's wife."

Franco pretended he hadn't heard the last sentence. If he thought about it too much, he might be tempted to tell the truth and he couldn't do that. Luc had his faults— bedding the boss's wife chief among them—but he was Franco's friend. Luc had been there for him when he needed someone most.

Franco owed Luc, and it was time to pay up.

"That's over." Franco swallowed. "I'm in love."

He waited for a lightning bolt to appear out of the sky and strike him dead.

Nothing happened. Franco just kept standing there, holding the squirming puppy and watching the horses being led toward the practice field.

He missed this. He missed spending so much time with his horses. He'd been exercising them as often as possible, but it couldn't compare with team practice, day in and day out.

Diana had to miss it, too. He knew she did.

Diamond is dead. That's my problem.

Franco felt sick every time he remembered the lost look in Diana's eyes when she'd said those words.

Her vulnerability had caught him off guard. It affected him far more than her disdain ever could. He didn't mind being hated. He deserved it, frankly. But he *did* mind seeing Diana in pain. He minded it very much.

Again, not his problem. He was here to get himself, not Diana, back in the saddle.

"In love," Ben repeated. His gaze dropped to the rich soil beneath their feet. "I'm happy to hear it. I am. But I'm afraid it's going to take more than a few pictures in the paper to convince Ellis."

Franco's jaw clenched. "What are you saying?"

But the coach didn't need to elaborate, because the field was filling up with Franco's team members. They were clearly preparing for a scrimmage because, instead of being dressed in casual practice attire, they were wearing uniforms. Franco spotted Luc, climbing on top of a sleek ebony mount. But the sight that gave Franco pause was another player. One he'd never seen before, wearing a shirt with a number situated just below his right shoulder—the number 1.

Franco's number.

"Perhaps Ellis would feel differently if you were married. Or even engaged. Something permanent, you know. But right now, it looks like a fling. To him, anyway." Ben shrugged. "Surely you understand. Try to put yourself in his shoes, son. Imagine how you'd feel if another man, a man whom you knew and trusted, hopped into bed and ravished Miss Drake."

Franco's gaze finally moved away from the player wearing his number. He stared at the coach, and a nonsensical rage swelled in his chest. A thick, black rage, which he could only attribute to the fact that he'd been replaced. "Don't talk about her that way."

Ben held up his hands. "I'm not suggesting it will happen. I'm simply urging you to try and understand where Ellis is coming from."

"This isn't about Diana." Franco took a calming inhale and reminded himself that losing his cool wasn't going to do him any favors. "It's not even about Ellis and his wife. It's about the team."

The coach gestured toward the bright-green rectangle of grass just west of the barn. "Look, son. I need to get going. We've got back-to-back scrimmages this afternoon."

Franco jerked his chin in the direction of the practice field. "Who's your new number 1?"

Ben sighed. "Don't, Franco."

"Just tell me who's wearing my jersey, and I'll leave."

"Gustavo Anca."

"You can't be serious." Franco knew Gustavo. He was a nice enough guy, but an average player at best. Ellis was playing it safe. Too safe. "You know he won't bring in the wins."

"Yes, but he won't sleep with the owner's wife, either." The older man gave him a tight smile.

Franco's gaze flitted ever so briefly to Luc sitting atop his horse, doing a series of twisting stretches. He turned in Franco's direction, and their eyes met.

Franco looked away.

"Listen. Can I give you a piece of advice?"

Whatever he had to say, Franco didn't want to hear it.

"Move on. Let the other teams know you're available. Someone is bound to snap you up."

He shook his head. "Out of the question."

The Kingsmen were the best. And when Franco had worn the Kingsmen jersey, he'd been the best of the best. He'd earned his place there, and he wanted it back. His horses were there. His teammates. His heart.

Also, if the Kingsmen were already scrimmaging, it could only mean the rosters had been set for the coming

season in Bridgehampton. If Franco wanted to play anywhere before autumn, he'd have to go Santa Barbara. Or
even as far as Sotogrande, in Spain.

He couldn't leave. He'd made a promise to the Drakes.
And for the time being, his position as the face of Drake
Diamonds was the only thing paying his bills.

His hesitancy didn't have a thing to do with Diana. At
least, that's what he wanted to believe.

"Think about it. Make a few calls. If another team
needs a reference, have them contact me." Ben shifted
from one foot to the other. "But I can only vouch for your
playing. Nothing else."

"Of course." The tangle of fury inside Franco grew
into something dark and terrible. He clamped his mouth
shut.

"It was good to see you, but please understand. The situation isn't temporary." His coach gave him a sad smile.
"It's permanent."

"Miss Drake, you have a visitor." The doorman's voice
crackled through the intercom of Diana's borrowed apartment. "Mr. Andrade is on his way up."

Diana's hand flew to the Talk button. "Wait. What?
Why?"

Franco was here? Now?

There had to be some sort of mistake. They weren't
scheduled to arrive at the Harry Winston party for another hour and a half. She wasn't even dressed yet. Besides, she'd given the driver strict instructions to pick
her up first. She didn't need Franco anywhere near her
apartment. Their lives were already far more intertwined
than she'd ever anticipated.

She'd even talked to him about Diamond. Briefly, but
still. It had been the closest she'd come to admitting to

anyone that she was having trouble moving past her accident. It had also been the first time she'd said Diamond's name out loud since her fall.

She'd spent the intervening days since the Fur Ball carefully shoring up the wall around her heart again. She went through the motions with Franco, speaking to him as little possible. He was the last person she should be confiding in. His casual reference to Diamond had caught her off guard. She'd had a moment of weakness.

It wouldn't happen again.

Even if the sight of him with that adorable puppy in his arms made her weak in the knees…she was only human, after all.

The doorman's voice crackled through the intercom. "I assumed it was acceptable, given the nature of your relationship, that I could go ahead and send Mr. Andrade up."

The nature of their relationship. Hysterical laughter bubbled up Diana's throat.

She swallowed it down. "It's fine. Thank you."

She took a deep breath and told herself to get a grip. She couldn't reprimand the doorman for sending the purported love of her life up to see her, could she?

The building that housed Dalton's apartment was one of the most exclusive addresses in Lenox Hill. She wholeheartedly doubted the doorman would be indiscreet. But the press was always looking for a scoop. The last thing she and Franco needed was a headline claiming she'd turned him away from her door.

Diana shook her head. Not she and Franco. She and Artem. The Drakes were the ones who were on the same team. Franco was just an accessory.

A dashing, dangerous accessory.

Three solid knocks pounded on the door and echoed

through the apartment. Diana tightened the belt of her satin bathrobe and opened the door.

"Franco, what a pleasant surprise," she said with forced enthusiasm.

"Diana," he said flatly.

That was it. No loving endearment. No scandalous quip about her state of near undress. Just her name.

She motioned for him to come inside and shut the door.

Her smile faded as she turned to face him. There was no reason for pretense when they were alone together. Although, now that she thought about it, this was the first time since embarking on their charade that they'd been alone. *Truly* alone. Everywhere they went, they were surrounded by drivers, photographers, doormen.

A nonsensical shiver passed through her as she looked up at him. His eyes seemed darker than usual, his expression grim.

"What are you doing here?"

Had something happened? Had word gotten out that they'd been faking their love affair? Surely not. Artem would have said something. She'd talked to him on the phone only moments ago, and everything had seemed fine.

"We have a date this evening, do we not?" His words were clipped. Formal.

Diana never thought she'd miss his sexually charged smile and smug attitude, but she kind of did. At least that version of Franco was somewhat predictable. This new persona seemed quite the opposite.

"We do." She nodded and waited for him to ogle her. She was wearing a white satin minibathrobe, for crying out loud.

He just stood there in his impeccably cut tuxedo with

his arms crossed. "Where are we going tonight, any-way?"

"To a party at Harry Winston."

"The jewelry store?" He frowned. "Isn't Harry Winston a direct competitor of Drake Diamonds?"

"Yes, but the Lambertis are going to be there."

"Who?" he asked blithely.

Seriously? They'd been over this about a million times. "Carla and Don Lamberti. They own the diamond, re-member? *The* diamond."

"Right." His gaze strayed to her creamy satin bath-robe. Finally. "Shouldn't you be getting dressed?"

"I *was*. Until you knocked on my door." This wasn't the night for Franco to go rogue. Absolutely not. "What's with you tonight? Is something wrong? Why are you even here?"

His eyes flashed. Something most definitely wasn't right. "You're my girlfriend." He used exaggerated air quotes around the word *girlfriend*. "Why shouldn't I be here?"

"Because the car was supposed to pick me up first, and then we were going to collect you in Tribeca. That's why."

He eyed her with an intensity that made her feel warm and delicious, like she'd been sipping red wine. "I'm tired of following orders, Diana. Surely I'm not expecting too much if I want to make my own decision regarding trans-portation to a party."

"Um…"

"A real couple wouldn't be picked up at two separate locations. Real lovers would be in bed until the moment it was time to leave. Real lovers would, at the very least, be in the same godforsaken apartment." An angry muscle twitched in his jaw. Diana couldn't seem to look away from it. "We need this to look real. *I* need it to look real."

She'd never seen Franco this serious before. It shouldn't have been nearly as arousing as it was. Especially on a night as important as this one.

Diana nodded and licked her lips. "Of course."

She hadn't realized he'd cared so much about either the company or the diamond. Wasn't this whole lovey-dovey act just a paycheck for him? A way to get a little publicity for the Kingsmen?

Why *did* he care so much?

She realized she didn't actually know why he'd agreed to participate in their grand charade. Artem had said something about Franco changing his image, but she hadn't pressed for details. She just wanted to get through their twenty-one days together as quickly and painlessly as possible.

Franco prowled through her living room with the dangerous grace of a panther. "Where's your liquor cabinet? I need something to pass the time while you're getting ready."

Clearly this wasn't the moment for a heart-to-heart.

She crossed the living room, strode into the kitchen and pulled a bottle of the Scotch that Dalton favored from one of the cabinets. She set it on the counter along with a Waterford highball glass. "Will this do?"

Franco arched a brow. "It'll work."

"Good. Help yourself." She watched as he poured a generous amount and then downed it in a single swallow.

He eyed her as he picked up the bottle again. "Is there a problem, or are you going to finish getting dressed?"

Alarm bells were going off in every corner of her mind. Franco was definitely upset about something. She should call Artem and cancel before Franco polished off the rest of Dalton's Scotch.

But that wasn't an option. Not tonight, when they were

finally going to come face-to-face with the Lambertis. Their 1,100-carat diamond was the sole reason she was in this farce of a relationship.

She took a deep inhale and pasted on a smile. "No problem at all."

Not yet, anyway.

Chapter Eight

Diana held her breath as they climbed into the Drake limousine, hoping against hope that Franco's strange, dark mood would go unnoticed by everyone at the gala.

She kept waiting for him to slip back into his ordinary, devil-may-care persona, but somehow it never happened. They made the short trip to Harry Winston in tense silence, and for the first time, the strained, quiet ride seemed to be Franco's choice rather than hers.

She kept trying to make conversation and loosen him up, but nothing worked. She was beginning to realize how badly she'd behaved toward him over the course of the past week. *This must be how he feels every night.*

She shouldn't feel guilty. She absolutely shouldn't. This wasn't a real date. Not one of the past seven nights had been real. It had been business. All of it.

It needs to look real. I need it to look real.

As the car pulled up to the glittering Harry Winston

storefront at the corner of 5th Avenue and 57th Street—
just a stone's throw from Drake Diamonds—she turned
toward Franco.

"Are you sure you're ready for this?" she asked.

He met her gaze. The slight darkening of his irises was
the only outward sign of the numerous shots of Scotch
he'd consumed back at her apartment. Last week she
wouldn't have known him well enough to notice such a
subtle change.

"Yes. Are you?"

She felt his voice in the pit of her stomach. "Yes."

*There's still time to back out. Artem will be inside. Let
him charm the socks off the Lambertis.*

But making sure the owners of the diamond chose
to work with Drake Diamonds was her responsibility.
Not her brother's. And considering it was pretty much
her *only* responsibility, she shouldn't be passing it off
to Artem.

She'd already survived a week as Franco's faux love
interest. Surely they could pull this off for another four-
teen days. Franco would get himself together once they
were in public. He'd be his usual, charming self.

He had to.

But even walking past the mob of paparazzi gathered
in front of the arched entrance and gold-trimmed gate
at Harry Winston's storefront felt different. Franco felt
stiff beside her.

Diana missed the warmth of his hand on the small of
her back. She missed his playful innuendo. God, what
was happening to her? She hadn't actually enjoyed spending time with him.

Because that just wasn't possible.

The moment they crossed the threshold, Artem and
Ophelia strode straight toward them. When her brother

first told her they were coming, Diana had been filled with relief. Tonight was important. She could use all the reinforcements she could get. Now she wished he wasn't here to witness what suddenly felt like a huge disaster in the making.

"Diana." Artem kissed her on the cheek, then turned to shake Franco's hand. "Franco, good to see you."

The two men exchanged pleasantries while Diana greeted Ophelia. Dressed in a floor-length tulle gown, her sister-in-law looked every inch like the ballerina she'd been before taking the helm of the design department of Drake Diamonds. The diamond tiara Artem had given her as an engagement present was intricately interwoven into her upswept hair.

"You look stunning," Diana whispered as she embraced the other woman.

"Thank you, but my God. Look at yourself. You're glowing." Ophelia grinned. "That sapphire suits you."

Diana touched the deep blue stone hanging from the diamond and platinum garland around her neck. She'd worn it every night she'd been out with Franco as an homage to their billboard. "Well, don't get used to it. I doubt my brother is going to let me keep it once this is all over."

"He won't have to, remember? He won't be your boss anymore." Ophelia winked and whispered, "Girl power!"

Diana's stomach did a nervous flip. *Powerful* was the last thing she felt at the moment.

Franco bowed his head and murmured in her ear, "I'm going to fetch some champagne. I'll be right back." He was gone before she could say a word.

Artem frowned after him. "What's wrong with your boyfriend?"

Diana cast him a meaningful glance. *He's not my boyfriend.*

"Sis, I'm being serious. What's wrong with Franco?" Artem murmured.

So much for Franco's somber mood going unnoticed.

"He's fine, Artem. He's doing a wonderful job, as usual." Since when did she jump to Franco Andrade's defense?

"Really? Because he seems a little tense. You're sure he's all right?"

Ophelia looped her arm through her husband's. "Artem, leave Diana alone. She's perfectly capable of doing her job."

Thank God for sisters-in-law.

"I never insinuated she wasn't." Artem gave Diana's shoulder an affection little bump with his own. "My concern is about Andrade. He's letting this whole mess with the Kingsmen get to him."

Diana blinked. "What mess with the Kingsmen?"

"The fact that he's been dropped from the team. I'm guessing by his mood that he hasn't been reinstated yet. But I'm sure you know more about it than I do." Artem shrugged.

Franco had been *fired*?

So that's why he'd signed on with Drake Diamonds. He had as much to gain from their pretend courtship as she did.

But he was one of the best polo players in the world. Why would the Kingsmen let him go? It didn't make sense. She stared at him across the room and wondered what other secrets he was keeping.

Whatever the case, she wasn't about to tell Artem that she didn't have a clue Franco had been cut. This seemed like the sort of thing his girlfriend should know. Even a fake girlfriend.

"He's fine." She forced a smile. Doing so was becoming alarmingly easy. She probably shouldn't be so good at lying. "Really."

"How is it we're here, anyway? I feel like we've breached enemy territory," Ophelia whispered.

Diana looked around at the opulent surroundings—pale gray walls, black-and-white art deco tile floor, cut crystal vases overflowing with white hydrangeas—and tried not to be too impressed. She'd never set foot in Harry Winston before. As far as she knew, no Drake ever had. Their father was probably rolling in his grave.

"We were invited. All the high-end jewelers in the city are here. It's a power move on Harry Winston's part. I think it's their strategy to show the Lambertis that Harry Winston is the obvious choice to cut the diamond. It's bold to invite all your competitors. Confident. You have to admire it."

"Well, I don't." Diana rolled her eyes. "When you put things that way, the invitation is insulting. How dare they insinuate Drake Diamonds isn't good enough? We're the best in the world."

Artem winked at her. "My sister, a CEO in the making."

Franco returned to their group carrying two champagne flutes and offered them to Diana and Ophelia. "Ladies."

"Thank you," Ophelia said.

Diana reached for a glass and took a fortifying sip of bubbly. It was time to make her move.

She wasn't about to let the Lambertis be swayed by Harry Winston. If the egotistical power players behind this party thought she was intimidated, they were sorely mistaken. Drake Diamonds was about to totally steal the show.

We need this to look real.

She stole a glance at Franco and took another gulp of liquid courage. Someone needed to make it look real, and clearly it wasn't going to be him for once.

She moved closer to him, slipped her hand languidly around his waist and let her fingertips rest on his hip.

His champagne flute paused halfway to his lips. He glanced at her, and she let her hand drift lower until she was caressing his backside right there in Harry Winston in front of all of New York's diamond elite.

Franco cleared his throat and took a healthy gulp of champagne.

Another couple joined their small group. Artem introduced them, but their names didn't register with Diana. Her heart had begun to pound hard against her rib cage. All her concentration was centered on the feel of Franco's muscular frame beneath the palm of her hand.

"What are you doing?" he whispered.

"I'm doing exactly what you wanted. I'm making it look real." Her gaze drifted to his mouth.

He stared down at her, and the thunder in his gaze unnerved her. "This is a dangerous game you're playing, Diana. And in case you haven't noticed, I'm not in the mood for games."

She handed off her champagne flute to a waiter passing by with a silver tray. "Come with me."

"We're in the middle of a conversation." He shot a meaningful glance at Artem, Ophelia and the others.

"They won't even miss us, babe." She slid her arm through his and tugged him away.

They ended up in a darkened showroom just around the corner from the party. The only light in the room came from illuminated display cases full of gemstones and platinum. Diamonds sparkled around them like stars against the night sky.

"*Babe?* Really?" Franco arched a brow. "Why don't you just call me *honey bun*? Or *boo*?"

He could make fun of her all he wanted. At least she was trying. "You're blowing it out there. You realize that, don't you?"

A muscle flexed in his jaw. He looked as lethal as she'd ever seen him. "You're exaggerating. It's fine."

"Fine isn't good enough. Not tonight. You said so yourself." She couldn't let his icy composure get to her. Not now. "Talk to me, Franco. What has gotten into you? Did you have a bad day on the polo field or something? Did your polo pony trip over your massive ego?"

She crossed her arms and waited for him to admit the truth.

He raked a hand through his hair, and when he met her gaze, his dark eyes went soulful all of a sudden. If Diana had been looking at anyone else, she would have described his expression as broken. But that word was so wholly at odds with everything she knew about Franco, she was having trouble wrapping her head around it.

"I didn't ride today," he said quietly. "Nor have I ridden for the past month. So, no. My pony did not, in fact, trip over my massive ego."

"I know. Artem just told me." Her voice was colder than she'd intended.

She wasn't sure why she was so angry all of a sudden. She'd been the one to insist they keep things professional. And now was definitely not the time or place to discuss the fact that he was no longer playing polo.

But she couldn't seem to stop herself. The emotions she'd been grappling with since Artem so casually mentioned Franco was no longer playing with the Kingsmen felt too much like betrayal. Which didn't even make sense. Not that it mattered, though, because words were coming out of her mouth faster than she could think.

"Why didn't you say something? Why didn't you tell me?" The last thing she wanted was for him to know she cared, but the tremor in her voice was a dead giveaway.

He looked at her, long and hard, until her breath went shallow. He was so beautiful. A dark and elegant mystery.

Sometimes when she let her guard down and caught a glimpse of him standing beside her, she understood why she'd chosen him all those years ago. And despite the humiliation that had followed, she would have chosen him all over again.

"You didn't ask," he finally said.

She gave her head a tiny shake. "But…"

"But what?" he prompted.

He was going to make her say it, wasn't he? He was forcing her to go there. Again.

She inhaled a shaky breath. "But I told you about Diamond."

Their eyes met and held.

Tears blurred Diana's vision, until the diamonds around them shimmered like rain. Something moved in the periphery. She wiped a tear from her eye, and realized someone was coming.

Her breath caught in her throat.

Carla and Don Lamberti were walking straight toward them. Diana could see them directly over Franco's shoulder. Panic welled up in her chest.

The Lambertis couldn't find them like this. They most definitely couldn't see her crying. She was supposed to be in love.

In love.

For once, the thought didn't make her physically ill.

"Kiss me," she whispered.

Franco's eyes glittered fiercely in the shadows, drawing her in, pulling her toward something she couldn't quite identify. Something dark and familiar. "Diana…"

There was an ache in the way he said her name. It caught her off guard, scraped her insides.

A strange yearning wound its way through her as she reached for the smooth satin lapels of his tuxedo and balled them in her fists.

What was she doing?

"I said kiss me." She swallowed. Hard. "Now."

Franco's gaze dropped to her lips, and suddenly his chiseled face was far too close to hers. Her heart felt like it would pound right out of her chest, and she realized she was touching him, sliding her fingers through his dark hair.

She heard a noise that couldn't possibly have come from her own mouth, except somehow it had. A tremulous whimper of anticipation.

You'll regret this.

Just like last time.

Franco took her jaw in his hand and ran the pad of his thumb over her bottom lip as his eyes burned into her. His other hand slid languidly up her bare back until his fingertips found their way into her hair. He gave a gentle yet insistent tug at the base of her chignon, until her head tipped back and his mouth was perfectly poised over hers.

She felt dizzy. Disoriented. The air seemed too thick, the diamonds around them too bright. As her eyes drifted shut, she tried to remind herself of why this was happening. This wasn't fate or destiny or some misguided romantic notion.

She'd chosen it. She was in control.

It doesn't mean anything.

It doesn't.

Franco's mouth came down on hers, hot and wanting. Every bone in her body went liquid. Warmth coursed through her and, with it, remembrance.

Then there was no more thinking. No more denial. No more lying.

Not even to herself.

This kiss was different than their last.

Franco thought he'd been prepared for it. After all, this wasn't the first time his lips had touched Diana Drake's. They'd been down this road before. He remembered the taste of her, the feel of her, the soft, kittenish noise she made right when she was on the verge of surrender. These were the memories that tormented him as he'd lain awake the past seven nights until, at last, he'd fallen asleep and dreamed of a hot summer night long gone by.

But now that the past had been resurrected, he realized how wrong he'd been. A lifetime wouldn't have prepared him for a kiss like this one.

Where there'd once been a girlish innocence, Franco found womanly desire. Kissing Diana was like trying to capture light in his hands. He was wonderstruck, and rather than finding satisfaction in the warm, wet heat of her mouth, he felt an ache for her that grew sharper. More insistent. Just…

More.

He actually groaned the word aloud against the impossible softness of lips and before he knew what he was doing, he found himself pressing her against the cold glass of a nearby jewelry display case as his fingertips slid to her wrists and circled them like bracelets.

What the hell was happening?

This wasn't just different than the last time he'd kissed

Diana. It was different from any kiss Franco had experienced before.

Ever.

He pulled back for a blazing, breathless moment to look at her. He searched her face for some kind of indication he wasn't alone in this. He wanted her to feel it too—this bewildering connection that grabbed him by the throat and refused to let go. Needed her to feel it.

She gazed back at him through eyes darkened by desire. Her irises were the color of deep Russian amethysts. Rich and rare. And he knew he wasn't imagining things.

"Franco," she whispered in a voice he'd never heard her use before. One that nearly brought him to his knees. "I…"

Somewhere behind him, he heard the clearing of a throat followed by an apology. "Pardon us. We didn't realize anyone was here."

Not now.

Franco closed his eyes, desperate not to break whatever strange spell had swallowed them up. But as his pulse roared in his ears, he was agonizingly aware of Diana's wrists slipping from his grasp. And in the moment that followed, there was nothing but deep blue silence.

He opened his eyes and focused on the glittering sapphire around her neck rather than turning around. He needed a moment to collect himself as the truth came into focus.

"Mr. and Mrs. Lamberti." Diana moved away from him in a swish of tulle and pretense. "We apologize. Stay, please."

It had been an act. All of it. The caresses. The tears. The kiss.

He took a steadying inhale and adjusted his bow tie as he slowly turned around.

"Mr. Andrade, we'd know your face anywhere." A woman—Mrs. Lamberti, he presumed—offered her hand.

He gave it a polite shake, but he couldn't seem to make himself focus on her face. He couldn't tear his gaze away from Diana, speaking and moving about as if she'd orchestrated the entire episode.

Probably because she had.

"Franco, darling. The Lambertis are the owners of the diamond I've been telling you about." Diana turned toward him, but didn't quite meet his gaze.

Look at me, damn it.

"It's a pleasure to meet you both," he said.

"The pleasure is ours. Everywhere we turn, we see photos of the two of you. And now here you are, as real as can be." Mr. Lamberti laughed.

"Real. That's us. Isn't it darling?" Franco reached for Diana's hand, turned it over and pressed a tender kiss to the inside of her wrist.

Her pulse thundered against his lips, but it brought him little satisfaction. He no longer knew what to believe.

How had he let himself be fool enough to fall for any of this charade?

"It's nice to see a couple so in love." Mrs. Lamberti brought her hand to her throat. "Romance is a rarity these days, I'm afraid."

"I couldn't agree more." Franco gave Diana's waist a tiny squeeze.

Diana let out a tiny laugh. He'd been around her long enough now to know it was forced, but the Lambertis didn't appear to notice.

They continued making small talk about their diamond as Diana's gaze flitted toward his. At last. Franco saw an unmistakable hint of yearning in the violet depths of her eyes. He knew better than to believe in it, but it made his chest ache all the same.

"Wait until you see it." Mr. Lamberti shook his head. "It's a sight to behold."

"I hope I do get to see it someday," Diana said. "Sooner rather than later."

Good girl.

She was going in for the kill, as she should. That baseball-sized rock was the reason they were here, after all. Another polo player was wearing Franco's jersey, and the prospect of keeping up the charade alongside Diana suddenly seemed tortuous at best.

But he'd be damned if it was all for nothing.

"We'll be making an announcement about the diamond tomorrow, and I think you'll be pleased." Mrs. Lamberti reached to give Diana's arm a pat. "Off the record, of course."

Diana beamed. "My lips are sealed."

Mr. Lamberti winked. "In the meantime, we should be getting back to the party."

"It was lovely to meet you both," Diana said.

Franco murmured his agreement and bid the couple farewell.

The moment they were gone, he stepped away from Diana. He needed distance between them. Space for all the lies they'd both been spinning.

"Did you hear that?" she whispered, eyes ablaze. "They're making an announcement tomorrow. They're going to pick us, aren't they?"

Us.

He nodded. "I believe they are."

"We did it, Franco. We did it." She launched herself at him and threw her arms around his neck.

Franco allowed himself a bittersweet moment to savor

the feel of her body pressed against his, the soft swell of her breasts against his chest, the orchid scent of her hair as it tickled his nose.

He closed his eyes and took a deep inhale.

So intoxicating. So deceptively sweet.

He reached for her wrists and gently peeled her away.

"Franco?" She stood looking at him with her arms hanging awkwardly at her sides.

He shoved his hands in his pockets to prevent himself from touching her. "Aren't you forgetting something? We're alone now. There's no reason to touch me. No one is here to see it."

She flinched, and as she stared up at him, the look of triumph in her eyes slowly morphed into one of hurt. Her bottom lip trembled ever so slightly.

Nice touch.

"But I…"

He held up a hand to stop her. There was nothing to say. He certainly didn't need an apology. They were both adults. From the beginning, they'd both known what they were getting into.

Franco had simply forgotten for a moment. He'd fallen for the lie.

He wouldn't be making that mistake again.

"It's fine. More than fine." He shrugged one shoulder and let his gaze sweep her from top to bottom one last time before he walked away. "Smile, darling. You're getting everything you wanted."

Chapter Nine

A *Page Six* Exclusive Report

New York's own Drake Diamonds has been chosen by the Lamberti Mining Company as the jeweler to cut the world's largest diamond. The massive rock was recently unearthed from a mine in Botswana and weighs in at 1,100 carats. Rumor has it Ophelia Drake herself will design the setting for the record-sized diamond, which will go on display later this month at the Metropolitan Museum of Art.

No word yet on the exact plans for the stone, but we can't help but wonder if an engagement ring might be in the works. Diamond heiress Diana Drake stepped out again last night with her current flame, polo-playing hottie Franco Andrade, at a private party at Harry Winston. Cell phone photos snapped by guests show the couple engaged in some scorching hot PDA. Caution: viewing these pictures will have you clutching your Drake Diamonds pearls.

Chapter Ten

Pop!

The store hadn't even opened yet, and already the staff of Drake Diamonds was on its third bottle of champagne. The table in the center of the Drake-blue kitchen was piled with empty Waterford glasses and stacks upon stacks of newspapers.

Drake Diamonds and the Lamberti diamond were front-page news.

"Congratulations, Diana." Ophelia clinked her glass against Diana's and took a dainty sip of her Veuve Clicquot. "Well done."

"Thank you." Diana grinned. It felt good to succeed at something again. Although it probably should have felt better than it actually did.

Stop. You earned this. You have nothing to feel guilty about.

She swallowed and concentrated her attention on Ophelia. "Congratulations right back at you. Have you started sketching designs for the stone yet?"

Ophelia laughed. "Our involvement has only been official for about an hour, remember?"

Diana lifted a dubious brow. "So until now you've given the Lamberti diamond no thought whatsoever?"

Ophelia's expression turned sheepish. "Okay, so maybe I've been working on a few preliminary designs… just in case."

Diana laughed. "It never hurts to be prepared."

Artem's voice boomed over the chatter in the crowded room. "Okay, everyone. The doors open in five minutes. Party time's over."

Ophelia set her glass down on the table. "I'm off, then. Duty calls."

"Something tells me your job won't be in jeopardy if you hang out a little while longer," Diana said in a mock whisper.

"I know, but I seriously can't wait to get to work on the design now that I know I'm actually going to get my hands on that diamond. I almost can't believe it's happening. It hasn't quite sunk in yet." Her eyes shone with wonder. "This is real, isn't it?"

Diana took a deep breath.

This is real, isn't it?

The memory of Franco's touch hit her hard and fast… the dance of his fingertips moving down her spine…the way his hands had circled her wrists, holding her still as he kissed her…

She was beginning to lose track of what was genuine and what wasn't.

"Believe it. It's real." She swallowed around the lump in her throat and gave Ophelia one last smile before she found herself alone in the kitchen with Artem.

Diana reached for one of the tiny cakes they kept on hand decorated to look like Drake-blue boxes and bit into it. Ah, comfort food. She could use a sugary dose of comfort right now, although she wasn't quite sure why.

You're getting everything you wanted.

Why had she felt like crying when Franco uttered those words the night before?

"Can we talk for a moment, sis?" Artem sank into one of the kitchen chairs.

"Sure." Diana sat down beside him. She was in no hurry to get back to Dalton's empty apartment. She'd rather be here, where things were celebratory.

When she'd first read the news that the Lambertis had, indeed, chosen Drake Diamonds, she'd been propped up in bed sipping her morning coffee and reading her iPad. Seeing the official press announcement hadn't given her the thrill she'd been anticipating.

If she was being honest, it almost felt like a letdown. She didn't want to examine the reasons why, and she most definitely didn't want to be alone with her thoughts. Because those thoughts kept circling back to last night.

Kissing Franco. The feel of his mouth on hers, wet and wanting. The look on his face when he spotted the Lambertis.

"You okay?" Artem looked at her, and the smile that had been plastered on his face all morning began to fade.

Diana leaned over and gave him an affectionate shoulder bump. "Of course. I'm more than okay."

But she couldn't quite bring herself to meet his gaze, so she focused instead on the table in front of them and its giant pile of newspapers. The corner of *Page Six* poked out from beneath the *New York Times*, and she caught a glimpse of the now-familiar grainy image of herself and Franco kissing.

Her throat grew tight.

She squeezed her eyes closed.

"I hope that's true, sis. I do. Because I have some concerns," Artem said.

Diana's eyes flew open. "Concerns. About what?"

He paused and seemed to be choosing his words with great care.

"You and Franco," he said at last.

She blinked. "Me and Franco?"

Artem's gaze flitted to *Page Six*. "I'm starting to wonder if this charade has gone too far."

"You can't be serious. The whole plan was your idea." She waved a hand at the empty bottles of Veuve Clicquot littering the kitchen. "And it worked. We did it, Artem."

"Yes. So far it's been a remarkable success." He nodded thoughtfully. "For the company. But some things are more important than business."

Who was his guy and what had he done with her brother? Everything they'd done for the past few weeks had been for the sake of Drake Diamonds. "What are you getting at, Artem?"

But she didn't have to ask. Deep down, she knew.

"This." He pulled the copy of *Page Six* out from beneath the *Times* and tossed it on top of the pile.

She didn't want to look at it. It hurt too much to see herself like that.

"It was just a kiss, Artem." Her brother was watching her closely, waiting for her to crack, so she forced herself to look at the photograph.

It was worse than the enormous billboard in Times Square. So much worse. Probably because this time she hadn't been acting. This time, she'd wanted Franco to take her to bed.

Her self-control was beginning to slip. Along with her

common sense. The kiss had pushed her right over the edge. It had made her forget all the reasons she despised him. Even now, she was still struggling to remember his numerous bad qualities. It was like she was suffering from some kind of hormone-induced amnesia.

Artem lifted a brow. Thank God he couldn't see inside her head. "That looks like more than *just a kiss* to me."

"As it should." She crossed her arms, leaned back in her chair and glared at him. He was pulling the overprotective brother act on her now? *Seriously?* "The whole point of our courtship is to make people believe it's real. Remember?"

"Of course I remember. And yes, I'm quite aware it was my idea. But I never said anything about kissing." He shot her a meaningful glance. "Or making out in dark corners. Where was this picture taken? Because this looks much more like a private moment than a public relations party stunt."

It took every ounce of will power Diana possessed to refrain from wadding up the paper and throwing it at him. "I can't believe what I'm hearing. For your information, the only reason I kissed him was because the Lambertis were walking straight toward us. I had to do something. I didn't want them to think Franco and I were arguing."

"Were you?" Artem raised his brows. "Arguing?"

She sighed. "No. Yes. Well, sort of."

"If there's nothing actually going on between you and Franco, what do you have to argue about?"

Diana shifted in her chair. Maybe Artem *could* see inside her head.

Of course he couldn't. Still, she should have had a dozen answers at the ready. People who weren't lovers argued all the time, didn't they?

But she couldn't seem capable of coming up with a

single viable excuse. She just sat there praying for him to stop asking questions.

Finally, Artem put her out of her long, silent misery. "Is there something you should tell me, Diana?"

"There's nothing going on between Franco and me. I promise." Why did that sound like a lie when it was the truth?

Worse, why did the truth feel so painful?

You do not *have feelings for Franco Andrade. Not again.*

"You're a grown-up. I get that. It's just that you're my sister. And as you so vehemently pointed out less than two weeks ago, Franco is a man whore." Artem looked pointedly at the photo splashed across *Page Six*. "I'm starting to think this whole farce was a really bad idea."

"Look, I appreciate the concern. But I can handle myself around Franco. The kiss was my idea, and it meant nothing." It wasn't supposed to, anyway. "End of story."

She stood and began clearing away the dirty champagne flutes and tossing the empty Veuve Clicquot bottles into the recycling bin. She couldn't just sit there and talk about this anymore.

"Got it." To Diana's great relief, Artem rose from his chair and headed toward the hallway.

But he lingered in the doorway for a last word on the subject. "You know, we can stop this right now. You've proven your point. You have a lot to offer Drake Diamonds. I was wrong to put you in this position."

"What?" She turned to face him.

Surely she hadn't heard him right.

He nodded and gave her a bittersweet smile. "I was wrong. And I'm sorry. Say the word, and your fake relationship with Franco can end in a spectacular or not-so-spectacular fake breakup. Your choice."

Her choice.

But she didn't have a choice. Not really.

A week ago, she would have given anything to get Franco out of her life. Now it didn't seem right. Not when she'd gotten what she needed out of the deal and Franco apparently hadn't.

Smile, darling, you're getting everything you wanted.

He'd played his part, and she owed it to him to play hers. Like or not, they were stuck together until the gala.

"You know that's not possible, Artem. We haven't even finalized things with the Lambertis. They could take their diamond and hightail it over to Harry Winston."

"I know they could. I'm beginning to wonder if it would really be so awful if they did." Artem sighed, and she could tell just by the look on his face that he was thinking about the photo again. *Page Six.* The kiss. "Is it really worth all of this? Is anything?"

"Absolutely." She nodded, but a tiny part of her wondered if he might be right. "You're making a big deal out of nothing. I promise."

It was too late for doubts. She'd made her bed, and now she had to lie in it. Preferably alone.

Liar.

Artem nodded and looked slightly relieved, which was still a good deal more relieved than Diana actually felt. "I suppose I should know better than to believe everything I read in the papers, right?"

She picked up the copy of *Page Six*, intent on burying it at the bottom of the recycling bin. It trembled in her hand.

She tossed it back onto the surface of the table and crossed her arms. "Exactly."

How was she going to survive until the gala? She

dreaded seeing Franco later. Now that he seemed intent on not kissing her again, it was all she could think about.

Even worse, how could she look herself in the mirror when she could barely look her brother in the eye?

Franco gave the white ball a brutal whack with his mallet and watched it soar through the grass right between the goal posts at the far end of the practice field on his Hamptons property.

Another meaningless score.

His efforts didn't count when he was the only player on the field. But he needed to be here, as much for his ponies as for himself. They needed to stay in shape. They needed to be ready, even if it was beginning to look less and less like they'd be returning to the Kingsmen.

Last night had been a reality check in more ways than one. He wasn't sure what had enraged him more—seeing his number on another player's chest or realizing Diana had asked him to kiss her purely for show.

He knew his fury was in no way rational, particularly where Diana was concerned. Their entire arrangement was based on deception. He just hadn't realized he would be the one being deceived.

But even that shouldn't have mattered. He shouldn't have cared one way or another whether Diana really wanted his mouth on hers.

And yet…he did care.

He cared far more than he ever thought he would.

I'm not yours, Mr. Andrade. Never have been, never will be.

Franco wiped sweat from his brow with his forearm, rested his mallet over his shoulder and slowed his horse to an easy canter. As he watched the mare's thick muscles move beneath the velvety surface of her coat, he thought of Diamond.

He thought about Diana's dead horse every time he rode now. He thought about the way she could barely seem to make herself say Diamond's name. He thought about her reluctance to even hold Lulu. She was afraid of getting attached to another animal. That much was obvious. Only one thing would fix that.

She needed to ride again.

Of course, getting Diana back in the saddle was the last thing he should be concerned about when he couldn't even manage to get himself back on his team.

That hadn't stopped him from dropping Lulu off at Drake Diamonds before he'd headed to the Hamptons. Artem's secretary, Mrs. Barnes, had looked at him like he was crazy when he'd handed her the puppy and asked her to give it to Diana. Maybe he *had* gone crazy. But if he'd forced the dog on Diana himself, she would have simply refused.

She needed the dog. Franco had never in his life met anyone who'd needed another living creature so much. Other than himself when he'd been a boy...

Maybe that's why he cared so much about helping Diana. Despite their vastly different upbringings, he understood her. Whether she wanted to admit it or not.

Let it go. You have enough problems of your own without adding Diana Drake's to the mix.

She didn't want his help, anyway, and that was fine. He was finished with her. As soon as the gala was over and once he had his job back, they'd never see each other again. He was practically counting the minutes.

"Andrade," someone called from the direction of the stalls where Franco's other horses were resting and munching on hay in the shade.

Franco squinted into the setting sun. As he headed off the field, he spotted a familiar figure walking toward him across the emerald-green grass.

Luc.

Franco slid out of his saddle and passed the horse's reins to one of his grooms. *"Gracias."*

It wasn't until he'd closed the distance between himself and his friend that he recognized a faint stirring in his chest. Hope. Which only emphasized how pathetic his situation was at the moment. If the Kingsmen wanted him back, the coach wouldn't send Luc. Santos would be here. Maybe even Ellis himself.

He removed his helmet and raked a hand through his dampened hair. "Luc."

"Hola, mano." Luc nodded toward the goal, where the white ball still sat in the grass. "Looking good out there."

"Thanks, man." An awkward silence settled between them. Franco cleared his throat. "How was the scrimmage yesterday?"

Luc's gaze met his. Held. "It was complete and utter shit."

"I wish I could say I was surprised. Gustavo Anca. Really? He's a six-goal player." Not that a handicap of six was bad. Plenty of world-class players were ranked as such. But Franco's handicap was eight. On an average day, Gustavo Anca wouldn't even be able to give him a run for his money. On a good day, Franco would have wiped the ground with him.

Luc nodded. "Well, it showed."

Franco said nothing. If Luc was hoping for company in his commiseration, he'd just have to be disappointed.

"Look, Franco. I came here to tell you I can't let this go on. Not anymore." Franco shook his head, but before he could audibly protest, Luc held up a hand. "I don't want to hear it. We've waited long enough. The Kingsmen are going to lose every damn game this season if we don't get you back. I'm going to Jack Ellis first thing in the morning, and I'm going to tell him the truth."

"No, you're not," Franco said through gritted teeth.

He'd made a promise, and he intended to keep it. Even if that promise had sent his life into a tailspin.

"It's not up for discussion. I don't know why I let you talk me into this in the first place." Luc shook his head and dropped his gaze to the ground.

He knew why. They both did.

"It's too late to come clean." Would Ellis even believe them if they told the truth this late in the game? Would anyone? Franco doubted it, especially in Diana's case. She'd made up her mind about him a long time ago.

But why should her opinion matter? She had nothing to do with this. Their lives had simply become so intertwined that Franco could no longer keep track of where his ended and hers began.

"I don't believe that. It's not too late. I love you like a brother. You know I do. You don't owe me a thing, Franco. You never did, and you certainly don't owe me this." Luc looked up again with red-rimmed eyes.

Why was he making this so difficult? "What's done is done. Besides, what's the point? If you tell the truth, you know what will happen."

"Yeah, I do. You'll be in, and I'll be out, which is precisely the way it should be." Luc blew out a ragged exhale. "This is bigger than the two of us, Franco. It's about the team now."

He was hitting Franco where it hurt, and he knew it. The team had always come first for Franco. Before the women, before the partying, before everything.

Until now.

Some things were bigger. Luc was family. Without Luc, Franco would never have played for the Kingsmen to begin with. He would have never even left Buenos Aires. He'd probably still be sleeping in a barn at night, or worse. He might have gone back to where he'd come from. Barrio de la Boca.

He liked to think that horses had saved him. But, in reality, it had been Luc.

He exhaled a weary sigh. "What's the point anymore? The Kingsmen can't lose you, either. If you do this, the team will suffer just as much as it already has."

"No. It won't." A horse whinnied in the distance. Luc smiled. "You're better than I am. You always were."

Franco's chest grew tight, and he had the distinct feeling they weren't talking about polo anymore.

"I came here as a courtesy, so you'd be prepared when Ellis calls you tomorrow. This is happening. Get ready." Luc turned to go.

Franco glared at the back of his head. "And if things change between now and tomorrow?"

Luc turned around. Threw his hands in the air. "What could possibly change?"

Everything.

Everything could change.

And Franco knew just how to make certain it would.

Chapter Eleven

Diana was running out of ball gowns, but that wasn't her most pressing problem at the moment. That notable distinction belonged to the problem that had four legs and a tail and had peed on her carpet three times in the past two hours.

As if Franco hadn't already made her life miserable enough, now he'd forced the puppy upon her. After Diana's awkward encounter with Artem in the Drake Diamonds kitchen, Mrs. Barnes had waltzed in and thrust the little black pug at her. She'd had no choice but to take the dog home. Now here they sat, waiting for Ophelia to show up with a new crop of evening wear.

Diana had never needed so many gowns, considering thus far she'd spent the better part of her life in riding clothes. But she'd worn nearly every fancy dress she owned over the course of her faux love affair with Franco, and she wanted to make an impression tonight. More than ever before.

The Manhattan Ballet's annual gala at Lincoln Center was one of the most important social events on the Drake Diamonds calendar. Ophelia had once been a prima ballerina at the company. Since coming to Drake Diamonds, she'd designed an entire ballet-themed jewelry collection. Naturally, the store and the Manhattan Ballet worked closely with each other.

Which meant Artem and Ophelia would be at the gala. So would the press, obviously. Coming right on the heels of the Lamberti diamond announcement, the gala would be a big deal. Huge.

It would also be the first time Diana had seen Franco since The Kiss.

But of course that had nothing to do with the fact that she wanted to look extra spectacular. Then again, maybe it did. A little.

Okay, a lot.

She wanted to torture him. First he'd had the nerve to get upset that she'd asked him to kiss her, and now he'd dropped a puppy in her lap. Who behaved like that?

Lulu let out a little yip and spun in circles, chasing her curlicue tail. The dog was cute. No doubt about it. And Diana didn't completely hate her tiny, velvet-soft ears and round little belly. If she'd had any interest in adopting a puppy, this one would definitely have been a contender.

But she wasn't ready to sign on for another heartbreak in the making. Wasn't her heart in enough jeopardy as it was?

Damn you, Franco.

"Don't get too comfortable," she said.

Lulu cocked her head, increasing her adorable quotient at least tenfold.

Ugh. "I mean it. You're not staying."

One night. That was it. Two, tops.

The doorbell rang, and Lulu scrambled toward the door in a frenzy of high-pitched barks and snorting noises. Somehow, her cuteness remained intact despite the commotion.

"Calm down, you nut." Diana scooped her up with one hand, and the puppy licked her chin.

Three nights...maybe. Then she was absolutely going back to Franco's bachelor pad.

"A puppy!" Ophelia grinned from ear to ear when Diana opened the door. "This must the one I read about in the paper."

Diana sighed. She'd almost forgotten that every detail of her life was now splashed across *Page Six*. Puppy included. "The one and only."

"She's seriously adorable. Franco has good taste in dogs. He can't be all bad." Ophelia floated through the front door of Diana's apartment with a garment bag slung over her shoulder. She might not be a professional ballerina anymore, but she still moved liked one, even with a baby strapped to her chest.

Diana rolled her eyes and returned Lulu to the floor, where she resumed chewing on a rawhide bone that was three times bigger than her own head. "I'm pretty sure even the devil himself can appreciate a cute puppy."

"The last time I checked, the devil wasn't into rescuing homeless animals." Point taken.

Ophelia tossed the garment bags across the arm of the sofa. "Enough about your charming puppy and equally charming faux boyfriend. I've come with fashion reinforcements, as you requested."

"And you brought my niece." Diana eyed the baby.

There was no denying she was precious. She had Artem's eyes and Ophelia's delicate features. Perfect in every way.

Diana just wasn't one of those women who swooned every time she saw a baby. Probably because she'd never pictured herself as a mother. Not after the nightmare of a marriage her own mother had endured.

"Here, hold her." Ophelia lifted little Emma out of the baby sling and handed her to Diana.

"Um, okay." She'd never really held Emma before. She'd oohed and aahed over her. Plenty of times. But other than the occasional, affectionate pat on the head, she hadn't actually touched her.

She was lighter than Diana had expected. Soft. Warm.

"Wow," she said as Emma took Diana's hand in her tiny grip.

"She growing like a weed, isn't she?" Ophelia beamed at her baby.

Diana studied the tender expression on her face. It wasn't altogether different from the one she usually wore when she looked at Artem. "You're completely in love with this baby, aren't you?"

"It shows?"

"You couldn't hide it if you tried." Diana rocked Emma gently from side to side until the baby's eyes drifted closed.

"It's crazy. I never pictured myself as a mother." Ophelia shrugged one of her elegant shoulders.

Diana gaped at her. "You're kidding."

"Nope. I never expected to get married, either. Your brother actually had to talk me into it." She grinned. "He can be very persuasive."

"I had no idea. You and Artem are like a dream couple."

"Things aren't always how they appear on the outside. But I don't need to tell you that." Ophelia gave her a knowing look.

Diana swallowed. "I should probably be an expert on the subject by now."

"I love your brother, and I adore Emma. I've never been so happy." And it showed. Bliss radiated from her sister-in-law's pores. "This life just isn't one I ever imagined for myself."

Maybe that's how it always worked. Maybe one day Diana would wake up and magically be ready to slip one of those legendary Drake diamonds onto her ring finger.

Doubtful, considering she was terrified of keeping the puppy currently making herself at home in Diana's borrowed apartment. "Can I ask you a question?"

"Sure. That's what sisters are for," Ophelia said.

"What changed? I mean, I know that sounds like a difficult question..."

Ophelia interrupted her with a shake of her head. "No. It's not difficult at all. It's simple, really. Love changed me."

"Love," Diana echoed, as the front-page image of herself being kissed within an inch of her life flashed before her eyes.

Please. That wasn't love. It wasn't even lust. It was pretend.

Keep telling yourself that.

"I fell in love, and that changed everything." Ophelia regarded her for a moment. "I may be way off base here, but do these questions have anything to do with Franco?"

"Hardly." Diana laughed. A little too loudly.

She couldn't ignore the truth anymore...she had a serious case of lust for the man. Everyone in New York knew she did. It was literally front-page news.

But she would have to be insane to fall in love with him. She didn't even like him. When she'd had her accident, she hadn't hit her head so hard that she lost her memory.

The day after she'd lost her virginity to Franco had been the most humiliating of her life. She'd known what she'd been getting into when she slept with him. Or thought she had, anyway.

She'd been all too aware of his reputation. Franco Andrade was a player. Not just a polo player...a *player* player. In truth, that was why she'd chosen him. His ridiculous good looks and devastating charm hadn't hurt, obviously. But mainly she'd wanted to experience sex without any looming expectation of a relationship.

She'd been twenty-two, which was more than old enough to sleep with a man. It hadn't been the sex that frightened her. It had been the idea of belonging to someone. Someone who would cheat, as her father had done for as long she could remember.

Franco had been the perfect candidate.

She'd expected hot, dirty sex. And she'd gotten it. But he'd also been tender. Unexpectedly sweet. Still, it was her own stupid fault she'd fallen for the fantasy.

She'd rather die than make that mistake again.

"Nothing at all? If you say so. There just seems to be a spark between you two," Ophelia said. "I'm pretty sure it's visible from outer space."

Diana handed the baby back to her sister-in-law. "Honestly, you sound like Artem. Did he put you up to this?"

Ophelia held Emma against her chest and rubbed her hand in soothing circles on the back of the baby's pastel pink onesie. Her brow furrowed. "No, actually. We haven't even discussed it."

Diana narrowed her gaze. "Then why are you asking me about Franco?"

"I told you. There's something special when you're together." She grinned. "Magic."

Like the kind of magic that made people believe in relationships? Marriage? *Family?* "You're seeing things. Seriously, Ophelia. You're looking at the world through love-colored glasses."

Ophelia laughed. "I don't think those are a thing."

"Trust me. They are. And you're wearing them." Diana slid closer to the garment bag and pulled it onto her lap. "A big, giant pair."

Ophelia shook her head, smiled and made cooing noises at the baby. Which pretty much proved Diana's point.

"By the way, there's only one dress in there." Ophelia nodded at the garment bag. "It's perfect for tonight. You'll look amazing in it. I was afraid if I brought more options, you wouldn't have the guts to wear this one. And you really must."

"Why am I afraid to look at it now?" Diana unzipped the bag and gasped when she got a glimpse of silver lamé fabric so luxurious that it looked like liquid platinum.

"Gorgeous, isn't it? It belonged to my grandmother. She wore it to a ballet gala herself, back in the 1940s."

Diana shook her head. "I can't borrow this. It's too special."

"Don't be silly. Of course you can. That's why I brought it." Ophelia bit her lip. "Franco is going to die when he sees you in it."

First Artem. Now Ophelia. When had everyone started believing the hype?

"Not if I kill him first," she said flatly.

The more she thought about his reaction last night, the angrier she got. How dare he call her out for doing exactly the same thing he'd been doing every night for a week?

Did he think the nicknames, the lingering glances and the way he touched her all the time didn't get to her? Newsflash: they did.

Sometimes she went home from their evenings together and her body felt so tingly, so alive that she had trouble sleeping. Last night, he'd even shown up in her dreams.

Her head spun a little just thinking about it. "I have no interest in him whatsoever."

"Yeah, you mentioned that." Ophelia smirked.

A telltale warmth crept into Diana's cheeks. "I'm serious. I'm not interested in marriage or babies, either. Certainly not with him."

"I believe you." Ophelia nodded in mock solemnity.

Even the puppy stopped chewing on her bone to stare at Diana with her buggy little eyes.

"Stop looking at me like that. Both of you. I assure you, it will be a long time before you see an engagement ring on my finger. And *if* that ever happens, the ring won't be from Franco Andrade."

He was about as far from being husband material as she was from being wife material. Diana should know...

She'd spent an embarrassing amount of time thinking it through.

Dios mio.

A little under twenty-four hours had hardly been enough time to rid Franco of the memory of kissing Diana. But the moment he set eyes on her in her liquid silver dress, everything came flooding back. The taste of her. The feel of her. The sound of her—the catch of her breath in the moment their lips came together, the tremble in her voice when she'd asked him to kiss her.

No amount of willful forgetting would erase those

memories. Certainly not while Diana was standing beside him in the lobby of Lincoln Center looking like she'd
been dipped in diamonds.

A strand of emerald-cut stones had been interwoven
through the satin neckline of her gown and arranged
into a glittering bow just off-center from the massive
sapphire draped around her neck. She looked almost too
perfect to touch.

Which made Franco want to touch her all the more.

"You're staring," she said, without a trace of emotion
in her voice. But the corner of her lush mouth curved into
a grin that smacked of self-satisfaction.

Franco had a mind to kiss her right there on the spot.

He smiled tightly, instead. She hadn't said a word yet
about the puppy stunt, which he found particularly interesting. But she was angry with him. For what, exactly,
he wasn't quite sure. He was beginning to lose track of
all the wrongs he'd committed, and tomorrow would be
far worse. She just didn't know it yet.

He cleared his throat. "I can't seem to look away. Forgive me."

She shrugged an elegant shoulder. The row of diamonds woven through the bodice of her dress glittered
under the chandelier overhead. "You're forgiven."

Forgiven.

The word and its myriad of implications hung between them.

He raised a brow. "Am I?"

He knew better than to believe it.

"It's a figure of speech. Don't read too much into it."
She shifted her gaze away from him, toward the crowd
assembled in the grand opera-house lobby.

Franco slipped an arm around her and led her down
the red-carpeted stairs toward the party. He'd been dread-

ing the Manhattan Ballet gala since the moment he'd woken up this morning. He'd lost his head at the Harry Winston party. He couldn't make a mistake like that again. Not now. Not when there was so much riding on his fake relationship. The Drakes may have gotten what they wanted, but Franco hadn't.

He would, though.

By tomorrow morning, everything would change.

"Diana, nice to see you. You look beautiful." Artem greeted his sister with a smile and a kiss on the cheek. When he turned toward Franco, his smile faded. "Franco."

No handshake. No small talk. Just a sharp look that felt oddly like a warning glare.

"Artem." Franco reached to shake his hand.

Something felt off, but Franco couldn't imagine why. Artem Drake should be the happiest man in Manhattan right now. His family business was front-page news. Everywhere Franco turned, people were talking about the Lamberti diamond. A few news outlets had even rechristened it the Lamberti-Drake diamond.

Would the Lambertis have even chosen Drake Diamonds if not for the pretend love affair? Franco wholeheartedly doubted it. The Lambertis had looked awfully comfortable at Harry Winston.

Until the kiss.

The kiss had been the deciding factor. Or so it seemed.

The way Franco saw things, Artem Drake should be high-fiving him right now.

Maybe he was just imagining things. After all, last night had been frustrating on every possible level. Most notably, sexually. Franco still couldn't think straight. Especially when Diana's silvery image was reflected back at him from all four walls of the mirrored room. There was simply no escaping it.

"Nice to see you again, Franco," Ophelia said warmly.

"Thank you. It's a pleasure to be here." He moved to give Ophelia a one-armed hug. Artem's gaze narrowed, and he tossed back the remainder of the champagne in his glass.

"I'm sure it is," Artem muttered under his breath.

Franco cast a questioning glance at Diana. He definitely wasn't imagining things.

"Shall we go get a drink, darling?" she said.

"Yes, let's." A drink was definitely in order. Possibly many drinks.

Once they'd taken their place in line at the bar, Franco bent to whisper in Diana's ear, doing his best not to let his gaze wander to her cleavage, barely covered by a wisp of pale gray chiffon fabric. It would have been a tall order for any man. "Are you planning on telling me what's troubling your brother? Or do I have to remain in the dark since I'm just a pretend boyfriend?"

Diana's bottom lip slipped between her teeth, a nervous habit he'd spent far too much time thinking about in recent days. After a pause, she shrugged. "I don't know what you're talking about."

"Do you really think I can't tell when you're lying?" He leaned closer, until his lips grazed the soft place just below her ear. "Because I can. I know you better than you think, Diana. Your body betrays you."

Her cheeks flared pink. "I'm going to pretend you didn't just say that."

"I'm sure you will." He looked pointedly at her mouth. "We both know how good you are at pretending."

"May I help you?" the bartender asked.

"Two glasses of Dom Pérignon, please," Franco said without taking his eyes off Diana.

"You're impossible," she said through gritted teeth.

"So you've told me." He handed her one of the two saucer-style glasses of champagne the bartender had given him. "Multiple times."

Her eyes flashed like amethysts on fire. "You've had your hands all over me for weeks, and I'm not allowed to be affected by it. But I kiss you once, and you completely lose it. You're acting like the world's biggest hypocrite."

The accusation should have angered him. At the very least, he should have been bothered by the fact that she was one hundred percent right. He was definitely acting like a hypocrite, but he couldn't seem to stop.

He'd thought the kiss was real. He'd *wanted* it to be real. He wanted that more than he'd wanted anything in a long, long time.

But he was so shocked by Diana's startling admission that he couldn't bring himself to be anything but satisfied at the moment. Satisfied and, admittedly, a little aroused.

"You like it when I touch you," he stated. It was a fact. She'd said so herself.

"No." She let out a forced laugh. "Hardly."

Yes.

Definitely.

"It's nothing to be ashamed of," he said, reaching for her with his free hand and cupping her cheek. "Would you like it if I touched you now?"

He lowered his gaze to her throat, where he could see the flutter of her pulse just above her sapphire necklace. In the depths of the gemstone, he spied a hint of his own reflection. It was like looking into a dark and dangerous mirror.

"Would *you* like it if I kissed you?" She lifted an impertinent brow.

Franco smiled in response. If she wanted to rattle him, she'd have to try harder.

"I'd like that very much. I see no need to pretend otherwise." He sipped his champagne. "I'd just prefer the kiss to be genuine."

"For your information, that kiss was more genuine than you'll ever know. Which is exactly why Artem is angry." Her gaze flitted toward her brother standing on the other side of the room.

Franco narrowed his gaze at Artem Drake. "Let me get this straight. Your brother wanted us to make everyone believe we were a couple, and now he's angry because we've done just that?"

Diana shook her head. "Not angry. Just concerned."

"About what exactly?"

She cleared her throat and stared into her champagne glass. "He thinks we've taken things too far."

Too far.

As irritating as Franco found Artem Drake's assessment of the situation, Diana's brother might be on to something.

He and Diana had crossed a line. Somewhere along the way, they'd become more to each other than business associates with a common goal.

Perhaps they'd been more than that all along. Every time Franco caught a glimpse of that massive billboard in Times Square he found himself wondering if they were somehow finishing what they'd started three years ago. Like time had been holding its breath waiting for the two of them to come together again.

He knew it was crazy. He'd never believed much in fate. Was it fate that he'd been born into the worst slum in Buenos Aires? No, fate wouldn't be so cruel. He was in control of his life. No one else.

But kissing Diana had almost been enough to make a believer out of him.

They weren't finished with each other. Not yet.

"And what about you, Diana? Do you think we've taken things too far?" He leveled his gaze at her, daring her to tell the truth.

Not far enough. Not by a long shot.

Chapter Twelve

When had things gotten so confusing?

A month ago, Diana had been bored out of her mind selling engagement rings, and now she was standing in the middle of the biggest society gala of the year being interrogated by Franco Andrade.

He shouldn't be capable of rattling her the way he did. The questions he was asking should have had easy answers.

Had they taken things too far?

Absolutely. That had happened the instant he'd fastened the sapphire around her neck. She should never have agreed to pose with him. That one photo had set things in motion that were now spinning wildly out of control.

Then she'd gone and exacerbated things by agreeing to be his pretend girlfriend. Worse yet, since she'd asked him to kiss her, she'd begun to doubt her motivation.

Did she really want to be co-CEO of Drake Diamonds? Had she ever? Or had the promotion simply been a convenient excuse to spend more time with Franco?

Surely not. She hated him. She hated everything about him.

You like it when I touch you.

Damn him and his smug self-confidence. She would have loved to prove him wrong, except she couldn't. She loved it when he touched her. The barest graze of his fingertips sent her reeling. And now she'd gone and admitted it to his face.

She lifted her chin and met his gaze. "Of course we haven't taken things too far. We're both doing our jobs. Nothing more."

"I see. And last night your job included kissing me." The corner of his mouth curved into a half grin, and all she could think about was the way that mouth had felt crashing down on hers.

"You seriously need to let that go." How could she possibly forget it when he kept bringing it up? "Besides, *you* kissed *me*."

"At your request." He lifted a brow.

Her gaze flitted to his bow tie. Looking him in the eye and pretending she didn't want to kiss him again was becoming next to impossible. "Same thing."

"Hardly. When I decide to kiss you, you'll know it. There will be no mistaking my intention." There was a sudden edge to his voice that reminded her of Artem's offer to end this farce once and for all.

Say the word, and your fake relationship with Franco can end in a spectacular or not-so-spectacular fake breakup. Your choice.

Her choice.

She'd had a choice all along, whether she wanted to admit it or not. And she'd chosen Franco. Again.

She was beginning to have the sinking feeling that she always would.

She'd tried her best to keep up her resistance. She really had. The constant onslaught of his devastating good looks paired with the unrelenting innuendo had taken its toll. But his intensity had dealt the deathblow to her defenses.

He cared. Deeply. He cared about Diamond. He cared about why she refused to ride again. That's why he'd forced her hand about the puppy. She'd known as much the moment that Mrs. Barnes had dropped the wiggling little pug into her arms.

Despite his playboy reputation and devil-may-care charm, Franco Andrade cared. He even cared about the kiss.

A girl could only take so much.

"What are you waiting for, then?" she asked, with far more confidence than she actually felt. She reminded herself that she knew exactly what she was doing. But she'd thought the same thing three years ago, hadn't she? "Decide."

A muscle tensed in Franco's jaw.

Then, in one swift motion, he gathered their champagne glasses and deposited them on a nearby tray. He took her hand and led her through the crowded lobby, toward a shadowed corridor. For once, Diana was unaware of the eyes following them everywhere they went. She didn't care who saw them. She didn't care about the Lambertis. She didn't care about the rest of the Drakes. She didn't even care about the press.

The only thing she cared about was where Franco was taking her and what would happen once they got there.

Decide, she'd implored. And decide he had.

"Come here," he groaned, and the timbre in his voice seemed to light tiny fires over every exposed surface of her skin.

He pushed through a closed door, pulling her alongside him, and suddenly they were surrounded on all sides by lush red velvet. Diana blinked into the darkness until the soft gold glow of a dimly lit stage came into focus.

He'd brought her inside the theater, and they were alone at last. In a room that typically held thousands of people. It felt strangely intimate to be surrounded by row upon row of empty seats, the silent orchestra pit and so much rich crimson. Even more so when Franco's hand slid to cradle the back of her head and his eyes burned into hers.

"This is for us and us alone. No one else." His gaze dropped to her mouth.

Diana's heart felt like it might beat right out of her chest. *You can stop this now. It's not too late.*

But it was, wasn't it? She'd all but dared him to kiss her, and she wasn't about to back down now.

She lifted her chin so that his mouth was perfectly poised over hers. "No one else."

He grazed her bottom lip with the pad of his thumb, then bent to kiss her. She expected passion. She expected frantic hunger. She expected him to crush his mouth to hers. Instead, the first deliberate touch of his lips was gentle. Tender. So reverent that she knew within moments it was a mistake.

She'd fought hard to stay numb after her fall. The less she felt, the better. So long as she kept the world at arm's length, she'd never have to relive the nightmare of what she'd been through. But tenderness—especially coming from Franco—had a way of dragging her back to life, whether or not she was ready.

"Diana," he whispered, and his voice echoed throughout the room with a ghostly elegance that made her head spin.

She'd wanted him to kiss her again since the moment their lips parted the night before. She'd craved it. But as his tongue slid into her mouth, hot and hungry, she realized she wanted more. So much more.

Was it possible to relive only part of the past? Could she sleep with him again and experience the exquisite sensation of Franco pushing inside her without the subsequent heartache?

Maybe she could. She wasn't a young, naive girl anymore. She was a grown woman. She could take him to bed with her eyes wide open this time, knowing it was purely physical and nothing more.

My choice.

He pushed her against a velvet wall and when his hands slid over the curves of her hips, she realized she was arching into him, pressing herself against the swell of his arousal. She could spend all the time in the world weighing the consequences, but clearly her body knew what it wanted. And it had made up its mind a long time ago.

Your body betrays you.

He'd been right about that, too, damn him.

"Franco," she murmured against his mouth. Was that really her voice? She scarcely recognized herself anymore.

But that only added to the thrill of the moment. She was tired of being Diana Drake. Disciplined athlete. Diamond heiress and future CEO. Perpetual good girl.

She wanted to be bad for a change.

"Yes, love?" His mouth was on her neck now, and his hands were sliding up the smooth silver satin of her dress to cup her breasts.

She was on fire, on the verge of asking him to make love to her right there in the theatre.

No. If she was going to do this, she wanted it to last. And she wanted to be the one in control. She refused to get hurt this time. She couldn't. Wouldn't.

But as she let her hands slip inside Franco's tuxedo jacket and up his solid, muscular back, she didn't much care about what happened tomorrow. How much worse could things get, anyway?

"Come home with me, Franco."

Franco half expected her to change her mind before they made it back to her apartment. If she did, it would have killed him. But he'd honor her decision, obviously.

He wanted her, though. He wanted her so much it hurt.

By the time they reached the threshold of her front door, he was harder than he'd ever been in his life. Diana gave no indication that she'd changed her mind. On the contrary, she wove her fingers through his and pulled him inside the apartment. The door hadn't even clicked shut behind them before she draped her arms around his neck and kissed him.

It was a kiss full of intention. A prelude. And damned if it didn't nearly drag him to his knees.

"Diana," he groaned into her mouth.

Everything was happening so fast. Too fast. He'd waited a long time for this. Three excruciating years. Waiting…wanting.

"Slow down, love." He needed to savor. And she needed to be adored, whether she realized it or not.

She pulled back to look at him, eyes blazing. "Just so you know, this is hate sex."

He met her gaze. Held it, until her cheeks turned a telltale shade of pink.

Keep on telling yourself that, darling.

He drew his fingertip beneath one of the slender straps of her evening gown, gave it a gentle tug and watched as it fell from her shoulder, baring one of her breasts. He didn't touch her, just drank in the sight of her—breathless, ready. Her nipple was the palest pink, as delicate as a rose petal. When it puckered under his gaze, he finally looked her in the eye.

"Hate sex. Obviously." He gave her a half smile. "What else would it be?"

"I'm serious. I loathe you." But as she said those words, she slid the other spaghetti strap off her shoulder and let her dress fall to the floor in a puddle of silver satin.

I don't believe you. He stopped short of saying it. Let her think she was the one in control. Franco knew better. "I don't care."

History swirled in the air like a lingering perfume as she stood before him, waiting. Naked, save for the dark, sparkling sapphire resting against her alabaster skin.

She was gorgeous. Perfect. More perfect than he remembered. She'd changed in the years since he'd seen her this way. There was a delicious curve to her hips that hadn't been there before, a heaviness to her breasts. He wouldn't have thought it possible for her to grow more beautiful. But she had.

Either that, or this meant more than he wanted to admit.

Hate sex. Right.

She gathered her hair until it spilled over one shoulder,

then reached behind her head to unfasten the sapphire-and-diamond necklace.

"Leave it." He put his hands on the wall on either side of her, hemming her in. "I like you like this."

"Is that so?" She reached for the fly of his tuxedo pants and slipped her hand inside.

Franco closed his eyes and groaned. He was on the verge of coming in her hand. As much as he would have liked to blame his lack of control on his recent celibacy, he knew he couldn't. It was her. Diana.

What was happening to him? To them?

"Diana," he whispered, pushing her bangs from her eyes.

He searched her gaze, and he saw no hatred there. None at all. Only desire and possibly a touch of fear. But wasn't that the way it should be? Shouldn't they both be afraid? One way or another, this would change things.

His chest felt tight. Full. As if a blazing sapphire like the one around Diana's neck had taken the place of his heart and was trying to shine its way out.

"I need you, Franco." Not want. *Need.*

"I know, darling." He grazed her plump bottom lip with the pad of his thumb. She drew it into her mouth, sucked gently on it.

Holy hell.

"Bedroom. Now." Every cell in his body was screaming for him to take her against the wall, but he wanted this to last. If they were going to go down this road together…again…he wanted to do it right this time. Diana deserved as much.

She released her hold on him and ducked beneath one of his arms. Then she sauntered toward a door at the far end of the apartment without a backward glance.

Franco followed, unfastening his bow tie as his gaze

traveled the length of her supple spine. She moved with the same feline grace that haunted his memory. He'd thought perhaps time had changed the way he remembered things, as time so often did. Surely the recollection of their night together shone brighter than the actual experience.

But he realized now that he'd been wrong. She was every bit as special as he remembered. More so, even.

He placed his hands on her waist and turned her around so she was facing him. She took a deep, shuddering inhale. The sapphire rose and fell in time with the beating of her heart.

She was more bashful now, with the bed in sight. Which made it all the more enticing when her hands found his belt. But her fingers had started trembling so badly that she couldn't unfasten the buckle.

"Let me," he said, covering her hands with his own.

He took his time undressing. He needed her to be sure. More than sure.

But once he was naked before her, her shyness fell away. She stared at his erection with hunger in her gaze until Franco couldn't wait any longer. He needed to touch her, taste her. Love her.

He hesitated as he reached for her.

This isn't love. It can't be.

The line between love and hate had never seemed so impossibly small. As his hands found the soft swell of her breasts, he had the distinct feeling they were crossing that line. He just didn't know which side they'd been on, which direction they were going.

He lowered his head to draw one of her perfect nipples into his mouth, and she gasped. An unprecedented surge of satisfaction coursed through him at the sound of her letting go. At last.

That's it, Wildfire. Let me take you there.

He teased and sucked as she buried her hands in his hair, shivering against him. He reached to part her thighs, and she let out a soft, shuddering moan. As he slipped a finger inside her, he stared down at her, fully intending to tell her they were just getting started. But when she opened her eyes, he said something altogether different.

"You have the most beautiful eyes I've ever seen. Like amethysts."

The words slipped out of his mouth before he could stop them. He loved her eyes. He always had. But this wasn't the sort of thing people said during hate sex. Even though he wasn't at all convinced that's what they were doing.

Still. This wasn't the time to turn into a romantic. If she needed to pretend this was nothing but a meaningless release, fine. He'd give her whatever she needed.

"There's a legend about amethysts, you know," she whispered, grinding against him as he moved his finger in and out.

"Tell me more."

He guided her backward until her legs collided into the bed and she fell, laughing, against the down comforter. He stretched out beside her and ran his fingertips in a leisurely trail down the perfect, porcelain softness of her belly.

Then he was poised above her with his erection pressing against her thigh, and her laughter faded away. Her eyes turned dark, serious.

"According to legend, they're magic. The ancient Romans believed amethysts could prevent drunkenness. Some still say they do."

Franco didn't believe it. Not for a minute. He felt

drunk just looking into the violet depths of those eyes. "Nonsense. You're intoxicating."

"Franco."

He really needed to stop saying such things. But he couldn't seem to stop himself.

If the circumstances had been different, he would have said more. He would have told her he'd been an idiot all those years ago. He would have admitted that this charade they'd both been dreading had been the most fun he'd had in ages. He might even have told her exactly what he thought of her breathtaking body…in terms that would have made her blush ruby red.

But circumstances weren't different. They'd been pretending for weeks. He'd just have to pretend the words weren't floating around in his consciousness, looking for a way out.

There was one thing, however, he definitely needed to say. Now, because come morning it would be too late. "Diana, there's something I need to tell you."

She shook her head as her hands found him and guided him toward her entrance. "No more words. Please. Just this."

Then he was pushing into her hot, heavenly center, and he couldn't have uttered another word if he tried.

What am I doing?

Diana's subconscious was screaming at her to stop. But for once in her life, she didn't want to listen. She didn't want to worry about what would happen tomorrow. Her entire life had been nothing but planning, practice, preparation. Where had all of that caution gotten her?

Nothing had gone as planned.

She was supposed to be on her way to the Olympics.

And here she was—in bed with Franco Andrade. Again. By her own choosing.

On some level, she'd known this was coming. She might have even known it the moment he'd first strolled into Drake Diamonds. She most definitely had known it when he'd kissed her at Harry Winston.

But the kiss had been her idea, too, hadn't it?

Oh, no.

"Oh, yes," she heard herself whisper as he slid inside her. "Yes, please."

It doesn't mean anything. It's just sex. Hate sex.

"Look at me, Wildfire. Let me see those beautiful eyes of yours." Franco's voice was tender. So tender that her heart felt like it was being ripped wide open.

She opened her eyes, and found him looking down at her with seriousness in his gaze. He kept watching her as he began to move, sliding in and out, and Diana had to bite her bottom lip to stop herself from crying out his name.

After months and months of working so hard to stay numb, to guard herself against feeling anything, she was suddenly overwhelmed with sensation. The feel of his body, warm and hard. The salty taste of his thumb in her mouth. The things he was saying—sweet things. Lovely things. Things she'd remember for a long, long time. Long after their fake relationship was over.

It was all too much. Much more than she could handle. The walls she'd been so busy constructing didn't stand a chance when he was watching her like that. Studying her. Delighting in the pleasure he was giving her.

"That's it, darling. Show me." Franco smiled down at her. It was a wicked smile. A knowing one.

He didn't just want her naked. He wanted her exposed

in every way. She could see it in the dark intent in his gaze, could feel it with each deliberate stroke.

This didn't feel like hate sex. Far from it. It felt like more. Much more.

It felt like everything.

It felt…real.

"Franco." His name tasted sweet in her mouth. Like honey. But as it fell from her lips in a broken gasp, something inside her broke along with it.

She shook her head, fighting it. She couldn't be falling for him. Not again.

It's all pretend. Just make believe.

But there was nothing make believe about his lips on her breasts as he bowed his head to kiss them. Or the liquid heat flowing through her body, dragging her under.

She arched into him, desperate, needy. He gripped her hips, holding her still as he tormented her with his mouth and his cock, with the penetrating awareness of his gaze.

This was all her doing. He knew it, and so did she.

They hadn't been destined to fall into bed together. Not then. Not now. She'd wanted him. For some nonsensical reason, she still did. Every time he touched her, every time he so much as glanced in her direction, she burned for him.

She'd made this happen. She'd seduced him. Not the other way around.

It wasn't supposed to be this way. It was supposed to be quick. Simple. But every time her climax was in reach, he slowed his movements, deliberately drawing things out. Letting her fall.

And fall.

Until everything began to shimmer like diamond dust, and she could fall no farther.

She began to tremble as her hips rose to meet his,

seeking release. Franco reached for her hands and pinned them over her head, their fingers entwined as he thrust into her. Hard. Relentless.

"My darling," he groaned, pressing his forehead against hers.

I'm not yours.

She couldn't make herself say it. Because if she did, it would feel more like a lie than any of the others she'd told in recent days. Whether she liked it or not, he held her heart in his hands. He always had, and he always would.

The realization slammed into her, and there was no use fighting it. Not now. Not when everything seemed so right. For the first time in as long as she could remember, she felt like herself again.

Because of him.

He paused and kissed her, letting her feel him pulse and throb deep inside. It was exquisite, enough to make her come undone.

"This is what you do to me, Diana." His voice was strained, pierced with truth. She felt it like an arrow through the heart. "No one else. Only you."

In the final, shimmering moment before she came apart, her gaze met his. And for the first time it didn't feel as though she was looking at the past.

In the pleasured depths of his eyes, she could see a thousand tomorrows.

Chapter Thirteen

Diana woke to a familiar buzzing sound. She blinked, disoriented. Then she turned her head and saw Franco asleep beside her—*naked*—and everything that had transpired the night before came flooding back.

They'd had sex. Hot sex. Tender sex. Every sort of sex imaginable.

She squeezed her eyes shut. Maybe it had all been a dream. A very realistic, very *naughty* dream.

The buzzing sound started again, and she sat up. Something glowed on the surface of her nightstand. Her cell phone. She squinted at it and saw Artem's name illuminated on the tiny screen.

Why was Artem calling her at this hour?

She couldn't answer the call. *Obviously.* But when she grabbed the phone to silence it, she saw that this was his third attempt to reach her.

Something was wrong.

"Hello?"

"Diana?" Artem's CEO voice was in overdrive…at six in the morning. Wonderful. "Why are you whispering?"

"I'm not," she whispered, letting her gaze travel the length of Franco's exposed torso. God, he was beautiful. *Too beautiful.*

Had her tongue really explored all those tantalizing abdominal muscles? Had she licked her way down the dark line of hair that led to his manhood?

Oh, God, she had.

She yanked one of the sheets from the foot of the bed and wrapped it around herself. She couldn't be naked while she talked to her brother. Not while the face of Drake Diamonds was sexually sated and sleeping in her bed.

"Diana, what the hell is going on?" She couldn't think of a time when she'd heard Artem so angry.

He'd found out.

Oh, no.

She slid out of bed, tiptoed out of the room and closed the door behind her. Her confusion multiplied at once when she saw heaps of feathers all over the living room. The air swirled with them, like she'd stepped straight from the bedroom into a snowfall.

A tiny black flash bounded out of one of the piles.

Lulu.

The puppy had disemboweled every pillow in sight while Diana had been in bed with Franco. Now her life was a literal mess as well as a metaphorical one. Perfect.

"Look, I can explain," she said, scooping the naughty dog into her arms.

Could she explain? Could she really?

I know I told you there was nothing going on between Franco and me, but the truth is we're sleeping together.

Slept together. Past tense. She'd simply had a bout of temporary insanity. It wouldn't happen again, obviously. It couldn't.

Hate sex. That's all it was. She'd made that very clear, and she'd stick to that story until the day she died. Admitting otherwise would be a humiliation she just couldn't bear.

"You can explain? Excellent. Because I'd really like to hear your reasoning." Artem sighed.

This was weird. And overly intimate, even by the dysfunctional Drake family standards.

"Okay...well..." She swallowed. How was she supposed to talk about her weakness for Franco's sexual charms to her *brother*? "This is a little awkward..."

Lulu burrowed into Diana's chest and started snoring. Destroying Dalton's apartment had clearly taken its toll.

"As awkward as reading about my sister's engagement in the newspaper?" Artem let out a terse exhale. "I think not."

Engagement?

Diana's heartbeat skidded to a stop.

Engagement?

Lulu gave a start and blinked her wide, round eyes.

"W-w-what are you talking about?" Diana's legs went wobbly. She tiptoed to the sofa and sank into its fluffy white cushions.

She hoped Franco was sleeping as soundly as he'd appeared. The last thing she needed was for him to walk in on this conversation.

"You and Franco are engaged to be married. It's in every newspaper in the city. It's also all over the television. Look, I know I gave you free reign as VP of public relations, but don't you think this is going a bit far?"

"Yes. I agree, but..."

"But what? The least you could have done was tell me your plans. We just talked about your relationship with Franco yesterday morning, and you never said a word about getting engaged." Artem sounded like he was on the verge of a heart attack.

Diana felt like she might be having one herself. "Calm down, Artem. It's not real."

"I know that. Obviously. But when are you going to clue everyone else in on that fact? While you're walking down the aisle?"

A jackhammer was banging away in Diana's head. She closed her eyes. Suddenly she saw herself drifting slowly down a path strewn with rose petals, wearing a white tulle gown and a sparkling diamond tiara in her hair.

What in the world?

She opened her eyes. "That's not what I mean. The announcement itself isn't real. There's been a mistake. A horrible, horrible mistake."

"Are you sure?" There wasn't a trace of relief in Artem's voice. "Because the article in the *Times* includes a joint statement from you and Franco."

"I'm positive. A statement? That's not possible. They made it up. You know how the media can be." But he'd said the *Times*, not *Page Six* or the *Daily News*.

The *New York Times* had fact checkers. It was a respectable institution that had won over a hundred Pulitzer Prizes. A paper like that didn't fabricate engagement announcements.

Now that she thought about it, the weddings section of the *Times* was famous in its own right. Society couples went to all sorts of crazy lengths to get their engagement announced on those legendary pages.

Her gaze drifted to the closed bedroom door. Ice trickled up her spine.

He wouldn't.

Would he?

No way. Franco would be just as horrified at this turn of events as she was. He wouldn't want the greater population of New York thinking he was off the market.

You and I are monogamous.

She'd actually laughed when he'd said those words less than two weeks ago. But she'd never pressed for an explanation.

This can't be happening. I can't be engaged to Franco Andrade.

Sleeping with him was one thing. Letting him slip a ring on her finger was another thing entirely.

Forget Franco. Forget Artem. Forget Drake Diamonds. This was her life, and she shouldn't be reading about it in the newspapers.

She took a calming breath and told herself there was nothing to worry about. There had to be a reasonable explanation. She didn't have a clue what that might be, but there had to be one.

But then she remembered something Franco had said the night before. Right before he'd entered her. She remembered the rare sincerity in his gaze, the gravity of his tone.

I need to tell you something.

The engagement was real, wasn't it? The statement in the *Times* had come from Franco himself. He'd even tried to warn her, and she'd refused to listen.

She hadn't wanted words. She'd wanted to feel him inside her so badly that nothing else mattered.

And now she was going to kill him.

"Artem, I have to go. I'll call you back."

She pressed End and threw her phone across the room. She glared at the closed bedroom door.

Had Franco lost his mind? They could *not* be engaged. They just couldn't. Even a fake engagement was out of the question.

Of course it's fake. He doesn't want to marry you any more than you want to marry him.

That was a good thing. A very good thing.

She wasn't sure why she had to keep reminding herself how good it was over and over and over again.

The tightness in Diana's chest intensified. She pressed the heel of her palm against her breastbone, closed her eyes and focused on her breath. She was on the verge of a full-fledged panic attack. All over an engagement that wasn't even real. If that didn't speak volumes about her attitude toward marriage, nothing would.

Breathe. Just breathe.

Maybe she was losing it over nothing. Maybe whatever Franco had wanted to tell her had nothing at all to do with the press. Maybe the *Times* wedding page had, indeed, made an unprecedented error.

She looked at the dog, because that's how low she'd sunk. She was seeking validation from a puppy. "Everyone makes mistakes. It could happen, right?"

Lulu stretched her mouth into a wide, squeaky yawn.

"You're no help at all," Diana muttered, focusing once again on the closed bedroom door.

There was only one person who could help her get to the bottom of this latest disaster, and that person didn't have four legs and a curlicue tail.

Franco slept like the dead.

He opened his eyes, then let them drift shut again. He hadn't had such a peaceful night's rest in months. He forgot all about the Kingsmen, Luc's ultimatum and the overall mess his personal life had become. It was remarkable what great sex could do for a man's state of mind. Not just great sex. Phenomenal sex. The best sex of his life.

Sex with Diana Drake.

"Franco!"

He squinted, fighting the morning light drifting through the floor to ceiling windows of Diana's bedroom.

Someone was yelling his name.

"Franco, wake up. Now." A pillow smacked his face.

He opened his eyes. "It's a little early in the morning for a pillow fight, Wildfire. But I'm game if you are."

"Of course you think that's what this is. For your information, it's not." She stood near the foot of the bed, staring daggers at him. For some ridiculous reason, she'd yanked one of the sheets off the bed and wrapped it around herself. As if Franco hadn't seen every inch of that gorgeous body. Kissed it. Worshipped it. "And I've asked you repeatedly not to call me that."

"Not last night," he said, lifting a brow and staring right back at her.

What had he missed? Because this wasn't the same Diana he'd taken to bed the night before, the same Diana who'd cried his name as he thrust inside her. It sure as hell wasn't the same Diana who'd told him how much she'd needed him as she unzipped his fly.

"I'm being serious." She tugged the bedsheet tighter around her breasts.

Franco pushed himself up to a sitting position, rested his back against the headboard and yawned. When his eyes opened, he caught Diana staring openly at his erect cock. *That's right, darling. Look your fill.* "See something you like?"

Her gaze flew upward to meet his. Franco was struck once again by just how beautiful she was, even flustered and disheveled from a night of lovemaking. He preferred her like this, actually. Fiery and flushed. He just wished she'd drop the damned sheet and climb back in bed.

"Cover yourself, please," she said primly.

"Sure. So long as I can borrow your tent." He stared pointedly at her bedsheet-turned-ballgown.

"Nice try." She let out a laugh. Laughter had to be a good sign, didn't it? "But I'll keep it, thank you very much."

Franco shrugged. "Fine. I'll stay like this, then."

Her gaze flitted once again to his arousal. If she kept looking at him like that, he might just come without even touching her. "Suit yourself. Naked or not, you have some explaining to do."

"What have I done this time?"

"I think you know." She titled her head and flashed him a rather deadly-looking smile. "My dear, darling *fiancé*."

Fiancé.

Shit.

The engagement announcement. He'd meant to tell her about it before it hit the papers. He'd even tried to bring it up the night before, hadn't he? "So you've seen the *Times*, I presume?"

"Not yet. But Artem has. He's also seen the *Observer*, *Page Six* and the *Daily News*. It's probably the cover story on *USA TODAY*." She threw her hands up, and the sheet fell to the floor. But she'd worked herself into such a fury, she didn't even notice. "Explain yourself, Franco."

"Explain myself?" He climbed out of bed, strode toward her and picked up the pile of Egyptian cotton at her feet. Pausing ever so briefly to admire her magnificent breasts, he wrapped the sheet around her shoulders and covered her again.

Her cheeks went pink. "Thank you." For a brief second, he saw a hint of tenderness in her gaze. Then it vanished as quickly as it had appeared. "You heard me. I can't believe I even have to ask this question, but why does everyone on planet Earth suddenly think I'm going to marry you?"

He sighed and rested his hands on her shoulders, a sliver of relief working its way through him when she didn't pull away. He reminded himself the engagement was a sham. Their whole relationship was a sham. None of this should matter.

"Because I told them we're engaged."

"Oh, my God, I knew it." She began to tremble all over.

Franco slid his hands down her arms, took her hands in his and pulled her close. "No need to panic, Wildfire. It's nothing. Just part of the ruse."

A spark of something flared low in his gut. Something that felt far too much like disappointment. He'd never imagined he would one day find himself consoling a woman so blatantly horrified at the idea of being his betrothed. The fact that the woman was Diana Drake made it all the more unsettling.

She wiggled out of his grasp and began to pace around the spacious bedroom. The white bedsheet trailed behind her like the train on a wedding gown. "What were you thinking? I can't believe this."

She took a break from her tirade to regard him through narrowed eyes. For a moment, Franco thought she might slap him. Again. "Actually, I can. I don't know why I thought I could trust you. About anything."

He nearly flinched. But he knew he had no right.

As mornings after went, this one wasn't stellar. He wasn't sure what he'd expected to happen after last night.

The line between truth and lies had blurred so much he couldn't quite think straight, much less figure out whatever was happening between him and Diana. But he was certain about one thing—he'd seen the same fury in her gaze once before.

Of course he remembered what he'd said. He'd regretted the words the instant they'd slipped from his mouth.

He'd known he needed to do something dire the moment he'd woken up beside her, all those years ago. She'd looked too innocent, too beautiful with her dark hair fanned across his chest. Too damned happy.

Strangely enough, he'd felt almost happy, too. Sated. Not in a sexual way, but on a soul-deep level he hadn't experienced before. It had frightened the hell out of him.

He didn't do relationships. Never had. Never would. It wasn't in his blood. Franco had never even known who his father was, for crying out loud. As a kid, he'd watched a string of men come in and out of his mother's life. In and out of her bed. When the men were around, his mother was all smiles and laugher. Once they'd left— and they always left…eventually—the tears came. Days passed, sometimes weeks, when his mother would forget to feed him. Franco had gotten out the first chance he had. He'd been on his own since he was eleven years old. As far as he knew, his mother had never come looking for him.

He wouldn't know how to love a woman even if he wanted to. Which he didn't. If his upbringing had taught him anything, it was that self-reliance was key. He didn't want to need anyone. And he most definitely didn't want anyone needing him. Especially not a diamond heiress who'd opened her eyes three years ago and suddenly looked at him as if he'd hung the moon.

He'd done what he'd needed to do. He'd made certain she'd never look at him that way again.

Come now, Diana. We both know last night didn't mean anything. It was nice, but I prefer my women more experienced.

She'd had every right to slap him. He'd deserved worse.

"You can breathe easy. I have no intention of actually marrying you," he said.

"Good." She laughed again. Too lively. Too loud.

"Good," he repeated, sounding far harsher than he intended.

What exactly was happening?

He didn't want to hurt her. Not this time.

"What you fail to understand is that I don't want to be *engaged* to you, either." She held up a hand to stop him from talking, and the sheet slipped again, just enough to afford him a glimpse of one, rose-hued nipple.

His body went hard again. Perfect. Just perfect.

Diana glanced down at him, then back up. There wasn't a trace of desire in her eyes this time. "I can't talk to you about this while you're naked. Get dressed and meet me in the kitchen."

She flounced away, leaving Franco alone in a room that throbbed with memories.

He shoved his legs into his tuxedo pants from the night before and splashed some water on his face in the bathroom. When he strode into the kitchen, he found her standing at the coffeemaker, still dressed in the bedsheet. Lulu was frolicking at her feet, engaged in a fierce game of tug-of-war with a corner of the sheet. The dog didn't even register his presence. Clearly, the two of them had bonded, just as he'd hoped. He should have been happy. Instead, he felt distinctly outnumbered.

Diana poured a steaming cup, and Franco looked at it longingly.

She glanced at him, but didn't offer him any.

Not that he'd expected it.

"I'm sorry," he said quietly.

She lifted a brow. "For what, exactly?"

For everything.

He sighed. "I should have given you a heads-up."

Her expression softened ever so slightly. "You tried."

"I could have tried harder." He took a step closer and caught a glimpse of his reflection—moody and blue—in the sapphire still hanging around her neck.

She backed up against the counter, maintaining the space between them. "Just tell me why. I need to know."

A muscle flexed in Franco's jaw. This wasn't a conversation he wanted to have the morning after they'd slept together. Or ever, to be honest. "My chances of getting back on the Kingsmen will be much greater if I'm engaged."

She blinked. "That doesn't make sense."

Don't make me explain it. He gave her a look of warning. "It matters. Trust me."

"Trust you?" She set her coffee cup on the counter and crossed her arms. "You've got to be kidding."

"For the record, it would be even better if we were married." What was he saying? He was willing to go pretty far to get his job back, but not that far.

Diana gaped at him. "I can't believe this. You're a polo player, not a priest. What does your marital status have to do with anything…" Her eyes grew narrow. "Unless… oh, my God…"

Franco held up his hands. "I can explain."

But he couldn't. Not in any kind of way that Diana would find acceptable. Even if he broke his promise to

Luc and told her the truth, she'd never believe him. Not in this lifetime.

"You did something bad, didn't you? Some kind of terrible sexual misconduct." She fiddled with the stone around her neck, and Franco couldn't help but notice the way her fingers trembled. He hated himself a little bit right then. "Go ahead and tell me. What was it? Did you sleep with someone's wife this time?"

He looked at her long and hard.

"You did," she said flatly. The final sparks of whatever magic had happened between them the night before vanished from her gaze. All Franco could see in the depths of her violet eyes was hurt. And thinly veiled hatred. "How could I be such an idiot? *Again?* Who was it?"

Less than an hour ago, she'd been asleep with her head on his chest as their hearts beat in unison. How had everything turned so spectacularly to crap since then?

A grim numbness blossomed in Franco's chest. He knew exactly what had gone wrong. The past had found its way into their present.

Didn't it always?

He'd written the script of this conversation years ago.

He wanted to sweep her hair from her face and force her to look him in the eye so she could see the real him. He wanted to take her back to bed and whisper things he'd never told anyone else as he pushed his way inside her again.

He wanted to tell her the truth.

"It was Natalie Ellis," he said quietly.

"Ellis? As in *Jack* Ellis?" She pulled the bedsheet tighter around her curves, much to Franco's dismay. "You had an affair with your boss's wife? That's despicable, Franco. Even for you. You must think I'm the biggest fool you've ever met."

"I'm the fool," he said.

She shook her head. "Don't, okay? Just don't be nice to me right now. Please."

"Diana…"

Before he could say another word, the cell phone in the pocket of his tuxedo pants chimed with an incoming text message.

Damn it.

Diana rolled her eyes. Lulu barked at the phone in solidarity. "Go ahead. Look at it. It's probably from one of your married girlfriends. Don't let me stand in your way."

Franco didn't make a move. Whoever was texting him could wait.

His phone chimed again.

Diana glared at him. "You disgust me, Franco. And I swear, if you don't answer that right now, I'm going to reach into your pocket and do it for you."

Franco sighed and looked at the phone's display.

See you at practice today at 10 sharp. Come ready to play. Don't be late.

The engagement announcement had worked. He was back on the team.

And back on Diana's bad side.

She hated him.

Again.

Chapter Fourteen

Diana didn't bother returning Artem's call. Instead, she decided to get dressed and go straight to Drake Diamonds and explain things in person.

But there was no actual explanation, was there? She was engaged. *Pretend* engaged, but still. Engaged.

She had no idea what she was going to say to her brother. If she admitted she'd known nothing about the engagement, it would look like she'd lost control over her own public image. And as VP of public relations, the Drake image was pretty much the one thing she was responsible for. On the other hand, if she pretended she'd known all about the faux engagement, Artem would be furious that she'd kept him in the dark. It was a catch-22. Either way, she was screwed.

She had to face him sooner or later, though. She desperately wanted to get it over with. Maybe she'd go ahead and tell him he'd been right. The charade had gone too far. She should end it. The Lambertis would walk away, of course. And she'd never be co-CEO. She might not even be able to keep her current position. Artem had told her she'd proven herself, but that had been before the engagement fiasco. Who knew what would happen if she broke up with her fake boyfriend now? She could end up right back in the Engagements department.

But that would be better than having to walk around pretending she was going to get married to Franco, wouldn't it?

Yes.

No.

Maybe.

The only thing she knew for certain was that she shouldn't have slept with him the night before. How could she have been so monumentally stupid? She deserved to be fired. She'd fire herself if she could.

He'd carried on an affair with a married woman. That was a new low, even for a playboy like Franco. And it made him no different than her father.

So, of course she'd jumped into bed with him. God, she hated herself.

"Is he in?" she asked Mrs. Barnes, glancing nervously at the closed office door. What was her brother doing in there? He rarely kept his door closed. He was probably throwing darts at the wedding page of the *Times*. Or possibly interviewing new candidates for the VP of public relations position. She shook her head. "Never mind, I know he wants to see me. I'm going in."

"Wait!" Mrs. Barnes called after her.

It was too late, though. Diana had already flung Artem's door open and stormed inside. Artem sat behind his desk, just as she'd expected. But he wasn't alone. Carla and Don Lamberti occupied the two chairs opposite him.

Ophelia was also there, standing beside the desk with what looked like a crystal baseball.

The diamond.

It was even larger than Diana had imagined. She paused just long enough to take in its impressive size and to notice the way it reflected light, even in its uncut state. It practically glowed in Ophelia's hands.

All four heads in the office turned in her direction.

Any and all hopes she had of sneaking out the door unnoticed were officially dashed. "I'm so sorry. I didn't mean to interrupt."

She practically ran out of the office, but of course she wasn't fast enough.

"Diana, what a nice surprise!" The brightness of Carla Lamberti's smile rivaled that of her diamond.

Diana forced a smile and cursed the four-inch Jimmy Choos that had prevented her speedy getaway. Why, oh why, had she worn stilettos?

Probably because there had been a dozen paparazzi following her every move all day, thanks to Franco's little engagement announcement. The doorman had warned her about the crowd of photographers gathered outside her building before she'd left the apartment. If her picture was going to be splashed on the front page of every newspaper in town, she was going to look decent. Especially considering that Franco's walk of shame out of her building earlier in the morning had already turned up on no less than four websites.

Not only had she made the terrible mistake of sleeping with him, but now everyone with a Wi-Fi connection knew all about it.

"It looks like you're busy. I just needed to talk to Artem, but it can wait." She turned and headed for the door.

"Don't be silly. Join us. We insist. Right, Mr. Drake?" Carla glanced questioningly at Artem, who nodded his agreement. "I want to hear all about your engagement to Mr. Andrade. I can't seem to pry a word out of your brother."

The older woman turned to face Diana again. Behind her back, Artem crooked a finger at Diana, then pointed to the empty place on his office sofa.

Okay, then. Diana took a deep breath, crossed the room and sat down.

"So, tell us everything. As I said, Artem won't breathe a word about your wedding." Carla cast a mock look of reprimand in Artem's direction.

Your wedding.

Diana did her best not to vomit right there on the Drake-blue carpet.

Ever the diplomat, Ophelia jumped into the conversation. "I'm sure Diana and Franco would like to keep some things private. It's more special that way, don't you think?"

Diana released a breath she hadn't realized she'd been holding. She owed Ophelia. Big-time.

Mr. Lamberti rested a hand on his wife's knee. "Goodness, dear. Leave Diana alone. She's here to join our meeting about the plans for the diamond, not to discuss the intimate details of her personal life."

Carla let out a laugh and shrugged. "I suppose that's true. Please pardon my manners. I was just so excited to read about your engagement in the paper this morning. I knew from the moment I saw you and Franco together at the Harry Winston party that you were destined to be together. The way that man looks at you…"

Her voice drifted off, and she sighed dreamily.

Artem cleared his throat. "Shall we proceed with the

meeting? Ophelia has drawn up some beautiful designs for the stone."

"Of course. Just one more question. I promise it's the last one." Mrs. Lamberti's gaze shifted once again to Diana. She prayed for the sofa to somehow open itself up and swallow her whole, but of course it didn't. "It's true, isn't it? Are you and Mr. Andrade really engaged to be married?"

This was the opening she'd been waiting for. She could end the nonsensical charade right here and now, and she'd never even have to set eyes on Franco again. All she had to do was say no. The papers had made a mistake. She and Franco weren't engaged. In fact, they were no longer seeing each other. The Lambertis would obviously be disappointed, but surely they wouldn't pack up their diamond and leave.

Would they?

Diana swallowed. *Do it. Just do it.*

Why was she hesitating? This was her chance to get her life back. It was now or never. If she didn't fess up, she'd be stuck indefinitely as Franco's fiancée.

Speak now or forever hold your peace.

She was already thinking in terms of wedding language. Perfect. She may as well climb right into a Vera Wang.

She glanced from the Lambertis to Artem to Ophelia. This would have been so much easier without an audience. And without that ridiculously huge diamond staring her in the face. It was blinding. Which was the only rational explanation for the next words that came out of her mouth.

"Of course it's true." She smiled her most radiant, bridal grin. "We're absolutely engaged."

* * *

All the way to Bridgehampton, Franco waited for the other shoe to drop. He fully expected to arrive at practice only to be ousted again. The moment he'd left Diana's apartment, she'd no doubt picked up the phone and called every newspaper in town to demand a retraction.

He wasn't sure what to make of the fact that she hadn't. His cell phone sat on the passenger seat of his Jag, conspicuously silent.

He arrived at the Kingsmen practice field at ten sharp just as instructed, despite having to break a few traffic laws to get there on time. He still hadn't heard a word from Diana when he climbed out of his car and tossed his cell into the duffel bag that carried his gear.

He needed to quit worrying about her. About the two of them. Especially since they weren't an actual couple.

It had only been hate sex.

He slammed the door of his Jag hard enough to make the car shake.

"And here I thought you'd be thrilled to be back," someone said.

Franco turned to find Coach Santos standing behind him. "Good morning."

"Is it? Because you seem pissed as hell." His gaze swept Franco from top to bottom. "A tuxedo? At ten in the morning? This doesn't bode well, son."

Franco was lucky he kept a bag packed with his practice gear in the trunk of his car. There hadn't been time to stop by his apartment. "Relax. I wasn't out partying. You caught me at my fiancée's apartment this morning. I'm a changed man, remember?"

"Let's hope so. Ellis isn't so sure, but he's willing to give it a shot. For now." Santos looked pointedly at Franco's rumpled tux shirt. "But try not to arrive at practice look-

ing like you just rolled out of someone's bed. It's not helping your cause. Got it?"

"Got it." Franco gave him a curt nod and tried not to
think about that bed. Or that particular *someone*.

He needed to have his head in the game, today more
than ever. But he hated the way he and Diana had left
things. He'd thought this time would be different.

If he was being honest with himself though, it was for
the best. Diana Drake had always been out of his league.
He didn't have a thing to offer her.

Time hadn't changed who he was. It hadn't changed
anything. He and Diana had ended back where they'd
begun.

"We've got a scrimmage in an hour. And don't forget
about Argentine Night at the Polo Club tonight. Ellis ex-
pects you there with your doting fiancée on your arm."

Franco's gut churned. Getting Diana anywhere near
the Polo Club would be next to impossible. It seemed as
though she hadn't gotten within a mile radius of a live
horse since her accident.

There was also the slight complication that she hated
him. Now, more than ever.

"What are you waiting for? Get suited up." Coach
Santos jerked his head in the direction of the practice
field, where the grooms were already getting the horses
saddled up and ready.

Before Franco had come to America—before all the
championship trophies and the late-night after parties—
he'd been a groom. He'd been the one who brushed the
horses, running a curry comb over them until the Argentine sunshine reflected off them like a mirror. He'd
bathed them in the evenings, grinning as they tossed
their heads and whinnied beneath the spray of the water
hose. Franco had lived and breathed horses back then.

When he wasn't shoveling out stalls, he was on horse-back, practicing his swing, learning the game of polo.

Sometimes he missed those days.

But grooms didn't become champions, at least not where Franco had come from. He was one of the lucky ones. Not lucky, actually. Chosen. He owed Luc Piero everything.

"You did it, man." Luc greeted Franco with a bone-crushing hug the moment he stepped onto the field. "You're back."

"I told you there wasn't anything to worry about." Franco shrugged and fastened his helmet in place.

"Engaged, though?" Luc lifted a brow. "Tell me that's not real."

"Does it matter?" Franco planted one of his feet into a stirrup, grabbed onto the saddle and swung himself onto his horse's back. His grooms had gotten the horses to the field just in the nick of time.

"Yes, it matters. It matters a whole hell of a lot. I mean, you've never been the marrying kind."

"So I hear." He was being an ass, and he knew it. But he wasn't in the mood to discuss his marriageability. Not when he couldn't shake the memory of the hurt in Diana's gaze this morning.

He sighed. "Sorry. I just don't want to discuss Diana Drake. Or any of the Drakes, for that matter."

They had been the means to an end. Nothing more. Why did he keep having to remind himself of that fact?

Luc shrugged. "I can live with that. You're back. That's what important. Nothing else. Right?"

Franco shot him a grim smile. "Absolutely."

He rode hard once the scrimmage got underway. Fast. Aggressive.

By the close of the fourth chukker, the halfway point

of the game, the scoreboard read 11 to 0. Franco had scored each and every one of the goals. He managed four more before the end of the game. He was back, indeed.

His teammates gathered round to congratulate him. Ellis applauded from his box seat, but didn't approach Franco. And that was fine. Franco didn't feel much like talking. To Ellis or anyone. The urge he felt to check his cell phone for messages was every bit as frustrating as it was pressing. When he finally did, he had over forty voicemails, all from various members of the media.

Not a single word from Diana.

He shoved his phone in his back pocket and slammed his locker closed. What was he supposed to do now? Were he and Diana engaged? Were they over?

He had no idea.

He stopped by his apartment in Tribeca and packed a bag, just in case. No news was good news. Wasn't that the old adage? Besides, he couldn't quite shake the feeling that if Diana Drake had decided to dump him, he would have heard it first from the press...

Because that's how monumentally screwed up their fake relationship was.

But the mob of photographers outside Diana's building didn't say a word about a breakup when Franco arrived on the scene. They screamed the usual questions at him, along with a few new ones. About the wedding, of course. He kept his head down and did his best to ignore them.

The doorman waved Franco upstairs, just as he had before. That didn't necessarily mean anything. Diana probably wouldn't have broken the news first to her doorman, but Franco was beginning to feel more confident that he, indeed, had a fiancée waiting for him in the penthouse.

Sure enough, when Diana answered the door, there

was a colossal diamond solitaire situated on her ring finger. "Oh, it's you."

For some nonsensical reason, the sight of the ring rubbed Franco the wrong way. If their engagement had been real, he would have chosen a diamond himself. And it wouldn't be a generic rock like the one on her hand. He would have selected something special. Unique.

But what the hell was he thinking? *None* of this was real. The ring shouldn't matter.

It did, though. He had no idea why, but it mattered.

"Nice ring," he said through gritted teeth.

"I picked it up at Drake Diamonds today since my *fiancé* forgot to give me one." She lifted an accusatory brow. "What are you doing here, anyway?"

He gave her a grim smile and swished past her with his duffle and a garment bag slung over his shoulder. "Honey, I'm home."

She gaped at him. "I beg your pardon?"

Lulu shot toward him, all happy barks and wagging tail. At least someone was happy to see him. He tossed his bags on the sofa and gathered the puppy into his arms.

Diana frowned at Lulu, then back at Franco. *Someone looks jealous.* "What's going on? Surely you don't think you're moving in with me."

"We're engaged, remember? This is what engaged people do."

She shook her head. "Please tell me you're not serious. I've already taken in one stray. Isn't that enough?"

It was the wrong thing to say.

"You're comparing me to a stray dog now?" he said through clenched teeth.

She opened her mouth to say something, but Franco wouldn't let her. He'd heard enough.

"I've put up with a hell of a lot from you and your family in the past few weeks, Diana. But you will not speak to me that way. Is that understood, wifey?"

She blinked. "I…"

He held up a hand. "Save it. We can talk later. We have a date tonight, anyway. You should get dressed."

"A *date*?"

"We're going to Argentine Night at the Polo Club. If you have a problem with it, I don't want to hear it. I've accompanied you to every gala and party under the sun in the past few weeks. You can do one thing for me." He gave Lulu a scratch behind the ears. "Unless you'd like to kick both of the strays out of your life once and for all?"

She wouldn't dare. If she wanted him gone, she wouldn't be wearing that sparkling diamond on her ring finger. Franco honestly didn't know why she wanted to play along with the engagement, but he no longer cared.

You care. You know you do.

If he didn't, the stray dog comment wouldn't have gotten under his skin the way it had.

"Well?" he asked.

"I'll be ready in half an hour." She plucked the dog from his arms. "And Lulu isn't going anywhere."

She sauntered past him with the little pug's face peering at him over her shoulder and slammed the bedroom door.

Franco wanted to stay angry. Anger was good. Anger was comfortable. He knew a lot more about what to do with anger than about what to do with the feelings that had swirled between them last night.

But seeing her with the dog took the edge off. He'd been right to force the puppy on her. He'd done something good.

For once in his life.

Chapter Fifteen

Diana had spent the better part of her life around horses, but she'd never been to the Polo Club in Bridgehampton. Show jumping and polo were clearly two separate sports. She'd known polo players before, obviously. She'd certainly seen Franco at her fair share of equestrian events. But she'd never run in the same after-hours circles as Franco's crowd.

Even before the night she'd lost her virginity to Franco, she'd noticed a brooding intensity about those athletes that both fascinated and frightened her. They rode hard and they play hard. Deep down, she knew that was one of the qualities about Franco that had first drawn her toward him. He didn't care what anyone else had to say about him. He behaved any way he chose. Both on and off the field.

Diana had no idea what that might feel like. She was a Drake, and that name came with a myriad of expectations.

If she'd been born a boy, things would have been different. Drake men were immune to rules and expectations. At least, that had been the case with her father. He'd spent money as he wished and slept with whomever he wished, and everyone in the family had to just deal with it. Her mother included.

"You look awfully serious all of a sudden," Franco said as she stepped out of the Drake limousine at the valet stand outside the Polo Club. "What are you thinking about?"

"Nothing." *Marriage.* Why was she even pondering such things? Oh, yeah, because she was engaged now. "I'm fine. Let's just go inside."

"Very well." He lifted her hand and kissed it before tucking it into the crook of his elbow.

Diana looked around, expecting to see a group of photographers clustered by the entrance of the club. But she didn't spot a single telephoto lens.

"Good evening, Mr. Andrade and Miss Drake." A valet held the door open for them as Franco led her into the foyer.

"Wow," she whispered. "This is really something."

The stately white building had been transformed into a South American wonderland of twinkling lights and rich, red decor. Sultry tango music filled the air. Diana was suddenly very glad she'd chosen a red lace gown for the occasion.

She and Franco were situated at a round table near the center of the room, along with his coach and several other players and their wives. When she took her seat, the man beside her introduced himself as Luc Piero.

"It's a pleasure to meet you," she said.

"The pleasure's all mine, I assure you." Luc grinned from ear to ear. "I've known Franco for a long time, and

I've never seen him as captivated with anyone before as he is with you. I've told him time and again that I wanted to meet you, but he's been hiding you away."

"I've done no such thing," Franco countered.

"That's right. Your pictures have been in the newspaper every day for two weeks running. How could I forget?" Luc smiled.

Diana kind of liked him. She probably would have liked him more if she weren't so busy searching the room for Natalie Ellis. She had a morbid curiosity about the woman Franco had apparently considered worth risking his entire career over. Diana had seen the woman on a handful of occasions, but she wanted a better look. She wasn't jealous, obviously. Simply curious.

Right. You're a card-carrying green-eyed monster right now.

"I'm going to go get us some drinks, darling." Franco bent to kiss her on the cheek, which pleased her far more than it should have. "I'll be right back."

She reminded herself for the millionth time that she hated him, then turned to Luc. "You say you've known Franco a long time?"

"All our lives. We grew up together in Argentina."

"Really?" Franco had never breathed a word to her about his childhood. She couldn't help being curious about the way he'd grown up. "Tell me more."

"He's loved horses since before he could walk. You know that, right?"

She didn't. But she understood it all too well. "That's something we have in common."

"My father owned one of the local polo clubs in Buenos Aires. I used to hang out there when I was a kid, and that's where I met Franco."

"Oh, was he taking riding lessons there?"

Luc gave her an odd glance. "No, Franco's one hundred percent self-taught. A natural. He was a groom at my father's stable."

"I see." She nodded as if this wasn't stunning new information. After all, she should probably have some sort of clue about Franco's childhood since he was her fiancé.

But a groom?

In the equestrian world, grooms and riders belonged in two very different social classes. Not that Diana liked or condoned dividing people into such groups. But it was an unpleasant fact of life—she'd never known a groom who had gone on to compete in show jumping. Maybe things were different in the sport of polo.

Then again, maybe not.

"It's unusual, I know. But Franco was different, right from the start."

Indeed. Her throat grew tight.

She should be furious with him after the stunt he'd pulled. He'd strong-armed her into an engagement, plain and simple. An engagement she didn't want.

And she'd let him. She wasn't sure who she was angrier at—Franco or herself.

"Different. How so?" She glanced at Franco across the room, where he stood standing beside a man she recognized from equestrian circles as Jack Ellis, the owner of the Kingsmen.

Her breath caught in her throat. No matter how many times she looked at Franco—whether it was from the other side of a crowded room or beside him in bed—his physical perfection always seemed to catch her off guard. He was the most handsome man she'd ever seen. Ellis, on the other hand, appeared immune to Franco's charms. The expression on his face was grim. Even the woman on Jack Ellis's arm didn't seem to notice Franco's charming smile or dark, chiseled beauty. Natalie Ellis looked almost bored as she glanced around the room. When her gaze fell on Luc, her lips curved into a nearly imperceptible smile.

Odd.

"Well…" Luc continued, dragging her attention back to their conversation. "Like I said, he was a talented rider. Fearless. Instinctual. Even as a kid, I knew I was witnessing something special. He had a bond with the horses like nothing I'd ever seen. They were his life."

A chill went up Diana's spine. She had a feeling she was about to hear something she shouldn't.

"His life," she echoed.

"I found out he was sleeping in the stables and kept it a secret from my father for over year before he found out." Luc gave her a sad smile. "I thought he'd be angry and kick Franco out. Instead, he gave Franco a room in our family home."

She most definitely shouldn't be hearing this. Franco had never said a thing to her about his life in Argentina. Now she knew why. These were the sort of intimate details only a lover should know. A real lover.

She should change the subject. Delving further into this conversation would be an invasion of Franco's privacy. But she was so distraught by what she'd heard that she couldn't string together a single coherent sentence.

She'd called Franco a stray.

And he'd been homeless.

Oh, God.

"Are you all right, Diana?" Luc was watching her with guarded curiosity. "You look like you've seen a ghost."

No, just a monster. And that monster is me.

"Fine." She cleared her throat. "Is that when Franco

started playing polo? After he moved in with your family?"

Luc shrugged. "Yes and no. He was still working as a groom, but I'd begun playing. Franco was my training partner. In the beginning, he was just there to help me improve my game. That didn't last long."

"He's that good, isn't he?" She forced herself to smile like a doting bride.

What was happening? She was acting just like the nauseatingly sweet engaged couples she'd loathed so much when she worked in Engagements.

It *was* an act, wasn't it?

"He's the best. He always has been. His talent transcends any traditional rules of the game. That's why my father put him on the team." He smiled at Franco as he approached the table. "We've been teammates ever since."

A lump formed in Diana's throat. "I'm glad. Franco deserves a friend like you."

"He's more like a brother than a friend. He's always got my back. The guy's loyal to a fault, but I'm sure you know that by now."

Loyal to a fault...

Before Franco had walked through the door of Drake Diamonds a month ago, Diana would have never used those to words to describe him. Now she wasn't so sure.

She'd seen a different side to Franco in recent weeks. It all made sense now...the way he'd jumped at the chance to adopt a homeless puppy, his commitment to their fake relationship. Franco was a man of his word.

She was beginning to question everything she'd believed about him, and that wasn't good. It wasn't good at all. Their entire relationship had been built on a lie, and Diana preferred it that way. At least she knew where she stood. She operated best when she could look at the world in black and white. But things with Franco had blurred into a disturbing shade of gray.

She didn't know what she thought anymore. Worse, she wasn't sure what she felt. Because despite everything that had happened in the past, and despite the fact that just when she thought she could trust Franco he'd gone and announced to the world that they were engaged, she felt something for him. And that *something* scared the life out of her.

But he obviously had little or no regard for marriage, otherwise he wouldn't have bedded Natalie Ellis. Natalie Ellis, who seemed to have no interest in Franco whatsoever.

What was going on?

"Hello, darling. Sorry to leave you alone for so long." Franco bent and kissed her on the cheek again. "I hope Luc hasn't been boring you."

"No, not at all." Quite the opposite, actually.

She smiled up at him and tried to forget all the things she'd just heard. But it was no use. She couldn't shake the image of Franco as a young boy, sleeping on a bed of straw in a barn. What had happened to him to make him end up there? Where was his family? So many unanswered questions.

The air between them was heavy with secrets and lies, but somewhere deep inside Diana, an unsettling truth had begun to blossom.

She had feelings for Franco. Genuine feelings.

"The tango contest is about to begin." He offered her his hand. "Dance with me?"

She stared at his outstretched palm, and words began to spin in her head.

Do you take this man to love and to cherish, all the days of your life?

She was losing it.

"Yes." *I do.* She placed her hand in his. She didn't even know how to tango, but she didn't much care at this point. "Yes, please."

The music started and Franco wrapped his right arm around Diana until his hand rested squarely in the center of her back. When he lifted his left arm, she placed her hand gently in his.

"I should probably mention that I don't exactly know how to tango." She blushed.

"Not to worry. I'm a rather strong lead."

"Why am I not surprised?" she murmured. He took a step forward, and she moved with him in perfect synchrony. "Luc had some lovely things to say about you just now."

They reached the end of the club's small dance floor, and Franco spun her around. "He's probably had more than his fair share of champagne."

"Don't." Diana shook her head and slid one of her stilettos up the length of his leg. "I'm being serious. He loves you like a brother."

Franco nodded. Her leg had traveled nearly up to his hip. He pulled her incrementally closer. "You're right. He does. And I'd do anything for him."

He deliberately avoided glancing in Natalie Ellis's direction.

This wasn't the time or place for a heart-to-heart, but something about the way Diana was looking at him all of a sudden made it impossible for him to keep giving her flippant responses.

She slid her foot back to the floor and they resumed stalking each other across the floor to the strains of the accordion music.

"I had no idea you could dance like this, Franco." Diana swiveled in his arms. "You're full of surprises."

"It's an Argentine dance." He lifted her in the air, and her legs wrapped around his waist, then flared out before she landed on the floor with a whisper. For someone who claimed not to know how to tango, Diana was holding her own. Someone had clearly been watching *Dancing With the Stars.*

This was beginning to feel less like dancing and more like sex. Not that Franco was complaining.

"Tell me more about your life in Argentina," she whispered as her hand crept to the back of his neck.

Should he be this aroused at a social function? Definitely not. He was a grown man not a horny fifteen-year-old kid. "Other than the dancing?"

"Yes, although I'm a little curious about the dancing, as well."

He pulled her closer, but kept his gaze glued in the opposite direction. The quintessential tango posture. Convenient, as well, since he never discussed his family upbringing. But he'd witnessed a staggering amount of Drake family dynamics over the past few weeks. Hell, he was beginning to almost feel like a Drake himself. If she was asking questions, he owed her a certain degree of transparency.

"I grew up with a single mother in Barrio de la Boca. I never knew my father."

"I see," she murmured.

He cast a sideways glance in her direction, hoping against hope he wouldn't see a trace of pity in her gaze. Having Diana Drake look at him in such a way would have killed him. She wasn't, though. She seemed more curious than anything, and for that, Franco was grateful.

"My mother was less than attentive. I ran away when

I was eleven. Luc's father took me in. The rest is history, as they say."

They reached the end of the dance floor again, but instead of turning around, Diana slid her foot up the back of his calf. "I wish I would have known about this sooner."

He reached for the back of her thigh and ground subtly against her before letting her let go. "Would it have changed anything?"

"Yes." She swallowed, and he traced the movement up and down the elegant column of her neck. "I'm sorry, Franco. I should have never said what I did earlier."

He lowered her into a deep dip and echoed her own words back to her from the night before. "You're forgiven."

"Ladies and gentlemen, the winners of the annual tango contest are Franco Andrade and Diana Drake."

The room burst into applause.

"I can't believe this," Diana said as Franco pulled her upright. "We won!"

Franco wove his hand through hers and held on tightly as Jack Ellis approached them, holding a shiny silver trophy.

His mouth curved into a tight smile as he offered it to Franco. "Congratulations."

"Gracias." The fact that Ellis was so clearly upset by his presence probably should have bothered Franco to some extent, but he couldn't bring himself to care at the moment.

Diana was speaking to him again. They'd only exchanged a handful of words since their engagement had been announced, and somehow he'd managed to get back in her good graces. Better than that, it felt genuine. He was starting to feel close to her in a way he seldom did with anyone.

Don't fool yourself. It's only temporary, remember.

"Miss Drake, it's a pleasure to make your acquaintance." Ellis shook Diana's hand. "Will you be joining us at tomorrow's match?"

Diana went instantly pale. "Tomorrow's match?"

"The Kingsmen have a game tomorrow. Surely Franco's mentioned it." Ellis frowned.

A spike of irritation hit Franco hard in his chest. Ellis could talk to him however he liked, but he wasn't about to let his boss be anything but polite to Diana. "Of course I have. Unfortunately, Diana has a previous engagement."

She nodded. After an awkward, silent beat, she followed his lead. "I'm afraid Franco's right. I have a commitment tomorrow that I simply can't get out of."

"That's too bad," Ellis said. "Another time, perhaps."

"Perhaps." She smiled, but Franco could see the panic in her amethyst gaze. She had no intention of watching him on horseback. Not tomorrow. Not ever.

Ellis said his goodbyes and walked away. The band began to play again, and Franco and Diana were swallowed up by other couples.

"Come with me." He slid his arm around her and whispered into her hair.

"Where are we going?" She peered up at him, and he could still see a trace of fear in those luminous eyes.

Franco would have given everything he had to take her distress away. But no amount of money or success could replace what she'd lost the day she'd fallen. He'd never felt so helpless in his life. Nothing he could do would bring Diamond back to life.

But maybe, just maybe, he could help her remember what it had been like to be fearless.

If only she would let him.

* * *

"Close your eyes," Franco whispered. His breath was hot on her neck in tantalizing contrast to the cool night air on her face.

Franco's voice was deep, insistent. Despite the warning bells going off in Diana's head, she did as he asked.

"Good girl."

A thrill coursed through her and settled low in her belly. What was she doing? She shouldn't be out here in the dark, taking orders from this man. She most definitely shouldn't be turned on by it.

She inhaled a shaky breath. *Open your eyes. Just open your eyes and walk away.*

But she knew she wouldn't. Couldn't if she tried. Something had happened out there on the dance floor. She felt as if she'd seen Franco for the first time. She'd gotten a glimpse of his past, and somehow that made the dance more meaningful. Not just their tango…the three-year dance they'd been engaged in since they'd first met.

"This way." His hand settled onto the small of her back. "Keep your eyes shut."

He started walking. Slowly. Diana kept in step beside him, letting him lead her. Unable to see, her other senses went on high alert. The sweet smell of hay and horses tickled her nose. The light touch of Franco's fingertips felt decadent, more intimate than it should have.

She licked her lips and let herself remember what it had felt like to take those fingertips into her mouth, to suck gently on them while he'd watched through eyes glittering like black diamonds. She wanted to feel that way again. She wanted *him* again, God help her.

"Be careful." Franco's footsteps slowed. She heard a door sliding open.

"Can I open my eyes now?" He voice was breathy, barely more than a whisper.

Franco's hand slid lower, perilously close to her bottom. "No, you may not."

How close was his face? Close enough to kiss? Close enough for her to lean toward him and take his bottom lip gently between her teeth?

She swallowed. This shouldn't be happening. None of it. The sad reality of Franco's childhood shouldn't change the ridiculous truth of their situation. The only thing they shared was a long string of lies. This was the same man who'd called the newspapers and told them he was marrying her. It was the same man who'd so callously dismissed her the morning after she'd lost her virginity.

They were pretending.

But it no longer felt that way. Not now that she'd seen the real him.

"Franco," she whispered, reaching for him.

He caught her wrist midair. "Shhhh. Let me."

She waited for a beat and wondered what would come next. Franco slid her hand into his, intertwining their fingers. Then her hand made contact with something soft. Warm. Alive.

She stiffened.

"It's okay, Diana. Keep your eyes closed. I'm here. I've got you." Franco's other arm wrapped around her, pulling her against him. He stood behind her with his hand still covering hers, moving it in slow circles over velvety softness.

A horse. She was touching a horse. She knew without opening her eyes.

I'm here. I've got you.

Did he know this was the closest she'd come to a horse since she'd fallen? Did he know this was the first time she'd touched one since that awful day? Could he possibly?

Of course he did. Because he saw her. He always had.

She felt a tear slide down her cheek, and she squeezed her eyes shut even harder. If she opened them now and saw her fingers interlocked with Franco's, moving slowly over the magnificent animal in front of them, she wouldn't be able to take it. She'd fall apart. She'd fall...

But this time, Franco would be there to catch her.

Or not.

How could this man be the same one who'd slept with Natalie Ellis and gotten himself fired?

It didn't make sense. Especially now that she knew his background. She could see why he pushed people away. She could even see why he'd said such awful things after she'd slept with him three years ago. Intimacy—real intimacy—didn't come easily to Franco. It couldn't. Not after what he'd been through as a boy.

If anyone could understand that, Diana could. Hadn't her own childhood been filled with a similar brand of confusion? They'd each found their escape on horseback. Which is why nothing about his termination made sense.

Polo meant everything to Franco. More than she'd ever imagined. Why would he risk it for a meaningless romp with his boss's wife?

There had to be more to the story. She wished he would tell her, but she knew deep down he never would. And she didn't particularly blame him.

"I lied, Franco." She kept her eyes closed. She couldn't quite bring herself to look at him. "It wasn't hate sex."

"I know it wasn't." He pulled her closer against him. When he spoke, his lips brushed lightly against the curve of her neck, leaving a trail of goose bumps in their wake.

"I don't hate you. I never did." She was crying in earnest now. Tears were streaming down her face, but she didn't care. She was tired of the lies. So very tired.

"Don't cry, Wildfire. Please don't cry." He pressed an openmouthed kiss to her shoulder. "It kills me to see you hurting. It always did, even back then."

Her heart pounded hard in her chest. There were more things to say, more lies to correct. She wanted to set the record straight. She *needed* to. Even if she never saw him again after next week.

You won't. He's going away, and he's not coming back.

"For three years, I've been telling myself I chose you because I knew you'd let me down. It's not true. I chose you because I wanted you. I wanted you back then. I wanted you the other night. And I want you now." She opened her eyes and turned to face him.

They were standing in a barn. She'd known as much, and she'd expected to feel panicked when confronted with the sight of the horses in their stalls. But she didn't. She felt right, somehow. Safe.

She'd dreaded coming here tonight, and now she realized it had been a gift.

"How did you know this is what I needed?" she asked.

He cupped her face, tipped her chin upward so she looked him in the eyes. "I knew because, in many ways, you and I are the same. I want you, too, Diana. I want you so much I can barely see straight."

"Take me home, Franco."

Chapter Sixteen

Franco didn't dare touch Diana in the backseat of the limo on their ride back to New York. If he did, he wouldn't be able to stop himself from making love to her right there in plain view of the driver and every other car on the long stretch of highway between Bridgehampton and the city.

It was more than just an exercise in restraint. It was the longest ninety minutes of his life.

They rode side by side, each trying not to look at the other for fear they'd lose control. An electric current passed between them. If the spark had been visible, it would have filled the lux interior of the car with diamond light.

As the dizzying lights of Manhattan came into view, he allowed his gaze to roam. It wandered down Diana's elegant throat, lingering on the tantalizing dip between her collarbones—the place where he most wanted to kiss her at the moment so he could feel the wild beating of her pulse beneath his lips. He wanted to taste the decadent passion she had for life. Consume it.

Diana felt each and every one of her emotions to its fullest extent. It was one of the things he'd always loved about her. Being by her side these past weeks had caused Franco to realize the extent to which he avoided feelings. Since he'd moved to America, he'd done his level best to forget the world he'd left behind. His memories of Argentina were laden with shame. The shame of growing up without a father. The shame of the way his mother had all but abandoned him.

He'd tried to outrun that shame on the polo field. He'd tried to drown it in women and wine. But it had always been there, simmering beneath the surface, preventing him from forming any real sort of connection with anyone. At times he even kept Luc at arm's length.

Luc knew the rules. He knew not to bring up the past. He knew not to push. Why he may have done so this evening was a mystery Franco didn't care to examine too closely.

He thinks this is different. He thinks you're in love.

This *was* different.

Was it love? Franco didn't know. Didn't want to know. Because what he and Diana had together came with an expiration date. He'd known as much from the start, but for some reason it was just beginning to sink in. The date was growing closer. Just a matter of days away. And now that he was a member of the Kingsmen again, he'd be leaving just as soon as their arrangement came to an end.

He should be happy. Elated, even. This was why he'd gotten himself tangled up with the Drakes to begin with. This was what he'd wanted.

But as his gaze traveled lower, past the midnight blue

stone that glittered against Diana's porcelain skin, he had the crippling sensation that everything he wanted was right beside him. Within arm's reach.

Screw the waiting.

He pushed the button that raised the limo's privacy divider and slid toward her across the wide gulf of leather seat in under a second. Diana let out a tiny gasp as his mouth crushed down on hers, hot and needy. But then her hands were sliding inside his tuxedo jacket, pulling him closer. And closer, until he could feel the fierce beat of her heart against his chest.

Not here. Take it slow.

But he couldn't stop his hands from reaching for the zipper at her back and lowering it until the bodice of her dress fell away, exposing the decadent perfection of her breasts. He stared, transfixed, as he dragged the pad of his thumb across one of her nipples with a featherlight touch.

The gemstone nestled in her cleavage seemed to glow like liquid fire, burning blue. On some level, Franco knew this wasn't possible. But he'd lost the ability for rational thought. All he knew was that this moment was one that would stick with him until the day he died.

He'd never forget the feel of Diana's softness in his hands, the way she looked at him as the city whirled past them in a blur of whirling silver light. Years from now, when he was nothing but a distant memory in her bewitching, beguiling mind, he'd remember what it had felt like to lose himself in that deep purple gaze. He'd close his eyes and dream of radiant blue light. God help him. He'd probably never be able to look at a sapphire again without getting hard.

"Diana, darling." He groaned and lowered his lips to her breasts, drawing a nipple into his mouth.

He was being too rough, and he knew it, nipping and biting with his teeth. But he couldn't stop. Not when she was arching toward his mouth and fisting her hands in his hair. His hunger was matched by her need, which didn't seem possible.

It was like falling into a mirror.

How will this end?

Badly. No question.

He couldn't fathom walking away from Diana Drake. But he knew he would. He always walked away. From everyone.

"Mr. Andrade." The driver's voice crackled over the intercom.

Franco ignored it and peeled Diana's dress lower. He was fully on top of her now, spread over the length of the backseat. He was kissing his way down her abdomen when the driver's voice came over the loud speaker again.

"Mr. Andrade, there are photographers at the end of the block, just outside the apartment building."

Diana stiffened beneath him.

"It's okay," he whispered. "Don't worry. Everything will be fine."

He gently lifted her dress back into place, cursing himself for being such an impatient idiot.

What were they doing? They weren't teenagers on prom night, for crying out loud. He was a grown man. The choices he made had consequences. And somehow the consequences of his involvement with Diana seemed to grow more serious by the day.

Diana sat up and brushed the chestnut bangs from her eyes. Her sapphire necklace shimmered in the dark.

Franco looked away and straightened his tie from the other end of the leather seat.

"We're here, Miss Drake, Mr. Andrade," the driver announced.

"Thank you," Franco said, squinting through the darkened car window.

The throng of paparazzi gathered at the entrance to the building was the largest he'd ever seen. The press attention was getting out of hand. The wedding would be a circus.

Get a grip.

He shook his head. There wasn't going to be a wedding. Ever. The engagement was a sham, despite the massive rock on Diana's finger.

The ring was messing with Franco's head. He was having enough trouble maintaining a grasp on reality, and seeing that diamond solitaire on Diana's hand every time she reached for him, touched him, stroked him just added to the confusion.

The back door opened, and he and Diana somehow managed to find their way inside the building amid the blinding light of flashbulbs. The photographers screamed questions at them about the details of the wedding. Would it be held at the Plaza? Who was designing Diana's wedding dress?

It occurred to Franco that he would have liked to see Diana dressed in bridal white. She would look stunning walking toward her man standing at the front of a church in front of the upper echelons of Manhattan society. A lucky man. A man who wasn't him.

They managed to keep their hands off each other as they navigated the route to Diana's front door. When had touching each other become something they did in private rather than for show? And why did that seem so dangerous when that's the way it should have always been?

Diana slid her key into the lock. She pushed the door open, and they paused at the threshold.

Franco caught her gaze and smiled. "I'm sorry about what happened in the car and the close call with the photographers. That was…" He shook his head, struggling for an appropriate adjective. *Careless. Intense. Fantastic.* They all fit.

The corners of her perfect bow-shaped lips curved into a smile that could only be described as wicked. "I'm not sorry."

Franco swallowed. Hard.

Like falling into a mirror.

But mirrors broke when they fell. They ended up in tiny shards of broken glass that sparkled like diamonds but cut to the quick.

He didn't care what happened to him next month. Next week. Tomorrow. He just knew that before the night was over, he would bury himself inside Diana again. Consequences be damned.

The moment they stepped inside the apartment and the door clicked shut behind them, Diana found herself pressed against the wall. Franco's mouth was on hers in an instant, kissing her with such force, such need that her lips throbbed almost to the point of pain.

A forbidden thrill snaked its way through her. This was different than it had been the night before. They'd been somewhat cautious with each other then, neither of them willing to fully let down their guard. But she knew without having to ask that tonight wouldn't be like that. Tonight would be about surrender.

"Take off your dress," he ordered and took a step backward. His gaze settled on her sapphire necklace as he waited for her to obey.

She stood frozen, breathless for a moment, as she tried to make sense of what was happening. She shouldn't enjoy being told what to do, but this was for her pleasure. His. Theirs. And the molten warmth pooling in her center told her she liked it, indeed.

She reached behind her back for her zipper, but her hands were already shaking so hard that they were completely ineffectual. Franco moved closer, his face mere inches from hers. Her neck went hot, her knees buckled and she desperately wanted to look away. To take a deep breath and calm the frantic beating of her heart. But she couldn't seem to tear her gaze from his.

The corner of his mouth lifted into a barely visible half smile. His eyes blazed. He knew full well the effect he had on her. In moments like this, he owned her. He knew it, and so did she.

It should have frightened her. Diana had never wanted to belong to anyone, let alone him. And she wouldn't. Not once their charade was over and they'd gone their separate ways.

But just this once she wanted it to be true. Just for tonight.

"Turn around, love." His voice was raw, pained.

She did as he said and turned to face the wall. With excruciating care, he unzipped her gown. Red lace slid down her hips and fell to the floor. Franco's hands reached around to cup her breasts as his lips left a trail of tantalizing kisses down her spine.

"*Preciosa*," he murmured against her bare back. *Lovely.*

His breath was like fire on her skin. She was shimmering, molten. A gemstone in the making.

She sighed and arched her back. Franco's hands slid from her breasts to her hips, where he hooked his fingers around her lacy panties and slid them down her legs. She stepped out of them, turned to face him, but he stopped her with a sharp command.

"No." He took her hands and pressed them flat against the wall, then whispered in her ear. "Don't move, Diana. Stay very still."

This was like nothing she'd ever experienced before. She'd never been with anyone besides Franco, but this was even different than the times they'd been together. The brush of his designer tuxedo against her exposed skin made her consciously aware of the fact that, once again, she was completely undressed while he remained fully clothed. She couldn't even see him, but that seemed to enhance the riot of sensations skittering through her body. She could only close her eyes and feel.

He brushed her hair aside and kissed her neck, her shoulder. His hands were everywhere—on her waist, her bottom, sliding over her belly. She was suddenly grateful for the wall and the way he'd pressed her hands against it. It was the only thing holding her up. Her legs had begun to tremble, and the tingle between them was almost too much to bear. She was so overwhelmed by the gentle assault of his mouth and the graceful exploration of his hands that she didn't even notice he'd nudged her legs apart with his knee until his fingertips reached between her thighs and found her center.

"I could touch you forever," he said and slid a finger inside her.

Forever.

It was a dangerous word, but this was a dangerous game they were playing. For all practical purposes, they were playing house. Living as husband and wife. And to Diana's astonishment, she didn't hate it.

On the contrary, she quite enjoyed it.

Especially now, bent over with Franco's fingers moving in and out of her. She moaned, low and delicious. She needed him to stop. Now, before she climaxed in this brazen posture. But she'd lost control of her body. Her hips were rocking in time with his hand, and she was opening herself up for him like a flower. A rare and beautiful orchid. Diamond white.

"Franco," she begged. "Please."

"Come," he whispered. "For me. Do it now."

Stars exploded before her eyes, falling like diamond dust as her body shuddered to its end. She collapsed into his arms, and he carried her across the apartment to the bedroom, whispering soothing words.

She'd gone boneless, yet her skin was alive. Shimmering like a glistening ruby. The King of Stones. And as he gingerly set her down and pushed inside her, she felt regal. Adored as no woman had ever been.

She was a queen, and Franco Andrade was her king.

Chapter Seventeen

Diana took her place at a reserved table situated near midfield, where Artem and Ophelia sat beneath the shade of a Drake-blue umbrella. She tried not to think too hard about the fact that this is what life would be like if she and Franco were together.

Really together.

Sundays at the Polo Club, sipping champagne with her brother and his wife, surrounded by the comforting scents of fresh-cut grass and cherry blossoms. A real family affair.

It wouldn't be so bad, would it?

Her throat grew tight. It felt quite nice, actually. Far too nice to be real.

Surrender.

It would have been so easy to give in. The past month had been more than business. It had been such a beautiful lie that she wondered sometimes if she actually believed it.

I could touch you forever.

Forever.

The word had branded itself on her skin, along with Franco's touch.

"Here he comes," Ophelia said.

Diana dragged her attention away from the night before and back to the present, where Franco was riding onto the field atop a beautifully muscled bay mare. The horse's dark tail was fashioned into a tight braid, and the bottoms of its legs were wrapped with bright red bandages. These were protective measures, necessary to guard against injury during play, rather than fashion statements. But the overall effect was striking just the same. The horse was magnificent.

But not as magnificent as its rider.

Diana had never seen Franco in full polo regalia before. Riding clothes, sure. But not like this…

He wore crisp white pants and brandy-colored boots that stretched all the way above his knees. The sleeves of his Kingsmen polo shirt strained at his biceps as he gave his mallet a few practice swings. She couldn't seem to stop looking at the muscles in his forearms. Or the way he carried himself in the saddle. Confident. Commanding. The aggressive glint in his eyes was just short of cocky.

He winked at her, and she realized he'd caught her staring. Before she could stop herself, she wiggled her white-gloved fingers in a tiny wave.

Beside her, Artem cleared his throat. "Are you ready for this, sis?"

She dropped her hand to her lap and nodded. "I am."

He was talking about the horses, of course. As far as Artem knew, she hadn't been this close to a horse since the day of her accident. She thought about telling him what Franco had done for her, but she couldn't find the words. She wasn't even sure words existed to describe what had happened when he'd taken her hands and placed them on the warmth of the gelding's back.

But the main reason she didn't try and explain was that she wanted to keep the grace of the moment to herself. To preserve its sanctity. Almost every move she and Franco had made for the past month had been splashed all over the newspapers. Every touch. Every kiss. Every lie. The truth between them lived in the quiet moments, the ones no one else had seen. And she wanted to keep it that way as long as she possibly could.

Because so long as no one knew how much he really meant to her, she could pretend the end didn't matter. She could hold her head high when the gossip pages screamed that she and Franco were over.

Right in front of her, the players were clustered together in the center of the field. The two teams faced each other, waiting for the throw-in—the moment when the umpire tossed the ball into play. Diana forced herself to watch, to concentrate on the present rather than what hadn't even happened yet. But as the bright white ball fell to the ground, she couldn't help but feel like time had begun to move at warp speed. And, with a resounding whack of Franco's mallet, it did.

The ball sailed across the grass, a startling white streak against bright, vivid green. Franco leaned into the saddle, and his horse charged forward. The ground shook beneath Diana's feet as the players charged toward the goal.

Franco led the charge, and when he hit the ball with such force that it went airborne, her heart leaped straight to her throat.

She held her breath while she waited for the official ruling. When the man behind the goal waved a flag over his head to indicate the Kingsmen had scored, she flew to her feet and cheered.

Franco caught her eye as his horse galloped toward the opposite end of the field. He smiled, and her head spun a little.

God, she was acting like an actual fiancée. A wife.

But she was supposed to, wasn't she? She was just doing her job.

It was more than that, though. There was no denying it. She wasn't acting at all.

Oh, no.

Her legs went wobbly, and she sank into her white wooden chair.

You're in love with him.

"He's amazing, isn't he?" Ophelia clapped and yelled Franco's name.

"He is, indeed." Diana felt sick.

How had she let this happen? Sleeping with Franco again—*twice*—had been stupid enough. Falling in love with him was another thing entirely. Off-the-charts idiotic.

The players flew past again in a flurry of galloping hooves and swinging mallets, and Diana's gaze remained glued to Franco. She shook her head and forced herself to look away, to concentrate on something real. The silver champagne bucket beside the table. The feathered hat situated at a jaunty angle on Ophelia's head. Anything. She counted to ten, but none of the little tricks she'd once used to stop herself from thinking about Diamond worked. She couldn't keep her eyes off Franco.

In the blink of an eye, he scored three more goals. It was a relief when the horn sounded, signaling the end of the first chukker. The break between periods was only three minutes, but she needed those three minutes. Every second of them. She needed a break from the intensity of the action on the field. Time to collect herself. Time to convince herself that she wasn't in love with the high-scoring player of the game.

Artem refilled their champagne flutes. "Franco's on fire today."

Diana watched him trot off the field toward a groom who stood by, ready and waiting, with Franco's next horse and mallet. By the time the match was finished, he'd go through at least seven horses. One for each chukker.

"Diana?" Artem slid a glass in front of her.

"Hmm?" she asked absently.

Franco had removed his helmet to rake his hand through his hair, a gesture that struck her as nonsensically sensual. Even from this distance.

"Could you peel your eyes away from your fiancé for half a second?" There was a smile in Artem's voice.

Sure enough, when she swiveled to face him, she found him grinning from ear to ear. Ophelia's chair was empty. Diana hadn't even noticed she'd left the table.

"Fake fiancé," she said. The back of her neck felt warm all of a sudden. She sipped her champagne and wished Artem would find something else to look at.

"You can stop now," Artem said. "I know."

"Know what?" But she was stalling. She knew exactly what he'd meant. He *knew*.

"About you and Andrade." His gaze flitted toward Franco climbing onto his new horse. This one was a sleek, solid-black gelding. Just like Diamond.

Diana's heart hammered in her chest. "Who told you?" Franco? Surely not.

But no one else knew.

"No one." Artem let out a laugh. "Are you kidding?

No one had to. I'm not blind, sis. It's written all over your face."

She shook her head. "No. We're not... I'm not..."

I'm not in love. I can't be.

"Don't even try to pretend it's an act. I'm not buying it this time." His gaze flitted from her to Franco and back again. "How long?"

Diana sighed. She was suddenly more exhausted than she'd ever been in her life. So many lies. She couldn't tell another one. Not to her brother. "I don't know when it happened, exactly."

Slowly. Yet, somehow, all at once.

Was it possible that she'd loved him all along, since the first night they'd been together, back when she was twenty-two?

"This is awful. Artem. What am I going to do?" She dropped her head into her hands.

Artem bent and whispered in her ear. "There are worse things in the world than falling for your fiancé."

She peered up at him from beneath the brim of her hat. "You seem to be forgetting the fact that we're not actually engaged. Also, I know for certain that you hate the thought of Franco and me."

His brow furrowed. "When exactly did I say that?"

She sat up straight and met his gaze. "The day of the Lamberti diamond announcement. And the morning the engagement was listed in the newspaper. And possibly a few other times over the course of the past four weeks."

He shook his head. "Clearly you weren't listening."

"Of course I was. You're not all that easy to ignore, my darling brother. Believe me, I've tried." She gave him a wobbly smile.

She felt like she was wearing her heart on the outside of her body all of a sudden. It terrified her to her core.

The giddy, bubbly feeling that came over her every time she looked at Franco was probably the same thing her mother had experienced when she'd looked at Diana's father. His long list of mistresses had no doubt felt the same way about him, too.

Fools, all of them.

Artem reached for her hand and gave it a squeeze. "I never said I didn't like the idea of you and Franco having a *genuine* relationship."

Could that be true? Because it wasn't the way she remembered their conversations. Then again, maybe she'd been the one who found the idea so repugnant, not Artem.

He leveled his gaze at her. "I was concerned about your pretend relationship. It seemed to be spinning out of control, far beyond what I intended when I make the mistake of suggesting it. But if it's real…"

If it's real.

That was the question, wasn't it?

She would have given anything in exchange for the answer.

Ophelia returned to the table as the next chukker began. Diana redirected her attention to the field, where Franco cut a dashing figure atop his striking black horse. Seconds after the toss-in, he was once again ahead of the other players, smacking the ball with his mallet and thundering toward the goal.

But just as he reached the far end of the field, a player from the other team cut diagonally between him and the ball.

"That's an illegal move," Artem said tersely.

Diana could hear Franco yelling in his native tongue. *Aléjate! Away!* But the player bore down and forced his horse directly in front of Franco's ebony gelding.

Somewhere a whistle sounded, but Diana barely heard

it. Her pulse had begun to roar in her ears as Franco and his horse got lost in the ensuing fray. She flew to her feet to try and get a better look. All she could see amid the tangle of horses, players and mallets was a flash of dazzling black.

Just like Diamond.

Her throat grew tight. She couldn't breathe. Couldn't speak. She reached for Artem, grabbed his forearm. The emerald grass seemed too bright all of a sudden. The sky, too blue. Garish. Like something out of a nightmare. And the black horse was a terrible omen.

No. She shook her head. *Please, no.*

There was a sickening thud, then everything stopped. There was no more noise. No more movement. Nothing.

Just the horrific sight of Franco lying facedown on top of that glaring green lawn. Motionless.

Franco heard his body break as it crashed into the ground. There was no mistaking the sound—an earsplitting crack that seemed as though it were echoing off the heavenly New York sky.

The noise was followed by a brutal pain dead in the center of his chest. It blossomed outward, until even his fingertips throbbed.

He squeezed his eyes closed and screamed into the grass.

Walk it off. It's nothing. You've been waiting for this chance for months. You can't get sidelined with an injury. Not now.

He moved. Just a fraction of an inch. It felt like someone had shot him through the left shoulder with a flame-tipped arrow. At least it wasn't his playing arm.

Still, it hurt like hell. He took a deep breath and rolled himself over with his right arm. He squeezed his eyes closed tight and muttered a stream of obscenities in Spanish.

"Don't move," someone said.

Not *someone*. Diana.

He opened his eyes, and there she was. Kneeling beside him in the grass. The wind lifted her hat, and it went airborne. She didn't seem to notice. She just stared down at him, wide-eyed and beautiful, as her dark hair whipped in the wind.

For a blissful moment, Franco forgot about his pain. He forgot everything but Diana.

If she was putting on an act, it was a damned convincing one. Something in his chest took flight, despite the pain.

"You're a sight for sore eyes, you know that?" He winced. Talking hurt. Breathing hurt. Everything hurt.

Especially the peculiar way Diana was looking at him. As if she'd seen a ghost. "Why are you sitting up? You shouldn't be moving."

"And you shouldn't be on the field. You're going to get hurt." She was on her hands and knees in the grass, too close to the horses' hooves. Too ghastly pale. Too upset.

She remembers.

He could see it in the violet depths of her eyes—the agony of memory.

"*I'm* going to get hurt? Look at you, Franco. You *are* hurt." She peered up at the other riders. "Someone do something. Get a doctor. Call an ambulance. Please."

Luc had already dismounted and stood behind her with the reins to his horse as well as Franco's in his hand. He passed the horses off to one of their other teammates and knelt beside Diana. "The medics are coming, Diana. Help is on its way. He's fine. See?"

She blinked and appeared to look right through him.

Franco wished he knew what was going on in her head. Which part of her horrific accident was she remembering?

He'd known she was having trouble coming to terms with what had happened to her…with what had happened to Diamond. But he'd never once suspected that she remembered her accident. She'd had a concussion. She'd been unconscious. Those memories should have been mercifully lost.

No wonder she'd had such a hard time moving on.

"Diana, look at me." He reached for her, and a hot spike of pain shot through his shoulder. He cursed and used his right arm to hold the opposite one close to his chest.

A collarbone fracture. He would have bet money on it.

It was a somewhat serious injury, but not the worst thing in the world. With any luck he'd be back on the field in four weeks. Six, tops.

But he didn't care about that right now. All he cared about was the woman kneeling beside him…the things she remembered…the fear shining in her luminous eyes.

He'd been such an idiot.

The list of things he'd done wrong was endless. He shouldn't have pushed her to overcome her fears. He shouldn't have ridden a jet-black horse today. He damn well shouldn't have pressured her into watching him play.

He wished he could go back in time and change the things he'd said, the things he'd done. He would have given anything to make that happen. He'd never set foot on a polo field again if it meant he could turn back the clock.

If that were possible—if he could step back in time, he'd walk…run…all the way to the first moment he'd touched her. Not last night. Not last week.

Three years ago.

"Diana, I'm fine. Everything is fine."

But his assurances were lost in the commotion as the medical team reached him. He was surrounded by medics, shouting instructions and cutting his shirt open so they could assess his injuries. Someone shone a light in his eyes. When the spots disappeared from his vision, he could see the game officials clearing the horses and riders away. Giving him space.

He couldn't see Diana anymore. Suddenly, people were everywhere. Jack Ellis loomed over him, his expression grave. The emergency medical team was carrying a stretcher out onto the field.

Franco looked up at Ellis. "Is all of this really necessary? It's a collarbone. I'll be fine."

"Let's hope so," Ellis said coldly. "We need you on the tour."

Luc cleared his throat. His gaze fixed on Franco's, and Franco felt...

Nothing.

For months this was all he'd wanted. Polo was his life. Since he'd left home at eleven, he'd lived and breathed it. Without it, he'd been lost. The thought of losing it again, even for a few weeks, combined with the look on Ellis's face should have filled him with panic.

He wasn't sure what to make of the fact that it didn't.

"Diana," he said, ignoring Ellis and focusing instead on Luc. "Where is she? Where did she go?"

"She's with her brother." Luc jerked his head in the direction of the reserved tables.

"Go find her." Franco winced. The pain was getting worse. "Bring her to the hospital. Please."

Luc nodded. "The second the game is over, I will."

The game.

Franco had all but forgotten about the scrimmage. He'd turned his life upside down to get back on the team, and in a matter of seconds it no longer mattered.

Slow down. This is your life. She's a Drake. You're not. Remember?

Diana would be fine.

She was a champion. She'd come so far in conquering her fears in recent weeks. She was close. So close. His fall had been nothing like hers. Of course she'd been rattled, but by the time he saw her again, she'd be okay.

He clung to that belief as the paramedics strapped him to a stretcher and lifted him into an ambulance.

But the look on Diana's face when she walked into his hospital room however many hours later hurt Franco more than his damned arm did. The person standing at his bedside was a ghost of the woman he'd taken to bed the night before. Memories moved in the depths of her amethyst eyes.

Painful remembrance.

And stone-cold fear.

Franco had seen that look before in the eyes of spooked horses. Horses that had been through hell and back, and flinched at even the gentlest touch. It took years of patience and tender handling to get those horses to trust a man again. Sometimes they never did.

"You're here." He shifted on the bed, and a spike of pain shot from his wrist to his shoulder. But he didn't dare flinch. "I'm glad you came."

She gave him an almost invisible smile. "Of course I came. I'm your fiancée, remember? How would it look if I weren't here?"

So they'd gone from making love to just keeping up appearances. Again. Marvelous.

"Sweetheart." He reached for her hand and forced himself to speak with a level of calmness that was in direct contrast to the panic blossoming in his chest. "It's not as bad as it looks. I promise."

She nodded wordlessly, but when she quietly removed her hand from his, the gesture spoke volumes. He was losing her. It couldn't happen again. He wouldn't let it, damn it. Not this time. Not for good.

"Diana…"

"I'm fine." There was that forced smile again. "Honestly."

He didn't believe her for a minute, and he wasn't in the mood to pretend he did. Hadn't they been pretending long enough? "You're not fine, Diana."

She stared at him until the pain in her gaze hardened. *Go ahead, get mad. Just feel something, love. Anything.* "Be real with me."

She shook her head. "We had an agreement, Franco."

"Screw our agreement." She flinched as if he'd slapped her. "There's more here than a fake love affair. We both know there is."

"Stop." She exhaled a ragged breath. "Please stop. The gala is in two days, and so is the Kingsmen tour."

"Do I look like I'm in any kind of condition to play polo right now?" He threw off the covers and climbed out of the hospital bed. There was too much at stake in this conversation to have it lying down.

"You're going on the tour. Luc said Ellis is insisting that you come along. As soon as your injury heals, you'll be right back in the saddle." Her gaze shifted to his splint, and she swallowed. Hard.

"I'll always ride. It's not just my job. It's my life." Using his good arm, he reached to cup her cheek. When she didn't pull away, it felt like a minor victory. "It's yours, too, Diana. That's one of the things that makes us so good together. You'll ride again. You will. When you're ready, and I intend to be there when it happens."

She backed out of his reach. So much for small victories. The space between them suddenly felt like an impossibly vast gulf. "Go on tour, Franco. You'll be fired again if you don't."

Franco sighed. "I highly doubt that."

"It's true. Ask Luc. Apparently your coach wants to keep an eye on you." Her gaze narrowed. "I guess he doesn't want to leave you behind with his wife."

Shit. That again.

"Natalie Ellis means nothing to me, Diana. She never did."

"That's not such a nice way to talk about a woman you slept with. A woman who was *married*, I might add."

Franco followed her gaze to her ring finger, where her Drake Diamonds engagement ring twinkled beneath the fluorescent hospital lighting. He watched, helpless, as she slid it off her hand.

No. Every cell in his body screamed in protest. "What do you think you're doing?"

"I'm breaking up with you." She opened her handbag and dropped the ring inside. Her gaze flitted around the room. She seemed to be looking anywhere and everywhere but at him.

"Why remove the ring? It's not as if I actually gave it to you." Would she have been able to remove it so easily if he had?

He hoped not, but he couldn't be sure.

"I still think it's a good idea to take it off. You know, in case the press…"

"You think I still give a damn what the press thinks? Here's a headline for you—I don't. This isn't about our agreement. It's not about Drake Diamonds or Natalie

Ellis. It sure as hell isn't about the press. What's happening in this room is about you and me, Diana. No one else."

He'd fallen off his horse—something he'd done countless times before with varying degrees of consequences. Over the course of his riding career, he'd broken half a dozen bones and survived three concussions. But never before had a fall caused so much pain.

"Diana, you're afraid. But I'm fine. I promise. Now stop this nonsense. We have a gala to attend in two days."

She shook her head. "We had a deal, and now it's over. We both got what we wanted. It's time to walk away."

"Don't do this, Wildfire." His voice broke, but he couldn't have cared less. The only thing he cared about was changing her mind.

He wasn't sure when, but somewhere along the way he'd stopped pretending. He had feelings for Diana Drake. Feelings he had no intention of walking away from.

"Marry me."

Her face went pale. "You're not serious."

"I am. Quite." He'd never wanted this. Never asked for it. But he did now. The future suddenly seemed crystal clear.

She saw it, too. He knew she did. She could close her eyes as tightly as she wanted, but it was still there. Diamond bright.

"I'll marry you right now. We could go straight to the hospital chapel. Just say yes." They could have a fancy ceremony later on. Or not. Franco didn't care. He just wanted to be with her for the rest of his life. "Come on the tour with me, Diana. I don't want to do this without you."

"No." She shook her head. "You're not. You're just confused. I am, too. But it's not real. *We're* not real. You know that as well as I do."

"All I know is that I'm in love with you, Diana."

"Is that what you told Natalie Ellis? Were you in love with her too?" Diana's gaze narrowed. "You slept with a married woman, Franco. Your boss's wife. Do you even believe in marriage?"

What was he supposed to say to that?

I never slept with her.

I lied.

She'd never believe him. "There's never been anyone else, Diana. Only you."

"That doesn't exactly answer my question, does it? I can't marry you, Franco. Don't you see that? I might be a Drake, but I'm not my mother. She stood by the man she loved, even as he slept with every other woman who crossed his path. It killed her. It would kill me, too."

Then Diana turned and walked right out the door, and Franco was left with only the devastating truth.

He knew nothing.

Nothing at all.

Chapter Eighteen

The Met Diamond gala was supposed to be the most triumphant moment of Diana's fledgling career as a jewelry executive, but she dreaded it with every fiber of her being. She should have been walking up the museum's legendary steps on Franco's arm. She couldn't face the possibility of doing so alone. Not when every paparazzo in the western hemisphere would be there, wondering what had happened to her famous fiancé. She'd rather ride naked through the streets of Manhattan, Lady Godiva-style. But she'd made a promise, and she intended to honor it.

Thank God for Artem and Ophelia. Not only did they ride with her in the Drake limo, but they also flanked her as she climbed the endless marble staircase. She didn't know what she would have done without them. Artem slipped her arm through his and effectively held her upright as she was assaulted by thousands of flashbulbs and an endless stream of questions.

"Diana, where's Franco?"

"When's the wedding?"

"Don't tell us there's trouble in paradise!"

She wanted to clamp her hands over her ears. She could hear the photographers shouting even after they'd made it inside the museum.

"Are you okay?" Artem eyed her with concern.

God, she loved her brother. This night was every bit as important for him as it was for her, but his first concern was her broken heart.

She forced a smile and lied through her teeth. "I'm fine."

"No, you're not," Ophelia whispered. "You're shaking like a leaf. Artem, call our driver back. Diana should go home."

As good as that sounded, she couldn't. She'd made it this far. Surely she could last another few hours. Besides, she couldn't hide forever. The world would find out about her breakup eventually. It was time to face the music.

She was shocked no one had learned the truth yet. Two days had passed since she'd ended things with Franco. He hadn't breathed a word to the press, apparently. Which left her more confused than ever.

"Diana, I'd like you to stay." Artem glanced at his watch. "At least for half an hour. Then you can go straight home. Okay?"

"Artem…" Ophelia implored.

He cast a knowing glance in his wife's direction, one of those secret signals that spouses used to communicate. Diana would never be on the receiving end of such a look. Obviously.

"Thirty minutes," he repeated. "That's all I'm asking."

"No problem. I told you I'm fine, and I meant it." For the thousandth time since she'd walked out the door of

Franco's hospital room, the pad of her thumb found the empty spot where her engagement ring used to be.

A lump sprang to her throat.

She wasn't fine. She hadn't been fine since the moment she'd seen Franco fall to the ground at the polo match.

She'd thought she'd been ready to be around horses again, but she hadn't. She'd thought she'd been ready for a real relationship, one that might possibly lead to a *real* engagement and a *real* marriage, but she'd been wrong about that, too.

She couldn't lose anyone again. She'd lost both her mother and her father, and she'd lost Diamond. Enough was enough. She couldn't marry Franco. Not now. Not ever. If she did and something happened to him—if she lost him, too—she'd never be able to recover.

She shouldn't even want to marry him, anyway. The man had zero respect for the sanctity of marriage. He'd been fired for sleeping with his boss's wife, which meant that Diana had somehow fallen for a man who was exactly like her dad.

She'd have to be insane to accept his proposal.

Even though she'd almost wanted to…

"Excuse me." A familiar voice broke into their trio.

Diana turned to find the last person in the world she ever expected to see. "Luc?"

What on earth was Luc Piero doing at the Met Diamond gala? Had Franco not even told his closest friend that the engagement was off?

"Luc, I'm sorry. There's been a change of plans. Franco's not with me tonight." *Or any other night.*

He shook his head. "I'm not here for Franco. I came to talk to you."

"Me?" She swallowed.

What could she and Luc possibly have to talk about?

"Yes. You." He looked around at their posh surroundings. The Met was stunning on any given day, but tonight was special. Faux diamonds dripped from every surface. It was like standing inside a chandelier. "Is there someplace more private where we can chat?"

She shouldn't leave. She had a job to do. She had to speak to the Lambertis and pose for photos. And just looking at Luc made her all the more aware of how much she missed Franco.

She shook her head, but at the same time she heard herself agreeing. "Come with me." She glanced at Artem and Ophelia, who'd been watching the exchange with blatant curiosity. "I'll be right back."

She led Luc past the spot where the Lamberti diamond, which had just been officially rechristened the Lamberti-Drake diamond, glowed in a spectacular display case in the center of the Great Hall. Her stilettos echoed on the smooth tile floor as they rounded the corner beneath one of the Met's sweeping marble archways. When they reached the darkened hall of Greek and Roman art, her footsteps slowed to a stop.

They were alone here, in the elegant stillness of the sculpture collection. Gods and goddesses carved from stone surrounded them on every side. Secret keepers.

Diana was so tired of secrets. She'd spent her entire life mired in them. No one outside the family knew the circumstances surrounding her mother's death. Diana hadn't been allowed to talk about it. Nor did the public know the identity of Artem's biological mother. To the outside world, the Drakes were perfect.

So much deception. When would it end?

She turned to face Luc. "What is it? Has something happened to him?"

She hadn't realized how afraid she'd been until she uttered the words aloud.

Luc wouldn't have sought her out if what he had to say wasn't important. The moment he'd asked to speak to her in private, her thoughts had spun in a terrible direction. She remembered what it had felt like to find her mother's lifeless body on the living room floor...the panic that had shaken her to her core. It had been the worst moment of her life. Worse than her accident. Worse than losing Diamond. Worse than watching Franco's body break.

Every choice she'd made since the day her mother died had been carefully orchestrated so she'd never feel that way again. And where had it gotten her?

Completely and utterly alone.

But that wasn't so bad. She could handle loneliness. What she couldn't handle was the way her heart had broken in two the moment she'd seen Franco's lifeless body on the ground.

She'd fought her love for him. She'd fought it hard. But she'd fallen, all the same.

"No, he's fine." Luc's brow furrowed. "Physically, I mean. But he's not fine. Not really. That's why I'm here."

Her heart gave a little lurch. "Oh?"

Franco couldn't possibly love her. Not after the way she'd treated him. He'd been real with her. Unflinchingly, heart-stoppingly real. And she'd refused to do the same.

Worse, she'd judged him. Time and again. She'd acted so self-righteously, when all along they'd both been doing the same thing—running from the past. She'd chosen solitude, and in a way, so had Franco. Neither one of them had let anyone close. Until the day Franco asked her to marry him.

He was ready to leave the past behind. He was moving

beyond it, and he'd offered to do so hand in hand with Diana. But she'd turned him down.

She'd spent years judging him, and now she knew why. Not because the things he'd done were unforgivable, but because it was convenient. So long as she believed him to be despicable, he couldn't hurt her.

Or so she'd thought.

But he hadn't hurt her, had he? She'd hurt herself. She'd hurt them both.

"He's in love with you, Diana," Luc said.

She shook her head. "I don't think so."

She'd made sure of that.

"You're wrong. I've known Franco all his life, and I've never seen him like this before." The gravity in his gaze brought a pang to her chest. "He misses you."

She shook her head. "Stop. *Please.*"

Why was he doing this? She'd nearly made it. Franco was leaving with the Kingsmen in less than twenty-four hours. Once he was gone, she'd have no choice but to put their mockery of a romance behind her and move on. She just had to hold on for one more day.

A single, heartbreaking day.

She swallowed. "I'm sorry, Luc. But I can't hear this. Not now."

She needed to get out of here. She'd thought she could turn up in a pretty gown and smile for the cameras one last time, but she couldn't. All she wanted to do was climb into bed with her dog and a pint of ice cream.

She gathered the skirt of ball gown in her hands and tried to slip past Luc, but he blocked her exit. He jammed his hands on his hips, and his expression turned tortured. "You're going to make me say it, aren't you?"

Diana was afraid to ask what he was talking about. Terrified to her core. She couldn't take any more. Refusing Franco had been the most difficult thing she'd ever had to do.

But she couldn't quite bring herself to ignore the torment in Luc's gaze. "I don't know what you're talking about."

Luc shook his head. "Franco is going to kill me. But you deserve to know the truth."

The truth.

A chill ran up Diana's spine. She had the sudden urge to clasp her hands over her ears.

But she'd been turning her back on the truth long enough, hadn't she?

No more secrets. No more lies.

"What is it?" Her voice shook. And when Luc turned his gaze on her with eyes filled with regret, she had to bite down hard on the inside of her cheek to keep from crying.

His gaze dropped to the floor, where shadows of gods and goddesses stretched across the museum floor in cool blue hues. "Look, I don't know what happened between the two of you, but there's something you should know."

Diana nodded wordlessly. She didn't trust herself to speak. She couldn't even bring herself to look at him. Instead, she focused on the marble sculpture directly behind him. Cupid's alabaster wings stretched toward the sky as he bent to revive Psyche with a kiss.

A tear slid down her cheek.

"Tell me," she whispered, knowing full well there would be no turning back from this moment.

Luc fixed his gaze with hers. The air in the room grew still. Even the sculptures seemed to hold their breath.

"It was me," he said.

Diana began to shake from head to toe. She wrapped

her arms around herself in an effort to keep from falling apart. "Luc, what are you saying?"

"I was the one who had an affair with Ellis's wife, not Franco." He blinked a few times, very quickly. His eyes went red, until he stood looking at Diana through a shiny veil of tears. "I'm sorry."

Diana shook her head. "No."

She wanted him to take the words back. To swallow them up as if she'd never heard them.

"No!" Her voice echoed off the tile walls.

Luc held up his hands in a gesture of surrender. "It wasn't my idea. It was Franco's. I left my Kingsmen championship ring in Ellis's bed. He found it and knew it belonged to one of the players. Franco confessed before I could stop him."

"I can't believe what I'm hearing." But on some level, she could.

Franco loved Luc like a brother. He wanted to protect him, just as Luc had protected him when he'd been living in his barn and then his home.

She should have figured it out. From the very beginning, she'd suspected there was more to Franco's termination than he'd admitted. Then, at Argentine Night at the Polo Club, Natalie Ellis had looked right through him.

And Diana had known.

Franco had never touched her.

But Diana had been so ready to believe the worst about him, she'd pushed her instincts aside. What had she done?

"He never anticipated being cut from the team. He was too valuable. But Ellis couldn't stand the sight of him. I tried to tell the truth. Over and over again. Franco wouldn't have it."

She wanted to pound her fists against his chest. She wanted to scream. *You should have tried harder.*

But she didn't. Couldn't. Because deep down, she was just as guilty as he was. Guilty of letting the past color the way she saw her future.

I should have believed.

Franco wasn't her father. Loving him didn't make her into her mother. And she *did* love him, despite her best efforts not to.

She'd spent every waking second since her accident trying to protect herself from experiencing loss again, and it had happened anyway. She'd fallen in love with Franco, and she'd lost him. Because she'd pushed him away.

"Tell me this changes things." Luc searched her gaze. His eyes were red rimmed, but they held a faint glimmer of hope.

"I wish it could." Her heart felt like it was going to pound out of her chest. She pressed the heel of her hand against her breastbone, but it didn't make a difference. She was choking on her remorse. "He asked me to marry him, Luc. And I turned him down."

Luc's brow furrowed. "What do you mean? I thought you were already engaged. It was in all the papers."

"He didn't tell you?" Her voice broke, and her heart broke along with it. "It was never real."

"He never said a word."

The fact that Franco never told Luc their relationship was a sham meant something. Diana wasn't sure what… but it did. It had to. He'd been willing to sacrifice everything for Luc, but he'd let his closest friend believe he was in love. He'd let him think he was going to marry her.

And that made whatever they'd had seem more genuine than Diana had ever allowed herself to believe.

It was real. It had been real all along.

She needed to go to him. What was she doing standing here while he was preparing to leave? "Sorry Luc, there's something I need to do."

She turned and ran out of the sculpture gallery, her organza dress swishing around her legs as she ran toward the foyer. But when she rounded the corner, she collided hard against the solid wall of someone's chest.

A hard, sculpted chest.

She'd know that chest anywhere.

"Franco, you're here." She pulled back to look up at him, certain she was dreaming.

She wasn't. It was him. He was wincing and holding his arm in the sling where she'd banged against it, but it was him. She'd never been so happy to see an injured man in all her life.

"I am." He smiled, and if her heart hadn't already been broken, it would have split right in two.

It felt like a century had passed since she'd walked out of his hospital room. A century in which she'd convinced herself she'd never see him again. Never get to tell him the things she should have said when she'd had the chance…

"Franco, there's something I need to say." She took a deep breath. "I'll go with you on tour. Please take me with you."

His smile faded ever so slightly. "Diana…"

"I just want to be with you, Franco. *Really* be with you." She choked back a sob. "If you'll still have me."

She felt as if she'd just taken her broken heart and given it to him as an offering. Such vulnerability should have made her panic. But it was far easier than she'd expected. Natural. Right. The only thing making her panic was the thought that she'd almost let him leave Manhattan without telling him how she felt.

She took a deep, shuddering inhale and said the words

she'd tried all her life not to say. "I love you. I always have. Take me with you."

Around them, partygoers glided in the silvery light. The air sparkled with diamond dust. They could have been standing in the middle of a fairy tale.

But as Franco's smile wilted, Diana plunged headfirst into a nightmare.

"It's too late." He took her hands in his, but he was shaking his head and his gaze was filled with apologies that she didn't want to hear.

She'd missed her chance.

She should have believed.

She should have said yes when she'd had the opportunity.

"I understand." She pulled her hands away and began gathering her skirt in her fists, ready to run for the door. Just like Cinderella.

The ball was over.

Everything was over.

"It's okay." But it wasn't. It would never be okay, and it was all her fault. "I just really need to go…"

"Diana, wait." Franco stepped in front of her. "Please."

She couldn't do this. Not now. Not here, with all of New York watching. Couldn't he understand that?

But she'd fallen in love while the world watched. She supposed there was some poetic symmetry to having her heart broken while the cameras rolled.

"I can't." It was too much. More than she could take. More than anyone could.

But just as she turned away, Franco blurted, "I quit the team."

Diana stopped. She released her hold on her dress, and featherlight organza floated to the floor. "What?"

"That's what I meant when I said it's too late. You

can't go with me on the road because I'm not going."
His mouth curved into a half grin, and Diana thought
she might faint. "Did you really think I could leave you?"

He's not my father.

She'd turned him down, sent him away. And he was
still here. He'd stuck by Luc, even when it had come at
great personal cost.

Now he was sticking by her. He was loyal in a way
she'd never known could be possible.

"You're afraid," he said in a deliciously low tone that
she felt deep in her center. "Don't be."

He moved closer, cupped her face with his left hand.
She'd missed him. She'd missed his touch. So, so much.
She could have wept with relief at the feel of his warm
skin against hers.

"I'm not afraid. Not anymore." She searched his gaze
for signs of doubt, but found only rock-solid assurance.
His eyes glittered, as sharp as diamonds.

He dropped his hand, and her fingertips drifted to her
cheek, to the place where he'd touched her. She hadn't
wanted him to release her. *Too soon*, she thought. She
needed his hands on her. His lips. His tongue.

Everywhere.

"Wildfire." Franco winked, and she felt it down to
the toes of her silver Jimmy Choos. "I have something
for you."

He reached into the inside pocket of his tuxedo and
pulled out a tiny Drake-blue box tied with a white satin
ribbon. It was just like the ones she'd once sold to all the
moonstruck couples in Engagements.

Diana stared at it, trying to make sense of what was
happening. For as long as she could remember, she'd
hated those boxes. But not this time.

This time, the tears that pricked her eyes were tears of joy.

"Franco, what are you doing?" How had he even gotten that box? Or whatever was inside of it?

Her gaze flitted over Franco's shoulder, and she spotted Artem watching from afar with a huge grin on his face. So her brother was in on this, too? That would certainly explain where the tiny blue box had come from. It also explained his insistence that she stay for the beginning of the gala.

Is this really happening?

"Isn't it obvious what I'm doing?" Franco dropped down on one knee, right there in the Great Hall of the Met.

It *was* happening.

A gasp went up from somewhere in the crowd as the partygoers noticed Franco's posture. Diana could hear them murmuring in confusion. Of course they were baffled. She and Franco were supposed to be engaged already.

Let them be confused. For once, Diana didn't care what anyone was saying about her. She didn't care what kind of headlines would be screaming from the front page of the papers tomorrow morning. All she cared about was the man kneeling at her feet.

"It occurred to me that I never asked properly for you to become to my wife. Not the way in which you deserve. So I'm giving it another go." He took her hand and gently placed the blue box in it.

Her fingertips closed around it, and their eyes met. Held.

"I love you, Diana Drake. Only a fool would walk away from something real, and I don't want to be a fool anymore. So I'm asking you again, and I'm going to keep asking for as long as it takes." But there would be no more proposals, because she was going to say yes. She could barely keep herself from screaming her answer before he finished. *Yes, yes, yes.* "Will you marry me, Diana Drake?"

"I'd love to marry you, Franco Andrade."

The crowd cheered as he rose to his feet and took her into his arms. Diana was barely conscious of the popping of a champagne cork or the well-wishers who offered their congratulations. She was only aware of how right it felt to be by Franco's side again and how the tiny blue box in her hand felt like a magic secret.

She waited to open it until they were back at her apartment. The time between his proposal and the end of the party passed in a glittering blur. She needed to be alone with him. She needed to step out of her fancy dress and give herself to him, body and soul.

After they left the gala and finally arrived at her front door, Diana wove her fingers through Franco's and pulled him inside.

"Alone at last," he said, gazing down at her as the lights of Manhattan twinkled behind him.

"Sort of." Diana laughed and lifted a brow at Lulu, charging at them from the direction of the bedroom.

Franco scooped the puppy into the elbow of his uninjured arm and sat down on the sofa. Lulu burrowed into his lap, and he gave the empty space beside him a pat. "Come sit down. Don't you have a box to open?"

She sat and removed the little blue box from her evening bag. She held it in the palm of her hand, not wanting the moment to end. She wanted to hoard her time with Franco like a priceless treasure. Every precious second.

"Open it, Wildfire."

She tugged on the smooth satin ribbon and it fell onto her lap, where Lulu pounced on it with her tiny black paws. As the puppy picked it up with her mouth, she fell over onto her back between them, batting at the ribbon with her feet. The comical sight brought a lump to Diana's throat for some strange reason.

Then she realized why…

The three of them were a family.

She lifted the lid of the box, but the large rose-cut diamond solitaire nestled on top of the tiny Drake-blue cushion inside was unlike any of the rings in the shiny cases of the Engagements section of Drake Diamonds. Jewelers didn't typically style diamonds in rose cut anymore. This ring was different. Special. Familiar in a way that stole the breath from Diana's lungs.

"This was my mother's ring." She hadn't seen this diamond in years, but she would have recognized it anywhere. When she was a little girl, she used to slip it on and dream about the day when she'd wear sparkling diamonds and go to fancy black-tie parties every night, just as her parents did.

That had been in the years before everything turned pear-shaped. Before they'd all learned the truth about her father and his secret family. Back when being a wife and a mother seemed like a wonderful thing to be.

Diana had forgotten what it was like to feel that way.

Now, with breathless clarity, she remembered.

"How did you get this, Franco?" It was more than a stone. It was hope and happiness, shining bright. Diamond fire.

"I went to Artem to ask for your hand, and he gave it to me. He said it's been in the vault at Drake Diamonds for years. Waiting." Franco took the ring and slid it onto her finger. Then he lifted her hand and kissed her fingertips.

The diamond had been waiting all this time. Waiting for her broken heart to heal. Waiting for the one man who could help her put it back together.

Waiting for Franco.

At long last, the wait was over.

Epilogue

A *Page Six* Exclusive Report

Diamond heiress Diana Drake returns to New York today after winning a gold medal in equestrian show jumping at the Tokyo Olympics. The win is a shocking comeback after Drake suffered a horrific fall last year in Bridgehampton that resulted in the death of her beloved horse, Diamond. Drake's new mount—a Hanoverian mare named Sapphire—was a gift from her husband, polo-playing hottie Franco Andrade.

Andrade was on hand in Tokyo to watch his wife win the gold, where we hear there was plenty of Olympic-level PDA. We can't get enough of Manhattan's most beautiful power couple, so *Page Six* will be front row center this weekend when Andrade returns to the polo field as captain of the newly formed team, Black Diamond, which he co-owns with his longtime friend and teammate, Luc Piero.

All eyes will certainly be on Diana, who is returning to the helm of her family's empire Drake Diamonds as co-CEO. Rumor has it she declined a glass of champagne at the party celebrating her Olympic victory, and we can't help but wonder...

Might there be a baby on the horizon for this golden couple?

Only time will tell.

* * * * *

Love finds the Drake siblings in the glittering world of jewels and New York City.

If you enjoy IT STARTED WITH A DIAMOND, be sure to check out the first two books in the
DRAKE DIAMONDS *series,*
HIS BALLERINA BRIDE and
THE PRINCESS PROBLEM
wherever Mills & Boon Cherish books and ebooks are sold.